WHEN THE SKY FELL APART

Caroline Lea was born and raised in Jersey. She studied English Literature and Creative Writing at Warwick University and has had poetry published in *Phoenix New Writing* and *An Aston Anthology*, which she also co-edited. *When the Sky Fell Apart* is her first novel.

When the Sky Fell Apart

CAROLINE LEA

TEXT PUBLISHING MELBOURNE AUSTRALIA

textpublishing.com.au

The Text Publishing Company
Swann House
22 William Street
Melbourne Victoria 3000
Australia

First published in 2016 by The Text Publishing Company
Reprinted 2016

Cover and page design by Imogen Stubbs
Cover image based on the painting 'The Inlet' by Alice Kent Stoddard, David David Gallery / Getty Images
Typeset by J&M Typesetting

Printed in Australia by Griffin Press, an Accredited ISO AS/NZS 14001:2004 Environmental Management System printer

National Library of Australia Cataloguing-in-Publication entry:
Creator: Lea, Caroline, author.
Title: When the sky fell apart / by Caroline Lea.
ISBN: 9781925240719 (paperback)
ISBN: 9781922253392 (ebook)
Subjects: War stories.
Dewey Number: 813.6

This book is printed on paper certified against the Forest Stewardship Council® Standards. Griffin Press holds FSC chain-of-custody certification SGS-COC-005088. FSC promotes environmentally responsible, socially beneficial and economically viable management of the world's forests.

For my wonderful sons Arthur and Rupert.

Part 1

WHEN he was on fire, the man smelt bitter. Like the stink when Claudine had once tried to burn Maman's old wool blankets because they had itched.

Even after they had tipped buckets of sea water over him, he still smelt. But sweeter. It reminded her of Maman's Sunday lunch: roast pork with blackened skin and the cooked fat seeping out through the cracks.

Claudine's mouth watered. She clutched Francis's sweaty little hand and tried not to cry. She didn't go too close. Minutes earlier, he had been a talking, laughing man. Now he was a monster, without any skin. And full of noise. Bellowing, writhing, screaming.

She closed her eyes and tried to pretend it was something from a story: once upon a time, a girl and her baby brother huddled on the beach, watching the death throes of a dangerous giant—or, better yet, a dragon. She breathed in the smoke, imagined the man's roars to be the dragon's last breaths, flames sirening from his broken mouth. She saw herself beside him: small, grubby, dark-haired.

But when the man howled again, the story dissolved.

Heart thudding, Claudine stayed back near the sea. Francis's face had crumpled and he had started sniffling. Quietly, but any minute it would turn into a bawl. The grown-ups were fussing and shouting at each other; their raw voices and wild eyes filled Claudine with fear.

She dragged her gaze to the stones that had been smoothed by the mouth of the sea, looking for something familiar to clutch on to. Somewhere, there must be a treasure she could use to distract her brother. Perhaps an unbroken crab shell on the tide line—she could skitter it over his skin, pretending it was alive. *It's coming to nip your nose!* His lip would stop quivering; they would laugh and things would start to make sense again.

But whole crab shells were rare—the sea devoured and crunched them to pieces. Usually, by the time she had finished milking Rowan and Elderflower and given Francis his oatmeal and put the bread in the larder to prove, all the treasures along the beach had been taken by other children.

Today was no different, despite the burning man, the panicking people and the smoking bomb holes. All the shells and pretty stones had been scooped up hours earlier, when the sea was still somewhere to swim and the sand was still somewhere to dig.

Claudine had once found a piece of pink granite in the shape of a love heart. She had cradled it against her chest and then stuffed it into her apron pocket, but Papa had scolded her. He didn't want stones left lying around in the house. Francis might try to swallow them, or throw them at a window.

'You should know such things, clever clogs that you are.'

Even though he had smiled, his voice had been hard. It had made her recall when she'd given Maman and Papa the letter from school: moved ahead two classes. 'Clever girl,' they said. But their narrowed eyes said something different. *Too clever by half.*

A few days later, she had found the love heart stone on the kitchen table, with some writing on it, very tiny and in Papa's hand—the big loops on the letter Y.

'What is this, Maman?'

Her mother hadn't turned from scrubbing the nappies over the sink.

'Your papa gave it to me. You may take it, if you wish.'

Claudine carried it in her pocket for the rest of the day. It banged a bruising tattoo on her hip, pulling purple flowers from beneath her skin, but she didn't give a fig because Maman and Papa both loved her: why else would she have been allowed such a wonderful treasure?

It was only later in her room, with Francis grumbling next to her and sucking on his little fist in his sleep, that she wondered why Maman would have given away the stone when Papa had written the message on it for her: *To Sarah—my only heart.*

The burnt man was now groaning, as cows do when they are calving and the little one is stuck in the birth canal. The grown-ups were puce-faced from bawling at each other. A woman was crying, *'Non! Non! Non!'* It was Madame Hacquoil, her face screwed up and red; when she screamed, blue veins bulged like ropes in her neck. She tried to stroke the burnt man's face, but the others seized her arms and dragged her back.

And Claudine realised, with a sickening wrench of her

insides, that the blackened, moaning beast must be Clement Hacquoil, the butcher. He was kindly and well respected and often gave Claudine crisp slivers of bacon rind to chew on while she waited for Maman to do the shopping.

Now he looked like a charred chunk of meat. Claudine shuddered.

Monsieur Le Gallais was waving a big pointy piece of granite and shouting in Jèrriais, too fast for Claudine to understand. And Clement, the monster-man, moaned even louder and clawed at the air, as if he were trying to grasp the rock. As if he *wanted* to be pounded about his roaring skull with that toothed piece of granite.

His hands were like firewood. And his arms too—black and cooked-looking. Where his skin wasn't black, it was bright red: tongued by the flames. No clothes, no skin. Just the blood and the wetness underneath. The word *oozing* came into Claudine's head. She whispered it under her breath: a word with a taste in it.

There was a series of splashes, which Claudine made-believe was wheeling birds slapping into the sea in search of fish, but which she knew was the sound of pails of sea water being emptied over the man.

A shout made Claudine turn.

'Stop that! Are you trying to kill him!'

An older woman rushed out of the crowd, waving her arms.

With a complicated twist in her stomach, Claudine recognised Edith Bisson, the woman who used to help Maman to care for her and Francis. She hadn't seen Edith in months—Maman had forbidden it—but she was unchanged: grey-haired but straight-backed, and eyes sharp.

As Claudine watched, Edith took the pail from the man's

6

hands and dumped the water out on to the sand.

'Oi!' The man glared. 'Want Clement to cook, do you?'

Edith glared back. 'Use *clean* water, for goodness sake.'

'It's fresh from the sea.'

'Fresh indeed! A fine plan to shower poor Clement in fish shit and heaven knows what else.'

She threw the pail to another man. 'Stop gaping, Hedley, and fetch some water from a hosepipe.'

Hedley shut his mouth with a click and scurried off to fetch the water.

'And Anton,' Edith said to the first man, 'run for Dr Carter, would you?'

Edith continued to direct people while they waited: she sent Madame Hacquoil to fetch some potatoes and some tea.

Claudine heard someone ask Edith what use potatoes would be to poor Clement.

Edith gave a grim smile. 'No more than his wife's hysterics. It'll calm her to be doing something.'

Claudine would have liked to run and embrace Edith: she remembered the comforting reassurance of those strong arms. But Maman's voice was loud in her memory: *Keep away from that woman!* So Claudine hung back, near the gently plashing waves.

By the time Dr Carter arrived, Clement Hacquoil had stopped bellowing. Every breath was a gasping wheeze, punctuated by a horrid sucking noise: the sound when wet boots are tugged from clags of clinging mud.

Once or twice, Claudine had tried to go closer, but the

grown-ups had shooed her away. Even Edith.

You can't be of any help here, dear. This isn't a sight for children. Go on and play now; be off with you!

Dr Carter was a tall man. Long arms and legs, and a face that made Claudine think of the pictures of hawks and eagles in Papa's bird book. He was the new English doctor—Claudine knew none of the grown-ups really liked him.

Thinks he knows everything, old Mrs Fauvel had wheezed to Maman. *Told me to cut back on my cigarettes. Well, I ask you, how can they be making my lungs worse, at my age, when I've smoked them all this time with no trouble at all?*

But whether they liked him or not, all the grown-ups let him through now.

'Will he die?' Claudine whispered, but no one was listening. She felt a sudden, fierce longing for Maman—the old Maman, who might have held Claudine close, or picked her up and kissed her, but she hadn't done those things for a long time, not since before Francis was born.

As Claudine crept closer, she saw how Dr Carter said very little but the grown-ups were talking at him, all at once:

'Well, I ran, of course, as soon as I heard the plane.'

'Running's not cowardice; it's good common sense when there are barbarians bombing an undefended island.'

'We should have all evacuated before now and never mind the shame of it...'

Dr Carter didn't say very much, only 'yes' and 'really?' and 'hmmm'. The way Maman did when she was trying to sleep and Claudine wanted to tell her about the sandhoppers she had collected.

Clement howled and writhed as if his skin were still alight.

Dr Carter blinked nervously—but surely grown-ups didn't feel nervous?—and put a hand gently on Clement's unburnt shoulder, leaning in close to the charred and bloody stump that must have been an ear.

'Can you hear me?'

Dr Carter's voice was kindly, his manner gentle. Claudine wondered why none of the islanders liked him.

'Monsieur Hacquoil,' Dr Carter said, 'I'm here to help you. You are in enormous pain, which will only worsen once we attempt to move you. So I am going to give you an injection. To make the pain go away. Do you understand?'

Clement screamed. Blood and spittle sprayed across Dr Carter's glasses.

Claudine held Francis close, but he seemed less distressed than she was, and watched with wide-eyed bafflement.

Dr Carter filled the syringe with a clear liquid that looked like water and stabbed the needle into Clement's arm. His face immediately changed: like ice melting, all the hardness went out of it. His breathing sounded less jagged.

Dr Carter took a deep breath too. 'You should be feeling more comfortable,' he said. 'That's a good man.'

Clement made no noise at all. No movement.

'Oi, Doctor!' Monsieur Fauvel shouted. 'He's not breathing. You've gone and killed him. By *Crie*, he's only bloody gone and killed him, hasn't he?!'

Claudine's stomach lurched. But it was true: Monsieur Hacquoil had slumped forward so his cheek was resting in the sand. His eyes were half open and cloudy.

Everyone rushed forward.

'Throw sea water on him.'

'Don't be a fool, Marian, do you want to drown him?'

'Tickle his neck.'

'What good is that going to do? Blow smoke up his backside, that'll have him going again. Who has some bellows?'

'Don't be disgusting, Fauvel.'

'He hasn't killed him at all!'

It was Edith, shouldering through the crowd.

'Look, he's still breathing. Dead indeed! For goodness sake! Out of my way, if you please. You too, Doctor. Come on, chop chop!'

Claudine remembered that tone: it was the exact same voice she'd used to usher Claudine into bed when she was being *overexcitable and giddy*. Claudine almost smiled to see the grown-ups jumping out of Edith's way exactly as she used to herself.

Edith drew a glass jar of liquid from her apron pocket, and a handkerchief, which she soaked in the liquor from the jar. Even in the open air with a strong breeze, Claudine could smell the sharp tang of soil and onions and herbs. It was a smell Edith always had about her, in varying degrees, and it reminded Claudine of comfort and warmth, even as it made her eyes water. The grown-ups took another step back: Edith's potions were legendary.

She held the soaked handkerchief under Clement Hacquoil's nose. After a breathless, silent few seconds, his eyelids began to flutter and he gulped a deep lungful of air.

Everybody began to clap, but Edith waved her hand in the air impatiently. Cradling his head in her lap, she pressed the glass jar to Clement's lips and said, 'Come along, then. Down the hatch!'

Clement drained the jar, and within a few minutes he was

breathing evenly, as if he was sleeping, wrapped up in his own bed, with his skin in one piece.

Claudine was used to seeing Edith work her magic, but even she found herself staring, open-mouthed.

—

EDITH could hardly credit the dilly-dallying and fussing.

Once poor Clement was breathing again, everyone stood gawping. Did they expect him to jump to his feet and dance a jig? Even that English doctor, who'd seemed an unflappable sort—even he was gaping at her.

She clapped her hands together, as though she was shooing her chickens into their coop. And in less time than it took to skin a rabbit, Clement had been laid out on a bedsheet and then carried up the beach to the tractor and trailer, which would take him to the hospital. Everyone followed, chattering and gossiping, like children at a saint's day feast.

Dr Carter waved at Edith to follow him up to the trailer. Those big eyebrows of his were drawn down and his lips were pressed into a thin line. It crossed her mind that perhaps she had trodden on his toes a little, swooping in like that and taking over. Still, Clement hadn't been breathing, and she was jiggered if she was going to stand and watch a man die purely because she wanted to show good manners and kiss the English doctor's proverbial backside. So she frowned right back at him, ready to give him an earful if he so much as blinked at her in that know-all way that doctors have.

Instead, he coughed. 'A fine job there,' he said. 'Quite

miraculous, really, reviving the fellow like that. I'd have expected to perform some sort of forced respiration—what you might call mouth-to-mouth, if you understand me?'

His words were all rounded vowels, like listening to a BBC News broadcast. He was still frowning, but perhaps that was just his way: some folk have faces that'd look glum even if they found a ten shilling note in their breeches.

Edith tried not to grin too widely.

Dr Carter continued. 'It was most impressive, I must say. What exactly was that concoction you administered? I'd like to procure some for my own practice.'

She blinked. There must have been a question somewhere in that jumble of gibberish.

'Forgive me,' he said. 'I'm being terribly rude. Timothy Carter. I shouldn't expect you to offer up your miracle cures to virtual strangers.'

He smiled—like the sun coming up—and held out his right hand. With his other hand, he checked Clement's pulse. Gentle hands, she could see that.

She smiled back. This was something. The last doctor had called her a witch—told all his patients that they shouldn't go to see a charlatan. But this one seemed…amiable.

'So, what was it? Or is it a secret?'

'Beg your pardon, Doctor?'

'What miracle concoction did you give the chap to bring him round?'

'Oh, *that?*'

The cart jolted forward. She sat down next to him.

'Simple enough, really. Only some mint, rosemary and pepper with a touch of vinegar. Oh, and a drop of honey to take the edge off it: burns something awful otherwise. It's a job convincing folks to drink it without the honey—they sick it straight back up. And that doesn't do anyone a bit of good, particularly not if it's on my house shoes, which has been known.'

'Just a few herbs and some vinegar! Is that all?'

'And a little onion juice, of course. Gets the blood going; works a treat.'

He shook his head. 'Well, I never.'

'It's the shock of it, you see, Doctor. I don't know if you caught a whiff, but the stuff stinks to high heaven. Stick it under your nose and it'll make you gasp. Gives you a real kick up the backside. Let my cat sniff it one time. The poor thing ran around in circles, yowling like he was being chased by the devil himself.'

When Clement groaned, Carter squeezed his hand again. 'Steady now, nearly there,' he murmured. 'Good fellow, well done.'

Edith watched. He was kindlier than folk had described him. And there was a calm intelligence and wisdom behind those blue eyes, despite his manner of frowning when he spoke.

'So,' she said, pointing to the sky. 'Do you think we can expect more of this, then?'

'I don't know, Mrs... Please forgive me, I don't know your name.'

'Edith Bisson.'

'Mrs Bisson, I really couldn't say. I can't see any particular advantage to the Germans in wiping out the lot of us. But, then, why bomb a defenceless island in the first place? It's crossed my mind that I should have evacuated while the opportunity was there.'

'You should have, Doctor. English by birth, aren't you? So

you've no loyalties here. And the rest of your lot went last week. You didn't think to go with them?'

'No, not really. I haven't much to return to back in England. Only Father and…' He busied himself checking Clement. 'I felt, well—it didn't…sit right with me, the thought of leaving.' He kept his eyes down.

What are you hiding? Edith wondered.

But she nodded along as Carter continued. 'We've no idea what medical care will be necessary if they do invade. Leaving would have seemed, well—I almost said *traitorous*, but perhaps that's a foolish term to use.'

'I heed you, Doctor. You wouldn't catch me leaving, either. But then I'm rooted to this soil—years of my blood in it. I just couldn't understand it, folk upping and leaving like that, thousands of them. Rats from a sinking ship.'

'Well, there will be no more of that—the chap who fetched me said that there's more smoke over St Helier. Rumour has it they've bombed the harbour.'

Edith felt a fluttering of fear. *'Bombed* the harbour? By *Crie!* They mean business then?'

He gave a thin, humourless smile; he really did have a kind face, and a sort of sadness in those eyes.

'It would seem so,' he said. 'We're entirely isolated now.'

'We've been cut off for two weeks already, Doctor, what with England leaving us to our own devices. Demilitarisation? A fine name to pretty up leaving your dependants to be blown up and invaded, don't you think? We're supposed to be under Crown protection. The English took every single one of their soldiers. The Germans could come and butcher the lot of us, for all they care.'

Carter blinked. His eyes were red-rimmed from the smoke or exhaustion. It hit her, for the first time: the weight of responsibility on this man's shoulders—English doctor in a land far from home, during a foreign invasion. Why would any soul make that choice? What must his family think?

He sighed. 'Yes, well. On some days, I'm ashamed to call myself English.'

'Now, Doctor. The shame isn't with you. It's those politicians sitting in London, smoking their cigars and drinking while other people—good, honest people—die for them. Seems they could drop bombs on us until we're nothing but a crater in the sea and the English wouldn't shift a muscle to help us.'

'If it's any consolation, Mrs Bisson, I can't see that happening. There's little doubt the Germans will invade now. But there oughtn't to be any more killing. What would be the gain for them, murdering innocent people?'

Edith felt a jolt of irritation: why didn't he understand the danger they were in? Where was his fear? His rage?

'What about what they've done in France then, eh?' she demanded. 'Burned farms to the ground, killed whole families, raped women... What makes you think it'll be any different here?'

'It *has* to be.'

'And why is that?'

He was quiet a while. Just the creaking of the cart, the soft wheeze of poor Clement's ruined lungs. The seagulls screeing in the open sky above them and the sea breathing behind them, inhaling and exhaling, mumble-mouthed over the stones. Some things remain the same, even when the sky over your head is ablaze.

He sighed. 'Because…because I have to *hope* it will be different.'

No answer at all. Once again, Edith was struck by the thought that Dr Carter was hiding something, or perhaps hiding *from* something.

The cart creaked over their silence. She turned to look at the sea. Flat stretch of water, blank and blue as the sky above. Pretty as a picture, except with black and grey craters where the bombs had fallen: as though some thuggish child had scrawled all over the picture out of spite alone.

And Dr Carter thought this time would be different? He was naïve, too young to remember the Great War, the way it ripped apart people and land and time. Still, no gain in making him fret over what couldn't be changed. Another few minutes and she would get off and leave him to travel the mile to the hospital. She hoped Clement would last the journey.

Near her fence, Edith called for the cart to stop. She turned to Carter.

'I must be off now,' she said. 'I live on that hill.'

'Of course. Well, very pleased to have met you.'

'Likewise.' She paused, put her head to one side. How far could she trust him? 'You were saying before—about the harbour being out. Not being able to leave. Were you looking to go yourself, after all? There's none would blame you. You've no ties here.'

A momentary flash of a haunted shadow in his eyes, and then he smiled and his professional briskness was back.

'I'm staying,' he said. 'It's only that I've some patients who would do well from receiving more specialist care on the mainland. But, of course, that's out of the question now…'

'I might know a way, Doctor, if you can be at La Rocque pier tomorrow morning. I've heard tell there's one last boat leaving. Mostly women and children, a few fellows set on fighting. Only a small collier, you understand. But it might do for those strong enough to stand a slow trip across the channel.'

He stared at her, hard, eyes narrowed. For a moment, her stomach dropped. Perhaps she had him all wrong?

But then he said, 'Very helpful, thank you, Mrs Bisson. I shall see you there tomorrow.'

He smiled, his longish nose pinking under the sun, like a tourist's.

Edith climbed off the trailer. When she looked back, Dr Carter was straight back to checking on Clement and counting out his pulse.

She had decided to walk the last part home along the sand. She'd spotted some devil's claw there that would come in handy for Clement—ever so good for burns, it was.

The tide was up. That deep blue and the surface like glass. The Germans could have pelted a hundred bombs into it, a thousand, and it wouldn't change a jot.

The mirror would shatter and then reform. Implacable. Eternal.

Behind her, the beach was smoking, the air thick and grey with the settling ash. Edith turned away. Some wounds are so shocking that looking on them too long stings the eyes and brings bile to the throat.

—

MAURICE had been at home bathing Marthe in front of the stove when the bombs struck the beach.

She'd had a miserable night and had woken sweaty and soiled. Her skin was ever so delicate, and he knew he would need to bathe her at once to stop the rashes and sores.

He carried her into the kitchen and stripped her down to her drawers. As usual, she didn't say anything. She stared at him as though she would like to thank him, but couldn't find the words.

Maurice kissed her lips, gently wiped away the white film and spittle that crusted her chin. Pulled down her drawers. Picked her up and cradled her in his arms, rocking her for a moment back and forth.

She would be thirty-one next month.

He had known her for all of those years, or as many of them as he could remember. The earliest moment he could recollect, when he was just a scrap of a boy, barely standing on his own two feet, was of little Marthe tottering over and pushing half of her biscuit into his mouth and then knocking him backwards in an embrace.

They married the day after she turned eighteen.

He had loved her as long as he had loved anything. Thinking of it made his eyes itch.

Marthe's head lolled against his arm. He shifted her a little. Dr Carter had warned him against letting her neck sag; she could suffocate under the weight of her own head, he'd explained, if her chin was folded into her chest.

Maurice caught a glimpse of himself in the looking glass above the mantle and started at the wild man he saw there: matted hair (he rarely had the time or inclination to comb it these days), sun-browned, wind-whipped skin and eyes carved with lines from squinting at the glare from sun and the sea. And something else, something new: deep brackets of pain around tightened lips.

He'd seen the same look on the face of another fisherman once. The man had tangled his hand in the snarled mess of his fishing net and, fingers swelling and blackening under the rope that tightened with every twist, had taken out his fishing knife and sawn off his own fingers.

Gently, Maurice lowered Marthe into the metal tub, all the while watching her face for any movement that might tell him that the water scalded or froze her. But she moved not a muscle—only stared at a point just beyond his shoulder. Perhaps the plates? He had meant to wash them that morning, but then her bath had been more pressing, what with the blasted rash. When they were first married, before the disease had fully gripped her, she had been ever so house-proud. Not a cup or a fork out of turn. His heart sickened to think of the scolding she should be giving him for those crocks.

He kissed her forehead. 'I'm sorry,' he whispered. 'Not enough hours in the day, my love.'

They had taken in a girl to help, when the disease became too much. The doctor said Marthe would need someone to tend to her while Maurice was out on the boat. They could have done with another girl now, he knew it. But he didn't trust anyone since the first girl turned out a damned thief and a liar—pinching Marthe's food and leaving her all alone during the day.

He had only found her out because he had come back early once. The wind was up and the sea would have swallowed his boat whole, so he left his nets and went home. The house had been silent: Marthe and the girl were nowhere to be found.

Gone for a walk, probably.

He'd planned to give the girl a ticking-off for dragging poor Marthe out on such a wild day. Without her woollen blanket, either—it lay in its usual spot by the door. Then he heard a noise, a whimper, such as a dog might make, coming from their bedroom.

When he went to look, there was a stench like a midden. The room was thick with it. And there she was, covered in her own mess, face in the bedspread and nearly smothered. Couldn't move a muscle to save herself, could she? Turned out the girl had been leaving her alone all day, without food or water. Stewing in her own filth. And then only cleaning her up when she came back from whatever jaunt she'd been out on, so Maurice was none the wiser.

He could have done her an injury, that girl, when she finally turned up. Pockets full of sweets and bobbins and ribbons she had bought with the money he paid her. His fingers had itched, but he hadn't belted her, not with Marthe watching. Told the butcher's wife about her, though—Madame Hacquoil. The girl hadn't worked since: the whole island and every soul on it knew her for the good-for-nothing thief she was.

Gossip seeped in with the sea water, insinuated itself like the salt and spread the rot from the inside. But some moulds have their uses.

Maurice soaked a rag in the water and sponged the wisps of fine, blonde hair back from Marthe's forehead. He had loved that hair when they first courted—the way it fell forward across her face when she was talking so she had to tuck it behind her ear. It made him recall that sweet child she once was.

He used to love the way her hair fell around his face when

they made love, too. A curtain, shutting out the world. There was just her. All eyes and lips—her soft breath on his face. The smell of her: grass and sea and sweet sweat. That hair of hers, all around them, like something to take deep into your lungs and drown with.

It was still as beautiful, her hair, still long and thick—the illness hadn't touched it. He used his fingers to comb it back from her face and worked the soap in gently, so as not to hurt her. Then he washed, ever so carefully, her neck, shoulders, back. He counted each bone in her spine. Her chest, so flat now, like a child's. The fuzz between her legs. He took extra care to rinse off all of the waste from her thighs and behind her knees, knowing she would flare up even redder if any trace remained.

Afterwards he wrapped her in a towel and held her on his lap in front of the kitchen stove to rub the warmth back into her bird bones. He thought how he would have done this with the children they should have had. The children she should have been nursing and rocking and kissing right now. The children who should have been hanging off her skirts as she stood at that stove and stirred the broth...

He stopped himself. Such thoughts did no one any good. He had driven himself mad over it all too many times to count.

He sang instead. 'Bobby Shaftoe' was Marthe's favourite—sometimes she snoozed as he sang.

He was on the second verse—*bright and fair*—when he heard the explosions. Felt them, really. A deep echo that moved through the walls and floor and up into his body. Into Marthe's delicate bones. A pause and then another boom as before, only louder.

Maurice stopped singing. Marthe's eyes snapped open.

Another boom.

He knew what it had to be. Everyone had been expecting it for weeks now, ever since the troops had left and they had announced on the wireless that the islanders would be left to fend for themselves.

Demilitarised.

A fancy word for abandonment.

He kissed Marthe's forehead, telling her he was sorry, so sorry, my love, as he laid her down on her blanket in front of the stove. She cried out, but he couldn't mind her, not just then.

He ran to the window. He could see the smoke billowing up as close as if it were from next door's bonfire.

Stomach jolting, blood singing, Maurice started to run.

By the time he reached the beach, it was a scene from the end of the world. Just the empty stretch of sand and the black, smoking craters, spewing smoke skywards. No aeroplanes in the sky; the sea was flat and blank. But in the air, the stink of burning *vraic* and something else he couldn't place. Something that made his mouth water. They'd already started the rationing—everyone's meat, butter and sugar had been restricted from the moment they knew England was cutting them off.

Back up the hill, smoke was spiralling from his chimney.

Marthe.

But he walked on towards the beach. He needed to see it for himself.

There wasn't another soul in sight. No fires either, now. Only huge, smoking holes, like blackened open mouths in the sand.

Warily, he inched over to the closest one. It was a vast crater with stones and *vraic* scattered all around. He peered in, guts roiling. *Deep enough to be filling up with water.* It was like a laceration, as though Jerry had clutched an enormous knife, reached across the ocean and dragged a blade across the face of the beach, gleefully stabbing and gouging.

Maurice felt suddenly chilled. His knees went and he sat down, cradled his head in his hands and tried not to think about who might have been on the beach when that bomb hit. Fishermen packing up their nets. Couples walking, hand in hand. Children playing...

He retched a little, insides churning with each fresh image, each fresh puff of smoke. He squeezed his eyes shut, pressed his fists against his eyelids. Everything was darkness until, when he pressed harder, silent stars or fireworks or explosions.

When Maurice opened his eyes, the bloody bomb holes were still there. Pockmarks on the face he had loved as long as he had drawn breath.

Damn Jerry. Damn the damned Bosche.

He hurled a stone into that hole that shouldn't have been there. It made a decent splash as it hit the water. He threw in another, then another. Then he kicked some of the sand in.

Suddenly he was scrabbling on hands and knees and pushing great armfuls of sand into the hole, as fast as he could, panting with the effort of it. His head was swimming but he carried on anyway. Armfuls and fistfuls and whatever he could push in. It made no difference at first, but after a while the water disappeared. He kept going. Each armful of sand burying the Bosche.

When he'd finished pushing all the sand back in, he sat back and tried to look at the shallow hole. Just as if he'd been walking along the beach and then happened upon it. Could have been made by children, pretending to dig their way to China. Black ash buried by the sand. Nothing to make you think of bombs or death. Just the beach, rumple-faced after a day of play, the same as ever.

Now for the others.

He had just started the second hole when he heard a voice behind him.

'What on *earth* are you doing?'

Maurice nearly jumped from his skin. Behind him stood a girl. God knows how long she'd been watching him. She was holding a shell in her hand. An ormer.

He felt his cheeks heat with embarrassment. 'What does it look like?' he said, gruffly. 'I'm filling in the holes.'

He pushed another armful of sand in.

'Can I help?'

He stopped and stared. She could only have been eight, nine at a push. She was narrow-chested, with tangled hair and a gaping hole in the leg of what looked like boys' trousers. She was half smiling, but her eyes were watchful.

'I'm Claudine. I'm ten.'

He smiled. 'I'm Maurice. I'm thirty-one.'

'Very pleased to meet you, Maurice.'

Then, without waiting for his say-so, she started hurling sand into the hole. She went about it like a burrowing animal, crouching over and flinging her arms so the sand went flying— some into the hole, but a good amount into his eyes and mouth too.

After a minute, she stopped, panting.

'Bombs made these holes, you know.'

Maurice gave a wry smile. 'I thought as much.'

'We're most likely to die, once the Germans arrive.'

He stopped digging and stared at the strange girl, with her scrawny legs and her clear voice: the matter-of-fact way she said *die*. Were all children like this? He struggled to find something reassuring to say.

'I'm sure no one will die.'

She pointed to the bomb craters all around. 'They're bombing us,' she said. 'And I'm not a fool. People always think children are fools. But I hear things. I've learnt about wars at school. People die and are killed. And everyone knows the Germans are evil. I heard the grown-ups say so. After they poured water all over the man who was on fire—the butcher.'

'On *fire*? Clement Hacquoil?'

'Yes. He looked like raw meat where he was burnt. You could see under his skin. All bones and blood, like in his butcher's shop. I didn't know people's bodies looked like raw animals inside.'

Maurice took a moment to realise she was waiting for a response. 'Dreadful,' he said. 'So Clement's in the hospital now?'

'Yes. Some other people died too, I think. Everyone kept telling me to run along. They said the Germans had bombed the harbour. The whole army will be here any day. And they have guns. *Real* guns for killing people.'

The girl's eyes were wide and her voice trembled a little with the horror of it but her words were bleak and merciless.

'Do *you* think the Germans will kill us all in our beds? Or bomb us again?'

Poor Clement. It was unimaginable. He'd seen him just the day before. Bought some chicken livers from him, for a good price too.

'No, of course not,' he said.

Claudine shrugged and started to twist her hair around her finger, again and again.

'Everyone else thinks so. And they all say women have to be very careful because the German men are like animals. I hope they aren't. I hope nobody else is killed.'

Her eyes shone with sudden tears.

Maurice flapped his hand towards her, unsure how to comfort her. He tried to make his voice calm.

'Now then, no one is going to kill us. Who's been filling your head with this rot?'

'It's not rot, it's the truth. Maman says so.'

'Does she? And what about your papa? What does he say?'

'Very little. Maman does most of the talking. He does a great deal of sitting. And he reads the newspaper. It's a sad state of affairs. Everyone says so. He's going to fight in the war, though. Will you go?'

Her gaze was brilliant and direct—with a child's intuition, she seemed to understand everything and yet nothing at all.

'No, I, ah—I have my wife to care for. She's...sickly.'

They carried on filling in the holes together. By the time they were finished, it was nearly nightfall and a wet coldness was creeping in across the sea.

Maurice turned to go back home, but the girl, to his horror, began to wade out into the water.

'You're not swimming now, surely?' he called. 'You should be getting home.'

She didn't turn around but carried on walking. 'Maman says I've to bring home something for dinner, so I'm digging up cockles with my toes.'

'That's ludicrous! Go home, would you?'

But she refused. In the end, the only way to persuade her to come out of the blasted water was by offering her some of his oysters. She came galloping out of the sea then, grinning and chattering beside him all the way up the hill.

Again, Maurice found himself wondering if all children carried this strange mixture of ignorance and intelligence.

The house was dark when they reached it and Maurice felt the familiar clutch of panic that always gripped him when he'd left Marthe alone.

He stopped outside the door. 'Just wait here, will you?' Then he opened it a little and squeezed though the gap.

Marthe lay where he had left her, eyes closed, breathing evenly. Maurice pressed his lips against her forehead, then picked her up and cradled her in his arms. The destruction he'd seen today had left him queasy: if the Germans would happily drop bombs on innocent fishermen and set the butcher on fire, what would that mean for him? For poor Marthe, who couldn't protect herself?

Suddenly he heard a voice: 'What is wrong with her?'

It was the girl, standing in his doorway and staring at Marthe.

Maurice jumped. 'Bloody hell, child! You scared the life out of me.'

It had been so long since he'd let anyone see Marthe that he'd forgotten how she must look, with her thin arms and legs and her slack face.

Claudine took a step forward. 'Is she—?'

Marthe began to groan and suddenly Maurice couldn't stand it: the shock on the girl's face, the horror in her eyes.

So he snapped, 'Wait here!' and settled Marthe in the bedroom before ushering the girl out of the house and down the path to fetch her damned oysters.

As they walked, Claudine prattled next to him: What was wrong with his wife? Why couldn't she walk? How long had she been poorly?

'Does it worry you,' she asked, 'that the Germans will hurt her?'

He stopped walking. It was like being underwater—the silence. It filled the space between them so there was no room for words. It stole the breath from him, the helpless rage at the thought of them hurting his harmless, defenceless wife.

'I shan't let them. They shan't lay a finger on her. I can promise you that.'

His voice sounded hard, flat, like someone else's.

Claudine nodded. She looked very young, very small. Too young and too small to be on an island that was about to be invaded.

Poor child.

He made his voice bright and kind. 'You must run along home. So, how many do you need?'

He dug around in the hole where he stored the oysters and pulled a net from the water.

Her face fell. 'But...oughtn't you throw oyster nets back into the sea? They belong to the French fishermen.'

He grinned at her. 'Yes, they do. Finest French oysters.'

—

THE mood in the hospital ricocheted between despair and hysteria.

Carter tried to remain calm, at least on the outside: no sense in pointless panic. But it was a challenge when the evidence of the Germans' brutality lay within the chill walls of the building, moaning, writhing, dying.

Carter sat by Clement Hacquoil's bedside whenever possible. Despite the cold, he insisted the patient remain uncovered. His wounds had to be kept meticulously clean and clear of any layers, save the thinnest of gauze dressings, otherwise infection would set in. Septicaemia and death would follow.

The poor chap shivered and moaned. The nurses who had to undertake his day-to-day care pleaded with Carter to allow him one blanket. Only one. He overheard one of the nurses calling him a callous so-and-so, but his ultimate concern was always for the patient's survival. Very little to be gained by making the man more comfortable and killing him in the process.

Carter tried to ignore the nurses' glares, tried to remember that they were in a hell of a state about the Germans arriving—panicking about the merits of last-minute escape attempts. Some of them, he knew, were terrified about the possibility of becoming the victims of the sort of barbaric acts that had been perpetrated against women across the rest of Europe.

Carter himself tried to remain level-headed: he remembered his father's lectures on surviving the trenches in the Great War: 'Tim, you must know that the only thing a panicking man earns is a bullet in his head.'

And while in some ways Carter's peaceful and nurturing career choice had perhaps been a way of avoiding the violent bravado that Father brandished like some sort of war decoration, he could see no gain in succumbing to the rising heat of hysteria that sparked with every mention of the German forces: fear only made bullies more powerful, after all.

Besides, the locals were relying on him to be calm, even as the island was groaning under the weight of speculation. Every shop and pub full of whispering huddles, all with the same mood of revulsion, terror and excitement. In a place where the most shocking news was usually the theft of a prize milker, the pending invasion caused wild-eyed panic in many quarters, despite Carter's attempts to quell it.

The initial call for evacuation had been issued two weeks earlier, when the German forces reached Cherbourg in France and it became clear that Hitler had set his sights on the Channel Islands. Over half the island signed up, many of the hospital staff included, even as Carter pleaded with them to stay.

In the end, to Carter's relief, shame at leaving and loyalty to the island that had birthed them meant that far fewer left— some 6500 people, and most of these were children or men of military age, keen to fight.

Many saw the act of leaving as an impossibility. Something about the island, its sun-spangled beaches and wind-nibbled cliffs—it had *moulded* them, as surely as seismic shifts in the earth's surface had carved the island from barren rock a hundred millennia ago. These people were a part of the landscape and the leaving of it seemed, for many of them, to represent a sort of *rending*.

But still, the dread bubbled as the threat of invasion grew.

A case in point occurred on the day after the bombings. At five o'clock that morning, three small aeroplanes had flown low over the island. Fearing another attack, the farmers milking their cows had run for cover. However, the aeroplanes did not deliver bombs but pieces of paper, relaying a clear message:

Surrender, or be annihilated.

Carter had learnt of all this at the hospital. He had been writing prescriptions and could hear the waiting area heaving with angry islanders—the overspill of bodies had surged into the corridor. It was mostly women, each in possession of an inordinate number of children. Everyone seemed to be crying.

Carter clapped his hands for attention. But the noise went unheard. He tried raising his voice and calling for hush—to no avail. In the end, he was reduced to bellowing: 'For God's sake! Will you all hold your tongues and let's have some quiet! There are patients sleeping on the wards. What the devil is going on here?'

In the resulting silence, every pair of eyes in the room turned to glare at him.

'Ladies, forgive me, please,' he stammered. 'But this behaviour is hardly helpful. What is the cause of all this upset?'

The woman closest to him, with arms like thighs and broken thread veins across her cheeks, thrust a paper in front of his face.

He blinked. 'What is—?'

The women all spoke up at once: 'We need shelter.'

'Sanctuary, isn't it, Doctor?'

'Walls like these could be hit by a bomb and you'd barely notice.'

He held up his hands and quelled the first quiver of fear in his gut by reminding himself of the sensation of the ruler slapping down on his palms if his hands had ever trembled as a boy.

31

Father's bellow: *Men don't feel fear, Tim.*

Thinking of Father reminded Carter of why he could never return to England.

He squeezed his eyes shut for a moment and kept his voice level.

'But if we are to surrender then we've nothing to fear from bombs. Your own homes will be as safe as within these walls. More comfortable too, I might add. We like to discourage our patients from outstaying their welcome.'

No one smiled at his joke.

'It's all very well for *you* to have a laugh at our expense, Doctor,' said a scowling, thin-lipped woman. 'It's us womenfolk will have to be watching ourselves. I'll be finding my grand-maman's high-collared dresses out of the attic, and no mistake.'

'I'm sure you have nothing to dread. We mustn't let the terror overwhelm—'

This was clearly the wrong thing to say. The women all shouted out at once:

'Who are *you* to tell us what to dread?'

'There have been women *raped* in France!'

'Would you be as calm if you feared for your own daughter, Doctor, for her modesty?'

'He hasn't children, Joan, remember?'

'No wife either. Lives by himself.'

'Does he now?'

'How strange...'

There was a pause in the tirade as they all turned to consider him. From their shared expression, he was found sadly wanting.

The woman with the mottled red cheeks spoke up again.

'In any case, we need shelter, Doctor. So we've come here

because that's your job, isn't it? To help people? And now you are trying to throw us out. To heaven knows what. And with the children too. Now let us through!'

Then the crowd grew ugly. The women started to shove their way past the nurses, who had gathered to block the way to the wards. The nurses tried to stand their ground but were quickly swamped and disappeared from sight behind the wall of angry flesh. A high-pitched wailing underscored the whole debacle, as more and more of the children began to cry.

Suddenly there was a deafening shout: 'Stop that! *Now!*'

Carter jumped. It was one of the ward sisters, Madame Huelin—she stood behind the crowd, hands on her hips and thunder on her face to make even the broadest and stoutest of the farmers' wives quail. There was silence, apart from the sobbing of a few of the younger children.

Sister Huelin spoke calmly and clearly, but there was no questioning her tone.

'Now, listen to me. It's dreadfully frightening, and it's clear that you need somewhere to shelter, but you cannot stay in the main hospital building. You may use the hospital basement for a short time, if it will make you feel safer. It is clean and secure and will provide plenty of space for you and the children. So if you'll just follow Nurse Le Sueur, she'll show you the way.'

After they had flocked out, Carter took a shaky breath and smiled at Sister Huelin.

'Thank you.'

She gave him a measuring look—she thought him a bumbling fool, he could see that. He would have liked to explain how it felt to be an alien in the midst of a community where everyone had rubbed shoulders for generations.

And now, with the threat of the Germans' invasion, he was yet another type of stranger to them. Another foreigner, of questionable nature: they seemed to doubt that he had the same passions and fears as them, saw the world through the same eyes, felt it with the same trembling hands. He had a duty to remain calm but because of it, they thought him cold and inhuman. War had made him into, if not an enemy, then an outsider. But he knew Sister Huelin would never understand this if he tried to explain.

'Well,' she finally said, 'they'll feel safe down there. Although they've nothing to fear from bombs—we'll be surrendering, I'm sure.'

Carter rubbed his hands over his chin: a fine stippling of stubble when he was usually meticulous about appearances.

'I believe you're right,' he said. 'But what else can we do without English support?'

'Ghastly business. Doctor, shouldn't you have evacuated by now? You may still have time to be on that last boat from La Rocque. It leaves this morning.'

'I thought that was a clandestine affair?'

She laughed and for a moment he felt something like friendliness, a shared understanding. But then her gaze settled back into the cold, appraising look he was so accustomed to seeing in the eyes of the locals.

'Nothing much stays hushed up on this island.' She used the kindly tone one might employ with a slow-witted child. 'You should know that by now. You'd best hurry if you're after a spot. It's that boat for you, or else heaven knows how long of living with the Bosche. I know what I'd choose, if I could.'

'Well, why don't you go, then?'

She blinked, stony-faced. 'I'm no rat, Doctor. I'm Jèrriais, born and bred. This is my home. I couldn't leave it any more than I could abandon my own bones.'

Carter felt a confusing tug of incomprehension and grief. He couldn't imagine that sort of savage attachment to another place, or even to another person—the one memory of heat and warmth and love he had (other than for his poor dead mother) he had pushed firmly down until it might as well have happened to somebody else.

~

EDITH lost count of the people crammed onto the little pier. Whole families clustered around one suitcase, which was all they could take with them. It was going to be a hot day, very little in the way of a breeze. It made for foul tempers all around, but at least those who were sailing would have a flat crossing.

She'd brought along some ginger root just in case. Expensive imported stuff, but Edith had always tried to only charge what people could afford to pay. For some, with a gaggle of six children and with all their worldly belongings stuffed into one small burlap sack, that was precious little. Still, she wouldn't stand for seeing children going off to sea without something to stop the sickness. No way of telling whom it would strike, either. Sometimes fishermen's children were the worst.

She handed out most of her supply. Hung on to a few pieces the size of her thumb in case any woman with a babe in her belly should need a ginger tea to settle the sickness.

Most were thankful. Of course, a few turned up their noses

and made the sign against evil behind their backs when they thought she wasn't watching.

It made her chuckle to imagine that some folk thought she had the devil's magic in her fingers. She didn't put stock in that mumbo jumbo. Lovely stories for children, to be sure, and the Bible was ever so good if she couldn't sleep of a night, but that was about the measure of it for her. She'd rather trust in Mother Nature than put faith in a god who was supposed to have happily killed off hordes of his own children, not forgetting his only son.

It was noted that she wasn't at church of a Sunday—she heard folks twittering about it. Still, those who wanted her help came to find her; the rest of them could do as they pleased.

She had some cod liver oil with her too, and a little St John's Wort, which she gave to those who looked especially glum. Some of the men were leaving to join the army on the mainland. It wasn't so many years ago that Jèrriais men had first swapped their pitchforks and fishing lines for guns and grenades and skipped off to fight the Germans in France. Half of them had stayed there for good.

Frank.

There was a compression within her chest whenever she thought of him, even after all these years. She remembered clinging around his neck; the shining gold on her new wedding band; the sour-wool smell of his uniform; the way her tears had stood like jewels on the stiff cloth, until he'd brushed them off, then turned to leave.

There were wives and sweethearts crying now. And, like a daguerreotype of twenty-five years before, there were plenty of howling children, clinging on to Papa's legs. Little ones pick up

36

on moods, even when they don't fully understand. People don't give children enough credit—they're born with old heads on their shoulders.

Edith did what she could to be of some comfort. Passed a sugared almond to a child here and there. Gave some of the women a tight embrace or a kind word. Held poor Rebecca Mourant's hair back while she vomited; made sure she didn't splash her good shoes.

She saw the Duret family but didn't try to speak to them. No one likes to make a scene and she'd not exchanged so much as a glance with them since Sarah had screamed her from their house six months ago: *And don't ever come back, you interfering old witch!*

Claudine's papa was the only one leaving, it seemed. He had a small bag and not much else. Off to fight, or he'd be taking the family with him, surely? None of Edith's business, of course. Not now, in any case.

Claudine had grown frail and fretful since Edith had last seen her. It tugged at her to think of how chubby she'd been as a tiny babe. Edith recalled blowing raspberries into her fat little stomach when she'd changed her nappy. Memories: holding her close, pressing kisses to a little mouth, squashed into a fish pout. Bicycling those plump legs while the chuckles juddered through her body. And now, Edith might as well have been a stranger for all the family looked at her.

Edith tried to see Claudine with an outsider's measuring gaze. She was thin-faced, sallow and ill-kempt. Wild, knotted hair and torn boys' trousers and a boy's shirt—grubby around the collar. Edith's fingers itched to go and comb out that hair and give her a good scrub and a kiss on the forehead.

37

Instead she watched, as Claudine turned to Sarah and said, 'Why can't we go with Papa?'

Sarah's voice was the same cigarette-harsh rasp that Edith remembered.

'Well, dear, they don't let women and children fight in the army.'

Claudine giggled. '*No*, Maman. I mean to live. So we're not here when the Germans arrive. Can't we go to England with Papa and leave the war here?'

'Be a good girl and hush yourself,' Sarah said. 'We're staying. No point in fussing. What would Rowan and Elderflower do without us? Besides, where would we live in England?'

Claudine nodded and poked at a stone with her toe. 'Who will care for us?'

Sarah's face was flat and impassive as she stared out at the departing boat. 'Wave to Papa, Claudine. We shall care for ourselves.'

'But *how*? Where will we get food? And money?'

Edith winced; she could see the hardness in Sarah's jaw and she half expected to hear the sound of a slap.

But Sarah glanced around at the surrounding crowd and knelt down in front of Claudine and took her shoulders in her hands. Edith could see Sarah's fingers digging into her daughter's flesh.

'Gracious, what have I told you about fussing? Those are *my* concerns. Not yours. We shall manage. Do you hear me? We've nothing to fret about. So, no tears. You've to be a big, strong girl now. Understand?'

Her knuckles were white and her arms shook with the force of her grip. Claudine was pale-faced but she didn't try to squirm away and she put Edith in mind of a rabbit, lying limp in a fox's jaws.

'No more questions then. Yes?'

Sarah's eyes were huge and bright and, for a moment, Edith could remember her as a child herself. So sweet and full of mischief. She had been like a tonic for Edith, after Frank's death—being widowed at twenty-six had stamped the life out of her, but she had slowly found herself again through the small child's laughter. Sarah had grown into a lovely young woman— generous, with a sharp wit, and Edith had been happy to help her with Claudine and then, later, with Francis, even though her forty-nine years sometimes made running around after children exhausting. But Sarah had become a different creature after Francis's birth—there was a hard darkness in her, which made her eyes and voice steel, made her quick to lash out: she reminded Edith of a caged animal, frantically snapping at any hand which came near.

Now, watching Sarah stiffen at her daughter's challenge, Edith found she was holding her breath. Then Claudine nodded and Sarah gave a quick, tight smile and let her go.

'That's the spirit. Good girl.'

But when she tried to light a cigarette, Sarah's fingers were trembling so much that she snapped three matches in half.

Edith turned away to watch the last remaining passengers boarding the boat.

Old Monsieur Le Brun, sitting on the quay, smoking and stroking his yellowed moustache, shouted out, 'Like rats, you are. Rats, buggering off at the first sign of trouble.'

One of the men on the gangplank stopped and called, 'Well, I'd rather be a living rat than a dead dog. You won't even see that boot coming until it kicks you in the ribs.'

Le Brun spat a thick yellow streamer of mucus on to the quay. 'May God forgive your desertion of your land in her time of need.'

The other men on the gangplank laughed harshly. One of them bellowed back, 'Yes, and God forgive *you*, you damned fool, bedding down with the enemy.'

The man next to him said, 'They'll all be speaking German the next time we see them. They'll have little moustaches. Even the women.' They laughed louder.

'And the babies. They'll be born with blond hair and their first words will be *Heil Hitler!*'

That raised the loudest laugh of all.

Dr Carter was at the quay too, but he wasn't leaving. He had a satchel on his shoulder, a bowl of water and a sponge. He was examining all the hospital patients who were well enough to be shipped off the island.

He took his time, talking to each of his patients and their families. He handed out tablets and gave injections here and there. But he was also redoing dressings and bandages—he even gave a quick sponge bath to one of the men who must have been completely bed-bound. Real donkey work, you might say. The last doctor, the one who thought Edith was the devil or close enough, would have had a flock of nurses seeing to all that for him.

Carter finished the last dressing and then came to stand next to her, eyebrows raised as if he were asking a question. No point in pretending she hadn't been gawking.

'Quite a bedside manner you have there, Doctor. They trust you, these folk, you know. And that's saying something.'

He gave a wry smile. 'I would say I'm flattered. But I suspect trust is a pleasant byproduct of being in charge of the medication for pain relief. I've found myself *most* popular with those patients in need of morphine.'

'Don't you believe it. We're an awkward bunch, we Jèrriais, or we can be, if we take against someone. But the people here don't mind you. Some might even like you. And that's something worth a pat on the back, when you've only been here a matter of months. Takes most visitors half a lifetime before they can make folk start to trust them, let alone *like* them.'

He turned to her with a quizzical smile. 'But I'm not a visitor. I plan to stay.'

'But you weren't born here. If you live here for the next half-century and draw your last breath on the island, you'll still be known as *that English doctor.*'

He laughed.

'I'm not jesting. Some families here can trace their blood back hundreds of years. Back to before the Conquest, or so they'd have you believe. And, as I say, we're a tricky bunch. See, we were part of French territory here, way back, but even when we were busy rebelling against the French, we were a law unto ourselves—we weren't ever *English*. We simply chose to side with them when it came to picking our loyalties for battles. But we're Jèrriais through and through. So if you're English then you're most certainly a visitor, Doctor, and a foreign one at that.'

He smiled. 'You paint quite a picture there. But surely you've all been English since 1066? Don't the Channel Islands belong to England nowadays?'

'Quiet with that sort of talk. There's people here would have your eyes for saying that we *belong* to anyone, let alone the

English. If anything, the English *belong* to us.'

'You're pulling my leg?'

'Not at all,' Edith said. 'It's like this you see: when William of Normandy took England for his own, we were part of Normandy. Part of the conquering army, if you like. Which means that we don't belong to England—England belongs to us. Our oldest possession, she is. Never you mind that smile, Doctor. There's some folk who've gone happily off to fight for the English, and that's their choice. But there are others who would no more leave here than peel off their own skins. I'll be buried here, even if it is the Germans who dig the hole.'

He had remarkable eyes when he smiled. Really quite blue. But why was he *smiling* when she mentioned the invasion?

'You're not frightened at all?' she asked.

He gave a tiny shrug. 'A little. I suspect we've chosen a raw deal. And you?'

'Of course, I'd be foolish not to be terrified.' She laughed, a high-pitched sound with an edge in it. It took her by surprise to say it out loud: she was petrified, losing sleep, queasy and knock-kneed with fear.

His eyes searched her face. 'You're thinking of the rumours of what they did in France?'

'Aren't we all?'

'And yet you chose to stay.'

'As did you. You could have left, very easily. I know you've said you felt a duty and that's very admirable. But there must be some other reason for a man like you to stay. Wouldn't you rather be near your family, at home?'

'Home...' He shook his head. 'No, I—I wanted to stay. Things cannot be as bad as all that, surely?'

She frowned. Was he a simpleton?

He looked at her for a long moment then leant forward and spoke quickly, earnestly. 'Because this isn't 1914. Because history doesn't repeat itself. Because it's only rumours, after all, and because the fear of the enemy is half the battle: if they have us running scared then they've already won, don't you see?'

She nodded, slowly. 'I think I do. You speak a fair amount of sense. For an Englishman, that is.'

He laughed and gave a small bow, as if at the end of a performance, and she suddenly wondered how much of what he said and did was just that: a performance, a brave face to scare the wolf of fear away.

⌒

A HAMMERING on the door dragged Maurice from sleep and he sat upright with a gasp. It took a moment for him to remember: the bombs, the evacuation, the Germans coming… For a confused moment he thought it might actually be soldiers battering on his door. But that wasn't possible, surely? Not so soon.

He rubbed his eyes. There was that hammering again.

Marthe grumbled in her sleep and Maurice heaved himself upright and opened the door an inch, squinting in the sudden sunlight.

That girl, Claudine, was standing on his doorstep, pink-cheeked as if she'd been running.

He frowned. 'Stop that hammering, will you? What are you doing here?'

'You've missed the boat,' she gasped. 'It's gone already. Just set sail. Papa has left, but you missed it.'

'Keep your voice down—Marthe is sleeping.'

'But Maurice, I thought you wanted to take Marthe.'

He rubbed his eyes. 'You're sharper than you look, young Claudine. I tried to leave, but she wouldn't come. Screamed the place down.' He tried to keep his voice calm. 'So now we're staying.'

'Aren't you worried the Germans will hurt her?'

He stared at her for a beat, then said, 'Yes. Perhaps I am.' And for an awful moment, he felt a rising tide of panic and thought he might weep in front of the girl. Then he drew a steadying breath.

'Well, it's too late to be fretting, in any case. It's wretched, but there's no escaping now.'

'But you've a boat of your own,' Claudine said. 'You could escape. You could row to England. With Marthe in the boat. You could rescue her—it would be such a thrilling adventure.'

For goodness sake. Was everything excitement and intrigue for this girl?

He shook his head. 'No, I can't take her anywhere alone. She's too far gone. I couldn't row and care for her as well...'

He couldn't force any more words past the cold stone of panic that crushed his chest.

And, bless the girl, she must have heard his voice tremble, because she looked out at the horizon while he calmed himself.

After a moment he managed to say, 'I've no choice but to stay now.'

'What rot! You simply need to find someone to go with you. And I'm going to help you. I will make it my very special task, to help you rescue Marthe and take her somewhere safe.'

For a moment, exasperating as it was, the child's blind optimism seemed as magical and unlikely as the stars: something that existed in spite of its own implausibility.

Maurice reached out and clasped her hand. Her fingers were small and cold in his and he was reminded of just how young she was. Ten, and a foreign army on the doorstep, but she wasn't cowering under the covers, howling in fear as he wanted to.

'Thank you,' he said. 'For wanting to help. You're a good girl. A marvel.'

After Claudine left, Maurice started scrubbing the floor, trying to pull himself together. But those stories skittered about in his head. What they said Germans did—what they'd done to the French when they invaded—it was enough to make a man sick. Perhaps the girl was on to something. Or perhaps not. Escaping once the Germans were here would be a bloody foolish business. Might as well take himself to the loony bin, or simply ask to be shot in the head.

He tried to think of something else; his fretting did Marthe no good. She sensed it and it made her restless and gripey.

She had settled back to sleep for the moment. Maurice had a mountain of washing, but that meant too much clattering with the scrubbing board and mangle. He could do the floor, though. It was a fine, quiet job. Just the scratch of the brush and the slosh of the water. If he set a good rhythm going then it helped to soothe her and she could sleep for hours. He liked to imagine she was dreaming about being out on the sea with him in the boat, back when they were courting and life stretched wide and open before them.

Dr Carter had told him there was nothing much going on in her head anymore, but sometimes she looked at him and Maurice could swear blind she was still there. Deep in those eyes, somewhere. So never mind the knife blade of pain in his back and the gunshot crack of his knees, he carried on scrubbing as long as he could bear it so she could have a good, long sleep. Perhaps find her way back to him while she was dreaming.

Maurice missed fishing terribly, of course. The oyster runs weren't the same: they were a rush out into the dark, snatch a net and back again. Rowing like the clappers; screaming muscles. All the while with his ears prickling for the sound of another boat, or a shout that might mean he'd been caught. Then it'd be a French prison for him, or a beating. Something worse, perhaps. And what would his Marthe do without him?

Fishing was different. He'd set off early in the morning, or in the dark breath of night sometimes, depending on the tide. Rowing steadily, keeping the same pace for an hour or more, until the island was a black smudge floating on the horizon. Far enough away for it to look like something he'd imagined, all the worries on it too distant to remember.

He'd cast his net out as if in a dream. A sort of magic to the action: like flinging out hope. Full of holes. Then sit and wait, every breath a prayer. Then tug and heave and dredge up wriggle-bodied treasure, slippery and gleaming.

There was nothing in the world like the enchanted stillness of the sea. Yes, there was a chorus of sounds: the water slapping on the wood and the whisper of his own breathing. Perhaps the cough of another fisherman, if he was close. But not one of those sounds crept under his skin. They were hums on the horizon. Outside of thought or care. As though they were buried fathoms under the sea, muffled by the weight and velvet darkness of the water.

And he could simply sit, silent. Wait for his net to fill with fish. Know that at home his wife would be rousing and washing, perhaps cooking something for his breakfast. When he returned he would be able to give her the money he'd raised from selling the fish: a conjuror to pluck gold from water. And she would help to sponge that sea smell from his body. And then perhaps they would both go back to bed for a touch of closeness. That face, those eyes. That sweet breath in his mouth and deep in his lungs. Fingers in his hair, nails on his back. He would sleep with her body wrapped around him. He would carry that peace with him all day.

He'd seen signs of the illness even before they married: changes in her mood, forgetfulness and a sort of *absence* in her eyes sometimes when she looked at him, as if she couldn't remember who he was.

Gradually, she'd become wilder: sometimes she lashed out at him for no reason. And they had both seen her mother's decline and knew how it might be for Marthe. But he loved her too much to leave her; he couldn't imagine existing without her. So they married and hoped that somehow Marthe's fate might be different.

Maurice had carried on fishing when Marthe's illness had worsened: they both pretended it wasn't happening, even as she became angrier, more absent, less herself. But then he would come home and find that she'd forgotten to fill the pan before she put it on the stove. The kitchen would be thick with smoke, stove smouldering, her coughing her insides up. Or she'd dropped a pile of dishes and then couldn't remember how to clean them up, had shredded her poor hands trying.

Every time he came home there would be something new she'd forgotten how to do—a piece of herself she had lost. Every time, she'd be crying and saying sorry over and over, as if she were somehow to blame for her illness.

But he knew he must stop the fishing when he came home and she'd spilled a pan of boiling water down her legs. She was rubbing at them—perhaps she had thought that might take the pain. But her skin was peeling off in her hands where the hot water had blistered it. Translucent parings of flesh, like white petals, which she threw to the floor, while underneath, her blood—so much blood.

He'd cried, 'What on earth?'

'I'm so sorry, darling,' she'd said. 'Look at this mess. Now just you sit tight and let me clean it up.'

She had tried to push him away when he sat her back down. She kept apologising for the state of the kitchen, and all the while she was sitting there with her legs raw and burnt and bloody. Holding her own skin in her hands.

He'd steered clear of the previous doctor, Dr Laird, up until then, but there was no escaping that time. He diagnosed Huntington's Chorea.

Maurice didn't care what it was called. He just wanted to know what to do, how they could avoid the fate her mother had suffered. But Laird had shaken his head and said there was nothing to be done. She would worsen and would need full-time care—sooner rather than later, as the disease progressed faster in younger people. 'Frightful business,' he'd murmured.

And, in the end, it would cause an infection, which would kill her.

Sorry, old chap.

Maurice had taken himself out for a walk. Stood on the cliff and bawled at the sea and the sky. Bent double with grief, he had screamed and sobbed until his breath ran out.

That was when he tried having that girl to tend her. But then, after he'd had to send her packing, he thought, *I can't do it. I can't leave Marthe with anyone again.*

Once the war started and France was occupied, Maurice would sometimes see the French fishermen who had managed to sneak out on to the sea, and they would tell stories of women being raped and gutted. Poked at with guns and knives before they were slit open like fish. Children shot at in the street for playing out after curfew. Or simply picked off, like stray dogs.

There were the other stories, too: Herr Hitler had it in for the Jews, it seemed—they were being rounded up all over Europe and put into camps where, Maurice imagined, they were forced to work for the Germans, or heaven knows what. And other types were taken off to work camps too: people who were crippled or too ill to care for themselves, gypsies. Homosexuals as well, but the fishermen laughed about that.

But he couldn't laugh at any of it. He could see that they didn't think it funny, not really. They laughed too loudly and for too long. And then there were lingering shards of silence when they all thought about their women and children.

So Maurice gave it all a good deal of thought while he scrubbed at the floor. By the time he had finished, he knew Claudine was right: they had to be out, before the Germans arrived. Never mind the journey—he would row until his back snapped in two.

He packed up a suitcase, just a few bits and pieces: clothes and so on for both of them, and some of the lavender soap that Edith had made for Marthe to help her sleep. Food and plenty of water, and that was it. He knew the soldiers were expected any hour.

His boat was moored up close to shore—he could carry Marthe down. She might sleep in the boat, if he was lucky. He could be on the mainland within two days, if he rowed hard.

But it was just as before, when he'd wanted to evacuate on that collier. Would Marthe leave the house? The tears began when he picked her up. Then, when he reached the door, she screamed and thrashed around as he'd seen small children do. Corded tendons on her neck, limbs flailing, lips stretched back so her face was more animal than human.

He tried to talk to her, to explain the way of it. *Shush, shush, this is for the best, my love. But shush and listen now. For God's sake, Marthe. For God's sake.*

But she was shrieking so loudly he didn't think she could hear him. And who knew if she could understand, in any case? He'd never seen anything like it—she was normally gentle as a kitten. He had always been the one with the temper.

He had to bundle her over his shoulder, pin her arms and legs. She kept straightening her limbs and flailing out so he couldn't pass through the door without hurting her. He hadn't a free hand for the suitcase, so he booted it in front of him.

Marthe was moaning something that sounded like the word *no*, even though she hadn't uttered a word to anyone in months. She began howling it, over and over again.

'Nononono!'

Next she started scrabbling her hands around and clawing at his back with her nails. Some days she couldn't even lift her own head from the pillow, but now she was flaying the skin from his back. And, as he began walking down the hill, the noise drew people from their houses. Folk began staring and whispering and then looking away and then back again, mouths agape.

Maurice ignored them and walked on. Let them talk.

At the bottom of the hill, Madame Le Cornu peered out from behind her washing. She tutted and shook her head.

A few fellows were digging a ditch nearby. They laid down their spades and scowled.

'There now, Maurice!' they called. 'Steady on!'

One of them, Benest, had his hands raised. Held them out in front of him, as if Maurice was brandishing a gun. 'Easy now, fellow. Let her go. Easy does it.'

Maurice pushed on, as though the chap were a strong wind. Noise to walk through, nothing more.

'Come, Maurice,' Benest said. 'No need to hurt her. Put her down.'

Hot lance of fear and rage. 'I'm *not* hurting her!'

Marthe screamed again.

Benest balled his hands into fists. 'Now, Maurice, I don't want to take her from you. But listen. Put her down. She's distraught. She's frantic. Put her down now, will you? There's a good man.'

Breath sobbing in his throat, Maurice set Marthe down on a nice, soft patch of grass, sank down next to her and buried his face in her hair. She was trembling all over.

He shushed her, and then he kissed her slack mouth. The fellows stood, gawping. Their hands still in fists.

Maurice took a juddering breath. 'Nothing to worry about,

lads. One of those days. The Germans coming—she's panicking. You know how it is.'

Benest nodded. 'It's a worry for the ladies. You'll look after her, Maurice. And gentle, eh?'

'Never you worry. I shan't let them touch a hair of her.'

He lifted her up and walked up the hill and back home, kissing her face with every step. The neighbours stood watching. Madame Le Cornu carried on pegging her washing—later she'd be off to tell Madame Hacquoil every detail.

Maurice tucked Marthe back up in their bed and stroked her hair from her forehead to help her to sleep. All the while he stared at the picture of the empty cross above their bed. A piece of the frame had been chipped away. *Oh, that needs fixing.*

Something to think upon.

He was glad, so glad, that when he next looked down she wasn't staring at him any longer. He wrapped his body around hers and tried not to think of those marching boots and shouting voices and their guns, growing closer, closer all the time. He half expected to hear a hammering on the door.

He worried it backwards and forwards for most of the night. He watched the dark shadows on the ceiling turning into snarling animals. Then men marching, unfurling like endless skeins of wool. Gleaming guns held high. Then he saw clouds. Then aeroplanes, their toothed stomachs vomiting out bomb after bomb.

When he opened his eyes, it was light outside. The shadows were memories and Marthe was stirring.

But, as if he was still trapped within his dream, there was a steady, insistent pulsing in his head, like the blood thrumming in his ears. He scrambled upstairs, drew back the curtain and pressed his face against the grubby glass.

Movement. He could see it on the road up from the beach. Blur of green, as if the very trees were marching.

He breathed out hot, panicked air on to the glass and scrubbed it with his sleeve, then pressed his face against the cold window.

The hazy green gradually formed itself into bodies and legs and marching boots. And bristling black guns, glinting in the morning sun.

Part 2

FROM a ramshackle jetty that had been hastily pieced together after the bombings, Dr Carter watched the enemy arriving.

The area around the harbour was packed with bodies, more so than the morning of the first large evacuation. Everyone jostling for a front-row view. But each was also reluctant to be standing in the firing line. They were all sweat and teeth and hot, rattled breath. Carter had the feeling that at any time chaos could erupt.

The Bailiff, Alexander Coutanche, had ordered white flags to be hung out in plain view wherever possible, as per the Germans' instructions. In defiance, some of the islanders had hung out long johns instead of bedsheets.

The ship had docked a few minutes earlier. It was a beastly thing: an enormous dark grey battleship, brash with guns, monstrous mouth gaping to allow the soldiers to march from its belly. It seemed to Carter, at that moment, as solid and immovable as the ground beneath his feet.

The soldiers were ordered and disciplined, forming lines and saluting as one before disembarking the ship. Their boots hit the ground in an exact *one-two-one-two* marching rhythm. It echoed through the ground, into his singing blood—before long it seemed that his heart pounded along to the same tempo.

Carter reviewed his vital signs as he might examine a patient: heart rate, raised; blood pressure, raised. Mouth quite dry, palms unpleasantly damp. His fear was useless, he knew: it would change nothing. And yet, seeing them for the first time, he was frightened. Enough to make him wish he had returned to England.

The men themselves were young: lads in their early twenties, for the most part, some younger. Each looked unwaveringly ahead, not allowing their eyes to wander for even a second, in spite of the strange surroundings. The personal and collective discipline put him in mind of a muzzled wolf.

They were all in rude health, too: ruddy cheeks and solid, well-muscled bodies, not a wheezer or a limper among them.

Carter tried not to feel nauseous. What a fool he had been to imagine that this invasion could be anything other than catastrophic. But still, just as his fear could not change the dreadful fact of the Germans' arrival, his panic would not improve matters.

So he returned to his post at the hospital with a cold fist of horror in his stomach but forced a spring into his step. He smiled and tried to reassure the farmers and fishermen who were winding their way uneasily back to their homes. He had always been conscious that one in his position must attempt to guide and protect those around him.

An appearance of unruffled calm was something he'd

cultivated since childhood. He could still remember the harsh bark of his father's laughter as he said, *'Trembling, are you? I'll give you something to tremble about.'* Then, inevitably, came the slipper, the cane, the back of his father's work-roughened hand. So, since fear changed nothing, Carter had taught himself not to feel it; or, at least to conceal it, even from himself.

The hospital staff were terrified—that much was clear as soon as he set foot on the ward.

The nurses looked up from their bandaging and all conversation stopped. Even the patients, those who were able, lifted their heads to stare. The same question was in every set of eyes.

Carter waited until he had complete silence and attention before announcing, 'Nothing to worry about. Not a thing. They seem civilised enough. Very ordered. There will be no riots or pillaging, I would bet my life on it. Now, how is Monsieur Hacquoil today?'

He didn't really need to ask. He could see even before he checked the charts that the poor chap was worsening.

Quite apart from his fever and rapid heart rate, which indicated the onset of infection, his colour was poor and his pupils unresponsive. His body was slowly shutting down, in spite of their best efforts. Much as it pained Carter to admit it, he'd need to move Hacquoil to a larger hospital with more sophisticated treatment methods and access to a wider variety of medication.

A larger hospital on the mainland might also be able to attempt skin grafts on his burns. The best they could do in Jersey was keep his wounds clean, change his bandages and drain the pus.

Carter had intended to evacuate him when the collier left but had worried that Clement might not survive the journey. Given his rapid deterioration, however, it was clearly a choice of moving him and giving him the chance of survival or keeping him on the island and attempting to provide for him a comfortable death.

It was this alternative that Carter planned to present to the Commandant later that day. He would need the German's permission to evacuate Clement to the mainland.

The Commandant had established himself in the States of Jersey Buildings in Royal Square—the seat of legislation in the island. All the locally elected officials and the King's own representative had offices there. It was the vacant office of the Lieutenant Governor (the King's representative) that the Commandant had chosen as his headquarters. This, too, was part of Jersey's complicated relationship with England, which had taken Carter some time to fathom: while the Channel Islands were free to make their own laws and exist almost entirely independently of the mainland, the King appointed the Lieutenant Governor to serve as de facto head of state.

Of course, that would all change now.

One of the Germans' instructions before arrival had been that the Lieutenant Governor was to leave, which seemed farcical given that his power on the island was negligible: he simply served as a royal figurehead, a reminder to the islanders that, although they might have French names, they still belonged to the English throne (although, after talking to Madame Bisson, this was not a thought Carter would voice aloud).

The departure of the Lieutenant Governor again reminded Carter that he really should have left for the mainland. He was

English-born and was not permitted by the Germans to remain on the island. But he was prepared to take that risk—his patients, after all, needed him.

Besides, his old life in England was over now: he had ruined everything. The memory of Father's fury and disappointment when they parted was painful to recall. Jersey had provided him with a fresh start. A clean slate, which would stay clean, as long as he remained careful.

Carter's move and his new life were born out of a desire to make amends, somehow, for the distress he had caused, to shape something like hope from the dead ashes of his past.

The Lieutenant Governor had clearly departed in a hurry— the Union flag was still displayed above the large oak desk. As Carter entered the office, the Commandant was overseeing the hanging of its replacement: the red and black swastika.

The Commandant was slightly corpulent and red-cheeked, but he seemed affable enough. He put Carter in mind of a child's imagining of St Nicholas. Except for the Nazi uniform, of course, and when Carter offered his hand to shake, the Commandant gave a straight-armed salute and barked, *'Heil Hitler!'*

Carter tried to push his mouth into a smile. 'Yes, quite. *Heil...* Very pleased to meet you. Apologies for my poor German—I don't speak it at all, really.'

The Commandant sat back in his leather chair, unblinking.

Carter took a deep breath. 'Thank you for agreeing to see me. I know how busy you must be, what with the, ah, *settling in* and so on... Please allow me to introduce myself. I'm Dr Timothy Carter.'

A faint smile now hovered around the Commandant's thin lips. Carter felt a surge of irritation.

'The local doctor...physician? Medical...?' He tapped on his stethoscope.

The Commandant's smile widened and the prim little mouth parted. '*Carter.* This is English name, yes?'

His voice was heavily accented with the guttural sounds so characteristic of native Germans, but his pronunciation was perfectly clear.

Oh Lord. If he admitted to being English then he instantly put himself at risk of imprisonment or deportation. While Carter's mind whirred, trying to fabricate a reason for his English name, the Commandant spoke again.

'And your voice—I understand this easily. You do not have the strange accent of Jersey.'

'I, ah—'

'Yes, you are English.' His eyes narrowed. 'No English should be here.'

'No, I—'

'But you are doctor. Medical men are useful, no? In war?'

He was moving too quickly for Carter to keep pace, though he did latch on to this last idea.

'Ah—yes, of course. I am very *useful*, as you say. I mainly work in the hospital, although I also engage in home visits, where necessary.'

The Commandant's pale eyes narrowed. '*Use*ful. Yes.'

Time swung like a scythe. Carter waited, his heart a clenched fist. *Don't show your fear.*

'The island is very pleasant. Much sunshine. This is healthful, yes?'

A reprieve. Carter exhaled.

'Oh, yes, sunlight is very beneficial. And I agree, the island is very beautiful. Of course, a little *less* beautiful after…recent events…' *Come on, Tim.* He coughed. 'The bombs. They have damaged the land and people were also injured in the…attack. Some died.'

The Commandant shrugged. 'Of course. This is war, yes. Injury, death. This happens.'

His tone hadn't altered from when they had been discussing the weather, and Carter felt a chill. The man simply didn't *care*. He spoke hurriedly now.

'Yes, so, what I mean to say is, ah, the…difficulty I have concerns one of my patients.'

'Yes?'

Carter stared at the black swastika above the German's head and clenched his jaw. His father's voice had entered his head. *For heaven's sake, Tim! The point is?*

Father had always been impatient with what he saw as his son's *scholar's sensitivity*. Carter was a long-limbed, fine-boned aberration in a family of stocky, brusque farmers, and Father, while proud of Carter as *a sharp lad*, had no time at all for his *airs and graces*.

In other words, his feelings.

Now, facing the Commandant, his legs shaking, Carter quashed this fear.

'The man in question is a burns victim.' He kept his voice firm, matter-of-fact. 'One of the bombs… Chap was caught in the blast and injured. Ah…very gravely injured indeed. Terrible burns. He's in a bad way, Commandant, I don't mind telling you. A *very* bad way.'

'I see. You are doctor, yes? But you wish medical advice from me?'

The Commandant still wasn't smiling, but his eyes glinted.

Carter frowned. 'No, no, ah, thank you. But I have reached the limit of my own and the hospital's capabilities. The patient requires advanced medical procedures, for which we have no trained staff, and medicines which we do not possess and have no hope of obtaining in the...current *situation*.'

'This is unfortunate.'

Carter felt a swell of relief: the man understood him.

'Yes. Quite. Unfortunate. So, as I'm sure you understand, it is vital that my patient receive medical care on the mainland.'

At this point, the Commandant leant back in his chair and stretched his pinched mouth into a wide smile.

'I have said, Doctor, this is unfortunate. But medical care from England? This is not possible. We are at war, *nichts*? And we have very good English doctor here, yes? We do not want Doctor to return to England. He will be useful here; he has said it.'

Was this a threat or was the Commandant being deliberately obtuse? Carter wet his lips.

'But...but I'm not asking to return myself. Nor am I requesting any sort of communication with England regarding the war. I'm simply entreating you to save a man's life. If we do nothing then the prognosis is horrifying. He simply *must* be evacuated.'

'Impossible.'

Carter blinked. 'Forgive me, Commandant, but I believe you misunderstand the magnitude of the situation. Without the correct medical care, this man will certainly die.'

'Unfortunate, yes. But this cannot be helped.'

'But *why*, for God's sake? This is ludicrous!'

Carter's voice cracked with anger. Surely the Commandant couldn't be such a brute? How was it possible to deny medical care to a dying man, regardless of the political situation?

The Commandant banged his hand upon the table, his fleshy face suddenly hard. 'Enough! You do not question or you will regret this! This is dangerous for you. You will stop now.'

Carter was dimly aware of the shortness of his own breath, of a tingling in his legs. He swallowed but his mouth was dry. He wanted, desperately, to rectify this confusion, to make the Commandant understand... But in the German's rebuke, he felt the shadow of a gun levelled at his forehead.

'You will not ask this again. No?'

Carter bit the inside of his cheeks, then shook his head.

The Commandant leant forward and whispered, as though he were imparting a great secret, 'I have said it, Doctor: we are at war.'

Carter was then dismissed. A guard came to escort him from the building. Despite the weakness in his legs, Carter managed to stand and turned to leave, fear and rage simmering in his gut.

Before he reached the door, the Commandant called, 'Wait please, Doctor.'

Carter's heart skipped: he had finally understood; he was not a monster.

But the Commandant only said, 'Your nails. Show me.' He held out his hands.

Carter almost hid his own hands behind his back like a child, then thought better of it and let the German examine his fingers. The Commandant smiled, fully then, although it was strange to watch: cracks creeping up a wall.

His touch was cold and his skin had a fleshy, slippery feel to it, like the scum on a dead fish. Carter forced himself not to snatch his hands away, although something possessive in the man's touch made his skin crawl.

'Your nails are very clean. How do you say, *immaculate*, yes?'

A strange detail to focus on, but Carter was so desperate to leave the room that he gabbled an agreement.

'Yes. I cannot afford to introduce bacteria to any of my patients. I am most fastidious.'

'That is good. I like that in a man. Dirt, I do not like. It is a sign of laziness. I do not like lazy men, Doctor.' His voice was smooth.

Carter thought of a flat-eyed snake. His stomach turned over, but not before the German dropped his hand and turned away.

~

EDITH couldn't lie: it had stolen her peace, watching them marching down the streets, setting up guards and patrols. Telling folk what to do. Edith had never been one for following orders, and didn't take too kindly to being told to stay in her house before sun-up and after sundown. So she didn't, and the Germans be jiggered—what could they do to an old woman like her, in any case?

The early morning just before dawn had always been her favourite time for gathering plants. When her husband, Frank, was alive, he used to complain when he woke and she was gone. Off rummaging in bushes for berries. *Stuff and nonsense.*

He never put much stock in her remedies, even though she'd

cured his headaches and his gout. Once, she'd bound up his broken arm with a herbal poultice, which took all the pain and helped knit the bones. But he laughed away the thought that it might have healed him. He said that he'd always mended well and had the constitution of a prime Jersey bullock. It didn't serve him very well in the trenches, mind. But there you are.

She never could face remarrying. She had no heart left to give after they brought her that envelope. Black-edged, as if the tidings it bore had scorched at the very paper. Sometimes she felt they must have buried the cinders of her still-beating heart with him in some field in France. The years living alone since had moulded her the way a prevailing wind will shape a stubborn tree into the most fantastic of fixed shapes. Independent, she was (*Bloody-minded*, Frank used to say), and that wasn't going to change for anyone, least of all for a gaggle of foreign soldiers.

They had always wanted children, Edith and Frank. Sometimes it still struck her that it would have been wonderful to see her husband's eyes in a young child's face, in the set of the jaw or the angle of the nose. The quick shout of his laughter, buffeting on a breeze. But then, she'd have been raising a child alone. Besides, there was a freedom in solitude. She could be out of bed in the middle of the night, ready to be rooting through bushes when the sun was up, and there wasn't a soul to tell her she should be elsewhere scrubbing bedsheets, or doling out the breakfast, or running herself ragged chasing grandchildren.

It was a week after the Germans had arrived and she had just discovered a wonderful patch of belladonna when Dr Carter found her. Not too much of the stuff around these days: most folks dug it up and burned it—a terrible shame and a waste. It was only poisonous if someone was fool enough to eat too much. Consumed in just the right amount it was a marvelous painkiller, even for the strongest birthing pains. It also made a truly excellent poultice for broken bones or burns and a wonderful tincture when steeped in hot water.

The previous doctor used to bemoan all manner of suspicious potions she made and plants she used, no doubt for nefarious means. *Witchcraft*, he'd called it. One of the things they had quarrelled about was that she kept belladonna in her garden.

Dangerous, he'd said. *Potentially lethal.*

She told him the truth: if folk will let their children run wild and dig around in other people's gardens and eat what they find there, then they're asking for trouble. She'd given the boy in question a good dose of warm salt and mustard water and he had vomited up all the berries, right then and there. All over her good bed of sorrel and sage, if you please. *That* was the fool mother's complaint: Edith had made her boy sick. He was bawling like she'd stuck pins in him, and when Edith told the pinch-faced mother that he was better off sick than dead, the child let out an almighty howl. The nit-witted woman shrieked at her and wouldn't believe that the salt and mustard mixture was actually the medicine her foolish child needed. So she took him to Dr Laird. He, of course, stuck his big beak in and told the mother Edith could have killed her boy.

They had tried to make her dig up the belladonna and burn it. The whole island was whispering witchcraft. Fires in their eyes, gleaming from the shadows like packs of hungry wolves. She couldn't go anywhere without people sneaking sideways glances at her and making the sign against evil behind her back. Rowan branches nailed above their doors, for heaven's sake. No one smiled when she said they'd be better off boiling up the bark and saving the liquid for winter coughs.

She'd said to Laird, 'I've put a label next to it that says *Deadly Nightshade* for a reason, you know, Doctor. The name is quite clear and in my best writing. See, the word *dead* is plain as your face or mine.'

But he'd stirred the island up against her. She had angry fathers hammering her door at three in the morning, which was an ungodly hour even for her (and she didn't sleep much of a night in any case). Folks threatening to torch her house. And friends of years refusing to meet her eye. Silence like a stone dropped from a cliff when she walked past. Eyes sidling slyly at her, noses upturned as if she were a rotten shank of mutton on the butcher's block.

It calmed down for the most part, though, after Dr Laird left to go back to the mainland because of an odd rash and vomiting illness, which kept bothering him as long as he was in Jersey, but disappeared whenever he left the island. Frightful luck. Edith had always thought it: belladonna was a marvelous plant.

So she was up to the elbows in a nice healthy patch with plenty of good, dark berries when the new doctor (Carter, she remembered) happened upon her. He seemed pleasant enough, but you never could tell. Besides, she liked her own company when she was gathering plants; it helped her to mull things over. Put the world to rights. She hoped that if she ignored him for long enough then he might move on.

But after a moment, he coughed loudly and she couldn't very well disregard that.

'Good morning to you, Doctor. Nasty cough there. Shouldn't you take something for that? It can't be good for business when the doctor himself is ill.'

'Ha, yes.' Carter paused, then said, 'Marvelous colours in the sky today.'

'Beautiful, isn't it?'

She didn't turn around; she had just spotted a very nice patch of ragwort. The farmers hated it because it poisoned the cattle, so she didn't often happen across it, which was a crying shame—it made for a most relaxing tea, in the right quantities.

She waited for him to be on his way. But she could see him from the corner of her eye, shuffling his feet in those fancy English leather shoes of his, and she sighed.

'Well, as long as you're going to be standing there, you might as well make yourself useful. Hold this, will you?'

She heaved her basket up. Carter staggered a little under the weight.

'You, ah—you do know that's…*ragwort*, don't you?'

'Well, if I didn't then I wouldn't be gathering it. Dangerous to pick plants you don't recognise. They could be poisonous.'

'So you're aware, then, that this is nightshade?'

'Why do you imagine I put a blanket at the bottom of the basket? You don't want the stuff on your hands or clothes, that's certain. Even a little of the juice can give you the runs for days.'

He laughed. But when he saw she was serious, he fell silent. She carried on digging while he stood staring out over the sand dunes and towards the sea.

The island was like a beautiful jewel: formed by years of pressure and compression, shaped by the elements and then constrained and combed and ordered by the metallic tools of man. The result was a savage, wild and rugged land with the long grasses gusted about by the wind, toothed rocks jutting from the soil, crusted with lichen: thousands of attentive gold and black ears, gaping at the slightest whisper of the wind.

Further inland, the precise hedgerows and straight lines of the farmer's fields, geometric crafting of grass and plough. And then the sea, the endless, gasping sea: when the tide swept away, the rocks jutted out of the mud like teeth from a smashed mouth. Stippled in limpets and winkles, heaving with seaweed: rock pools bubbling with life. To the east, picture-perfect houses, like clutches of crafted eggs, nestling by the golden beaches. To the west, the vast mudflats where children could pour salt into a hole in the mud and a razorfish might pop out like a conjuror's trick. The steady breaking and wombing of the sea, metronomic measure of seeping time.

But nothing ever the same: everything sharp and fresh, as if it had been cut out of paper new each day.

Now the land had Germans swarming across it, hacking into the landscape, roving over the hills, lounging on the beaches. The islanders didn't look at them, if they could help it: Edith had seen the way everyone's eyes slid from the soldiers practising their marching drills on the beaches where tourists usually sunbathed.

Edith liked to gawp at the scenery as much as the next person, for all she'd lived on the island more years than she'd care to count. But Dr Carter's eyes had a glassy look about them. *Away with the fairies,* Edith's mother used to say, and she'd give her a smart clip around the ear to bring her back sharpish.

'What do you want from me then, Doctor?'

He pulled his eyes from the view. 'Nothing in particular. That is to say, I don't know what I need, really.'

By *Crie,* by the time the man had come around to saying his piece they'd both be dead and buried.

'Well, Doctor, I can't help you then. *À bétôt.*'

She made a great show of struggling to heft her basket again. Carter took it from her. 'Please. Allow me.'

He fell in beside her as she walked. She set off, briskish, said not a word. Most folk would crack and say *something* in the end, given long enough in silence with a stranger.

Carter was no different from anyone else. 'So, what is your opinion then, on our current situation? Our visitors, I mean.'

'I'm not sure I can say, really. It's only been a week or so. Wretched situation—that goes without saying. But one foreigner is like any other to me, and at least it's not the bloody French, or the miserable lot from Guernsey invading us.'

'I've been unpleasantly taken aback by the Germans, I must admit,' Carter said. 'They don't seem to intend to be terribly *agreeable.*'

Laughter swelled. 'Agreeable?' Edith barked. 'Why ever did you dream they would be *agreeable?* We're the enemy. Makes no sense for them to be anything but downright unpleasant, if you ask me. And I imagine they want to make their mark. It's a war that's dropped on to our doorstep, remember. A *war.* They're not here for the sun and the fishing.'

'That's more or less what the Commandant said. I asked him, you see, if we could evacuate Clement to the mainland. Without the right treatment I'm convinced that he will die, slowly and painfully, I'm afraid—and soon.'

'The Commandant said no, of course.'

Carter nodded grimly. 'He seems to think the whole situation a terrific joke. It's horrendous.'

She was puzzled by Carter's bewilderment—not expecting such naïveté from an intelligent man. She stopped and put a hand on his arm.

'How old were you in the last war, Doctor?'

He stared at her hand, frowning. Then mumbled: 'Fifteen when it ended.'

'You've no memory then? How cheap men's lives can be.'

'I know of the terrible numbers of deaths and casualties.'

'Of course. But at the time, it didn't matter if five thousand men died, or five thousand and ten. Those ten men. What were they? Nothing. Not in the grand scheme of things, anyway. Only to those who loved them. Felt their absence like a lost limb.'

'But this is an entirely different situation—'

'Of course it isn't!' The sweet bafflement on Carter's face baffled her, almost irked her, but Edith softened her voice. 'What does it matter to the Commandant if ten men died in that bomb attack, or eleven? That extra man makes not a blind bit of difference to him. Only to Clement's family. Those of us who know him.'

'That's a *ghastly* approach to human life.'

'Right you are. But, Doctor, we are at war.'

'Even so...' He scrubbed his hand across his forehead and, for a moment she saw him for the kind-hearted, guileless boy he must have once been—and still was, in some ways.

'I simply cannot fathom it,' he said. 'A life is a *life*, after all, is it not? Would you justify letting a man die, simply because he was born in a different house to you?'

He didn't wait for her to reply but charged on, his words an urgent torrent.

'No, of course not. Why, then, let him die because he harks from a different town? A different country? I *cannot* grasp it...'

His eyes were wild and he was as impassioned as she had ever seen him.

'Not everyone has your heart, Doctor,' Edith said, gently. 'It's a noble thing: seeing the best in people, suffering to help them. It takes a great man. But it's a damned gallant fool who imagines that every other man feels anyone else's pain half as deeply as he does.'

The wind whipped through the long dune grasses and blew up flurries of sand. They squinted at the sensation, like needles on their faces. Out above the sea, hungry gulls were wheeling.

Carter fiddled with the plants in the basket. 'Found some fish, I expect.'

'Mackerel, probably.'

They watched them shrieking and diving again and again. Each gull filling his own belly and to hell with the rest of them.

'You've knowledge of health and medicine that supersedes that of many doctors I've seen,' Carter said. 'The way you revived Clement was really, well, it was...extraordinary. And I've heard other tales of how effective and impressive your remedies have been, in so many cases. As you know, the medication we are giving Clement is having little effect. So I, ah, I came to ask if you would...treat his burns and his fever. Try to, well...help me try to keep him alive.'

So *this* was what he wanted.

Edith nodded slowly. 'And if I can't?'

'Well, you may not be able to help him, of course. But at the moment he's dead without your help. So anything you can do, anything at all, would be...'

'Impressive? Extraordinary?' She grinned.

He gave a tiny smile. 'Precisely, yes... So, will you help?'

She stopped walking. What to say? Of course she was happy to help; such things came naturally to her. And even being asked was a pat on the back for Edith and a knife in the guts of the island gossips: one of the devil's own, helping in the hospital, working alongside real doctors? The church prayer group would be spitting feathers and fasting for a week.

And then, of course, there was the chance to save Clement's life. She'd have felt a callous brute if she'd not agreed to help. But her maman had always told her that it paid to have people believe that they owed you something or other.

The world doesn't run on kindness, Edith. It runs on guilt and favours and credit.

With the war on, who knew what the price would be on kindness for herself or for someone else?

So she said, 'I don't know, Doctor, I really don't...'

He had been smiling—so sure she would say yes. His face fell.

'But why on earth not? You'd be saving a man's life.'

'But that's just the thing, isn't it, Doctor: what if I don't? What if he dies? There's plenty of folk will be happy to think that I killed him off. The chap who was here before you *hated* me. He had everyone believing I was working hand in hand with the devil himself. And there's many were happy to believe it. If Clement died—well... They'd see me locked up for murder, I'm sure. Throw me in the sea to see if I float or sink.'

Carter tried to win her over to his way of thinking all the way back to her house, panting as he dragged the loaded basket. On and on and *on* he went. She let him talk. Folk always give more away when their thoughts run free.

By the time they reached her rickety old gate, he was begging and bargaining. He promised that he would do whatever he could to lift her good name with the rest of the islanders. To hear him talk, he planned to trumpet her praises at dawn from the top of Mount Bingham, whether Clement lived or no.

She took her basket back. The poor man was now quite exhausted.

Edith smiled. 'Thank you, Doctor. Most kind of you; you've saved my back, really you have. So, what time shall I call at the hospital tomorrow?'

He was silent for a moment while her words sank in. 'Then you'll do it? You'll help him? Wonderful woman, you won't regret this. You'll see! Thank you, you're a marvel! Thank you, bless you!'

And he actually kissed her on the cheek. Well, Edith couldn't help herself—she let out a shriek and a giggle and he chuckled right along with her.

Then he was suddenly serious. 'Perhaps you'd be so kind as to help me with something else then?'

'Try me, Doctor.'

'My aim—that is to say, my intention—is to, well...' He swallowed. 'To evacuate Monsieur Hacquoil. Medical equipment on the mainland so far exceeds our own. He stands a much better chance of survival.'

'I see. You need me to make him well enough to travel.'

'Precisely. And also—'

'You want my help taking him from the island?'

'Would you? I just wouldn't know where to start asking. For supplies, and the boat and so on. I don't want to risk asking in the wrong places. They're inclined to be garrulous, these island people.'

'Noticed that, have you? But it'll be a risky business: evacuating someone. There's signs up that say they'll shoot those who try to escape—and those that help could be shipped off to Germany. To one of their work camps.'

'You're absolutely right: it's too much to ask. Please forgive me and forget I mentioned—'

'Now, don't get ahead of yourself. I haven't said no, have I? Although it would be a foolish undertaking. And I couldn't even think of leaving myself.'

'No, of course not. But if you could point me in the right direction—'

'I'm hoping I won't need to do any pointing. If we can nurse Clement back to health then we won't be talking about leaving at all now, will we?'

'Certainly not. But—well, his condition is critical. It would be as well to have an idea of whom to ask if escape becomes our only option.'

'Stubborn so-and-so, aren't you?'

Edith thought for a moment. It was dangerous, of course, but even the thought of it was thrilling: helping someone to escape, right from under the Germans' noses, and saving Clement's life. She recalled what Carter had said, the wild passion in his eyes when he talked about the impossibility and barbarism of letting a man—any man—die.

She spoke slowly. 'I know a fisherman. He has a boat— unlicensed I suspect, so he doesn't have to give half his catch to the Bosche. He hasn't said so, but I'm sure he's anxious to be away from the island. I'll have a word, *if* I must. No guarantees, mind.'

'Of course.' He grinned, his face suddenly bright and youthful.

As she waved him off and watched him trudge through the long grasses, Edith felt a prickle of excitement and dread: the same sensation which swept through her when she jumped from a high rock into the dark sea, unsure if the water was deep enough to cradle her from the teeth of the hidden rocks beneath.

—

AFTER the Germans came, Claudine's mother hardly left the house. She sat in her chair and smoked. When her cigarettes ran out, she had Claudine fetch her some nettles and dry the leaves for her. The smoke smelt sour and made their eyes water.

Coughing, Claudine asked, 'What is the matter?'

Maman's eyes were dark and distant. 'Nothing. I simply—I miss your papa.'

Claudine remembered being curled up in her bed, the night before Papa had left on the boat. The sound of shouting. Maman crying, 'Why won't you stay?' Papa saying over and over that he wanted to fight. Saying that Claudine and Maman must stay to milk the cows and tend the chickens and keep the house from the German soldiers who might take it if it was left empty.

Maman had cried for a long time and then Claudine had heard her hiss, 'You don't want to fight. And you don't care a jot for us. You're *scared*. Yellow at the thought of the Germans—'

Claudine remembered a sound like a single clap. And then another. Applause bouncing off the walls—as if Papa were giving Maman an ovation for speaking her mind.

Claudine had known better. She knew better now, too. When Maman said, 'I miss your papa,' she meant something darker, and more complicated: an idea too knotted for Claudine to untangle into words.

It was very quiet in school in September when term began, after the Germans had rounded up all the English people and put them on to a boat—the children too. They were going to a work camp in Germany, everybody said.

Shocked, Claudine had watched the sobbing children clamber aboard, round-eyed and pleading. A German soldier had ruffled their hair and given them sweets. But the children had all spat them out over the side of the boat when the soldier wasn't looking, just in case they were filled with deadly poison.

It was harder to hide when the playground was quiet. Claudine remembered once seeing a dog chasing after a colony of rabbits, each tiny creature sprinting across the field, frantic paws drumming. The dog battered after them, weaving in all directions, yelping in frustration until it singled out a lone animal. Isolated from its companions, the creature was soon flop-bodied and broken.

One morning, a boy, Jacques Benest, found Claudine crouching next to the wall. He stood, staring at her, eyes burning.

Dry-mouthed, Claudine made daisy chains and pretended he was a rock or a tree.

'Hi there, *swot*,' he sneered. He sat down next to her—too close. 'Do you know that you will be taken away by the German soldiers one day?'

Claudine didn't look at him. 'No, I won't.'

'Yes, you *will*. Because you have black hair and brown eyes.'

'So?'

'So you look just like a filthy Jew. And *everybody* knows that the Germans hate the bloody, filthy Jews. My papa says they're rounding them all up and making them do all their work, like *animals.*'

Jacques Benest had a round, soft-cheeked face, blue eyes and fair hair that curled close to his scalp, like lambs' wool. He looked like the pictures of flying cherubs Claudine had seen in books, pale hands stretched out to touch Baby Jesus.

She stood and edged backwards until the wall was cold and hard against her spine.

He laughed. 'You shouldn't be dithering. You should be running away before they catch you and do you in. You and *all* the filthy Jews. My papa thinks the Germans should finish them all off. *Bang, bang, bang!* Right between the eyes. Loud as *anything.*'

He hooted with laughter. His breath smelt of apples and his mouth was crowded with strong, white teeth. Next to him, Claudine felt small and dark and grubby.

But his words made no sense to her: she knew that the Germans had made special laws which said that Jews weren't allowed into some shops and couldn't come out of their houses for most of the day. But that didn't mean that anyone was going to *shoot* them.

Jacques took a step towards her, still laughing, his fists clenched.

'Why do you call them *filthy Jews*?' she asked.

He stopped laughing and stared. 'Don't you know *anything*?' He smirked. 'I thought you were *clever*?'

As long as she kept him talking, perhaps it would keep his hard fists away from her.

'I haven't any books about Jews,' she said.

'They make a great deal of money. From other people. They *steal* it, all the money. That's what my papa says. *No one* likes them. They're a rotten lot. And you look *just* like them.'

Very softly—she couldn't help it, even though she knew it was comments like this that made other children call her *stuck-up* and *know-all*—Claudine said, 'But I'm *not* a Jew. Everybody knows that.'

Jacques curled his lips into a cruel smile, then pointed his fingers at her forehead and said, *'Bang!'*

Even her lessons were different, after the Germans came. The new teacher was called Madame Vibert. She put a picture of Hitler on the wall next to the chalkboard. They had to salute it every morning and say, *Heil Hitler!*

The children had to learn German, and they were not allowed to speak Jèrriais in case they were secretly plotting to blow up the Germans with a box of matches or build a boat from school desks and float across the channel to freedom. The thought made Claudine smile.

She quite enjoyed speaking German. Some words had a precision and a simplicity: *hier* and *gut* and *kommen* sounded almost like the English words. Two wonderful sentences were *das ist gut* and *kommen sie hier*. It was rather like speaking English with an absurd accent, and anyone could do that.

Longer words were imbued with beauty and elegance: her mouth watered over the drawn-out vowels and blurred consonants of *pflaumenkuchen*, and at night she said the word again and again and dreamed of a plum cake more delicious than anything she had ever tasted.

When she wasn't trying to learn German, she spent many of her hours in school lost in thought over the ways that Maurice could escape and whom he could take with him on the boat.

Dr Carter would have been a good choice, but he was confusing. Why hadn't he left with all the other English people? When she was collecting the meat ration, Claudine heard Madame Hacquoil saying that Dr Carter was 'a martyr to poor Clement's cause'. When she looked up *martyr* in the big school dictionary, it said *a person who is killed because of their religious or other beliefs*. She thought he must be a very good doctor to risk being killed for his patients.

Claudine wondered if she could persuade Maman to help, because she knew how to look after people and she was ever so kind when she wasn't in a black mood.

Her mother had worn her nightgown a great deal since Papa left, exactly as she had after Francis was born. When he was very little, he'd cried a lot, while Maman stayed in bed for days. Claudine had heard her hissing at Francis when he cried: *Shut up, shut up, shut up! I* hate *you!*

At first, Edith had come to help Maman every day, but one day, Claudine had arrived home from school and the air was hot with shouting. Maman was crying and Francis was screeching while Edith stood with her arms stretched out, saying, 'Just let me hold him, only for a minute. Just while you steady yourself. Some deep breaths, come now. I'll take him and quiet him, there now, Sarah.'

But Maman had held on tighter to Francis—the cords stood out on her neck and her lips curled back so she looked like a snarling animal. Francis's lips were blue from screaming and no noise came out, though his mouth was open wide.

Edith reached out to take him.

'Get away from me, you interfering old witch!' Maman growled.

Then she had made Edith leave and slammed the door after her.

At first, Edith had returned every day and knocked, imploring. When there was no answer, she left soup on their doorstep, or jars of herbs.

But Maman wouldn't let her in and she threw the offerings into next-door's pig trough. When Claudine heard Papa ask Maman what had happened, Maman had snapped, 'She was meddling.'

Maman's rages worsened after Edith stopped coming. That was when Papa had brought Francis into Claudine's room. He had slept in bed next to her ever since, soft-faced and huffing, fists like tightly curled shells, breath sweet with sleep.

She cuddled him in the night when he woke; he pulled on her hair in the mornings to rouse her, grinning gummily. But sometimes, as if from nowhere, a resentful thought snarled through Claudine's mind: *I wish you'd never been born!*

The ugliness of the thought shocked her, and she always held Francis closer and kissed him harder, so that he would never know that somewhere within her, there was a shrivelled soul that hated him.

One morning, in late September, two soldiers hammered on the door. They stared straight through Claudine and Maman and turned their hard faces from Francis's howls.

They had come to take Rowan and Elderflower and all

the chickens. They handed a letter from the Commandant to Maman, kept their eyes on the floor while she shouted protests. And then, deaf to the raw sound of Claudine's sobbing, they took the animals.

Maman continued to hurl Jèrriais curses at their retreating backs, but they carried on walking. Eventually, her shoulders sagged and she slumped back to bed. Claudine crept after her.

'Maman,' she whispered. 'I think the Germans are evil, don't you?'

Maman stared at the ceiling. She could have been made of candlewax, except that the rough flannel of her pink smock rose and fell, rose and fell. Claudine reached out and took her hand. Cold, but Maman didn't glare or snatch her hand away. Encouraged, Claudine climbed into bed next to her and stroked her hair, gently, as if she were caressing a wild cat.

'I *hate* the Germans,' she said, softly. 'Don't you?'

'Yes, dear,' Maman sighed. She rolled over and stared at the wall.

It was easier to talk to her back. Claudine counted her teeth with her tongue and said, 'I thought we might try to escape.'

There came a noise that might have been a laugh or a sob. 'Fancy being shot, do you, you goose? Fetch me a glass of water, my love.'

'But we would be careful. We could go at night.'

Maman rolled back over. Her eyes were fierce and her voice was ice again.

'Don't be a fool. We can't move without bumping into a German soldier. And how would we go unseen at night, with all the patrols after curfew?'

'But we *can't* stay here.' Suddenly panicked, Claudine

clutched Maman's sleeve. 'What will we do when all the food runs out?'

Maman shook her off. 'Don't be silly. I'm sure we'll manage. And we've enough food for today, even without the cows and the chooks. Don't trouble your head with tomorrow.'

Claudine tried to imagine not worrying. Maman may as well have asked her to be a dog, gaily wagging its tail and leaping through life without a care for where the next meal would come from. Even cows in the field lay down when they felt the threat of rain in the air. But she couldn't say as much to Maman: it might stop her talking, send her further into a black mood.

Instead, she said, 'But there must be *some*where else we can go? France, perhaps? I know they have German soldiers too, but there are more places to hide. It is bigger—'

Maman's laugh was high-pitched. 'And risk being caught and cooped up in a work camp? We're better off here, you cuckoo. Even with the ghastly Germans.'

'Perhaps we could go to England and be with Papa?'

Maman squeezed her so it was hard to breathe, kissing her nose roughly. 'And what do you think people would have to say about us running away?'

'It wouldn't matter. We wouldn't hear them in England.'

'You have some funny ideas, sometimes, my love.'

She stroked Claudine's hair and pulled her in close again. Claudine felt a shudder pass through Maman's body. When she peeked up at Maman's face, her cheeks were wet. She put her head back down on Maman's chest, in case she was ashamed to be seen crying. But Maman stroked her hair again and whispered, 'I love you. You *know* that, don't you?'

Claudine couldn't move, didn't want to move because of the

85

hum of those words, echoing in her chest like a tuning fork.

They shared an egg for breakfast between the three of them, laughing afterwards because their tummies were still grumbling. They shouted at Francis's tummy, 'Crying won't get you anywhere!' They used thick German accents and shouted, *'Halt den Munde!'* Sometimes pretending to be happy was enough.

But the walk to school was always miserable. Claudine walked by herself because the other children thought her strange, odd, touched. *Too clever by half.*

She walked the most pleasant way, which was along the beach, by the beaten metal of the sea. The sea and the sky yawned above and beside her. She felt she was at the centre of some enormous blue eye. The dunes towered over her; she was smaller than an ant, had less meaning than a grain of sand, or one of the blades of knife-edged, wind-whipped grass.

Claudine knew that the sea and sky she saw also touched the lives of thousands of people, miles away, in countries she had only ever seen in an atlas. But none of those people cared about Claudine, or knew that she breathed the same air as they did. Thinking about it hurt. Not like stubbing her toe, or even like the time she had fallen and cracked her arm bones—it was a *throbbing* in her head and her stomach. As if every vein in her body, every loop of her gut, every inch of her skin were a beating drum.

A line of poetry clattered around and around in her head: she'd had to learn it by heart and say it over and over again at school. *My heart aches and a drowsy numbness pains my sense.* Words of such loneliness and desperate longing for something unnamable. Not a *bad* feeling, not really. But a very *big* feeling. Too big for her child's body.

She distracted herself by watching the soldiers. They made Jersey look very different. Not only because there were thousands of them, covering the roads and beaches, grim-faced and hard-jawed and marching everywhere with the *stamp stamp stamp* of their boots, but they were building, too. Not sandcastles. Big blocks of concrete to make grey towers and bunkers on the dunes so that, from a distance, the land looked snaggletoothed. Cement to make bomb shelters. An enormous wall along St Ouen's beach, like the flat sinuous body of a sleeping snake. And guns. Everywhere guns and men's hands on them, their eyes looking down the sights.

By October, the nights started to close in and the cold and the dark crept in early over the sea. Claudine began running home after school with her head down, breath ballooning in her chest. The back of her neck itched with the feel of the glinting eyes watching her; the gleaming barrels of guns trained upon her.

After curfew, she lay in bed, the covers pulled up over her head. What would happen if she made a soldier angry? Would he shoot her and bury her in the big sea wall or under one of the huge concrete towers?

How long would it take for someone to find her bones, bleached white by sand, brined in seawater?

Running home through sand in the dark was like something from a nightmare; the ground shifted beneath her feet and sometimes there would be a dip in the sand and, for a moment, she would have the lurching sensation of plummeting off a cliff face with an unknown blackness gaping below. Then her foot would hit the sand and relief would jolt through her and she would run faster because who knew what German eyes with their German guns were lurking in the darkness?

One gloomy evening, she saw a bigger square of blackness on the dark grey of the beach and she stopped running.

What is it?

She crept closer, gasping to catch her breath. A giant hole in the sand, a little like all those craters from the explosions months ago, only with straight edges. As though someone had shaped and measured it. Almost like a shelter, but dug down into the sand, which was silly because it could easily collapse if there was ever another bomb.

She nearly turned back and walked home along the road. But that would have made her late home. She edged forward and peered in.

It was empty. Claudine lowered herself into it and felt around in the dark. Heart hammering, waiting for a monster to jump out.

No monsters. She patted her hands over a little crate, which seemed to be a table. And an empty tin, fashioned into a cup, half-filled with water. There was a crust of cabbage loaf, which felt a little dry and curled up at the edges, but at least it didn't have teeth marks in it or, when she sniffed it, smell of mouse.

She set it back down. The temptation to eat it was like a magnetic pull.

Hunger scrabbled in her gut. Food was scarcer all the time because the soldiers were helping themselves to everyone's bread and meat and stealing rabbits and chickens for their pots.

She tried talking to her stomach, and telling it that it wouldn't gain anything by complaining.

No one was watching. No one would know.

It was so dark. She couldn't see her own nose or hand. But

her hands remembered where the bread was. She tore off great mouthfuls, barely chewing. Some of it stuck in her throat. A lurching moment of airless, silent coughing. She imagined a soldier finding her in the hole in the morning, a slimy gobbet of unchewed bread lodged in her gullet.

She bent double and coughed, and then it came loose. She chewed and swallowed more carefully after that.

Then, over the sound of the sea and her chewing, she heard footsteps, crunching on the sand and stones.

A soldier!

No one else would dare be out after curfew. A soldier coming closer to the hole. Perhaps coming to eat his cabbage loaf. Tight-chested, Claudine stuffed the last of the bread in her mouth and crouched down. She squeezed her eyes shut and pressed herself into the side of the hole.

The footsteps stopped just above her. There was a silence. Then something heavy fell on top of her and knocked her face into the sand. She tried to scream but her mouth and nose filled up. She couldn't breathe.

Someone was shouting. A man's voice. But she couldn't understand the words.

Then he pulled her upright and started shouting in her face and holding a gun against her forehead. Cold metal on her skin. The man's spit went in her face and her eyes, which were gritty and stinging.

She tried to call for help, but when she opened her mouth, all that came out was sand. She coughed and sicked up. Sour acid and grit trickling down her chin. She managed to sob, 'Don't hurt me!'

The man suddenly stopped shouting and said, *'Kinder!'* and

pulled the gun away from her forehead. He slapped her on the back and hugged her and wiped the spit and shingle from her face. And he was saying something else—the same word over and again—but she couldn't understand.

She tried to spit the rest of the sand from her mouth and take a gulp from the tin cup of water he passed her. But her hands were shaking and she slopped most of the water over her shirt.

He laughed a little and held it for her, then tipped it towards her mouth, gently.

She tried to say thank you but no words came out—just a snort. Then she started to shake and her teeth clattered together, and she sat down on the wet sand and bawled.

The soldier took some matches from his pocket and lit a candle. His face, in the candlelight, was full of darkness and shadows. Like a picture of a skull she had once seen in the school copy of *Hamlet*. But then he moved the flame and the skull faded and she could see he had a pleasant face and kind eyes; he was smiling.

He held up one hand, like Maman did when she was telling Claudine to wait for something. He pulled out a long, thin piece of bark from his pocket and pressed it into her hand.

'Thank you,' Claudine said in a loud voice. '*Danke schön.*'

He beamed. '*Gute Deutsch.*'

'*Danke.*'

He chuckled. Then he pointed at the piece of wood and said, 'Schnap, schnap, schnap, eh? Schnap schnap!'

He clapped his hands together, awkwardly, and pointed at the wood again.

Claudine saw two things: firstly, that he must have cut the wood until it looked like a crocodile, with an eye and a tail and a mouthful of sharp, pointy teeth. The second thing she saw was that one of his hands was bunched up into a frozen, shiny fist, as though he had clenched his fingers for so long that the skin had grown over them. The thought of that strange paw brushing the sand from her face made her shudder.

The soldier had noticed her staring and she didn't want to anger him, so she held the wooden crocodile up and repeated, 'Danke schön.'

He nodded and grinned. He had ears that stuck out just a little and a biggish nose. But it was a fine nose, just the same.

She glanced again at that strange, menacing hand and then forced herself to look back to his cheerful face. And then, tentatively, shakily, she smiled.

He slapped his chest and said a word that sounded a little like 'friend'. He did this a number of times, until she nodded and copied him.

He shrugged. 'English very little.'

She thought for a moment. 'Ja. Mein Deutsch ist nicht gut.'

He laughed. 'Sehr gut!'

By the flickering, orange glow of the candle, the soldier showed her some more things he had put in the corner of the hole: a chair with a broken leg, leaning against the wall. And a badly scratched table to go with it. Some more cups made from tin cans. A doll without any eyes and a teddy bear with all the stuffing ripped out. A train with no wheels. Some sticks. Things people had lost or discarded that had been swallowed by the sea then hurled back up onto the beach.

Claudine picked up the doll and stroked the dark sockets where the eyes should have been. The blank face stared back at her.

'*Diese waren am Strand. Hier. Aber...*' He shrugged. '*Kaput. Alles kaput.*' And he put his hands together—the bunched-up fist with its curled fingers like coiled buds, and his good hand, whole and intact—and then pulled them apart.

Then he said that long word again, which she thought must mean *sorry*.

It was strange to find kindness in a German soldier and to hear softness in that foreign tongue used so often to bawl out commands. As if the words didn't matter so much as the warmth they carried, like a gift, a touch shared. Perhaps, Claudine thought, warmth and kindness didn't have a country or a language.

—

MAURICE had hated them on sight, of course: they were like some sort of machine, moving all in time without a single beating heart among the whole God-forsaken lot of them.

More of them arrived all the time. At first, it had been a thousand, which was bad enough, but by winter there were nearly twelve thousand of the bastards—one German for every four Jèrriais. And the rules, the endless bloody *rules*: the curfews and the rationing and, worst of all, no fishing.

Maurice had hidden his boat among the rocks at Devil's Hole and hoped that any Jèrriais who saw it wouldn't breathe a word. Most wouldn't want to see him come to harm, he was sure, but there were already a few loose tongues—people falling over themselves to settle old feuds by landing others in prison. Once the Germans had you in prison, who knew what would happen?

He recalled what one of the French fishermen had said about them—that the Germans were *dangereux* and *sans pitié*. It was after his brother had been caught sneaking his boat out of the St Malo Harbour. Slipping off to catch some fish for his children—staving off starvation with the hope of a silver-bodied fish.

The man had been beaten until near dead. Soldiers had raped his wife again and again, taking turns with her until she bled. Laughing while she screamed. The man and his wife and children had been put on a train and hadn't been heard from since.

The Frenchman knew his brother was dead. He believed he would be caught soon himself, and he knew that the same would happen to him. He comforted himself that he had no wife or children.

'*Les Allemands sont inhumaines.*'

When Maurice watched the soldiers marching around the island, those words were made flesh. It was the eyes. Cold pebbles. They found you out and then looked right through you, as if you were a dog in the street. Or a body in a ditch.

Maurice's panic swelled with every passing moment: Marthe wasn't safe. He couldn't be at home every minute of the day—they had to eat, even if it was just the oysters stolen from the French. But he couldn't be doing with knowing that one day he might go out on his boat to steal a netful and find himself captured.

If it was his friends, the French fisherman, who caught him, they'd give him a beating—at best. From the Germans, it would be a bullet in the head or a train to God only knew where. And all the while, poor Marthe at home alone, terrified, starving or dying of thirst or sitting in her own filth, juddering with hunger that melted flesh from her bones, believing he had abandoned her.

Or Maurice would worry about arriving home only to find that they'd stolen Marthe away and locked her up. Or shipped her off to have tests done on her. Everyone had heard the rumours. Their experiments on anyone who wasn't *normal* had been going on since before the war.

It was hunger that dragged him out to sea again. They had finished the oysters and all the hard bread and the seed potatoes. Even the pickled vegetables and the jams he had put by for the winter months. Gone, all gone.

He *must* go out on the boat. But what to do with Marthe? She needed constant care—all her food had to be mashed. She couldn't even swallow for much of the time. Each meal took hours, giving her tiny spoonfuls. She choked and choked, until she remembered she needed to swallow, her eyes dark pools of panic every time.

It was enough to make Maurice scream or want to rip his hair out by the roots. But he held her hand, told her she was a good girl.

My love, my dearest love.

He stroked her hair, kissed her fingers one by one, but all the while turning over what was to be done. He couldn't let them take her away. Torture her with their knives and their needles. Lock her up like some sort of diseased animal.

I'd rather kill her myself.

So he took her out one day, an hour or so before curfew. Not many patrols around at that time.

He had mashed some old windfall apples very fine, with a little milk and the last crust of bread. He'd dug out all the medicines she'd ever been given and he crushed each tablet and mixed everything together. He tried a little, on the tip of his tongue. Bitter enough to make him retch, so he added the last of their sugar ration too.

He had her blanket. Spare clothes for her, with deep pockets. Four large stones. He had it all planned out. Everything ready.

But as he picked Marthe up, she began to scream. Just like the time before. But this time, he couldn't afford to listen. Nothing for it but to keep walking.

He held her close, whispered against the soft skin of her ear—still perfect. Wisps of her hair tickling his face.

Don't think on that now.

'Come now, my love. We're just going to sit on the beach. We'll watch the sea together. Like we used to. Just you and me. See, I've brought a blanket for us to sit on. Remember the picnics when we courted? I've brought lunch—a little bowlful for us to share. Then we'll have a nice sleep on the beach. Just as we used to.'

She moaned as though the poison was already burning in her blood, as though the sea water was already bubbling in her mouth.

He didn't stop. *It's all for the best.*

They were halfway down the hill when Marthe kicked her legs out, hard. The bowl fell from his hand and smashed on the stone. Apples with milk and bread spattered all over the path, like vomit. The white crumbs of tablet and powder seeped into the soil.

Maurice cursed, tried to scrape it back into half of the bowl. The edges were sharp and he sliced his finger open, but he carried on. Stones and grit and drops of blood had all mixed in with it. He cursed again.

She would never swallow it.

He felt rage in the pit of his stomach, spreading up to his hands, his face, blood boiling through his veins until he felt like one of the damned German bombs. One false movement would detonate him.

So he put down the shattered bowl and walked to the cliff's edge and looked out at the flat blue sea and the unbroken sky. Never the same, yet unchangeable, immutable—even when the land was crawling with pissing, shitting dogs.

He drew in a steadying lungful of air. Sharp tang of salt in it. He listened to the seagulls screeching away and diving for fish. The same as ever, they paid no mind to the poison on the land. There must have been a decent shoal out there because there was a fair-sized flock of birds and they kept diving and coming up with wriggling silver in their beaks or gullets.

The sea had everything you needed, if you knew where to look. He had always fancied drowning would be a peaceful way to go. Just a few breaths, a burning while your lungs swelled for air and found water instead, and then darkness. How to miss the cliff face, though? That was the devil of it—avoiding being smashed to pieces on those rocks.

He was so lost in thought that when he heard the voice behind him he nearly jumped out of his skin and tumbled down the cliff there and then.

'Why hello there, Maurice. And Marthe too. Lovely view today. You can see clear across to France.'

Edith Bisson.

Maurice nodded and croaked a hello. He didn't say anything else, because how must it look with his sickly wife lying beside a cliff path while he stood gaping at the view?

Edith had always seemed kindly. She had never talked down to Marthe like she was some sort of baby—she'd always asked questions and spoken as if Marthe still understood what she was saying. And she had never been one to skirt around Maurice like he'd two heads, as so many folk did because they didn't know what to say to a man who was playing the nursemaid to his wife.

He didn't see too much of her in the normal run of things, but he knew that some people didn't trust her, had her marked out as a witch or some nonsense. He'd never taken much heed of gossip and she'd always been pleasant enough to him.

Sometimes, she'd found him out on market day and pressed a tea or a lotion into his hand, though she'd no reason to look after him or Marthe. The concoctions didn't hurt; some even seemed to make Marthe a little brighter, but Maurice had felt ashamed to ask for more when he didn't always have the money or the fish to pay.

He kept on staring out at the flat body of the sea, stretching off to lands where people had never heard of Germany—or Jersey, for that matter. Places where people had never heard the word *Nazi*.

Edith stood next to him, watching the seagulls. She had a quiet way about her that didn't intrude on your thoughts.

'Must be a fair few fish out there,' she said. 'Those gulls are having a feast.'

He nodded. 'I was thinking the same.'

'Good weather for it, I suppose—bit of a wind, but the water's clear enough to see the fish.'

'Yes, it's a north-easter.'

'Mackerel, then, you think?'

'Could be. Or bass. Something smaller, sand eels, perhaps. Difficult to tell at this distance.'

She stood a little closer. 'Had much to do with our German guests, then?'

'Not especially. I've not been out much. Best avoided, I think. You?'

'A little. They're het up with me because they keep catching me out before curfew ends in the early mornings. As if I could be making off to the mainland with nothing but a basket of nightshade.'

In spite of the turmoil churning in his gut, Maurice had to grin.

'I did offer one of the patrols a delicious nightshade tea,' she continued. 'He nearly drank it too. But one of his cronies spotted it, so I spent a few nights in Gloucester Street Prison. Which I wouldn't mind, but it's freezing at night in there and my old bones can't be doing with stone floors. Do you know, buggers didn't even give me a bed? At my age. Barbarians! Still, it gave me a chuckle to offer him the tea. I wouldn't have let him drink it. But then, you never know what you can do, once you're driven to it. I think most folks surprise themselves, when they're pushed.'

Maurice caught her glancing at the apple-mush and the smashed bowl, a few white flakes of tablet showing. He shifted his boot to cover them.

Edith looked back out to sea and carried on, just as if they were having a cosy chat in a tearoom.

'Still, it beats taking the whole thing lying down. I like to shake them up a bit—if we do everything they say then they really have beaten us. Speaking of which, have you been out on your boat yet?'

How does she know?

She reminded him of a tiny owl: head cocked to one side, eyes bright and sharp, looking right into him. So he didn't tell the story he had prepared for anyone who asked about his boat: that he had sunk it when he heard the Germans were coming.

Instead he said, 'Not since they arrived. I can't leave Marthe, you see.'

'Ah. Well, I've overheard a whisper that they're sending out a patrol to search the caves around the coast. Some swine has given out that people are hiding their boats there. Can you credit it? Folk giving information to the enemy, just for a little extra bread? I think it's sickening, I really do. Anyway, they're starting the search in an hour. They'll stop just before curfew tonight, I'd have thought, once they've been around all those caves.'

A muddle of words unspoken stretched between them. How did she know he'd moored his boat in one of the caves? It didn't matter, he supposed. But it did mean he had to get to his boat as soon as he could—keep it away from the island while the search went on.

Perhaps he could sneak out through one of the sheltered inlets where he wouldn't be seen? He could catch something decent, put it on the black market. Perhaps trade for some warmer clothes for the winter and some milk. Marthe did love her milk. But it was the same old problem: what could he do with her while he was gone?

As if she could read his reeling thoughts, Edith said, 'I can look after Marthe for you.'

He held up his hands, shook his head, 'No, no, I—'

'Why? What's the bother? You're at your wits' end, Maurice.

Any fool can see that. I suppose you haven't much food?'

He slumped, sighed.

'Well, neither have I,' she said. 'Just scraps and leftovers, and I enjoy fish now and then. So off you go. Go on, chop chop!' She smiled suddenly. 'I'll look after her as if she were my own, love her.' She stroked Marthe's hair and the tenderness in that touch decided him.

'*Mèrcie. Mèrcie!*'

'Don't be grovelling, I haven't done anything worth thanking me for yet. Now, off you go. And don't worry about her food in the meantime. We'll make do. But I'd love a mackerel for supper, if you chance across one.'

He laughed. 'Of course.'

'And once you're back, I have a boon to beg of you.'

'Yes, yes. Anything!' He felt as light as the winged gulls, swinging through the air.

'Don't run ahead of yourself, we'll talk later.'

She bent down and lifted Marthe gently, as if she weighed nothing at all.

'Come on, my love. We'll be all right, won't we?'

He kissed Marthe's forehead, once, twice, *I love you more than life, my soul.* And then he started to run down towards the caves. The wind buffeted Edith's words after him.

'There may come a day when I'll be holding you to that favour, mind!'

—

CARTER was near breaking point. It was November, nearly five months after the Germans' arrival and they were making patient care impossible. Not only was he contending with the lack of medication and the slippage in the standards of nutrition, which meant that more people were succumbing to fairly minor illnesses, but there were the rules, the endless blasted *rules*.

By the time winter set in, the number of laws issued by the Commandant was absurd. The curfew and blackout were expected by everyone, and as long as the ward sisters used a little common sense when they organised the shifts, then the law wasn't much more than a minor irritation, but other rules were ludicrous. For instance, the regulation forbidding more than four people to meet in one place at any one time. It made gaining a reasonable consult or discussing a patient's progress almost impossible. The soldiers who patrolled the hospital seemed especially suspicious of the nurses, as if their harmless chatter were a plot for insurrection.

One soldier in particular took this law very seriously and questioned any doctor, nurse or patient he observed in long discussion. His name was Hans Haas and he was a burly brute of a man, pig-faced, with skin like corned beef; he enjoyed being able to push others around. Many of Carter's conversations with his patients were interrupted by shouts of *'Beeil dich!'* with an accompanying wave of Hans's pistol if Carter did not immediately scuttle away.

Carter always obeyed, but felt like a boy again and suffered the familiar feeble, simmering rage that plagued him whenever faced with a bully, whether it was a snot-nosed boy in the schoolyard or his own father at home, towering above him, face brick-red from bellowing.

Carter and Father had parted, before he came to Jersey, on uncomfortable terms. Because of Will, of course.

Will had been a friend from university. At twenty-six, Carter was older than the other students, having already tried (and failed) to learn how to manage the farm alongside Father. So when he started his training, Carter knew he had to succeed, to prove to Father that he was not a dreamer, a feckless disappointment.

Carter had kept himself apart from the other students, preferring to spend his free time studying instead of drinking, and they soon stopped trying to talk to him. But Will, bright-eyed and sunny-natured, had gone out of his way to befriend Carter, always trying to pair with him in laboratory and dissection classes.

When Carter had looked askance at him, Will had grinned. 'Why on earth would I avoid you? You're my safest chance of qualifying, Tim.'

Tim. Carter had liked the warm way Will had said his name. And he began to like other things about him too: his easy laugh if a practical went badly; the way his blue eyes widened with joy when they had done well; the soft curve of his mouth when he met Carter's gaze. The way he shouted, 'Good man, Tim!' and pulled him into a quick, hard embrace when they gained the top marks in their class.

Carter felt like a stone against Will's warm body, but the memory of the touch settled into him, as water will seep into cracks in a rock, pushing the boulder apart, even as it freezes.

And, by slow degrees, Will became the only person Carter wanted to see. He spent nights in Will's tiny flat and slept on the sofa or on the floor. Gradually, it seemed perfectly natural to sleep side by side, in the same tiny, single bed, bodies crushed together. Despite Will's hipbones digging into his side and the way he flung his arms out and elbowed Carter in the face in the night, Carter felt blissfully peaceful, separate from the world. Life and everything in it had squeezed closed, like the contracted fist of a heart. The only things that existed were this room, this tiny bed, this bright-eyed man, who teased light and life into Carter's darkness: tickled him until he couldn't breathe; tenderly bit his shoulder; mumbled, through bleary half-sleep, 'You're *won*derful, Tim.'

The rhythm of Will's breath on his back, as he slept, rocked Carter as the sea rocks the land, as the pulsing heart rocks the body. He felt, for the first time in his life, utterly content.

Outside the room, among the other medical students, despite the dull thud of shame and fear Carter felt whenever he caught Will's eye, there was also something else: a secret thrill of belonging, of being *known*.

After they had finished training, Will returned to London.

'Come with me, Tim,' he'd pleaded, holding Carter's hands in his. 'We'll find a flat near one of the London hospitals. Imagine it—our own little hovel. We can live on boiled potatoes and wine.' He laughed.

'I...' Carter shook his head. 'I couldn't bring that shame on you. Your parents—'

'—don't give a damn about me.' Will finished, his eyes hard with a defiant sort of triumph. 'Mum and Dad are happy in the wilds of Cornwall and will swallow whatever lies I feed them. Anything to avoid confrontation, that's their motto.'

'I'm sorry.' Carter thought of his own father at home, seeking out confrontation at every opportunity. Imagining Father's snarling mouth, Carter shrivelled.

Will snapped his fingers in front of Carter's face. 'Tim. Say you'll live with me.'

But looking at Will's hopeful eyes, his wide and easy smile, Carter knew he couldn't do it. How could he rain shame and ruin upon this wonderful man, this bright boy who carried light and laughter wherever he went? Will would be better off without him. He would be happier, ultimately. And as he thought this, Father's growling seemed to quieten.

Carter returned home to Father and joined a small practice in the village. He missed Will dreadfully in the months that followed, and tried to forget about him, but Will sent letters every week and begged to be allowed to visit. Eventually, he relented, and when Will finally came up from London, it was impossible to resist the pull of his eager smile, his muffled laughter, his hot breath on Carter's skin.

Carter crept into Will's room every night and they talked and smoked and made love and then talked again, for hours—about Will's life in London and how Carter might join him one day. They laughed about escaping to live in a log cabin in the wilds of Canada.

'You can learn to fish and I'll go hunting with a spear,' Will chuckled. 'I hope you like eating rats.'

It was early one morning, when the watery sunlight was just seeping under the curtains. Will and Carter had been awake into the early hours and were now exhausted, or one of them would have startled at the thudding footsteps on the stairs. They would have roused before Father came bursting into the bedroom and saw his son and *that man*, limbs tangled together in sleep, naked.

It was a cool night, Carter had stammered. They had huddled together for warmth. Nothing perverse in that. Just high jinks, tomfoolery, don't you see?

But Father, disbelieving, disgusted, had raged at his son's *abhorrent behaviour*.

Carter had gabbled more excuses. But even as he spoke, his mind had been full of thoughts of Will: outlined against a window, dark shadow stitched in gold. Like a naked angel fallen to earth, still burning in Carter's arms. He was so beautiful—every part of him. How could he fail to love the man? What other option had he?

To his father, Carter had said, 'It isn't what it seems.'

But Father had scowled. 'I have always wondered what was wrong with you. Get *away* from me! You've always been weak. Now I see why. Re*pul*sive!'

He had allowed his son the time to dress and pack a suitcase, then thrown both him and Will into the street. He would not have a *deviant* under his roof. He would not listen to Carter's pleas and explanations.

Devastated, bewildered, nauseated by himself, Carter had left, and he and Will had walked to the park, where Carter had sat beneath a willow tree, hiding in the low hanging branches and trying not to weep.

Will had put his arms around him. 'It's dreadful for you, but now he knows. Now you can come and live with me.'

Carter had pushed Will away, roughly. 'Get off me. This is all your fault, don't you see?'

'My fault?' Will frowned. 'I know you're in a lather, but this is for the best. I want you to be happy, Tim—'

'*Happy?*' Carter spat. 'My life is in ruins and you want me to be *happy?*' His voice was an ugly growl, and now he couldn't stop the poison spilling out.

'You're a simpleton, Will. A sweet, vacant-headed fool. *How* could I come and live with you? Do you imagine they'd let you keep your job if they knew what you were?'

Will was white-faced but he stretched out a hand and put it on Carter's shoulder.

'Tim, it's...love. You know that.'

Carter brushed his hand away. This was the right thing to do. They needed to be free of one another. Perhaps he could make amends with Father. Will would be happier without him, in the end.

'Go. Get on your train.'

'But Tim—'

'*Go!*' Carter didn't turn around as he heard the crunch of Will's receding footsteps. Once the park was silent again, he sat on the bare earth and pulled his knees up to his chest.

He had never felt so utterly lost and entirely alone.

Carter moved into a small boarding house and tried, for two years, to build up a practice near Barford. He tried to forget about Will and attempted to regain Father's trust, visiting him weekly to sit in the drawing room, with the slow ticking clock marking out the distance between them. It would have been better, he knew, if he could have forced himself to marry, but he couldn't bring himself to do it.

Carter spent his nights lying awake, burning—longing for dreams of Will. But if the dreams came, they were unfulfilling. Sometimes Will was talking, but in another room, his words muffled. Sometimes he was laughing, but tantalisingly out of Carter's eyeline. Occasionally Will kissed him, long and deep, pressing his body against him, and Carter woke feeling his loss as the stinging pain of a fresh wound.

After two years of trying to forge a solitary life for himself, Carter admitted defeat and eventually decided to find a post elsewhere.

He wrote to Will, his phrasing stiff and formal, apologising for his behaviour at their last meeting and asking if he might possibly visit him in London.

Carter held little hope of a reply—after so long, he had no doubt that Will would have found no shortage of men, ready to fall in love with him.

But a return telegram arrived within the week, passed to him by Mrs Burton, who was purse-mouthed with displeasure.

Tim, you bloody fool. Come immediately.

'I don't approve of such language,' scowled Mrs Burton.

'I'll scold him roundly,' Carter grinned, practically skipping from the post office to pack a suitcase and board the next train to London.

Will greeted him as if they had never parted, clapping him on the back at the station and then, once they reached his tiny flat, embracing him and kissing him with a hot and open mouth, and Carter, who felt like he'd been frozen for two years, found his touch dizzying and he backed away, breathless, holding up his hands.

'I wanted to apologise—'

'Shut up, Tim.' Will grinned and kissed him again.

Carter lived in the London flat for the next five weeks, and the time spent within those walls, in the fug of summer heat and burning electricity of desire, were the happiest he had known. But as soon as he stepped outside the flat, with Will at his side, he was conscious of people's eyes on them, sidling glances, hushed whispers.

'They're laughing at us,' he said to Will, when they were safely back in the flat.

'Don't be ludicrous. How could they know? You're not branded with a *Q*, Tim.'

Carter frowned and Will hissed the word *'Queer'* with narrowed eyes, then chuckled and knocked his forehead lightly against Carter's. 'You're so very *grave*, Tim.'

Carter couldn't bring himself to laugh—the joke was too close to the bone. Even if people weren't giggling and staring now, they soon would be.

So when he saw the newspaper advertisement for the post in Jersey, he applied. As long as he was near Will, there was no escaping from the looming shadow of disgrace and shame, no matter how much pain it might cause them both. He just couldn't do it.

'I'm taking the post in Jersey. You're better off without me, Will. You'll see,' Carter said, miserably.

'For Christ's sake!' Will grabbed Carter's shoulders and shook him, roughly. 'How could I be better off without you?'

'If I stay, it'll ruin you. You don't understand—'

'No, *you* don't understand.' Will released Carter and paced the space of the flat, then turned to face him, his eyes blazing. 'You say you're concerned about gossip? About people up in arms because of how I live my life behind closed doors? I don't care what anyone else says, Tim.'

'But your job…your landlady. I've seen her staring. You could end up on the street—'

'I'll happily live in a wooden crate under a bridge, next to an open *sewer*, if you'll stay with me.' Will's eyes were frantic and he threw himself at Carter, wrapping his arms around him and kissing his face again and again. 'Don't you see, this is all that matters? *This*. Here. Both of us. You *must* see that.'

Will's mouth was fiercely alive and, in that kiss, Carter could feel all the pent-up years of longing. He could sense a glimpse of a future there, a possibility of hard-won happiness within his grasp. But something inside him shrank and he pushed Will gently away and shook his head.

'I…can't do it.'

'But *why*, for God's sake? Tell me that this isn't wonderful. It's perfect, you know that—'

'It's not *real*. Shuttered away like this. It seems perfect here, in these rooms. But it wouldn't last, out there.' Carter gestured to the door, to the cold, pitiless glare of the outside world.

Will exhaled and hung his head, then smiled, bitterly. 'I love every part of you, Tim. But I do wish you weren't such a bloody coward.'

'I'm sorry. I wish…' Carter shook his head. He didn't know how to wish to be different, for such a wish would have made him a more acceptable son for his father, a more respectable man to the world outside. Such a wish would have changed him so that he didn't desire Will, and Carter couldn't imagine wanting to change the love he felt at this moment, agonising as it was.

And yet he knew Will was right—Carter was a coward and he could not face the judgment and disapproval that he knew he would see in every set of eyes if he chose a life with Will.

Carter had spent his entire life seeking admiration from others, striving to earn Father's respect, working to be held in high regard. He knew that, if he stayed with Will, all that would disappear. Perhaps the only way to save himself was to carve out a life elsewhere.

'The post in Jersey is temporary,' he said, softly. 'I'll be back in five years.'

'Five *years*?' Will's face was pale with disbelief. 'And what then? Will you suddenly discover a backbone in that time, do you suppose? You'll return with the courage to be in love with me, even if only behind closed doors?' His tone was sharp with pain. Carter could not look him in the eye.

'I don't expect you to wait for me,' Carter whispered, forcing the words past the ache in his throat. 'You can find someone else—'

'I don't *want* anyone else!' Will slapped his hands on Carter's chest so that Carter staggered backwards. 'I want *you*. Ductus arteriosus, remember?'

Despite the rage in Will's voice, Carter smiled. It had been a joke of theirs, from very early on: the ductus arteriosus is a tiny blood vessel that diverts blood away from a baby's lungs in the womb. After birth, it closes and the blood vessel is no longer used. When Carter and Will first began their relationship, Will said his heart had changed forever, had shut off and closed to everything.

Apart from you, Tim.

For the next two weeks, they lived in a world of cut-glass silences and wounded glares. When they made love, it was with a doomed desperation, a grief-struck knowledge that their time was running out. And at the end of the fortnight, Carter, feeling every inch the coward, left for Jersey.

When news had arrived of the Germans' impending invasion, Carter had seen the opportunity to prove that he wasn't weak: a chance for repentance, for redemption. And then, when it was all over, when the world was a different place, he would have the courage to return to Will.

So when the Germans arrived, Carter's dedication to his patients increased immeasurably. He worked long into the night at the hospital and often rose in the early hours to make house calls and deliver medicine. Where possible, he used his influence to procure extra rations or medications for his patients. Will would have been proud of him, he knew it.

And the people under Carter's care responded to his diligent treatment. It was a blessed relief, and also the source of some tension that—confounding Carter's earlier prediction—within a few months, not only had he survived, but Clement Hacquoil finally began to show signs of improvement.

Under Edith's watchful eye, his fever had subsided. He had short periods of consciousness and lucidity and he was even able to eat very thin soups and gruels—with any luck, he might be able to manage a little of his meat ration for his Christmas dinner. His pain was also lessening by the day, making him more aware and alert.

Unfortunately, the raised keloid scar tissue had resulted in a number of contractures, particularly around the neck and shoulders, which would severely limit his movements, although he would regain some functional motion of his limbs if he completed stretches each day. The skin itself was oddly pigmented, raised and shiny and would probably cause him a great deal of pain and embarrassment—at least until he and everybody around him became accustomed to his altered appearance and abilities.

Carter's initial plan had been to evacuate him from the island as soon as he was well enough to travel. Edith had assured him that she knew a fisherman who would take them across the channel, and would be glad of the help while fleeing the island himself. Although she wouldn't give out his name until things were more certain. *Can't be too careful these days, Doctor.*

In the event, once he began to recover, Clement's improvement was so beyond anything Carter could have hoped for that it seemed ridiculous to risk escape.

When Carter whispered as much to Edith, she said, 'I can't pretend I'm disappointed. It would have been a madness.'

News had always travelled fast in Jersey. Everything was everybody's business. But that was often the case on small islands and in village communities—it had been the same in Barford, too.

Under occupation, gossip seeped from mouth to ear just as quickly, if not more so, the air thick with secrets and lies: the German forces, it seemed, knew as much as the locals. Possibly because the soldiers were everywhere. Nearly twelve thousand of them. Smoking on corners, marching down the streets. Sunbathing on the beaches, for goodness sake—even in the thin sunlight of December.

But gossip, Carter supposed, was an inevitable disease that spread with war: local informants, hungry mouths spilling with information and gaping for the extra food it brought them. Sad to think that members of his own staff at the hospital were in cahoots with the invading forces for a few extra grams of butter. He tried not to examine the faces of the nurses and the junior doctors, tried not to wonder who might have turned traitor. He tried not to wonder what the whispers were.

He didn't have to wait long to find out the latter, at least.

Two weeks before Christmas, Carter was hauled from the hospital to *die Sitzung:* a meeting with the Commandant. With a seeping feeling of dread, he tried to protest, but Hans Haas tapped his gun and snapped, *'Jetzt!'*

There was only one reason the Commandant would demand a meeting so urgently: somehow he'd discovered Carter's plans to escape.

Everyone stared and whispered as they marched through town. The rumours would have reached even the wilds of St Ouen by nightfall: farmers and fishermen alike cackling that the *foreign* doctor had been arrested and dragged in front of the Commandant.

Carter hadn't seen the Commandant since their last meeting when he had refused to evacuate Hacquoil. Carter had since kept his head down at the hospital, hoping the Commandant wouldn't suddenly change his mind and decide to deport him after all, simply for being English. But as he was poked and prodded and very nearly dragged across St Helier, Carter desperately hoped that this *was* the reason the Commandant wanted to see him. The alternative was too horrific to contemplate.

The room was darkened by heavy red curtains. The small circles of light produced by a few candles simply served to make it seem hotter, and smaller. There was a fug of expensive cigars and a sour slice of strong whisky, and something else, which reminded him of medical school—those times when animal carcasses had been given to them in dissection classes. A foetid muddle of rot and formaldehyde.

The office had been hastily refurbished and contained a number of comfortable leather chairs, as well as a dark mahogany desk. These had not been present at Carter's last visit, though quite how such items had been obtained in an occupied war zone was an enigma.

The desk was almost bare, save for an ashtray, a pen and a piece of paper, all lined up next to each other. The only other objects were three photographs: a formal portrait of a thinner, younger version of the Commandant, standing behind a dark-haired woman who sat with one child on her knee and another at her feet. They all stared out from the picture with a look of complete solemnity.

The other two were informal photographs, obviously captured by an amateur during some sort of family excursion: one showed the same young, thin Commandant throwing a baby high into the air—both man and baby had mouths stretched wide with joy. The other photograph was of the Commandant again, a little fatter, a little older, with a little less hair. But still smiling, embracing a young girl, while pretending to pull a chocolate from her ear. He gazed straight at the camera, in clear anticipation of his daughter's excitement.

The man in front of Carter didn't bear much likeness to that photograph. His thin lips were stretched into a wide smile. The resemblance to a toad was made more poignant by his slightly glazed stare (he had clearly indulged in no small amount of whisky, despite the hour) and by the bulk he had added to his already corpulent frame.

It was an impressive feat for the Commandant to have gained weight when food shortages squeezed the stomachs of the islanders and occupying forces alike. Carter's own clothes hung loosely upon him, and he had been obliged to make extra holes in his belt on at least three occasions.

In contrast to his grim glare at their last meeting, the Commandant smiled even more widely when he saw Carter.

'Aha, Doctor! Yes, he is here. Bring drink! And cigars, we must have cigars. And whisky, yes?'

His wide-lipped grin was unnerving. The warm, moist hand that Carter was obliged to shake, and such jovial familiarity, made his guts twist.

'I—no. No, thank you. I would rather not.'

The Commandant's smile didn't waver. 'But you *will*, Doctor. Cigar, whisky! Yes! You *must*.'

He stared until Carter held up both hands in defeat and sat down. The hospitality was, without doubt, a ruse, but it seemed he had no choice but to play along.

An attendant scurried over with a generous measure of whisky and a cigar. Carter sniffed: finest Cuban.

The Commandant sat back and sighed.

'Ah, Doctor, how pleasant to have you here again. You are very welcome.'

Carter's mouth was bone-dry as he waited for the accusation of treachery. The verdict of deportation. He took a sip of the whisky. Dark and peaty: a real Scottish single malt.

'My troops are enjoying their stay on your beautiful island.'

Carter thought of the luminous eyes he used to see in the undergrowth when he was a child. Foxes, perhaps, or, more likely, rabbits. But as a boy he had imagined wolves.

Hot-breathed, red-eyed, carnivore incarnate.

'Many of them believe they are on a long holiday,' the Commandant continued. 'The weather has been very good, even in winter. The people have made only small troubles.'

Another gulp of whisky so he could not give his initial response to this: one of these 'small troubles' had been the drawing of 'V' for 'Victory' signs around the island. For this offence, the Germans had imprisoned three boys who they believed to be responsible. Carter had been granted the unhappy task of treating the boys when they were released after nearly a week in the prison (and only then because the Bailiff, Coutanche, had begged for some leniency to be shown). They were sleep-deprived, covered in bruises, half starved and dehydrated.

Carter made no effort to conceal his contempt. 'They were not small troubles for those involved.'

'Ha! He speaks his thoughts. I like this in a man. But not too much. No.'

The German put down his cigar and steepled his fingers together, resting his chin on them. He had short, blunt fingers, with clubbing at the ends—a feature commonly associated with hereditary heart conditions. Carter also noted the telltale diagonal creases on both earlobes, a sure sign of cardiovascular disease.

That oily smile again. 'I believe I can trust you, Doctor.'

Creeping finger of sweat down his spine. *Of course.* He had discovered the plan to evacuate Clement. God only knew how he had found out. Edith? Surely she wouldn't have breathed a word. Perhaps the fisherman? Too many of the islanders were loose-tongued for the sake of an extra loaf of bread.

'Yes,' the Commandant said, 'you are honest and a good man, I think.'

He licked his lips—his tongue was quite pink. He gave a sudden bark of laughter.

'Doctor, you are a brilliant medical man or a brilliant liar. Which is it, I wonder?'

Carter's heart was hammering, his blood jolting as if waiting for the axe to fall. To hear the words: *treachery, insurrection, deportation.*

'Forgive me. I'm not sure I understand.'

The Commandant's voice was affable, his fat face hideously jovial.

'You say there is a man in your hospital. A man with burns. Very serious hurt, this man. He will not live, you say. He must be evacuated.'

Any moment. Any moment now, he would come to it: the planned escape. Carter smoked and tried not to cradle his soft underbelly. He counted the tugs and pushes of air in and out of his lungs.

The Commandant's voice was suddenly harsh. 'I find today that this man, this hurt man who will die—he survives, yes? He is eating. He is walking, yes? This is so?'

Carter said slowly, carefully, 'It is.'

'So, I ask again, are you a great doctor or a great liar?'

Carter forced himself not to blink, to meet those pale eyes, not daring to hope for a reprieve. It must be some sort of devilish plan, some way to entrap him. He pressed down his fear and matched the Commandant's sharp tone with his own.

'Neither. And it seems to be somewhat obtuse to assume that those are the only two alternatives.'

He laughed. 'He insults me! Brave, yes? *Mit große Hoden.*
Ah, Doctor, you are the amusing man, I think. But jokes, they
must stop now. This is no time for be shy. You save the man's
life—this is a great achievement, no? But, if he was not dying,
well...' The smile vanished.

The mention of that word, *dying*. Perhaps it was a veiled
threat?

Carter's mind whirred: what could he say when the plan was
mentioned? That he knew nothing of it? That the Commandant
was mistaken, must have been misinformed?

For the moment, he settled on the truth and was able to meet
the German's eyes quite boldly.

'As I told you before, Commandant, the man's life was indeed
in danger. Such was my conviction of the seriousness of his condition that I was prepared to let him travel, despite his weakness,
because I believed he would have a far greater chance of recovery
on the mainland. If he stayed here, I was perfectly convinced that
he would continue to deteriorate and he would die.'

'But he has not leave. And he has not die...' The
Commandant spread his hands, smiling, as if this was all an
entertaining puzzle.

Careful. When the Commandant mentioned the plan to
escape, should Carter keep his face impassive? Perhaps he should
seem shocked or affronted? His blood thudded in his skull as he
tried to decide on the facial expression that would appear most
innocent.

Carter swallowed another gulp of whisky, focused on the
burn of it and made himself continue to stare directly at those
cold eyes. They were bloodshot and heavily lidded, but still
sharp. A feral sort of intelligence lurked behind them.

'I take none of the credit, I am afraid, Commandant. If he had continued in my care alone, the man would certainly have died. However, after our...discussion, I enlisted the help of a local woman, renowned for her knowledge of herbs and natural remedies as cures for all varieties of illness. Clement has been under her care since that time and has made his remarkable recovery entirely because of her knowledge and wisdom.'

The Commandant sipped his drink and smoked. Silence scuttled into the room and squatted between them. Carter hoped that in mentioning Edith he had not incriminated her in any way, or confirmed her involvement in the plan to escape.

Eventually, the Commandant leant forward again and whispered, 'I have a gift. A sense—instinct. We say *telepathisch*. I know when a man lies.'

'Oh, yes?'

'And you, Doctor. *You* lie. I can *smell* it on you, this lie.'

'I assure you I am not—'

'*Do not deny it!*' The Commandant slapped his hand on the arm of the chair. 'I tell you, you *lie!* This is so! I say so!'

A vein on his temple pulsed. His already florid face turned puce.

Perhaps I will be lucky and be imprisoned. Most likely, I will simply disappear.

The hospital staff would notice, of course, but none would be foolhardy enough to challenge the German authorities, and he had no family in Jersey to question his vanishing. Father would be informed of his suspected death, he supposed, once the war had ended, and he would mourn, in his own way. Even as he saw his son's death as a neat solution to a humiliating problem.

But Will... Carter's heart clenched at the thought of him.

He could remember the first time he'd kissed him, every nerve burning, waiting for the inevitable recoil, rejection, revulsion.

But Will had embraced him, smiling. Sharp taste of tobacco and a stubbled urgency, kisses hard and hectic.

Carter's memories of that first night were of Will's mouth on his, hot and slick. The hard smoothness of the skin at the base of his spine. The wonderful, fumbling awkwardness of it all.

Will's arms wrapped around him had felt like touching the earth. Like coming home.

The Commandant interrupted his reverie. His voice was quiet—almost a whisper.

'Herbs and plants? How do you call it? *Natural remedy*? You think me a fool, Doctor. No man can be near die and then make whole with a leaf.'

He laughed again. There was no trace of his previous rage.

'And so, Doctor, I find you are a genius in medicine. But also *genügsam*, I think you say modest, no? Herbs? Plants? I am not fool. You should know this. This woman, she helped you, I know this. But she did not cure this man. *You* cured him, Doctor.'

'I did not, I assure you. She—'

His protests were waved away with his cigar smoke.

'No! *Enough!* Silence!' The Commandant's tone hardened. 'You lied to me. He was not dying. No need for evacuated. These are truth, these things. You see, I always find everything. You cannot hide from me.' He beamed, smugly.

Then he gestured at the empty glasses on the desk and bawled a harsh command; a serving man scurried from the shadows and poured both of them another generous measure, before disappearing again.

Carter allowed himself a moment to slump, to breathe, to thank whatever gods may be for the Commandant's apparent ignorance of the plan, to beg them for some further miraculous reprieve. And, in his relief, he lost focus on the man's words, thick-accented as they were, wasps throbbing from his mouth, so much so that suddenly he found himself nodding as the Commandant said, 'You are a great doctor. I must have a doctor. I will have you.'

Carter froze. 'But I—I can't. The…hospital needs me and I—well…'

'Ah, yes, the hospital. Do not fear. Other doctors work there, no? You will work for me, yes? *My* man to keep.'

Carter felt the blood seep from his face. Some primal instinct shrieked at him to run, to scream. But he sat, metal taste of adrenaline in his mouth, and forced himself to sip slowly on the last of his whisky while he searched for an escape.

'But surely you must have a doctor of your own? Someone who is…familiar with you. A German doctor. Someone you trust?'

'But I *trust you*. I trust that you will never tell anything about my body. If I have a German doctor? He whispers to soldiers of mine. They drink together, talk too much. My German doctor, he tells stories, about me, my body, yes? They laugh, drink. He tells all. What now? My men know everything. It is true, I can punish this doctor. But every one of my men? Ha! There are limits to every man's power, is that not so?'

Stupefied, Carter could only nod. What on *earth* was the man hiding? What medical condition could he have that must be concealed from his men? Syphilis, perhaps? Gonorrhea?

The Commandant smiled and clapped his hands together.

'So. We decide. You are my doctor. You must care for me—give me medicines. And you will not tell anyone about my body. You understand?'

Carter did. Suddenly, he understood completely. The knowledge slid into him, clean, effortless and efficient as a surgeon's blade.

Weight gain. Bloated face and ruddy complexion. Thinning hair. Tired, bloodshot eyes. Shortness of breath.

Cushings.

Carter wondered if the German knew, or if he suspected some disease of sexual origin. If Cushings was left untreated, it was almost always fatal. High blood sugar, high cholesterol and high blood pressure: heart attack or stroke. Of course, a simple prescription of steroids and some minor dietary changes could render the condition perfectly manageable.

But does he know that? Did he know what was making him suffer?

Carter examined those bloodshot eyes: ink from textbooks and scribbled pencil notes flashed through his mind: headaches and sleeplessness with accompanying chronic fatigue. If he suspected some sexual disease, then no wonder he felt shame and wanted to conceal it. Or perhaps he simply wanted to disguise any sign of weakness from his men.

The Commandant said, a little louder, 'You are *mine* now. Day, night. *Für mich*. All times. And you say nothing. Yes?'

Perhaps this knowledge was the shred of power Carter needed to keep himself alive. The German thought he was dying—that much was apparent. Carter had seen the haunted look in a thousand patients before. That mixture of anger and frustration, along with a pleading hope for the diagnosis to be incorrect or for the symptoms to instantly subside. And the consequences for Carter if the Commandant worsened were horrifying.

He shook his head. 'There are other doctors.'

'I have chosen you, *nichts?*'

'Yes, but…I wish to continue working in the hospital. I can do great good there.'

This drew a surprising and disturbing reaction: 'In hospital, yes? With the poor? The diseased? The rats and the lice? What have they done, these creatures, these *animals*, to have your time and care? You would rather treat men, I know, Doctor, than these stupid beasts. Is that not so?'

Carter's mouth dropped open.

The Commandant continued. 'I remember you are English too, no? Many of your English friends are in Ravensbrük. You like to join them, yes? You will need warm clothes. It is very cold, I think. Many do not feel when their toes fall off.'

He chuckled. It echoed around the room. When Carter still didn't speak, the Commandant took his silence for an agreement.

'You make the right choice, Doctor,' he said.

In the days after his meeting with the Commandant, Carter paced the landscape in directionless agitation. When he tried to recall it later, he found he had no memory of that chasm of time: whether he walked or ran, whom he might have seen or what he might have said. A blank vacuum in his memory, filled with the hiss of a glowing fuse.

He had a vague recollection of gazing out at the sea, but far clearer in his mind was the Commandant's sweating face. Those tiny, savage eyes. That harsh German voice as he called the populace *animals* and *filth*. His amusement at Carter's discomfort. The barely veiled threats.

Carter heard his blood hammering in his ears again. Sometimes that could be an indication of a brain tumour. He bent double, breathed into his cupped hands.

Pull yourself together, Tim.

He forced himself to straighten and to look at the view and to focus on the horizon. Gradually, the nausea subsided, his pulse dropped, and the black spots faded from his vision.

The landscape was a glazed expanse of sea, punctuated by rugged rocks and boulders. At high tide, these were almost completely covered, then exposed when the sea retreated. Jagged brown fangs rearing from clagged grey mud. Not a soul for miles. A world that had never been tamed and could not be civilised or inhabited. Barren, desolate, glaring.

He walked. Shingle crunched beneath his boots, which, he noted, needed repairing: a sole had started to peel away. Queasily, he remembered the Commandant's polished leather shoes, his pressed shirt, which showed no signs of wear.

I like a man to be neat.

The Commandant would not be refused—that much was clear. Were Carter fool enough to rebuff his 'offer', he had little doubt that he would find himself serving a lengthy sentence behind the walls of the local prison. If he were lucky. Given his illegal status in the island as an Englishman, however, it was more likely that he would be transported to mainland Europe.

Of the Jèrriais who had been sent to Ravensbrük, none had returned.

But the Commandant repulsed Carter, not only for his bloated, wheezing body, but for that diseased mind. He could not imagine handling the man with care, with humanity, when his beliefs and values were so utterly repellent.

You do not want to work with the filth. The animals.

And how could Carter look any Jerseyman in the eye, knowing himself a traitor? How would he be able to treat his chosen countrymen when they knew him to be a coward? All the trust he had built up with the Jèrriais community would be obliterated once news of his service to the Commandant became common knowledge.

He turned and started to stride home. He would wash and refresh himself, sluice the salt from his skin and the shingle from his shoes. Make himself *neat*.

He was allowed to see the Commandant immediately.

The German greeted him with a broad smile and a moist handshake, which lasted too long.

'You have good words for me, Doctor?'

'I'm sorry. But I must—decline. I am afraid. Most regrettably.'

He blinked. 'Decline? This means no?'

'Yes. I—I am afraid so. My presence at the hospital is really… it really is *most* vital. I cannot *abandon* my post.'

Chest tight, Carter waited for the rough hands of the guards. He half expected the Commandant to shoot him on the spot; even fearful, and desperate as he was, the comfort of his own integrity grounded and steadied him.

But he nearly collapsed when the Commandant smiled and

said, 'Of course. I understand. You are the hero, yes? A brave man, strong man. Big man, yes?'

He laughed and clapped Carter on the back, leaving his meaty hand to rest on his shoulderblade. Hot and heavy, the hand of fate.

Carter sweated all night over that laugh. What it meant. He didn't have to wait long to find out.

The next morning, he arrived at the hospital to find pandemonium. The corridors crammed with soldiers, some brandishing guns—the nurses in a hell of a state: running, shouting, waving their hands.

Sister Huelin found Carter immediately. Her face was pale.

'They say the building is needed for official business. We have to be out by midday. On the street. Patients and all. We've nowhere to go. For heaven's sake, some of the patients are under aseptic care. And what about drips?'

Panic gripped Carter. She must be mistaken, surely?

'What do you mean, we've to be *out*? This is the *hospital*. They can't evict us.'

'The soldiers say they need the building. They say we must leave.'

'That's absurd! There must be some misunderstanding.'

'That's what we thought. But they've a written order. From the Commandant. It's addressed to you.' Spots of colour burned in her cheeks and she gripped his arm. 'You must stop this, Doctor. It's madness.'

Carter recognised the soldier nearest to him as Hans Haas. He was ordering patients from their beds and herding them towards the door, waving his gun in their faces.

'Now look here,' Carter snapped. 'What is the meaning

of this? You cannot simply seize this building for your own purposes. It is the hospital, for God's sake. You must leave at once. At *once*! And put that damn gun away!'

But Hans didn't flinch.

'The Commandant, he say, *Danke schön, Herr Doktor.*'

Hans passed him a letter, the swastika emblazoned at the top, the Commandant's signature at the bottom.

> *This hospital is to be used as a military centre, effective immediately. The medical provision for Jersey residents must be completed in a different location. Failure to comply with this order will result in the imprisonment and deportation of hospital staff and patients to Germany.*
> *The Field Commandant*

Carter felt, with sudden horror, the petrifying sense of his own helplessness. He remembered vividly the ring of the Commandant's laughter.

'But this is...absurd. Where am I to take the patients?'

Hans smirked.

'This is too bloody. The whole business. It's foul. It will amount to murder, do you hear me? Putting these patients on to the street. Might as well take *this*'—Carter jabbed his finger at Hans's gun— 'and shoot them in the head.'

Half an hour later, Carter burst into the Commandant's office.

The German was sitting in his armchair, puffing on one of those damn cigars. For a moment, Carter allowed himself to imagine knocking it from the man's mouth and grinding it under his heel, then striking the Commandant's smug face with the glass ashtray. He'd heard of a man murdered that way. It was all a matter of force, timing and positioning.

The Commandant gave a broad smile. 'Ah, Doctor. I was thinking of you.'

Carter clenched his fists. 'What the devil do you think you're doing? Put a stop to it! I demand that you call off your...*dogs* this minute.'

The Commandant didn't move. 'Your friend,' he said slowly. 'The woman with plants. I think perhaps she is a witch, yes? This is what people say. My guards will take her to the prison. She will go tomorrow to Germany. And the butcher. He is *deformierten*. He makes me disgust. He will go too.'

'No! You can't!'

Rage. Pure, physical and visceral. Carter had never felt anything like it. He wanted to tear into the man's muscles with his bare hands. Sink his teeth into that smiling face. Slit his throat open and watch him bleed.

The Commandant's smile didn't falter. 'You will serve me, yes? This is the sensible thing. The *clever* thing. You are a *clever* man. You sit. A drink, yes. Cigar.'

Carter accepted the objects that were pressed into his hands. He drank. He smoked.

When he could gather breath to speak again, Carter made the Commandant promise not to touch the hospital patients or staff. Clement. Edith. And in return...

'It is done,' the Commandant said. 'Welcome, Doctor. No words for me now?' He patted Carter's cheek. 'Do not be sad. You have your hospital.'

Carter looked straight ahead at the flag, the desk. Those photographs.

'Thank you,' he rasped. 'Very much.'

The Commandant leant in very close. His hot breath stank of sour whisky. 'You will see the animals at the hospital one time each day,' he whispered. 'No more. You understand? The rest of the day, you are mine. For me. Yes?'

Carter nodded.

The Commandant chuckled and clapped Carter on the back, then slid his hand up to squeeze the nape of his neck. As one might clasp an errant dog.

'You are clever man. Do not do something foolish.'

Trapped, Carter unwillingly accepted a pair of new Italian leather shoes, which the Commandant ordered him to wear in place of his ruined pair.

When he hesitated, the Commandant said, 'You will be neat, yes? You obey me in all things now.'

—

WHEN Edith told Maurice that Dr Carter wouldn't be able to help him after all, she half expected him to lose his head over it.

But all he said was, 'Well, that's that then,' and carried on gutting the mackerel into her sink.

She looked up from the wild garlic she was crushing. It seeped into the blood, the smell of it. She would stink like a Frenchman for days.

'You're not angry?' she asked.

'Of course I'm angry! My wife might die or be taken from

me at any time. My chance of escape has gone. Without someone to care for her while I row, I'm stuck. Not enough food, except what I bring in the nets. Can't walk ten yards without seeing the Bosche. And any one of the filthy swine could be the one that reports on Marthe. Let alone the rats scuttling about in search of information to give the Germans for scraps of food. But I'm not letting them take her. So that's me done for.'

He stabbed the knife into another fish.

Edith set down her pestle and mortar. 'I'm sorry, Maurice. It's dreadful. If there were anything I—'

'Thank you. You've been marvelous, all you've done for Marthe. The care you take of her, of both of us.' His voice quavered.

She couldn't stand to see a man cry. 'Come now, dwelling on it won't change—'

'I'm not. I mean to say, I'm simply…I'm thinking on what's to be done.'

She patted his shoulder. 'We're safer staying and never mind the soldiers—we can protect Marthe, between us. Who knows what would have happened if we'd tried to escape? Nowhere to hide on the open sea, is there?'

Maurice's mouth was hard with trying not to weep; Edith felt a flash of guilt at the false hope she'd dangled in front of his nose when she'd mentioned escape, knowing she'd never believed it would come to that.

He sighed, pressed his finger against the tip of the knife.

'But it's *them* breathing down our necks, day in, day out. Not knowing who to trust. Do you know, I was talking to Richecoeur yesterday. He told me that Mary Blampied was taken off to prison for a week for having two wireless sets. She has an extra upstairs for her poor mother, who can barely shift out of bed because of her arthritis. It was a tip-off—a note from one of the neighbours, probably.'

Edith nodded and picked up the pestle again, crushed another garlic stalk.

'Petty jealousy. It's a poor turn of events when you're looking askance at the neighbours. I've heard all sorts about folk using the Germans to settle old scores.'

'Yes. That's the worst of it. Wondering who would want to see me taken down a peg. Thinking who I might have riled in the past. I'd have the lot of them, I would. German, Jèrriais. Do them in.' His hand gripping the knife shook.

'Hush, that's foolishness talking. You'll do no such thing. You'll carry on—we all will. Marthe will be well; you've me to look after her. Just keep your head down.'

She told him one of the better stories she'd heard: about Joanna Mourant, who had hidden a whole Christmas dinner from a patrol.

Maurice was still frowning. 'How did she manage that?'

'Pretended to be tucked up in bed and dying from smallpox. And the dinner tucked up with her.'

'She *didn't!*' A grin started nudging at the corners of his mouth.

Edith hooted. 'She did! A whole turkey and half a pound of potatoes in bed with her. More than an hour they searched that house—they were on a tip from Joan Hacquoil—and they didn't find so much as a single sprout.'

In the end, Maurice went off to his boat laughing and Edith could get back to minding Marthe without fretting over him.

Not that she resented tending to Marthe. A sweet thing, she

was. Besides, how else could Maurice have found food? There were enough folk starving by then, without Edith letting it happen on her own doorstep—and to an innocent like that poor girl.

Edith still thought of Marthe as a girl, even though she was in her thirties. But at nearly twenty years her senior, Edith felt old enough to be Marthe's maman, and what with her wide eyes and her tiny little body—not an ounce of spare flesh on it—Marthe put her in mind of a sickly child. Sat propped up in Edith's own bed, hair spilling over onto the pillows, she had stopped her groans, for the most part. Instead, she made little crooning noises as Edith combed out that blonde hair and gave her sips of hot, sweet tea. Made from potato peelings and dandelion leaves, of course—sweetened with the juice from slow-cooked barley.

Marthe had put on a little flesh under Edith's care, for all that she didn't believe in mushing up her food and spoonfeeding the girl.

When Maurice told Edith to mash her food, she smiled and nodded and shunted him out the door to his boat. Then she did exactly as she pleased. Put some pieces of carrot and potato, big as her finger, on a little tray in front of Marthe. Edith could see her staring. Then those big eyes flicked back to Edith, to see if she would be pulping them up and forcing them down her.

But not a bit of it—Edith carried on dusting, brewing up acorn coffee and boiling limpets, just as if she didn't know Marthe was there. And sure enough, in a minute or so, Marthe was patting her hand on that tray, trying to grasp the little sticks of carrot and potato which Edith had smeared with just a touch of butter that she'd traded her good housecoat for.

Couldn't do it, of course. Poor girl's hands and arms wouldn't do her bidding, hadn't done in these past two years. She gave a little yowl, and the tray and food toppled on to the floor.

Edith smiled. *There, there, never you mind.*

Then Edith held the sticks of potato and carrot up to the girl's lips; she chewed them as best she could. Sometimes she choked and gagged a little, but at least she knew what to expect and at least she *wanted* to be eating. It was a start.

Edith always tried to eat with her, and had similar things on her plate too, so she wouldn't feel babied. It's how she would have done things with her own child—the small, silent scrap of white flesh she'd buried as soon as it was born. Never took a breath but was perfect as if it had been lovingly moulded from clay. Little upturned nose, eyelashes fine as the wisps of dandelion seeds and so few, on those tiny eyes, squeezed shut against the bright glare and clamour of the world.

Would have been about Marthe's age by now, give or take a year or two. It seemed like a lifetime ago, back when Frank was still alive. They had hoped for a houseful. Edith wept as she buried the little thing. Not enough tears in the world for that grief. Still, she'd have wept longer and harder if she'd known Frank planned on having himself shot in a ditch in France before they had a chance to try for another.

She still ached for it, that babe buried at the back of the churchyard. No marker in the earth but her heart knew the exact spot. Lodestone. She sensed it, even after the yawning gape of the years—that remnant of her body under sand and soil. Never looked to see if it was a boy or girl. Simply wrapped it tight, laid it in the tiny hole she had dug with her own hands— ripping shreds of skin from her fingers as she burrowed. Pushed the earth back over that unmarked blue face, patted it down so it would be nice and warm. Sometimes, she wished she'd looked— boy or girl? She wished she'd given it a name.

Edith knew she had to move Marthe out into the fresh air. Like plants, folk needed sunlight on their skin. Marthe had been too long cooped up, when what she needed was to feel the wind buffeting her face and see the trees and the grass stretching skywards.

Marthe shouted the first time Edith took her out in the wind. Scared stupid, she was, heaven knows why. Edith didn't press her. Instead, she propped her on the doorstep with plenty of soft cushions around her. Then Edith sat. Knitted a little. Shelled some peas. Ground up some more acorns for coffee. All the while Edith kept chatting away, talking over what she was doing, speaking about the plants, the land, the colour of the light—yellow like beeswax.

Oh, but Marthe's grumbles made Edith anxious: what if a soldier marched past and wondered who she was, and why she was slumped and dribbling like an infant? Next thing they knew, Marthe would be carted off to one of those experiment camps and Maurice would have Edith's skin for a waistcoat.

They saw not a soul that first time outside. Soon enough, Marthe stopped her moaning and her eyelids dropped. Edith kept up her talking, soft and constant as the breeze. Then the girl was faintly snoring. Watery winter sunlight barely touching her neck, the wind scarcely moving that wispy hair of hers.

Before long, they were out there every day, weather permitting. Edith soon moved her from the doorstep to the garden. Marthe didn't complain or grumble a bit as Edith laid her out on her tiny square of grass so that the girl didn't have to slump on the potato patch and grow dirty, or be uncomfortable sitting on the thyme bushes. Edith chattered about whatever she was doing—knitting or making up poultices for poor Clement—or mixing some new salve which she thought might take the tightness from those burn scars. After a while, Marthe would fall into a doze and Edith would tuck the blanket around her or prop a cushion under her cheek or stroke that lovely golden hair from her forehead.

When a soldier finally walked past one day, he didn't take a second glance. Edith felt the blood drain from her cheeks but she kept her voice steady and said, 'My daughter.' He nodded. Then she added, 'Jennifer,' without even thinking. She'd no idea why. Marthe was a nice enough name, to be sure, and goodness knows where Jennifer came from. Just a name she had always liked. Pretty.

Moving to and from the hospital to help Clement was more of a battle and needed a little more thought. Marthe couldn't be left; she'd do herself an injury. Anyway, who would be there to give her food and water and soothe her to sleep? Edith couldn't carry her; she'd draw too much notice. Besides, her arms weren't up to it, for all the girl felt like she had the hollow bones of a bird.

So, in the end, she piled soft cushions and blankets in her old wheelbarrow and pushed her along, back and forth to the hospital, panting and sweating, but it was worth it to see the whisper of a smile on Marthe's slack mouth.

Edith got some odd glances, to be sure, but she hoped the Jèrriais folk knew to stay mum—even if some of them couldn't stand her and even though, between themselves, they were saying that Marthe had some sort of curse on her that was rotting her brain, they wouldn't see harm come to either of them, surely? That was what Edith liked to believe. They were all neighbours, after all, huddling in against the ravening cold and with bloody-mouthed wolves in their midst.

Happily, the soldiers didn't ask too many questions. If ever one came near, Edith shouted, 'Watch out, sir! She has a terrible sickness. Vomiting all night. Just taking her to hospital. Can't even walk, poor soul. Ooh, I wouldn't come too close if I were you—she's already caught my boots twice today.'

Perhaps the soldiers didn't understand a word of it, but Marthe would often oblige her by shouting or flapping her arms. Most of them hurried past, tried to look the other way. As if by looking at Marthe, really *looking*, they might catch whatever ailed her.

The performance wouldn't keep the soldiers at bay forever, but it did the trick for the moment. It helped that there were thousands of the blighters on the island—they didn't often see the same one twice.

Edith had been overjoyed when Clement took a turn for the better. Of course, it had folks gossiping about witchcraft. Maurice started calling her Edith Emmanuel and bringing dead fish for her to revive. Once, he kept a cod alive and sneaked it into her kitchen sink—heaven knows how—and then pretended to faint when it swam.

'It's a miracle!'

He clutched his head, as if overwhelmed, and then turned to Edith and prostrated himself at her feet.

'All hail the Queen of Cod!'

'Hush you! Up off my floor, you great lump! You'll have Sophie Renouf and the prayer group on our backs with that talk. And take that bloody fish out of my good sink!'

Later, when they were eating that miraculous cod, Maurice said, 'But you know they're saying you raised Hacquoil from the dead, not once but twice. People have started going on pilgrimages to the hospital with their sickly children.'

She grinned. It was a warm feeling.

'I'll bet the Germans are thrilled.'

'The nurses and doctors aren't best pleased, either. They found one woman rooting through the hospital laundry, digging out Clement's sheets to sleep on. I tell you, Edith, next thing you know you'll have a troupe of apostles and a book named after you.'

A gust of laughter. 'Quiet, you rogue!'

Maurice was right in one respect: it did wonders for Edith's business, Clement's recovery. She took payment in extra meat and eggs and butter, rather than the worthless paper scrip the Germans forced the islanders to use for money. And the more Clement improved, the more people came to Edith for remedies.

But even she was surprised by how sprightly he looked after some months with the teas and the poultices. She'd taken him off most of the injections and the tablets. It had been five weeks before he reopened his eyes. Then, layer upon layer, his skin had started to knit together. Like the very flesh was being woven over his bones, for all it was thick and shiny-looking and had the smooth, uncanny feel of an oilskin coat.

After Christmas, he had started moving again. Edith danced a few steps of a jig around his bed while he tried to shape that distorted face of his into a smile and rasped, *Thank you.* Then

Edith made him stretch out that scarred tissue so it couldn't knit too tightly and paralyse him inside his own skin.

She'd had him up and walking by the new year, leaning on her arm. His breath was still ragged, though: every exhalation was ripped from him. He couldn't speak in more than a harsh whisper and, lipless and frozen-faced as he was, it was a trick to untangle his words. But, piece by piece, she shaped him back into something that would pass for a man.

It was about that time that Dr Carter took an interest in Marthe. Scrawled down some notes. Asked her to move her arm, hold his pen, touch her nose, recite *she sells seas shells*.

Marthe moaned and flailed her arms; Carter scribbled away, shook his head, frowned. He did this every day for weeks, not a word to Edith about it—just kept writing.

The next Edith knew, he was waiting on her doorstep first thing in the morning.

'I do apologise, I simply—I wondered if you might allow me to examine Marthe?'

She blinked then smiled. 'Well, of course, if you can help her. Come in.'

'I'm unsure if I will be able to *help* exactly, but I've become intrigued recently by the idea of incurable cases—I've been studying my medical textbooks, you see, for a patient who has a…difficult condition. It made me wonder: you helped Clement Hacquoil to recover, and you seem to be doing a marvelous job with Marthe. I'm fascinated. Call it medical curiosity.'

His smile looked nervous. Edith nodded.

'Go on and please yourself, by all means. I'll be making some coffee. Parsnip today, I'm afraid.'

She went into the kitchen. As she boiled the burnt parsnip peelings and stirred the viscous, black liquid, she wondered again how Carter had managed to escape deportation. There were rumours, of course, that he was cosying up to the Germans, but she couldn't bring herself to believe them. Carter seemed so kind and he was so outraged by the Germans' cruelty. She remembered his touching naïveté, the way he'd called the Commandant *brutal* and *inhuman* in his carelessness with Clement's life, and she knew, without any doubt, that there must be some other explanation.

She watched him now, from the doorway, talking softly to Marthe, asking questions of her, looking for any response and then jotting notes in that little pad of his.

In the end, she said, 'Reporting back to someone, are you, Doctor?'

He started. 'Forgive me. I must seem terribly rude, ignoring you. It's simply that I find her fascinating.'

'Tragic through and through is what she is.'

'What I mean is, I examined her when I first arrived on the island. Her husband brought her because she had begun to exhibit the chorea so classic in Huntington's cases—'

'It's what?'

'Her disease. Huntington's Chorea. Juvenile onset, I would say, from her age and the rapid decline. What did you imagine was wrong with her?'

'Hadn't a clue, Doctor. I thought she was going mad, poor love. Like her mother before her.'

'Ah, it's more usually passed down from the father.'

'They say madness runs in families, don't they? There's

plenty whisper her family has been cursed. I don't put much stock in that rubbish, but her mother died very young. Beautiful, she was, just like Marthe.'

Carter sighed. 'It's not madness. Huntington's is a degenerative disease, which strikes the brain.'

Edith felt a surge of excitement. 'If you know what she has then you can cure her!'

Carter shook his head. 'Sadly, no. It's incurable,' he said, quite softly, and with a hand on her arm. 'She'll die, Edith. Like her mother. I'm so sorry.'

She had known it, of course. Seen her mother go. Folk said the same had happened to her grandmother too. But nothing like hearing the words to bring things home. A crushing sensation in Edith's chest and, before she could stop herself, she was sobbing on Carter's smart jacket with the leather elbow patches.

She was not usually given to tears. She took deep breaths, but they kept on coming. She concentrated on the rough wool and thought about how it smelt of sheep's urine when it was damp, which was why she never wore wool from Scotland, and she stopped crying quickly enough.

'Thank you,' she sniffed. 'You're a good man. A *kind* man.'

'If there's anything I can do. Anything at all...'

Carter patted her arm, turned to go and then stopped, suddenly.

'It occurs to me... If you're really determined to help her, then there are various lifestyle changes that may have a positive impact in terms of slowing the progression of the disease or improving her quality of life. But'—he smiled sadly—'I wouldn't advise you to give Maurice false hope.'

She understood. 'So, what must I do?'

Edith memorised Carter's every word: sunlight; lots of meat and fish; exercise every day, even if only helping her try to walk a few paces around the garden; plenty of fresh fruit and vegetables and lots of sleep and rest.

Simple enough. Except that the bloody greedy Germans had already eaten most of the stock of fresh meat and vegetables, which would have lasted the island the whole winter any other year. Edith would have to be clever about finding some extras. Good thing Clement was in her debt—extra meat was near on impossible to find. All the more reason to work on those scars and put him back behind the butcher's block as soon as possible.

—

HER soldier's name was Gregor.

Claudine walked past the bomb shelter every morning before school and every afternoon on her way home, and he was nearly always there, waiting. Except for when he had to do some important soldier work, guarding all the Russian and Italian *Häftlinge*. They were prisoners because they had done bad things to the German army in other countries. They were dangerous men, but the Germans kept them under control.

'Aren't you frightened of them, Gregor?'

'*Nein.* These are animals. Just broken animals.'

He seemed sad and he rubbed at the skin on his crooked arm, as he often did when he was troubled. Looking at the arm had upset Claudine at first, but she hardly noticed it now. He could still loop a bucket handle over the shiny stump and could use the bunched-up fingers to grip part of a spade and…it was simply part of him, like his thin face or his blue eyes or his quick smile.

'Shall we go into the sea? I can teach you to swim.'

Claudine wasn't horribly hungry like she had been after the Germans first arrived and gobbled all the food. There still wasn't much food, but Gregor often brought her presents, like pieces of meat, which no one else had very much of anymore.

Her eleventh birthday had been and gone. They had a little extra meat and Maman had wrapped an old dress of hers as a present. It was too long and Claudine kept tripping over the hem, but she laughed and they all skipped around the living room to stay warm.

Gregor had given her some extra meat for her birthday, too. Perhaps he had stolen it. She was too hungry to ask and ate it, greedily.

When Gregor couldn't find any meat, they tried to catch fish from the end of the pier—Gregor was allowed to fish because soldiers could do anything they pleased. Claudine sat far enough away from him that it wouldn't look odd if another soldier were to see them.

From three arms' lengths away, while looking out at the flat expanse of the sea, she taught him to fish: *Take a scrap of stale bread. Spit on it a little, like so, and mash it up with your finger, and then squash it into a hard ball on the end of your fishing line. Then when a big fish nibbles it, the hook will stick fast in his cheek.*

Sometimes, if no one was on the beach, they found a little ledge where both of them could sit side by side with their feet dangling just above the water. Their reflection could have been a sepia photograph from years before, the sort of thing tourists would have bought and sent home on a postcard as a memento of the idyllic island: *young girl fishing with her older brother.*

Once, Gregor caught a bass, laughed and shouted.

Claudine seized it and gave it a quick bash on the head with a sharp stone, just as Papa had shown her when he used to take her fishing when she was very little. Fish blood and brains spattered onto her hand and across her cheek.

She held the fish up to show Gregor. Silver scales glinting in the pale sunlight. She thought he would be happy, but his face was blank.

She asked if he wanted to hold it, to feel how heavy it was.

'It's *enormous*, Gregor, look!'

But he stepped backwards, his face twisted in revulsion. He was very quiet for a long time after that.

Sometimes Gregor was busy elsewhere with his soldier duties, so Claudine sat in the cold sand in the den and pretended to find monsters in the clouds. Or she climbed up on top of La Rocque pier. A long way away, she could see the soldiers marching. Like beetles, making dark grey shapes on the clean sand. Building, they were always building. Turning the island grey, shaping it into a fortress, bristling with weapons for the Germans to use. Within Claudine's gut was a frozen sort of sadness, like slowly melting ice. Or perhaps that was hunger.

On those days, Maman said, 'Where have you been, out until this hour? It's nearly curfew. I was worried sick.'

'Sorry. I was trying to catch another bass.'

'Silly goose. We'll just stretch out what we have. With the potatoes we've enough here for the three of us.'

Often that wasn't true, but Claudine didn't call her a liar, even when they all went to bed with insides that felt like they'd been scooped out with a jagged spoon.

The family huddled around the illegal wireless late at night, all tucked under one blanket to hear the BBC News broadcast. It was mostly names of strange places: Bardia, Tobruk, Eritrea. And something called the Blitz, which the newsreader described in a sombre voice—which meant, to Claudine's horror, that the Germans were killing people in England with bombs. She shuddered, reminded of the sour-sweet stench of Clement Hacquoil as he burned on the beach.

Still no news from Papa. Once a week, Claudine walked with Maman to the post office to see if he had sent a message to them through the Red Cross. Every week, Maman said, 'He must have forgotten us.'

The first time she said it, Claudine cried. But after months and months with no word, she started to say it too. Then she started to hope that it was true, because if he had forgotten them, it meant he was still alive.

On the beach with Gregor, she tried to forget the war and play games or tell stories. But the war seeped into everything, like the salt from the sea, like the gossip from people's mouths. War changed the colour and texture of everything, even the games of children.

Gregor was often quiet or sad and didn't seem to want to join in when she made up stories about people fighting battles or running and hiding from bombs.

Once, she asked him, 'Why are you here? In Jersey?'

'We are making a good world for all people.'

'But what about the people who are hurt? In London, people are dying. And in Germany too. I heard it on the news.'

He turned to her, his expression wretched. 'You should not have radio. Do not talk of this. It can bring trouble.'

She felt a small stab of the terror that had first engulfed her upon meeting him: a German soldier, with his gun. But then she blinked and he was Gregor again. Kind Gregor who gave her toys and shared his food with her, even though doing those things might get him into trouble.

'Is it rotten being a German soldier?'

'Sometimes, *liebchen*.' He kissed the top of her head, and then he stared out at the sea.

Claudine looked at the sharp planes of his German face, made sharper by hunger. Neither of them said anything. She noticed that the skin on his poor arm was redder than usual, and a little swollen. He had bruises on his neck and face: one made a scribbled circle around his eye. Smudges of blood under his skin: brown and yellowish. Old.

She took a breath to ask him: *What happened to your face?* But then she remembered how she used to feel a hot, sickening shame if anyone at school was nosy about the bruises she sometimes had on her legs and back, after Maman had been having one of her black weeks. So she simply sat with him, reached out, took his ruined stump of a hand. They watched the shifting, rumpled surface of the sea, wrinkling under the fingers of the wind.

When he was happy, Gregor taught Claudine German, which was very helpful at school. Soon she was the best in the class.

But the other children, faces twisted with spite, started calling her a *Jerry-Bag*, which was a nasty name for a Jèrriais woman who had a German boyfriend, or sometimes lots of German boyfriends. Another word for *traitor*.

Claudine tried not to mind, when they shouted it, but the

145

words cut deep, the sharp voices, the spiked anger. *Jerry-Bag! Jerry-Bag!*

She called them *Dreksau*, and then hid behind the big oak tree in the schoolyard so that no one would see her tears.

She tried to explain. 'Gregor isn't like a *proper* soldier; he's kind—he's a good sort. I hate the Germans too, but Gregor isn't *completely* German. Not *absolutely*.'

But the children just laughed and shouted, *Jerry-Bag! Jerry-Bag!*

Someone must have told Maman about Gregor, because one day, when Claudine came home, Maman's eyes were hard.

'I don't want you going on the beach by yourself anymore,' she said.

Claudine's stomach jumped. She told Maman about Gregor being different.

Maman said, 'But he's still German. He's still the enemy. You're too young to understand.'

Nothing would change her mind or the sad, disappointed downwards tug at the corners of her mouth. In the end, Claudine cried and put her head in Maman's lap, which smelt of the warm fug of potato peelings and ersatz tobacco.

Claudine waited until she hoped Maman had forgotten about Gregor and then she went back to playing with him, just as before, except she hurried home sooner, her chest like a squeezed balloon. She was also more careful about not being seen. The war had made tattletales of everybody.

At night, they listened to more news. The London Underground had been bombed and there was a 120-foot crater in the ground. Claudine tried to picture it but all she could see was the gaping mouth of a grey-and-black monster, crunching down on buildings, trains, people. She had nightmares and woke lathered in sweat.

Sometimes, when a nightmare roused her early, she crept out alone in the velvet hour of the morning, when everything was clean and blank and the patrols were mostly asleep or too bleary-eyed to notice a lone girl. She'd slip through the long grass towards the beach, where she sat on the sand, running the cold shingle through her fingers and staring at the sea. Black and grey too in the dawn gloom, like the flattened innards of the bombed city must be. When the tide went out, it left the mud and rocks covered in seaweed. No soldiers. No Jèrriais. Nothing but the roots of the sea.

—

OUT fishing, Maurice's main fear was the patrols. If they caught him sneaking out on his boat, it would be the finish for him.

He found ways to quell the fear and quash the risk: it wasn't so hard, learning the times of patrol switchover and memorising which soldiers were liable to fall asleep and which ones came on the job half cut or with a hangover.

Wednesdays were simple enough because the night patrol always knocked off early and went to sit on St Ouen's beach, smoking cigarettes they'd stolen or bought on the black market. Sundays were the worst: the changeover of duty was right near where Maurice liked to keep the boat moored because of the gentle tides and the straight route out to sea, with no worry about the biting reefs.

But he couldn't risk leaving the boat there with so many of

the Germans about, so every Saturday night he'd moor the boat half a mile north of the usual spot, hoping the jaws of the rocks wouldn't catch the bottom of the boat. It meant a hell of a time climbing in and out of the boat: if the tide was up then he had to swim the last stretch, holding the sack (heavy with his catch) between his teeth, the sensation of creaking hessian making his nerves jangle.

He was still anxious about Marthe, of course, but his fear faded: how happy she was with Edith and what good care she took of his wife. By the time new year had been and gone, Marthe even seemed to have a bit more flesh on her tiny bones, despite the rationing. Her cheeks had plumped. Sometimes, Maurice could look at her from the corner of his eye and see the girl he'd married.

But then Marthe would twitch or moan, and Maurice would lose her all over again; he would feel a strange sort of *aching* in his chest. Not anger or sadness—more akin to that moment of being startled from a beautiful dream.

It was a relief to escape from it all and meet with the French fishermen. They were a rough sort, down to the last man, with scars from God knows what—Maurice never wanted to ask. They were different to how they'd been a few years back, though. War changed everything and the French smiled at him more now. They liked him because he was doing the same as them: sneaking around on his boat every night to bring back fish so his friends and family didn't starve to death.

In war, your enemy's enemy becomes your friend.

By early 1941, they had settled into a pattern. Once a month, when the moon was down, they all sailed out to the little islands just south of Jersey called Les Minquiers. Big rocks with a few broken-down houses—no one lived there year-round, but people used to camp out there for the odd night, before the war. Of course, they were a dangerous place to stay too long—the Germans had wind of them as a hiding place for escapees and checked them often.

But, provided it seemed safe, Maurice and the Frenchmen arrived near midnight. Sometimes they'd simply crouch in the boats and talk. Other times, if there were no patrols and there was enough cloud cover, they would scramble on to those rocks and sit awhile, drinking and smoking and talking.

They only talked about the Germans on days when the French had brought along a bottle of brandy—black-market stuff that burned when Maurice swallowed. Sometimes, one of the handier Frenchmen might make a little fire with some dried twigs and a flint. He would always make sure it was low down in a sunken hole in the rocks, so the flames couldn't be seen.

Maurice was rarely close enough to feel the warmth in his bones, but the colour was a fine thing. Glimmer of orange hope in the darkness. Simply watching the faces of the Frenchmen in the glow took the chill from his own skin. It carried him back to nights in front of the fire when he was a boy. He could smell the sea water and fish stink coming from his papa's clothes as they dried. A dreadful, bitter stench, really, and it stuck in his nostrils for days afterwards, but now it seemed the smell of warmth and safety and faraway peace.

The French were full of tales about the Germans. Maurice never knew what to believe; hard to know how far a man can be trusted to tell the truth, especially a fisherman.

But the Frenchmen hooted and rolled about laughing with much of what they said. They had a story about a drunken

German soldier in France who had thought he was back in Leipzig with his own woman. He had climbed into bed with a Frenchman's wife while she was asleep. When the Frenchman came home from his meeting with the Resistance, he found his wife curled up next to a drunken German soldier. He shot them both.

The fishermen loved the story and they told it again and again until Maurice could have recited it word for word. He chuckled along with them. But something in the story plagued him. Before the war, Maurice couldn't have imagined an anger so consuming that it could turn an ordinary man into a murderer, but now he conjured the feeling with little effort.

The fishermen sniggered about the Commandant in Jersey, said they knew all about him—his face and stomach so bloated that they called him *pleine lune*. They said that he never stood for long at the top of a hill because he couldn't stop himself from rolling down to the bottom. That they could have used him as a buoy for mooring their boat but it would make the boat impossible to hide.

The jokes went on and on. Maurice laughed along with them: mocking the monster stole a little of his power, for a moment at least. The Frenchmen said the Commandant had syphilis and he'd caught it from his horse. Maurice laughed loudest at this but they all stopped to stare at him in surprise and said, *'Non, non! C'est vrai, c'est vrai!'* And then they all guffawed again and he didn't know if it was because the Commandant had caught syphilis from his horse, or because Maurice had believed them.

They also told other tales. Stories about women raped and murdered. Pregnant women—their stomachs split open and their babes burned before their eyes. Shops and businesses looted by the invading army, or torched—the shopkeepers screaming as they cooked. But when Maurice, heavy-hearted, asked them if any of these things had happened to them or to their wives, or their friends, they looked away and didn't reply.

When Maurice really pressed them, everything they said, all those terrible things, had happened to a friend of a friend in La Rochelle, or a neighbour's second cousin in Montmartre. Or it was only a story they had heard, probably not true.

Because the Germans couldn't truly be that evil, could they?

It was impossible in this new, shifting world called *Occupation*—a sort of stasis of enforced peace amid a war—to know whom to trust. But the stories made Maurice fret for Marthe all the same. The Germans hadn't hurt anyone in Jersey. Not really. Not irreparably. But it only took one soldier who thought too much of himself, or one Jerseyman to say something foolish. Or someone with a chip on their shoulder—and goodness knows there were enough of those about.

Often, Maurice left those meetings on the rocks feeling worse than he had before, and not only because of the terrible hangovers. His peace was gone. Those moments of emptiness when he dragged the nets in and all he thought about was putting one hand in front of the other and hauling till his back and shoulders burned and then counting the catch and throwing back any tiddlers with a blessing for the sea... Gone, all gone. All he could think of was Marthe and what would happen if a soldier found her alone.

The fish fetched a good price on the black market, which Clement Hacquoil was running now he was out of hospital. Maurice could take his catch into his shop and they might trade:

fish for meat. Or he could exchange for shoes or ersatz coffee. Clement hadn't been too happy to trade with Maurice, until he dropped Edith's name. Once Maurice said it was for Edith, the butcher would give him anything he wanted, as long as his wife wasn't listening in.

Maurice tried not to gape at Hacquoil's face. Eight months after the bombings and he still looked like a squid that had been left too long in the sun. *Candle Nose* the children called him. Some of the adults too, though you'd think they would know better. His movements were still odd—jerky and awkward. From the pain, Edith said. She thought it might ease with time. Then again, it might not.

They'd found the war tricky, the Hacquoils. Before, they'd had half the island at their beck and call. Partly because of the butcher's shop and the good meat that people wanted for their children's bellies. But, in the main, it was Joan. She collected people's secrets, hoarded them like those underground truffles rich folk would pay a fortune for. Then she dug them up, waved them around in the light: *Look at what I've discovered. How much is it worth?* Sometimes she used her knowledge to lord it over people, or turn them against each other at just the right time. Sometimes, they provided leverage to gain extra support—a few more votes for a friend who wanted to be a Senator or a Deputy. Sometimes she sat with that knowledge for years, enjoying having folk creeping around after her. A spider, just waiting.

But since the Germans had arrived, she'd been running the shop by herself and she'd lost some of her sway. Rumour had it, no sooner was Clement out of hospital than she was pushing him into black-market trading. She still collected secrets, where she could, from Jèrriais and Germans alike, by all accounts.

For his own part, Maurice stayed well away from her; he tried to earn favours from people, rather than grabbing and squeezing for them. He gave fish to this person and that: the grocer, a few policemen, the harbour-master. Sometimes he exchanged for just a scrap of meat or a few potatoes. Not a fair trade, but oftentimes he'd found it could be useful to have someone thinking they might owe you something one day. In the meantime, food bought people's silence.

Besides, it gave him some satisfaction to give some extra food to Edith and Marthe and Claudine. Just watching them eat gave him a glow.

Sometimes the girl wouldn't take the fish, though. She smiled and said, 'I'm full up, thank you.'

It had to be rubbish, of course—no one had been full for the longest time.

One day, Maurice said to her, 'Come, don't be a fool, child. There's no shame in taking the fish. Your maman will thank you for it.'

She smiled. 'We have plenty of food.'

'Well, then, I'll have to throw them away.'

She rolled her eyes. 'I sup*pose* I can take them then.'

He had just cooked up a bream to share with Marthe, fried it with some wild garlic and the little scraping of butter from his ration.

'Well, if you're full up, you won't be wanting any bream?'

'No, thank you.'

'It's a big fish and there's plenty to go around.'

'But I'm *really*, truly not hungry today.'

He was flaking the white fish flesh from the bones ready for

Marthe, but he set down the knife and fork and frowned. 'You're pulling my leg.'

'No, I'm not hungry.'

'But...*how?*' The rations were mostly vegetables and that wasn't enough to feed a growing child.

She smiled again and looked down at her shoes. 'I've a friend.'

'If it's Clement Hacquoil then you tell him that any extra meat is to come Edith's way too.'

'Not Monsieur Hacquoil. A better friend than that.' She was twisting her hair around her finger and smiling.

'Who is it then?' He went back to deboning the fish; no time to spare for children's games.

'His name is Gregor.'

His jaw dropped. 'That's a German name.'

'Yes, he's a soldier. But he is very kind and good, and he gives me extra food when he can spare it.'

Disbelief. Then anger. Maurice clenched his fists around the cutlery.

'A *soldier?* A *German* soldier is your friend? You foolish child.'

His knife slipped and a piece of fish shot off the plate and slapped wetly on to the floor. He cursed through gritted teeth.

'You foolish, *foolish* child.'

Claudine's face crumpled. 'I'm *not* foolish. He's my best friend.'

Maurice sighed. He stopped with the fish, washed his hands and sat down next to her. But his voice was still hard, lined with controlled rage.

'You're not my child to be ordering about. But honest to God,

Claudine, my love, a German soldier? You know better than that. Why can't you find some nice friends your own age? Good Jèrriais children?'

'Because they all *hate* me. They call me a Jerry-Bag.' Her eyes filled with tears.

He took her hand. 'Now you listen to me. They won't hate you. And they won't call you a Jerry-Bag if you stop spending time with this soldier. He's the enemy. It's common sense, Claudine. You must see that?'

The girl's lip trembled, but she nodded.

Maurice felt a stab of fear for her: she was such a strange and lonely little creature and it was plain to see that she thought highly of this soldier and truly believed he was different. But she didn't know—and why should she, child that she was—what devils men can be, especially Germans. And she couldn't see herself from the outside, how vulnerable she was and how a soldier could easily hurt a sweet and trusting child.

Silent tears shuddered down her cheeks; he clasped her in a quick, hard embrace.

'There now, it's all for the best. You'll see.'

But even as he held her, his thoughts turned to Marthe and of the risk Claudine's blind innocence brought for all of them.

He opened his mouth to ask Claudine if she'd mentioned anything about Marthe to this soldier but then forced himself to think clearly: the girl wouldn't be such a fool, surely? This war was making him believe the worst of everyone.

—

BY Easter of 1941, Dr Carter no longer needed Edith at the hospital. He was rarely there himself and, if the rumours were true, he was spending all of his time caring for the Commandant. She didn't ask him about it. Some things are best left unsaid.

Instead Edith made it her business to nurse Marthe. Rationing meant little enough meat for each of them, but Edith happily scooped most of hers onto Marthe's plate and she paid trips to the butcher whenever the whisper was that there was a bit extra over from France.

Clement Hacquoil was back behind his counter. After all those months in hospital, he was nothing but skin and bone. He put Edith in mind of a puppet, moving in short, tortured bursts and then collapsing. His wife was lurking in the background, of course, pulling the strings, stitched little lips sewn up into a scowl as she watched him.

Plenty of folk didn't recognise Clement. He was a shrunken shadow of the big, bluff man he had been. And then there was his skin—his face and arms were still pink and raw, even though he was healed and hardened. The melted skin had stretched his lips back from his teeth in a vicious leer, even when his eyes were smiling.

When he spoke, his voice was a wet rasp, and he had to pause every so often to suck the saliva back into his mouth or dab at his chin with a handkerchief. If children cringed, he'd put out his tongue (which looked quite normal), or magic a tiny scrap of cooked pork skin from thin air, for a baby to chew on. People would laugh and that jittery feeling in the room would fade, for the most part.

In fact, if anything, business was better than ever for the Hacquoils. Some went to gape, but many went to show their support—solidarity for the poor man whose world had been exploded forever by those bombs.

When first he was out of hospital, Clement greeted Edith like she was his own mother, giving her special cuts of meat he'd put aside. That broken leer, that squelching lisp as he proclaimed, 'This is the woman who saved my life. Worked miracles with her own hands, she did.'

Joan, eyes on her like little flints, would tut or glare. 'None of your blasphemy in here, Clement. The Lord alone saves. Look, there's a queue of customers waiting while you stand gassing.'

She was jealous of the attention, perhaps, or feared that Edith's influence might grow greater than her own.

Before long, Edith noticed Joan shouldering Clement aside so that she could serve her. He soon stopped standing up when Edith came in, stopped trying to stretch those ruined lips into a smile. He would nod a greeting to Edith and pass the time of day, but his eyes slid from hers. The parcels of meat that Joan gave Edith were smaller; the extras stopped. Soon, the packages were nothing more than fat and bloodied gristle.

Edith wouldn't have been so particular if it had just been for herself—years of making do meant she could rustle soup from anything and be glad of it. But it pained her to think of Marthe going without, especially since she knew that eating meat might be a way of easing the slow drag of the sickness that was unravelling her. So where before Edith would have nodded and hurried off with her miserly brown parcel of scraps, now she squared her jaw and glared. She started opening that little packet up, right in front of the other customers, presenting the bits of meat for all to see, as close to the window as she could.

'Ooh, but this is a bit ripe, don't you think? Maybe you

haven't quite the same sense of smell, Clement, after those nasty burns. But honestly, put your nose into that. This chicken stinks like it's been roosting in a midden. Have a sniff, will you, Joan?'

The other customers crowded in, muttering at the smell and the look of the bird she held up: greenish in places and reeking like mouldering cheese.

Joan glowered and growled something at Clement, who muttered, *Sorry, sorry*, and limped off to find Edith another chicken. Shamefaced, he thrust it at her, whispering more apologies and rubbing at those shiny scars of his.

It was that way for weeks when Edith went in: a cut of pork still with mud-clogged hair bristling the skin; a rabbit that looked more like a cat to Edith's eye—it had staved-in ribs and long ropes of intestines spilling out, as though it had been squashed by a motor car.

It was on that day that Edith asked Joan if she meant to give her cat-guts for one of her potions: 'They're very useful for calling up familiars, or so I hear.'

Joan's cheeks flushed and she shot a scalpel-sharp look at Clement. He cringed and shifted painfully out of her way as she disappeared out the back.

Clement coughed. 'Now, Edith, I'm ever so grateful to you. What you did for me—'

She kept her voice flat. 'Saved your life, you mean?'

'Yes, that…'

'No trouble, Clement. I wouldn't think to let a friend suffer.'

'Yes, I know you mean no harm, but Joan feels… That is, *we* think…'

He was twisting a pork loin in those big shiny claws. Normally, he was gentle with the meat, even with the awkwardness of moving his ruined hands.

Edith softened her tone. 'What are you trying to tell me, Clement, my love? I have to stop my provoking of your wife? Is that it?'

He drew a breath, closed his eyes. 'I'm obliged, you understand, for all you did for me, with the... But—' He winced and rubbed at his scars, and then it all tumbled out in a babble. 'You can't be coming here anymore to shop. It's not good for business. Having you and your sort about.'

Edith raised her eyebrows and let the silence stretch between them.

Clement opened his eyes and went back to twisting those ripped-up pieces of pork. Over his shoulder, Edith could see a shadow lurking behind the little piece of fabric that marked off where the shop ended and their home began.

Finally Edith said, nice and loud, so she knew Joan couldn't fail to hear, 'That's a shame, Clement. It's been such a *convenience* for both of us. Me shopping here, I mean. It really has. In the past, I've had some *lovely* meat from you. You'd have hardly known there was a war on. It's been handy for you too, hasn't it, me coming by? I do like to help people when I can. Even Joan, bless her. It's been hard on her too, with your injuries, I've heard...'

She watched Clement carefully. Face, eyes, mouth: all suddenly frozen. The shadow behind the curtain was still.

Edith affected a jovial air, as if she were asking about the meat delivery.

'Yes, Vibert was saying it's a terrible shame for a man to be locked out of his own bedroom of a night, and no matter how his scars might look. I can understand why you'd feel sour about it.'

Clement's expression was one of panic.

'If you like,' Edith whispered, loudly, 'I can mix a tonic to relax her. Perhaps she'll be less snappish if she at least lets you—'

Clement shoved a big package of meat at her. 'Here's a decent piece of pork for you, then. If you come back tomorrow, I might have a chicken. There are some due from France. I can put one by for you. No charge, of course.'

Edith tried not to smile too widely. 'Oh, bless you. Generous to a fault you are, Clement, my love. I'll be seeing you tomorrow.'

Joan's expression as Edith turned to leave was a treat. She'd poked that scrawny neck of hers around the curtain, practically spitting with rage.

Edith whooped as she stepped from the shop. It put her in a dancing mood, the laughter: a sort of fizz in her stomach. She skipped down the street, grinning from ear to ear. She could see folks covering their mouths, but they could sneer away because good meat would make Marthe better. And if that wasn't cause for a bit of skipping, even at Edith's age, then nothing was.

As she skipped, Edith imagined what Joan must be saying to Clement at that very moment, and that set off the giggles. In the end she had to lean against a wall because she had no puff left in her; just wave after wave of laughter.

Marthe was asleep when she arrived back home. Edith gave the neighbour's boy half a penny for watching the girl. He scampered off before she could notice that he'd been picking at the corners of her cabbage loaf again. Not that she minded. He was a skinny little runt with enormous eyes.

Edith had become used to the squeeze and grumble of her hollow belly, the feeling of being scrubbed out inside with wire wool and disinfectant. She could ignore the pinching gripe that twisted her guts most mornings. Coming over dizzy and light-headed was trickier to master. She'd taken to chewing on raw bulbs of wild garlic, which chased off the fug of exhaustion, though she didn't much care for the way it made her breath and clothes smell.

It was all worth it, though, to see Marthe thriving. The girl was sleeping better and was undoubtedly less twitchy—she hadn't scratched the skin off her face with her nails for weeks.

Edith kept waiting for Maurice to comment, but he didn't say a word. And, if Edith was to tell the truth, she didn't think he'd noticed. Not that he didn't love Marthe: he worshipped the very bones of her: it was plain as a wash of sudden sunlight on his face when he looked at her, or in the softness in his voice when he spoke to her.

The sea tugged at his thoughts constantly. Longing was in the shadows of his eyes: the constant need to provide, to do *something*. Perhaps it was men and war—a curious sort of feebleness for them, squeezed within the enemy's iron fist. So Maurice filled his time with *doing* things. Clutching at power wherever he could find it. Always off, out to catch a fish or find the best trade for warm clothes or more bread. Or off to meet those French fishermen and garner news that the wireless wouldn't tell him. And, for all he said he was simply looking out for Marthe and that he didn't really *want* to leave the house, Edith saw that little spring in his step when he walked out the door to go off to his boat—the same lightness had surged through her after that little run-in with Clement and Joan.

Her Frank had worn that same look before he went off to fight. He'd stroked her cheek and said he was doing it for her, so she'd be proud of him. But he had been deaf to her protests, her pleas, her tears. She *wouldn't* be proud, she'd said. She didn't *want* him to go. Didn't *want* him to fight.

He'd claimed not to believe a word of it. He was off to prove himself to her. But Edith had known, even then, as a young woman not long out of her father's house, Frank's reason for going was nothing to do with her. It was all about *him*. Chasing some little fragment of himself he thought was missing; the war offered him the chance to become someone else.

Edith had seen the way he'd smiled at the mirror once he had that uniform on. He had looked himself in the eyes and grinned like a doe-eyed, lovesick fool. *That's war*, Edith thought. Men trying to find themselves, searching out some misplaced strength, and they only found it in the mirror once they were dressed in their uniform with a gun.

Edith hoped Frank had found that splinter of himself he had been on the lookout for. She hoped he saw his reflection in some blood-black trench puddle and it made him smile. She hoped he was happy with himself and what he was worth before that bomb came and blew him all to bits.

The nights after they handed her the letter were the worst: she would lie awake for hours, burning up with the wanting of him, skin aflame with the need for *something*. The heat of a body. The chance for a life to blossom within her belly again. In those first years, she'd thought that if he walked in the door smiling and said that they'd made a mistake, it hadn't been him that was killed at all... Well, she thought she'd kill him there and then herself for all that he'd put her through.

Time ticked on and she grew to think that if he walked through her door, after all those aching, empty years and every-thing that had happened, she wouldn't dream of murder. She'd sit him down and make him a nice cup of tea, and press a kiss into his stubbled cheek. Then she'd sit and tell him how he'd scooped the life from her when he disappeared. Left her hollow and full of echoes. And then she might tread on his toes by accident. Or tip scalding tea into his lap by mistake.

But no more talk of killing. There was too much death and hatred already, Edith thought sadly, without her hurling more fuel on to the blaze.

—

BY the time the Germans had been on the island a year, Claudine's home was quiet and dark and cold and hungry. Maman stayed in her nightgown much of the time, often growling at Claudine for being bad—talking too loudly, or burning the potatoes, or accidentally letting the door slam and rousing Maman from her grey fog.

'You *selfish* child,' she snarled. 'You can see I'm sleeping.'

Claudine smothered her sobs and tried to be good but sometimes it was hard to know what *good* was. Good was quiet, she knew that, so she thought of rabbits—how they made themselves small and still and silent.

When she could, Claudine spent time with Maurice. He showed her how to braid broken fishing rope and debone a fish, even before it was cooked. Sometimes, when she sat next to him, watching the shimmering fish scales peel away like scattered sunlight under his knife, she could imagine he was Papa.

When Maurice first started going to Edith's house, Claudine thought she should stop seeing him, because Edith was a horrid old woman and Maman would be angry if she knew Claudine was there. But then she started to wonder if perhaps Maman's black moods made monsters from thin air.

Last year, Claudine had watched Maman scream at Edith and bundle her from the house and slam the door. Maman had called Edith 'that interfering old witch' and Claudine had nodded because grown-ups knew best. But then Claudine remembered more and more the way Maman had shouted at Francis and drawn her hand back to strike him, simply for crying. And Claudine recalled how soft and warm Edith had always been, the gentle lull of her voice, the rumble of laughter in her chest when Claudine squeezed her in a tight embrace, the smile that tugged her mouth upwards whenever she looked at the children. Once the black cloud in Maman's head lifted, Claudine hoped she might understand why she was seeing Edith again. Until then, she crept from the house and didn't mention Edith's name.

Claudine liked helping to care for Marthe. She wasn't frightening, not really. She reminded Claudine of a newborn calf, with her big liquid eyes and the way she trembled and moaned, as if life itself was a terror. Claudine kissed her cheeks and brushed her hair and told her stories. They liked *Little Red Riding Hood* best. Maurice and Edith listened too. Claudine was a good girl, they said to each other, smiling.

Maurice was late back from fishing one day. Edith was humming under her breath, but worry scrabbled in Claudine's gut just the same—she could see the fear in the deep creases around Edith's eyes and her mouth.

When Maurice finally returned, it was nearly dark.

'Where on earth have you been?' Edith snapped. 'We were worried sick. Imagining all sorts.'

He was soaking, his hair plastered to his head. His skin was the greyish-blue of a drowned man.

He collapsed in a chair and covered his face with his hands. 'Two soldiers stranded today,' he mumbled. 'Went out looking for limpets—fools were cut off by the tide.'

Edith gaped. 'What happened?'

'They were seen, of course. Germans took a boat out to pick them up. I had to hide in a cove until the boat was gone. Sorry to have worried you.'

'No bother, you're safe. That's what matters.'

His eyes were weary. 'I watched them for almost an hour, sitting on that rock. The water was creeping higher—they were panicking. Couldn't swim a stroke, I shouldn't wonder.' He gave a thin smile. 'I was hoping they'd drown.'

Claudine frowned. 'Didn't you want to rescue them?' It was confusing to her, the sort of anger that would let a good man like Maurice watch two terrified men drown.

His thin smile grew. 'Not a bit of it. If every single one of the soldiers on this island drowned, all twelve thousand of them, I'd be happy.'

'What about the good ones?'

'There aren't any good ones.'

'But you don't *know* any of them.'

'No, I don't. And I've no wish to. And you'd be best to keep away from them too. Wouldn't trust them an inch.'

Claudine flushed. He must know she was still spending time with Gregor. She felt a flash of alarm—what if Edith knew too? What if she thought Claudine was bad and foolish?

But then she felt a miserable sort of rage: everybody was angry with her for being friends with a soldier; they all thought her dim-witted and a silly little girl, but none of them *knew* Gregor. Why couldn't they understand, or at least try? Frustration made her voice shrill.

'But they're *kind*, some of them. They're real people. Just like us.'

Maurice laughed. Cold, hard sound, like a stone thudding against a brick wall.

'Bless you, but you're a simpleton, Claudine. They are *nothing* like us. I'm sure of it. How many countries have we invaded, eh? How many people have you killed today, child?'

He wasn't being fair but she couldn't find the words to explain it, not when he didn't want to understand.

'Not all of them are like that! Some of them are kind.'

'I suppose this is about that soldier of yours, eh?' he said, angrily. 'The one you've made friends with?'

Claudine glanced at Edith's shocked face, hoping to see a glimmer of sympathy, but Edith was silent.

'You're a hare-brained child,' Maurice said, 'and you'll end up hurt. If I were your papa, I wouldn't be letting you out of the house.'

'But you're *not*,' she snapped. 'My papa is fighting and you're *not*. So you *can't* tell me what to do!'

Edith gasped. '*Enough*, both of you! What's all this about a soldier, Claudine?'

Claudine hesitated. Edith would understand, surely?

'His name is Gregor and he is good, *truly*, he is.'

'But...a German soldier? Maurice is right, my love, it's foolishness to mix with them.'

'He's not just a soldier. He's my *friend*.' She knew her voice sounded wheedling but she couldn't help it.

Edith sat next to her and took her hand. The older woman's fingers were rough but her tone was gentle.

'I think you should stay with your own kind, child. It's safer. Who knows how far you can trust a soldier? I don't want you to get yourself into trouble.'

Claudine felt an ache of frustration: *none* of the grown-ups understood about the Germans. They'd made up their minds about every soldier, without knowing a single thing about them.

She said, very softly. 'You've never met him.'

'I don't need to meet him,' Maurice growled. 'He's German, isn't he? They're all monsters—'

'No need for that.' Edith held up her hand. 'The child is upset as it is.' She turned back to Claudine, pulled her in close and kissed her hair. 'You, my love, are a sweet, kind, trusting girl. And I'm afraid that a soldier might want to…hurt you somehow—'

'He hasn't ever hurt me. He wouldn't—'

'All the same, it's a risk, isn't it, my love? For all of us. And you know we want to keep Marthe hidden. What if this soldier follows you here?'

Claudine wanted to say that it wouldn't matter if he did; he would never harm them. But they wouldn't understand and so she bit her lip and nodded, miserably.

Edith kissed her again.

'Good girl. Almost time to listen to the wireless. Let's treat ourselves to some coffee. I'm trying acorns and sugar beet today.'

The coffee was hot and bitter. As Claudine sipped, she tried to forget what Maurice had said.

Gregor. A monster.

It didn't stop her spending time with him.

The only time Gregor wasn't jolly was when he had been working at night, guarding the *Häftlinge* from Russia and Spain and Poland in the prisoner-of-war camp. On those days he was quiet, his face pouchy and grey. Sometimes his ruined hand was redder than usual, or swollen—as if the shiny skin had been poked or twisted.

There were lots of prisoners for Gregor to care for, more of them all the time; they were part of Hitler's grand plan. When he felt like talking, Gregor told Claudine that there was work to do in Jersey, like building big walls in case the English soldiers tried to invade. Hitler wanted to construct an enormous wall that went all the way along all the parts of Europe he owned, and since the Channel Islands were going to be the most important part of that, they had to be well fortified. That was why the Germans needed so many prisoners of war, and why guarding them was such an important job.

Other times, when he was in a better mood, he told her silly stories. 'Sit here.' He would pat the sand next to him. 'A long time ago...'

Gregor's voice changed when he was telling stories: it was deeper but softer, and it made her think of warm, orange firelight, in spite of the cold, silver light that rebounded off the grey sea.

Her favourite story was called *The Golden Key,* and Gregor

told it in an exciting and mysterious voice which always made the hairs on the back of her neck stand up.

'A long time ago, in winter, there is snow. Much snow, very cold. There is a boy, very poor. His Mama send him into the forest. He must find wood for make the fire. He has find the wood, but he is very cold, this poor boy. So he stop and make the fire in the forest. First, he must make the ground clean of snow and leaves. He cleans the ground, this poor boy. He scratch with his cold fingers and you cannot guess what he finds...'

Claudine was always breathless as a small child, even though she had heard the story many times.

'What did he find?'

Gregor grinned. 'A key! Golden and very small. And this poor boy, he think, *There must be a box for this key!* So he dig and find a metal box. He think, *There must be much treasure in this box. I hope this key fit!* And it does!'

'And was there treasure?' Claudine giggled.

Gregor always turned to her with a mischievous chuckle. 'We cannot tell. We must wait for this boy to open the box so we can know what is inside.'

Claudine laughed. She loved the story; it had no answer and no real ending. She loved it even more when, one day, Gregor buried a little key and a box in the sand for her to find. The key didn't fit the box—in fact, the box had no keyhole at all.

Gregor shrugged apologetically. 'It is the only box I can find. It is for bullets.'

Claudine went to open it. 'But it doesn't have bullets in it now?'

He shrugged; his eyes twinkled. 'We do not know until we open. What should be in this box?'

She set it down on the sand and they stared at it while Claudine tried to think of the things she wanted most in the world. None of them would have fitted into the box.

When they were hungry, Claudine went to find cockles or to collect crabs from the rock pools. They tasted muddy and sour, not like *Chancre* crabs or *Araignye de mer*. But there was no chance of catching *Chancres* because they had all crawled into fishermen's pots or been gobbled by soldiers.

Cockles were Claudine's favourites but most of them had been eaten. So they pried limpets from the rocks with Gregor's knife. They were very chewy; sometimes she had to swallow them without chewing at all because the limpet bouncing off her teeth made her stomach twist. It was slimy when it slid down her throat, like a snail.

The best food they caught, when it was a very low tide in September, was sand eels. It was spring tide, which happened every month in the days after the full moon. The moon dragged the sea out until it was a scribble of blue on the horizon. Then they could scramble over the rocks for over two miles and reach the sandbank where the eels buried themselves.

'Sand eels are tasty, but they are difficult to catch. Watch me, Gregor!'

Claudine showed him how to run up and down the bank, stamping her feet very hard and sometimes stopping to slap the ground with her hands.

Gregor watched her, smiling, and then did the same. Claudine bent double with laughter at the sight of him, in his smart German uniform, running around and stamping and slapping. He pretended to fall and gave a mock cry of distress, but then he tripped backwards, arms windmilling and splashed on to his bottom in a puddle of sea water. Laughter ballooned out of them and bounced off the jagged brown rocks.

Gregor was puffing and soaked and covered in sand, but he still grinned. 'This is game, yes? No fish coming for us today. You have made a good joke on me, Claudine.'

'You need to wait. You'll see.'

Soon there was something shiny on the sand, wriggling. As if it was trying to jump back into the sea, but there was no sea. Just Claudine's deft hands and a sack.

She shouted, 'Look Gregor!' It was only a small one. She slapped it with her hand to kill it and then popped it into the sack. It was best to kill them very quickly. Otherwise it was cruel, Papa always said—they couldn't breathe in the air, so it was a sort of drowning for them: their little mouths going open-shut-open-shut, gasping for water.

Gregor wasn't very good at killing them. He waited too long, staring while the poor fish flapped.

'Smack them to kill them,' Claudine cried. 'Like this. Hard! Don't worry, it doesn't hurt. Look! There's one, kill it quickly.'

But he just stood there, so she smacked it and then popped it in the sack.

'Why wouldn't you kill it?'

Silence, except for the far-off breathing of the sea. They stared at one another, until Claudine saw more sand eels and ran to them.

Once they had a big sackful, they carried them back to the beach, scrambling over the rocks. Everything was grey and slimy and covered in slippery seaweed. They ran, because the tide raced in around Jersey. As fast as galloping horses, Papa used to tell her. Being surrounded by the sea meant drowning.

Before the war, visitors to the island would sometimes wander out and get stranded, bewildered by how quickly the world had turned watery. If there were no rocks, they drowned. Once, Papa found Claudine crying about it and said, 'That's why you must always be careful.'

She wondered if Papa was being careful, wherever he was.

One day, Claudine and Gregor collected what Papa would have called a *bumper catch* of eels. Gregor could hardly carry the brimming sack.

'We should cook some on the beach,' Claudine said.

'Yes, *Liebling*. But not a big fire. Very small fire.'

'But you are a German soldier, too. They won't tell you off, will they?'

'*Nein.*' He rubbed at his neck, where he sometimes had bruises.

'Good. I'll make a fire.'

She scampered off to find some big stones. Then she dug a pit in the sand and laid the stones at the bottom. She collected large pieces of driftwood and scattered little sticks on top as kindling. Then she found a flint and asked Gregor for his knife. He frowned but gave it to her and she banged the flint against the steel, just as Papa had shown her.

It took a long time and her hands throbbed; she bashed her fingers twice. But then, a little spark. She blew it gently, piled on more kindling and kept blowing, breathing life into the spark. Lick of flame, two, and suddenly a fire, alive, so hot she had to jump back.

Claudine damped the flames with seaweed until only the

red-hot ashes glowed. Thick, choking smoke billowed in their faces. She placed a large, flat stone on top of the damped fire.

'Ready,' she said, with a flush of pride.

She gutted the bigger eels, slicing open their bellies and tugging out the slippery entrails. It didn't matter with the little eels, though—the bitter innards were barely noticeable once the fish were crisp-skinned from the fire.

Claudine offered the knife. 'Do you want to gut one, Gregor?'

He shook his head. 'I do not like *this*...' He pointed at the pile of fish guts.

She laughed. 'But you're a *soldier*. Besides, you can wash your hands in the sea afterwards.'

He shook his head again, mouth set in a line, like Francis when he was being stubborn. Claudine shrugged and gutted the rest with quick fingers.

She laid the sand eels on the hot rock and they waited for the skin to turn dark brown—it was the best part: bitter and crunchy. The fish sizzled on the hot stone. Claudine flipped them with a piece of cuttlefish, so they were cooked on both sides. Some of the skins stuck to the rock but it didn't matter—they tasted delicious: sweet fish and hot, bitter smokiness.

A sudden crunching noise came from the darkness beyond the fire. Heavy footsteps.

Claudine thought of *Jack and the Beanstalk: I'll grind your bones to make my bread.*

Gregor pulled her close and put a hand over her mouth. His fingers were strong. His face was hard.

Beyond the glow of the dying fire, the darkness was like a blanket muffling her senses. Claudine listened carefully. Four sets of boots. Heavy and grown-up. Dread felt like a gaping hole in her chest; it was hard to breathe.

German soldiers, come to drag them to prison for breaking curfew.

Then she remembered: they wouldn't be angry. Gregor was a German soldier; he could do anything he wanted. Claudine looked at his face. Droplets of sweat on his forehead. He still had his hand over her mouth—it was shaking.

She saw their feet first, in the light from the fire. They wore big, sturdy black boots. They had guns too, and batons.

Gregor's face had turned the colour of curdled milk.

The soldiers glared at the campfire. Unblinking. Ready to attack. The sand eels on the fire were smoking, blackened, ruined, but Claudine didn't dare move.

Her brain whirred. She pushed Gregor's hand away, managed to rasp, '*Hallo. Mochten Sie ihnen...*' She stopped. What was the German for sand eels? She mumbled, 'Sand eels,' and pointed at the fire where the fish were unappetisingly charred.

None of the Germans said anything. Perhaps they didn't like sand eels. Perhaps the offer of burnt fish had made them angry?

All of a sudden they sat, laughing and talking, too quickly for Claudine to understand much of what they were saying. They began to gobble the eels, even though the hot flesh must have burned them.

For the first time, it occurred to Claudine that the German soldiers on the island were starving too. Everybody always said that they stole the islanders' food to supplement their generous rations; they made pigs of themselves, gluttonous beasts, and the islanders were famished because the soldiers were such guzzling, greedy swine. But these soldiers were like scarecrows—broomstick arms and long, thin noses. Claudine could see the harsh slant of bones jutting from their faces, sharp shadows; their fingers bumpy like broken twigs in winter.

She wondered if Papa was hungry, and if he had a sharp face and twig fingers now. Perhaps, when he came back home, she wouldn't know him. Claudine wondered if he would know her.

Perhaps war makes everything look different.

The soldiers finished the sand eels, so Claudine cooked more. They cheered and clapped. Her heart steadied and she felt a wave of happiness: she was helping Gregor's friends. She wondered why he hadn't brought them to meet her before.

They passed a bottle between them, gulping and sighing and wiping their mouths on their sleeves, belching and laughing. One of them—with very small eyes and thin lips—pretended to give the bottle to Gregor, only to pull the bottle away and snigger.

Then he shoved Gregor, hard. He fell backwards, arms and legs flailing like an upturned beetle. The soldier waited for Gregor to stand, and pushed him again. As Gregor stood up, the soldier twisted his ruined arm so that Gregor howled and sank to his knees.

Claudine shouted, 'Stop!' But her voice was swallowed by the soldier's laughter.

'*Aufstehen,*' he growled.

Gregor didn't move, just stared at the sand.

Again the soldier shouted, '*Aufstehen!*' and kicked Gregor in the stomach.

Over the beat of the thudding blood in her ears, Claudine heard one of the soldiers dragging Gregor away, laughing about *guarding the animals.*

When she opened her eyes again, Claudine saw the horror on Gregor's face, and for a moment she thought that he was scared for himself, and that the soldier was going to do something terrible to him. But then he struggled and tried to wrench his arms away and run back to her. He shouted, 'Claudine!' and his voice was raw.

His terror was for her.

The darkness engulfed him and she was alone with the other soldiers.

The soldier who had a nose that stuck up and out like a pig's snout pushed the bottle into her hand.

Claudine shook her head. 'I'm not thirsty.'

'*Nein. Trinken!*'

Her chest was being squeezed by an invisible fist, but she managed to whisper, 'I'm not thirsty, thank you.'

'*Jetzt trinken.*'

They moved around her. Their eyes were like glittering mirrors. The tall man took Claudine's head and wrenched it back. Another soldier held her hands in a crushing grip. She whimpered. The one with the piggy face tipped the bottle against her mouth and held her nose.

The glass was cold. She had to open her mouth. It tasted sour where they had been drinking from it, but she swallowed because she couldn't breathe. Lungs burning. Throat on fire. Then she choked and they roared with laughter, a noise like baying hounds.

When they finally released her, Claudine doubled over, wheezing, then she vomited. She started to wail, a childish howl she hadn't made in years. Legs and arms trembling, her face wet with tears and snot.

The soldiers stopped laughing. The one with the pig nose said, '*Ah, es tut mir leid.*' He put his arm around her, pulled her on to his lap and held her close, as if to comfort her. But his arms were hard, and when she struggled, he gripped her more tightly.

She froze and tried to stop crying.

His hands were around her waist, on her stomach. His fingers moved, very slowly, like tickling, but painful, digging into her flesh.

Let me go. Please.

The soldiers sat talking and drinking and eating sand eels for an endless yawn of gaping time. Claudine was queasy, and beyond terrified. She felt a tug of longing for her own bed with Francis's heavy little body half slumped over her chest, his thumb stuffed firmly into his mouth; at nearly two, his face was stubborn even in sleep.

The man wouldn't let her go. She tried to push his hands away, but it was like struggling against rock. Those hands, cold fingers possessive of her chest, then her stomach. He squeezed her leg, near the top, where Papa used to tickle her to make her giggle.

Claudine could barely breathe.

He moved his fingers up higher, inside her underthings. Still moving. Pushing hard, as if he was trying on a tight-fitting glove. Then came a swooping pain, in waves.

After she had counted the mouth of the sea crunching on to the sand three hundred and twenty-six times, the soldiers stood to go.

They had eaten most of the sand eels, but there were still

some left in the bottom of the sack. Claudine would take them home to Maman and Francis. Maman would need an explanation for her being out so late, a reason not to growl at her.

It was quiet and dark after they had gone.

Claudine counted fifty-three crunches of the waves on the sand while she tried to stop crying, tried to slow her breathing; her heart flipped in her chest, like a desperate, drowning fish.

After a long time, she stumbled home.

Part 3

DURING that first year, Carter learnt that the Commandant was both volatile and vicious. His essential nature was somewhat chimerical in any case, but the Cushings exacerbated these qualities. His sudden fits of rage might have seemed comical had he not been a man of such power and influence: his temper tantrums generally boded ill for those around him. Carter did his best to mitigate his anger and deflect his brutality from the islanders, but it was a struggle, when even the most insignificant blunders could induce apoplectic rage.

Take his breakfast: daily, he demanded two eggs, soft-boiled, with well-buttered toast cut into ten even 'fingers' made from white bread.

This breakfast caused many problems, not the least of which being that eggs, and chickens, were becoming rarer by the day. The poor, beleaguered cook managed to capture a young, plump bird and fed it precious grain and scraps, in return for its daily yield of one, sometimes two, eggs.

But in the autumn the bird disappeared one night, an event that coincided with a drunken patrol stripping off their uniforms and swimming naked in the sea. The men swore blind that they had not stolen the chicken and knew nothing of its whereabouts.

The Commandant's rage at an eggless breakfast knew no bounds. The entire patrol was sent to the front line in Russia.

In an attempt to assuage the effects of the Commandant's fury, Carter searched for another chicken: the Buff Orpington prime layer was replaced by an old, stringy bird who wore a careworn expression and rarely laid eggs.

The cook despaired. Even when eggs were available, there was almost always some other problem with the breakfast: the butter was sour or there was too little of it; the egg yolk was overcooked or undercooked; it was too small or too pale in colour; the toast fingers were different sizes... The Commandant's list of grievances with his breakfast seemed never-ending.

Each substandard breakfast put him in such a foul temper that his mood could only be lightened by issuing increasingly bizarre orders to the islanders. For instance, any two people travelling by bicycle together were forbidden from riding abreast. No islander could come within fifty miles of the French coast (the Commandant refused to acknowledge that nowhere on the island was it possible to be further than thirty-six miles *away* from the French coast). And the making of black butter was banned.

This last, in some ways, caused the most frustration: black butter was a highly flavoured jam, which was made using apples, sugar, cider and butter and various spices. It was an age-old, traditional recipe, and even rationing had only resulted in various improvised additional ingredients to make the jam.

The Commandant's displeasure lay not in the foodstuff itself, which was innocuous enough, but in the making of it. This was done in a celebratory manner, with whole communities congregating and cooking together, drinking cider while they worked and generally making merry.

Despite Carter's attempts to convince him otherwise, the Commandant believed that any such gathering posed the potential for insurrection. The penalty for making black butter was imprisonment or deportation, depending on the Commandant's mood and the standard of his breakfast that morning.

However, nothing more clearly exposed his brutishness and tyranny than his actions towards Frederique Soulette, the young Frenchman who was brought to the island in October, under arrest for escaping occupied France and for attempting to support the allied forces in Britain.

Carter first became aware of Soulette's capture when there was a great furore from the Commandant's office: shouting, banging and a thud, which sounded like furniture being overturned and then feet pounding down the corridor.

To his surprise and dismay, the Commandant himself strode into Carter's office.

'Doctor, come! I have surprise. You will like this, I think.'

He followed the Commandant to his office where he found a group of ten Frenchmen, bloody-faced and trembling.

The Commandant held up his hands, as if presenting Carter with a gift, and explained how they had been captured: Soulette and a group of nine other traitors had set sail from the Brittany Coast in the hope of reaching English shores and joining the free

French forces who opposed the Germans.

They landed on the shores of Guernsey and, thinking they had arrived on English soil, walked up the beach singing *La Marseillaise* and banging a drum.

'Stupid, yes?' The Commandant grinned.

Instead of the warm English welcome they had expected, they had been captured by a German patrol that had transported them to Jersey to be sentenced.

A few, Soulette among them, resisted arrest. Carter observed the sickening array of cuts, bruises and contusions on his face and arms.

The Commandant made all the Frenchmen kneel before him. When they refused, he booted each and every one of them until they collapsed to the floor.

Carter recalled a moment from his childhood: at the age of eight or nine, he had happened upon a group of older boys in the woods who had captured a dog, possibly feral—all bones, matted fur and wild, rolling eyes. The boys had wired shut the animal's snarling jaws and were taking turns poking at its eyes with a stick, laughing at the dog's high-pitched growls and its desperate, shuddering attempts to break free.

Carter had been half immobilised with fear, but his disgust and horror had been so powerful that he had flung himself at the boys, yelling and beating at them wildly with flailing fists. They had been in such shock at the outburst that they had let the dog go, and it had fled, howling, its poor jaws still wired firmly shut.

The biggest boy had rounded on Carter. 'What did ya do *that* for? We was only *playing*.'

The boys had set upon Carter and beaten him senseless.

The Commandant shouted for several minutes, showering all in the room in a fine spray of saliva. By this time, the Frenchmen were, for the most part, cowering from their position on the floor. Soulette alone returned the Commandant's stare.

Carter clenched his fists. *Look away. For God's sake, man, look away.*

Suddenly, the Commandant brought up his knee and smashed Soulette's jaw. A *crack* that sounded like gunfire as the bone shattered and Soulette crumpled. The Commandant began booting him in the abdomen.

Carter was torn: he desperately wanted to step forward to intervene but instead stood frozen. He despised himself for not protecting Soulette or attempting to calm the Commandant, yet *something* prevented him: a shameful, cancerous sort of fear that mushroomed with every act of violence he witnessed.

The Commandant ceased the assault only when he grew short of breath. Then he held up his hands, as if presenting a work of art, a masterpiece he had slaved over. Soulette's face was now grey and a ribbon of blood snaked from the corner of his mouth.

'So, Doctor, what do you say for our French visitors, eh? Ugly-looking bastards, yes?' The Commandant laughed. 'What must become of them? What must I do with these filth, these French animals?'

Some of the French still had the soft, rounded faces of boys. Plump cheeks that, no doubt, mothers had squeezed and kissed and wiped clean, not so many years ago. Even Soulette, whom Carter later discovered was the oldest at just twenty-one, even he looked as though he had not long needed use of a razor.

'It is not for me to make decisions, sir,' Carter finally

muttered. His stomach curled as he recognised that dangerous glint in the Commandant's eyes, which warned him that the German's patience had come to an end. He required an answer.

Carter thought of Edith, Clément, the patients in the hospital. All those who would suffer if he displeased the Commandant.

'But perhaps a spell, a, ah...*short* spell in prison...in France would be a suitable...punishment,' he managed to mumble.

'Prison, ha! You see, Doctor, you will never be the leader. Look at these men. What do you see?'

He exhaled. 'They are boys, *leibe Kommandant,*' he whispered. 'Just boys.'

'No!'

He walked a slow circle around the group. Soulette was still groaning on the floor. He knelt down, deliberately placing his knee on Soulette's hand. Crackle of shattering bones like walking across kindling. The Frenchman whimpered.

'No. Not boys,' the Commandant murmured. 'They are, I do not know your word...how do you say?...*ermordern.*'

'Murderers?'

'Yes. Murderers. These boys—you call them this—these *boys* would *kill* me.'

He spat these last words, his face puce. Carter found himself hoping that the rise in his blood pressure would be too much for his heart or brain. He visualised a blood vessel bulging, bursting.

But as quickly as the storm had arrived, it passed. The Commandant laughed again, throwing back his head so that Carter could see his yellowed teeth.

'*Nein.* These monsters, they will go to the *Konzentrasionslager,* *ja?* We will use these bodies. They will help to build. A good lesson, no, for these men who would—how do you say?...*zunicht machen.*'

'Destroy?'

The rumours from France were clear: the camps amounted to a death sentence. Murder, teased out with agonising slowness. But how to stop it? The double-barrelled gun of fate was loaded and cocked: a single false comment would direct it at Carter's own fragile skull.

The Commandant shook his head. 'No, we *build*. We *make*—this is our work, yes? To create? And these men, these *boys*, Doctor, they will help us.'

He booted Soulette in the abdomen. Carter couldn't prevent himself from shouting: 'Stop!'

The Commandant turned, glowering.

Throbbing with fear, Carter murmured, 'Sir, that young man is badly hurt. It seems unnecessary to inflict—'

'*You* would advise me?' The German stopped, his nose inches from Carter's. 'A *mouse* speak to a *man*? A *rat* give orders to a *god*? You dare to—'

'But the man requires—'

'*Silence!* Do not displease me, further, Doctor. You go too far.'

Carter drew a deep breath. 'Might I suggest—?'

'No! Enough! *No!* No suggestings. Your patient, the butcher. He recovers still, no?'

'Why do you—'

'He will not recover in prison, I think.'

Carter's heart dashed unevenly against his ribs. It was *impossible*: his every move against the Commandant was met with these wild threats.

187

He was about to protest further, but Soulette had struggled to sit up and was now staring at the Commandant with unconcealed hatred. The Commandant, who was an expert at reading even masked emotions in others, did not miss the defiance in the young Frenchman's glare. With calculated slowness, so as to draw maximum attention from his audience, he walked up to Soulette and kicked him in the groin, hard, twice.

Then he said, loud enough for everyone to hear over Soulette's whimpers, '*Die Eschreßenkommando für deise Fotze.*'

Then the Commandant came and patted Carter on the shoulder.

'You are confused, Doctor, no? The *Eschreßenkommando*? You call this the firing squad.'

Before Carter could say another word, the soldiers came and dragged the Frenchmen away.

———

AS their second winter under the crush of the jackboot closed in, Edith had more and more people coming to her for help. She knew the reason, of course: they were keeping away from the hospital because of talk that Dr Carter was helping the Commandant. He'd tried to do it on the hush at first, but people noticed that he was in and out of Royal Square every day, and once the rumours started, they spread like a fire on a thatched roof.

Carter had stopped visiting Edith altogether. He no longer checked on Marthe or questioned Edith about 'miracle cures'.

When she sat and thought about it, Edith wondered if he'd

been picking her brain for pieces of knowledge he might be able to use to help the Commandant. But perhaps she gave him too little credit: other folks' whispering voices drift into your head and shape the fibre of your thoughts until the fabric you see isn't anything you've had a hand in weaving.

In the quietest hours of the night, it had even crossed Edith's mind, although she tried not to linger on it, that Carter might have been spying for the Commandant. Reporting back, or assessing what should be done with Marthe when they came to take her. But she put the notion from her mind as soon as it appeared. If she'd not had to listen to people accusing him of all sorts of villainous motivations, she would have said Carter stayed away because he was ashamed. But who knew, really? Impossible to comprehend the texture of the darkness that squats in someone else's heart.

She saw him, early one September morning, on his way from the butcher's, she guessed, from the parcel he was carrying. The talk was that the Commandant had been sending him to collect the meat because he reckoned on Clement doing almost anything for the man who had saved his life. The bloody German wasn't wrong there—the rest of the island went short because of his gluttony. And for all Clement waved those mangled hands and said, 'What can I do? I owe the man my life,' the whispers went that the Hacquoils were in the pay of the Germans too.

So when Edith saw Carter hastening from the Hacquoils and towards Royal Square, she called out to stop him. He looked right at her, put his head down and hurried on. She had to shout twice more before he turned.

She smiled. 'Out and about early, Doctor? I've not seen you in months.'

He flicked his eyes to her face, then looked away. 'You know what they say: no rest for the wicked.'

'You're looking weary. We've missed you, Marthe and I. She's much the same, in case you were wondering.'

'Of course. Well, I'm glad to hear she hasn't worsened. And yes, I'm tired. I've been doing some late and early shifts at the hospital. To fit around ah…other…commitments.'

'Well, you mustn't run yourself ragged. What will we do for a doctor when the doctor is ill?'

He laughed—for a moment the years fell off him. 'Indeed. I must try to rest. But not this moment, I am afraid, Madame Bisson…'

'It's Edith, Doctor. You know that by now. Fine shoes. That's the second new pair I've seen on you in the past year.'

He shuffled his feet but said nothing.

'Fancy. Leather too. Where did you steal those from?'

He gave a tight smile and made as if to hurry off.

Edith called, 'Clement Hacquoil is steady in his improvement now. Scars don't seem to bother him as much. Some months back, I dropped a few salves around, but he didn't seem to have need of them. Says you've given him some fancy liniment. Something imported. I told him he must have it wrong.'

'I—I've seen him. And I've given him a cream to prevent more scars from turning keloid.'

'I hear you're picking up great parcels of beef that have been shipped from France. Where are you putting it all? I can't remember the last time I had beef.'

He was thin as a rail, even though people said that the Germans must be feeding him extra to buy his compliance.

'I must go.' Carter turned towards town.

'Doctor?'

He turned back.

'You look after yourself, won't you now?'

'Yes, I—Yes. Thank you. Edith.' There was a ghost of a smile. Then he was gone.

Edith had a hollow, jittery feeling in her gut for the rest of the day. She was trying to fathom what was different about him. He'd looked wretched—tired, and thin and ashamed of himself—but it was something more.

And then it slid home, knowledge like a knife: the man was terrified. He hadn't been bought by the Germans; he'd been bullied—threatened, perhaps.

Later that evening, she said to Maurice, 'I saw Dr Carter today.'

Maurice was rubbing one of Edith's salves into Marthe's chest. Lavender to help her to sleep. He didn't look up.

'Oh yes?'

'You must know that he has been looking after the Commandant for nigh on a year now?'

Marthe was asleep. Maurice leant her back a little in the chair so her chin didn't slump forward so.

'It's an ugly business,' he said.

'Do you think so?'

'Well, do you not? He's caring for that…that *fiend*, while there're people could use his help in the hospital.'

Edith sighed and rubbed her eyes. Exhaustion gnawed at her very bones.

'You're right, Maurice. It is a dreadful thing. He seemed a

decent sort. But who knows what folk will do, when—'

'There's nothing decent about helping out the Germans. Bad as the Jerry-Bags, he is. And there's no excuse in the world for that sort of traitor.'

'Yes, but...I saw him today, for the first time in so long and he looked...haunted. *Hunted*. I don't know. What's this war doing to us all?'

'*You*, Edith, don't have a thing to worry about. Nothing has changed you a bit. You're a wonder, that's what you are. Where would we all be without you, eh? So just stop worrying about Dr Carter. I can see you're fretting, even now, aren't you?'

For a moment, it crossed Edith's mind to tell him of Carter's visits to Marthe and the monstrous thought she'd had: that he might have been spying in some way, or storing up knowledge to use against them all in the future. Some sort of insurance against the terror that was chasing him. But instead she made some jest and Maurice chuckled and the moment passed.

But that night, when she lay down to sleep, Edith couldn't help remembering Carter's weary, hopeless face—the raw fear in those eyes.

———

IT was near Christmas. The air was sharp as if there was ice in it. Maurice was stumbling back from a fishing trip, brain fugged with exhaustion, when he first saw him: the soldier with the withered arm, sat outside the house, bold as if he lived there himself.

The seas had been wild, so Maurice hadn't caught much;

the nets tangled in the rocks and the reefs time and again. Two had ripped and the sea had swallowed one before he decided to give it up for a lost cause. They would just have to live off pickled mackerel and do without the money from selling, at least until the weather turned and the sea calmed. He'd caught two tiddlers for dinner, more by luck than anything—they'd snagged in his net somehow, even with the great rents in it.

On an ordinary day, it pleased him to throw the tiddlers back, with a little blessing. He didn't believe most of the rubbish fishermen swore by: always using the same nets on the same nights, or throwing the first fish back for the mermaids to eat, to slake their thirst for human blood, their hunger for a beating human heart between their jagged fish teeth.

All the same, he liked to be respectful to the sea so she treated him well. But on that morning he'd had such a run of poor luck that he thought the sea wouldn't mind overly if he took just two little ones back home—for Marthe. He stuffed them deep into his pockets—the coat smelt of fish anyway. Besides, it seemed foolish to drag back a great sack with but two tiny fish in the bottom.

But it meant that when he saw that soldier perched on his own back wall, he couldn't do what he would have any other day: stow his sack of fish in a bush. So Maurice dug his hands deep into his pockets, pressing them against the wet, slimy bodies of the dead fish, and strode past, head down.

He waited for the soldier to notice the bulges in his pockets, or catch the scent of those fish and call *Halt!* But he didn't say a word, simply carried on blowing smoke high up in the air and watching it drift away.

Surely he had to be play-acting? Any minute now, he'd pull

his gun, stop Maurice and search him. He'd discover those fish and that would be that. Prison at first, but a bullet straight through his skull was most likely, once they discovered the boat without a proper licence.

Maurice watched his feet as though they were someone else's, taking one step after another, across the grass, and then over the paving stones. His belly was churning. Those damn fish in his pockets, cold and slippery under his fingers.

Please let me see Marthe. To give her the fish. To say goodbye. Only let me say goodbye to her.

Suddenly, Maurice was safely past.

He could feel the soldier's eyes on his back. The hardest thing was not to run. He made himself stroll, and then closed the door gently. Just as though he hadn't a care or a worry in the world.

He could hear himself panting. He leant against the door, blinking black spots from his vision. The house felt too warm. But it was silent—Edith and Marthe must still be in bed. Maurice had taken to asking Edith to sleep in the house if he was going to be out all night, rather than taking Marthe to her house, which looked too suspicious if a patrol saw them. He would rather have raised eyebrows from neighbours who didn't know how to mind their own business than have soldiers baying at the door.

Perhaps that was why he was so shaken up by seeing one at the end of the garden. Bold as brass, as if he was waiting for someone in particular. Maurice peeped out the window, breath misting the glass, then ducked down again, cursing. Damn soldier was still there, his cigarette glowing.

As he crouched, he caught sight of the soldier's other hand.

It was curled into a tight fist, the skin was taut and shiny, as if it was too small for the bunched-up bones beneath.

It struck Maurice as something of a puzzle. If what the French fishermen said was true, then the Germans didn't put much stock in cripples. Why had such a specimen been allowed to survive, let alone put in the army? Shouldn't he be in some work camp somewhere? Or being tested? Or he should have been put against a wall and shot long ago, before the war even started.

Maurice yanked the curtains shut. None of his business and he wasn't going to join the pot-stirrers by mulling it over and gossiping to anyone who would listen.

The house was a mess. Edith was slovenly, although she was good with Marthe. Maurice had to clear the pots and crocks from the sink before he could wash the sea smell from his skin and the salt from his hair. He clattered the pots without thinking. He was usually careful and quiet as could be, especially if Marthe was sleeping.

He set the last pan down on the drainer and then stripped off to his smalls. Marthe used to pretend to retch at the smell of the sea on him—she said it made him stink like a fish. Sometimes, in the old days, Maurice used to tease her by coming back early and crawling into bed next to her, without washing. He'd press against her. Kiss the back of her neck. She would be half asleep, and so she would roll over and match kiss for kiss, hot breath and her body opening under him. But then she'd catch a whiff of the sea and she'd squeal and laugh and slap him away.

You're the very devil, Maurice Pipon!

She'd march him to the tin bath and throw buckets of cold water over him. Scrub his skin until it glowed red under her touch.

He would let himself be bossed and scolded and dragged about and scrubbed by this little wisp of a woman for just as long as he could restrain himself, but then his resolve would crumble and he'd yell and try to pull her into the bath with him. When she skittered away, he'd splash her, until she'd be standing there, nightdress clinging to that milky skin. Naked underneath. The rounded warmth of her body showing through the wet nightdress. Her head thrown back, laughing, hair soaked. Like a mermaid.

It was a crushing in his chest, that love he had for every part of her.

But now she was too ill to talk or stand or speak, Maurice always painstakingly rinsed every trace of sea smell from his skin. If he went to kiss her after he'd been out on the boat, he always did it quickly. Mouth closed. A brush of his lips against hers, and then he pulled away. Just in case she hated the smell but couldn't move or tell him. Because now, that mermaid's body was her prison. Her legs might as well have been fins for all the good they were to her.

He sighed and used the dishcloth to dry himself, which Marthe would have hated if she'd known. But it was either that or stand in the freezing air and shiver himself dry.

He had just about towelled most of the water off when he heard a rustling in the doorway. Thinking of the soldier, his heart alarmed and he jumped, but it was only Edith, grinning at him.

'Oh, I didn't see you there, I was…'

He dropped his fists back to his sides and held the dishcloth in front of himself and waited for her to leave or beg his pardon.

She bustled into the kitchen. 'Morning, my love. How were

the fish? I've left Marthe to sleep in. She woke around midnight and then struggled to settle—she'd wet her sheets, although I didn't notice at first. So her skin's a little tender this morning. You know how she is.'

Before Maurice could say a word, Edith was at the sink with last night's wet sheets in her hand. She barged him to one side and he dropped his cloth.

She didn't even look up. 'For heaven's sake, Maurice, put some clothes on, will you? Chop chop!'

All his clothes were in the bedroom—where Marthe was asleep—except for an old cardigan and some badly patched trousers which he kept down behind the armchair. He tried to reach the clothes without bending over and without dropping the cloth. All the while, Edith was humming away to herself and stirring those sheets around in the water—she must have known he was struggling, but she carried on smiling and stirring.

In the end, he managed to shunt the armchair to one side and grab the clothes. He dropped the cloth for a moment while he pulled his trousers on. He thought Edith might turn her back, or go outside, or do anything else you'd expect of a woman when there was a naked man in the room. Maurice couldn't be sure, but he thought she was sneaking a peek now and then, amused.

Once he was dressed, he said, 'What about that soldier, then?'

'What soldier, Maurice, my love?'

'The one sitting at the bottom of the garden. With the odd-looking hand.'

'Oh, *him!* Yes, he had me in a lather too, when I first noticed him. But honestly, Maurice, he seems harmless enough. And with that hand—what damage could he do?'

'Now just a minute. How long has he been here?'

'Oh, not long. Perhaps three days. Mostly when you've been out on the boat.'

'*Days?* Why on earth didn't you say something?'

'I didn't want you fretting. Look at you now—imagining all sorts of horrors and don't think I can't tell. And him not doing anything except sitting there.'

'Well of course he's not simply *sitting* there. He's on to me!'

'Come now, Maurice, there's no reason to think—'

He slumped at the table, trying to quash his panic. 'Well, what else would he be doing? I'm telling you, they know about the boat. It's the finish for me. For the lot of us, most likely.'

'Don't work yourself up. If they knew then they'd have come knocking already. I'd be in prison and you'd be halfway to Germany by now. He could be about something completely different.'

He jumped up and his chair clattered over. 'Marthe! Oh God, you think he's after Marthe? The prison camps! We must do something—'

'Oh for heaven's sake, calm down! If they were going to take her, they'd have done it by now.'

His heart thrummed unevenly in his chest. 'I'm going to look in on her.'

'Don't you dare! She's asleep. Just sit yourself down and close your eyes. You need the rest as much as she does. Panicking won't change a thing. We go about our usual business and wait.'

So Maurice stamped across the room, leant against the bedroom door and closed his eyes. He imagined Marthe on the other side of the door, sleeping with her hands up close to her face.

He felt a sudden urge to weep or scream. Instead he let his knees collapse under him and sank to the floor.

Edith was drying the dishes and humming again. She flashed him a sympathetic smile and then brought over a cup of nettle tea and squeezed his arm when he took it.

'It'll be well. We shan't let them have her.'

The tea was scalding. 'I wish we could leave. There's no way to keep her safe here—'

'I know. Try to rest.'

'I'm tired of all this talking. I want to do...*something*.'

She smiled, sadly. 'I know you do. But you can't fight the whole German army, Maurice. Even if you tried, you'd be shipped off or...' Edith sighed. 'The best thing any of us can do is hope for things to change. We've nothing but time, my love.'

—

CLAUDINE didn't see Gregor for a long time after that night with the sand eels and the soldiers. She walked to school a different way; she played with Francis on another part of the beach. Thinking of Gregor reminded her of the other soldier with the hard hands, and she felt ashamed and frightened. What if the soldiers had talked to one another and Gregor knew what the horrible soldier had done to her? And that she hadn't struggled to get away, but had *let* him touch her? She imagined the pity and the disgust on Gregor's face. Every time she saw him, she would remember that night.

So she avoided him and spent more time at home, helping Maman, who always wanted to lie in bed. If Claudine pleaded,

Maman made dinner. But while she did it, her face was frozen into a pained expression, her mouth twisted like Clement Hacquoil's, even though no fire had scorched her skin. She rarely smiled. When Claudine told her about school and German lessons, or the games they played, Maman blinked like a sleepwalker and said, 'Hmm.'

Once or twice, in moments Claudine treasured afterwards, Maman was more like her old self. From before Papa had left. Before Francis was born.

When it was Claudine's birthday, in November, Maman showed her how to cook bean crock, but they hadn't many beans and no pork at all, so they used potatoes instead. They peeled them together over the sink. They were seed potatoes, really—Claudine had dug them out of Mr Ozouf's vegetable patch when no one was looking.

'Were you planning on leaving any potato to eat,' Maman asked, 'or are you peeling it all for compost?'

'Sorry, I'm trying.'

'Well, try harder.' But her mouth was soft, her voice warm. 'Look, come here. Like this, and this. Gently does it. That's it.'

She held her deft hands over Claudine's, turning the potato quickly and slicing off the thinnest slivers—transparent, like wet petals.

When she had finished peeling, she pressed the potato back into Claudine's hands. 'Happy birthday, my love.' Then she kissed the back of Claudine's neck.

Claudine giggled. 'A *potato* for my birthday?'

Maman grinned. 'For your birthday *cake!*'

Claudine wondered if Maman would mind if she kissed her back. Next time, she definitely would.

But when it came to eating Claudine's potato birthday cake, Maman wasn't hungry: she trudged back to bed and pulled the quilt over her head. Claudine tried not to mind; she shared the potato and the bean crock with Francis. They gobbled every mouthful, even though the potatoes tasted bitter and had the powdery feel of dry flour between their teeth.

Claudine saved some for Maman—took a bowl of the bean crock into the bedroom for her, but Maman was asleep. Claudine gave it to Francis instead.

There was less and less fuel to heat up the water, so they all shared the same bathwater in the metal tub in front of the stove. Usually, Claudine bathed Francis first—she held his hand while he kicked and splashed her and chuckled that infectious toddler laugh that always made him sound fat and happy, even though he was scrawny as a plucked chicken and far too small for an almost three-year-old.

One evening, Claudine was struggling to bath Francis: he was making a great joke of drinking the bathwater and laughing, but she worried he would drown so she kept trying to pull his face up out of the water and he kept screaming, 'No! Dink!' and squirming free of her hand to slurp the water. He would choke for a moment, then giggle and say, 'Gain!'

'For heaven's sake!' Claudine snapped. 'Keep *still*, Francis!'

Maman came into the kitchen. 'Come on, trouble, in you go.'

Claudine raised her eyebrows. 'But I can't wash and stop Francis drowning himself. He thinks it's funny, look.'

Francis giggled. 'Dink!'

Maman rolled her eyes. 'So shuffle on up then.'

She helped Claudine climb into the tub and squeezed in behind her.

The water splashed over the sides when she sat down. It was a warm feeling in the cooling water: the closeness.

Maman held Claudine's hand when she climbed out.

'Thank you,' Claudine said, and kissed her on the shoulder. It was wet and tasted of coal tar soap.

After that, they squeezed into the tub together every night.

It was in the tub that Claudine started to notice Maman's bones. She was shrinking. When she stood up, her ribs were piano keys, stark white and striped with dark shadows.

She stopped liking meat, always pushed it straight on to Claudine's plate or fed it to Francis. Sometimes, if Claudine cuddled her and put her face against Maman's stomach, she could hear it growling.

At every meal, Claudine devoured every scrap of food (and sometimes licked the plate clean), but she still felt hollow. She didn't ask for more food because there wasn't any. But at night, she dreamed of eating a whole chicken and a loaf of bread and a bunch of bananas. She ate and ate until her stomach burst open and she still kept eating but the empty feeling never faded, even in her sleep.

And when she woke, the hunger hurt.

Before Christmas, everyone was ill. It started with a cough, which went to Francis's chest because there was no wood to burn the damp away. Then Claudine caught it too; they coughed each other awake at night, hacking up green phlegm, foreheads burning, eyes aching, mouths feeling like they had been stuffed with wire wool. Maman sat up in the chair in their room every night, sponging their skin, fanning them cool.

They were ill for over a week. But no sooner were they on the mend than Maman's face had the look of grey tallow and she was coughing day and night. Eyelids like bruises, breath rattling in her chest.

She went to bed for a week, but her cough worsened. She was awake all night with it; Claudine could hear her fighting to draw breath. When she coughed, there were dark shadows at her throat and her collarbones stood out like the beams of a broken-down house. Claudine could count every bone in her back, and the stacked bricks of her spine.

'Shall I fetch Dr Carter?' she asked.

'No, no…we can't—' Maman coughed, eyes bulging and then gasped, 'No money.'

'Well, then, I will give him my ormer shells. He can sell them when the war is finished. They are rare and pretty. They must be worth lots of money.'

Maman shook her head and carried on hacking. Hearing it, icy fingers clasped at Claudine's gut.

'I'll fetch Madame Bisson, then,' she blurted.

'Don't you dare! She'll interfere as she always does and—'

'But Maman, you are very poorly—'

'No means *no!*'

'But what if you die?' Claudine started crying.

Maman gave her a kiss and squeezed her close. 'I'm not going to die. Silly goose. No more crying, do you hear?'

But then she coughed, again, and it sounded like when the waves rattled stones on the beach. The rattling went on for a long time. Claudine knew that, over many years, the sea could scrape solid rock down to nothing, could make huge boulders disappear. She wondered how many coughs it would take for

Maman's lungs to be worn away to nothing.

The next morning, Claudine stopped at Dr Carter's house instead of going to school. She hammered on the door and the window until her knuckles stung. No answer. Then she saw him walking up the hill towards her. He didn't look thin and shadowy, like everybody else. But he looked smaller than she remembered. His eyes were sad and weary and full of little red veins.

Claudine tried to sound calm and grown-up but her voice was high-pitched and quavering with fear.

'My maman is very ill. Can you come now, please?'

He rubbed his eyes and said, 'Of course, young lady. Forgive my memory—it's Miss Duret, isn't it?'

She nodded. 'Claudine.'

He had a nice face when he smiled. 'Off we go then, Claudine.'

When they reached the house, Maman was asleep, but the kitchen was loud with the grating rattle of her breathing from down the hallway.

When Dr Carter came into the bedroom, she startled awake and snapped, 'Claudine! I told you—'

But then she started hacking. Her face went red, then white like wax, and then she fell back on to the pillows. She was gasping as though she had been running, and when she took the handkerchief from her mouth, there was a blossom of bright blood on it.

Claudine felt hot panic course through her. 'Can you help her, Doctor? Don't let her die!'

Dr Carter's mouth was a grim line. 'You should have called me before this, Madame Duret. Lie back. No, don't talk. Just nod or shake your head.'

Maman shook her head and glared.

'She is worried because we haven't any money to pay you,' Claudine said. 'But I can give you my ormer shells. Tourists will pay lots of money for them, after the war is over. Please take them.'

He listened to Maman's chest, nodding and smiling at Claudine.

'I will not take your shells, child,' he said.

'But how shall we pay you?' She showed him a shell, her eyes stinging with tears. 'Look, aren't they beautiful? See all the colours? They are very rare. They took an age to find. You can have *all* of them. Even this big one, look. Just don't... She *cannot* die, please.'

Dr Carter stood up. 'I'm afraid your maman is very poorly indeed,' he said. 'She will have to go into hospital. Don't worry about the cost. She may need to stay for a week or more, until she has recovered. She has something called pneumonia.'

Maman was shaking her head again; she tried to speak but she was coughing too much.

Claudine dropped her gaze to the floor. 'Maman has said that we are not a charity to live off other people's money. So you must take the ormers, *please.*'

Dr Carter smiled and patted her hand. 'I see. Well, perhaps I could collect them some other time, then? I'd like to move your maman to hospital as soon as possible. Do you have anywhere you can stay? Family who can look after you, perhaps?'

She thought of Edith. 'Maybe...'

'Good. I'll fetch my car.'

Claudine sat holding Maman's hot hand. Her hair was stuck to her forehead, so Claudine stroked it back.

The doctor soon returned with his motorcar, and he lifted Maman up from the bed and carried her out. He put her on to the back seat, very gently.

Claudine said, 'How strong you are!'

'Well, she's not very heavy. Hasn't been eating enough, I suspect.'

'She's not hungry.'

He nodded. 'Gives the food to you and the little boy, does she?'

He had very nice blue eyes, even though they were spidered with red veins. They were kind eyes. Before she could stop herself, Claudine blurted, 'People say you're a traitor. Why do they say that?'

He stopped smiling. 'Which people?'

'Nearly everyone, really. Edith doesn't say it. Madame Bisson, I mean. She says she suspects you're between a rock and a hard place.'

Dr Carter sighed. 'Yes, that's it, I suppose. Now look, I really must care for your mother. Do you have a neighbour, someone you can go to right now?'

'Yes, I think so. Do you like the Germans more than you like Jèrriais people, then?'

He was climbing into his car, but he stopped and leant down so he could look at Claudine when he talked. He spoke slowly.

'That's a difficult question. Simply speaking, no, I don't. Not at all. But I don't *dis*like them simply because they are *German*. They are men first, German second. Does that make sense to you?'

Claudine grew thoughtful. 'Don't you think the Germans are bad then?'

'Some of them, perhaps. But not all.'

He sat behind the wheel. Maman had fallen asleep.

'Do you like the Commandant?' Claudine asked. 'Everybody says he's a devil. Is it true?'

'Sometimes, I'm afraid so.'

'But then—why do you look after him?'

Dr Carter started his engine. 'Sometimes it's necessary to do the right thing,' he said. 'Sometimes the right thing is also wrong.'

Claudine watched the car bumping over the stones, and though she whispered his words to herself again and again, they still didn't make any sense.

At first, Claudine told herself that she would be able to stay at home while Maman was in hospital. But then she had to go to school, and she wasn't allowed to take Francis with her because he liked to scribble with the chalk and rip up the books and giggle during class prayer. She couldn't leave him with any of the neighbours because they glared every time they saw the Durets—sometimes when Maman was in a black mood she was very rude, even when she didn't mean to be.

Perhaps Edith won't mind looking after us for a little while? Just until Maman is better.

But she needed someone to watch her brother while she ran to Edith's house. Maman had offended many of the neighbours, so Claudine asked Madame Renouf, who lived ten doors away. She looked surprised at the request, but agreed to take Francis for the afternoon.

Claudine tried not to listen to Francis's wails as she walked away.

'I'll be back soon, I promise.'

She had to walk along the beach to reach Edith's house, past the shelter that she used to play in with Gregor. The sides were collapsing, like a gaping, septic wound where the ragged skin was crumpling into the body, unsupported by shattered bones. It smelt sour too, like an outhouse. Claudine tried not to look, tried not to breathe, tried not to think at all, but still memories of that night crept in. The soldier had whispered *'Leibchen'* as his fingers pressed into her.

Sometimes she thought that if she could make her mind completely blank, like the unbroken surface of the sand after the sea had scrubbed it smooth, then she might be happy, or at least not quite so lost and pitted and empty.

The sea and the sky were white and grey, like rumpled smoke. The air was sharp and cold, but dry. It snagged in her chest, that promise of winter.

She tried not to think of the wood and food and favours they would need to outlast the cold. Too many grown-up thoughts: they beat around in her head like moths in a jam jar. War had given her all of the worries of an adult, with none of the adult power to resolve them.

Then she heard a commotion along the beach. She ran and hid behind a sand dune, held her breath and waited.

The voices belonged to soldiers. A big patrol, perhaps two. They were shouting, but the wind whipped their words into shapeless, angry noise.

There were lots of men, old men, dragging themselves along beside the soldiers. They were dressed in ragged, dirty clothes. They were hunched over, heaving big spades or shoving wheelbarrows. Instead of shoes, they had rags tied around their feet—filthy cloth, splattered with brownish stains that looked like dried blood.

The old men came closer and Claudine's skin prickled with sudden comprehension: the men's faces weren't old at all. Some of them were young, not much older than Claudine. But their bodies were ancient. Stooped shoulders and sticks for arms and legs. And their skin hung loose on their scarecrow bones, as if they had borrowed the skin from much bigger men.

The men stopped walking and began to dig and heave rocks into piles. When they fell, the Germans shouted at them and kicked them until they stood again. That was all Claudine could hear—the sound of boots upon flesh, gasps of pain buffeted along by the cold wind.

These must be the prisoners of war, the ones that Gregor talked of.

A tall soldier was beating one of the prisoners for working too slowly. At first, the prisoner cried out and flailed his arms and legs. His cries were high-pitched, animal. The soldier struck rhythmically and the prisoner at last fell silent. But then the soldier kicked him, his boot to the back of the skull, and the prisoner's head whipped forwards and then backwards, as if he were a wooden mannequin. Then he lay very still. A streamer of blood spooled out from his skull and pooled on the sand.

The soldier gestured at two of the other prisoners and they lifted the man, who was now slack-bodied, into a wheelbarrow and carried him to the half-built wall, where they laid the body down and then piled bricks on top of it, followed by shovelfuls of cement. They patted it down as if it were a carefully prepared loaf of bread.

Claudine had heard it whispered, of course, that the sea wall was being built upon the bodies of prisoners. That one day, people walking along the wall would be stepping on the stacked bones of murdered men. But seeing the truth of it made her insides convulse.

A different soldier shouted, ordering the prisoners back over to him. His voice left no room for argument: there was work to be done. Hurry, he bellowed, the harsh German consonants ricocheting off the sea and sand. Then the soldier took his helmet off to wipe the sweat from his forehead.

It was Gregor.

Claudine crouched behind the dunes. A feeling like frost water prickled over her head and dripped into her stomach. Her heart was going like the clappers. Gregor didn't like her killing fish, and he'd never gutted the sand eels.

It *couldn't* be him, watching all of this. It must be a soldier who looked very much like Gregor. The real Gregor would have stopped the soldier from beating the prisoner, surely?

She peeped up over the dune again. He had Gregor's thin back, his curved shoulders. He had Gregor's nose. When he shouted, it was Gregor's voice, only harsher, more ferocious.

Claudine sat down again and stared out at the sea. None of the grey German buildings out there. No walls. No cement. No shouting, kicking, beating soldiers. No dead bodies of murdered prisoners packed away and hidden without a tear or a prayer. Except that... Perhaps it was happening too in another country across the sea. Perhaps it was the sort of thing that happened everywhere, all over the world, wherever there was a war.

There was no way to know.

Claudine closed her eyes, and rubbed her fists over her eyelids and she counted her teeth with her tongue. When she opened her eyes, nothing had changed.

—

THE Commandant had chosen a beautiful day at the end of December 1941 on which to put the young Frenchman, Soulette, in front of the firing squad. He ordered Father Gillard, the St Peter's parish priest, to give the boy his last rites, and charged Carter with the task of covering the Frenchman's injuries.

'Make him look beautiful for my men, Doctor. I want him—how do you say?—with no spot or scratch.'

He slapped Carter's shoulder and left his hot, heavy hand there a moment too long.

Carter nodded, compressing his lips into a smile. He took care not to look the Commandant in the eye.

The German had, despite rationing, also managed to develop diabetes. Ever since Carter had diagnosed him, he'd had to resist the urge to overdose him with insulin. As a form of murder, it was practically impossible to detect, as insulin was a natural secretion. If Carter injected between the toes, where coroners rarely checked during post-mortem, he stood a good chance of escaping discovery.

But a life, however monstrous, was still a life. And would not taking a life make Carter as immoral, as monstrous, as the Commandant?

Soulette's injuries were fairly extensive: three broken ribs, a mangled hand, a broken nose, a mouthful of smashed teeth, and a shattered cheekbone that lent his face a lopsided squint.

Carter did what he could for the boy, setting and realigning the broken bones where possible. Against the Commandant's instructions, he also administered a dose of morphine—if Carter was punished for this then so be it: he couldn't stand by and watch Soulette's agony.

But the Frenchman was stoic. 'Are you not afraid?' Carter asked, whispering so the guard would not report him. '*Avez-vous peur?*'

Soulette shook his head and said simply, '*Non. J'ai servi mon pays et mon Dieu.*'

By the following morning, the bruises were even more pronounced. The Commandant would be furious. Carter decided to ask for Edith's help, hoping she might know some variety of plant-lore that would alleviate the bruising.

He felt apprehensive. They had not spoken in the months since she had seen him near the butcher's and she must be aware, by now, of his position as the Commandant's physician. He feared the judgment he might see in her eyes. Part of him wondered if she would come at all.

But after no more than fifteen minutes of waiting, he heard her along the corridor.

'Take your paws off me! I've told you I'll walk, thank you. I don't need your great hams to help me along. Off me, I've said, unless you want to catch the pox? Riddled with it, I am. *Die Pocken*. Ha! Now, you're moving!'

Despite his black mood, Carter smiled. Edith was wild-haired and sharp-eyed as usual; she looked unperturbed by the three burly men and their guns. If anything, the soldiers were shying away from her as she shook her basket of herbs and ointments at them.

Her expression changed when she saw Soulette. She marched past Carter, pushing him aside, and looked the Frenchman over, tutting. Then she stroked the boy's hair, whispering, '*Ma chère enfant misérable.*'

She turned to the Carter, snapped, 'Who allowed this?'

He couldn't meet her gaze. Instead he fixed his eyes on their shoes: his were buffed and glowing, even in the dim prison light, while hers were battered and gaped at the toes. A wave of self-loathing washed over him.

Edith sighed. 'I thought as much. Well, I'll see what I can do. I'm making no promises, mind.'

'Thank you.'

She clapped her hands and within minutes had somehow persuaded the sulky guards to fetch a basin of hot water, some salt, sugar and vinegar—though from where and how, Carter had no clue. Then she set about making a paste, which she smoothed liberally on to Soulette's bruises.

She worked on his face first, holding his jaw steady with one hand while dabbing the strange concoction on with the other. Carter could see how it might work: a compound to constrict the tissues and thereby speed recovery.

But there was still a problem: 'He needs to look...as, ah, *normal* as possible, so to speak. For Thursday. For...well... *God*, what a bloody mess.'

At first he thought Edith hadn't heard. But then she said, still dabbing away at Soulette's face, 'In that basket, at the bottom, there's some wild garlic. No, not that—those are crocus bulbs, you buffoon!'

She elbowed Carter out of the way and dug around, then drew out some long, bright green leaves, peppered with tiny white flowers that he might have mistaken for clover. She threw them at him. The smell of garlic was overwhelming.

'Grind those up, will you? I want a smooth paste, mind—no lumps or stringy bits. There's a pestle and mortar in the basket.' And back she went to the Frenchman's face.

He flinched a little when she put the compound on the broken skin on his eyebrow: vinegar and salt on an open wound must have been excruciating.

She growled, 'Be still, will you!' then she patted his cheek, gently. 'Don't worry, the pain will be gone by Friday.'

A joke in poor taste, Carter thought: by Friday, the boy would be dead. But Soulette gave a harsh bark of laughter.

It took a great deal of time to grind up the leaves and flowers into a pulpy mess, even longer before Carter had anything approaching the smooth mixture Edith had demanded. But his arm was aching, so he showed Edith.

'I hope this will do.'

'It will have to, I suppose.'

Then she turned to Soulette. 'Now,' she said, in rapid French, 'one teaspoon every hour, morning and night. And don't scratch the tincture, I shan't make more.' She gave Carter a sad smile. 'It should take down the bruising and the swelling. Come Thursday, he'll look good as new. From a distance.'

A fist of tension in Carter's gut loosened. 'Excellent. Truly, excellent. Thank you.'

Edith nodded curtly, gave the Frenchman a brief, tight embrace and kissed him on both cheeks. He clung to her. His shoulders shook and he began sobbing.

Carter remembered the bite of Father whipping him with a willow wand when he wept: the sting of the switch across his buttocks or his palms. To toughen him up, Father had said, after Carter had come home with filthy, mud-spattered hair, his school clothes clagged with mud. Some other boys had chased him and pushed him into a ditch. Father had punctuated the whipping with admonishment: 'Next time *(Crack!)* turn and fight! *(Crack!)*'

After a long time, Edith emerged, wiping her eyes. She pushed past the guards and marched off down the corridor.

Carter had to scurry to keep up. 'Thank you, Edith. I am most grateful. You are a good woman, you really are.'

She waved her hand to shush him. 'Enough! It isn't right, this whole business, you see that?'

A hot flood of shame roared at his cheeks. 'You're absolutely correct. It's terrible.'

'Disgusting.'

'I wish I could do something.'

'You might as well be putting lipstick on a cow before it goes off to the slaughterhouse.' She stopped walking and glared. 'And what do you think you're doing, letting the child be beaten half to death like that?'

'I...I *tried* to stop it. But there was very little I could do.'

'Yes, I can see you did very little.'

She scowled, while he stood and stared at his shoes again. The rich glow of leather: sunlight on autumn leaves in a land before war. He wanted to hurl the damned things into the fire.

When Edith tutted and set off walking again, he followed. How could he make her understand, without putting her in danger? He could imagine only too well her response, if she knew the Commandant had threatened her: she'd march straight to Royal Square to give him a piece of her mind.

'You're a good man, Doctor,' she said. 'So how can you stand it? Treating the Commandant? Helping him, *supporting* him.'

'I'm not—'

She stopped again and held up her hand. 'None of your rubbish now. The *truth*. I've always thought that you're no traitor or collaborator. You're a decent man, stuck in a tricky spot.'

He gave a humourless laugh. 'It's more than a tricky spot—and not simply for myself.'

What to say? He couldn't endanger her by intimating anything of the Commandant's threats. But he also couldn't bear the disgust in her eyes.

He sighed. 'I'm quite powerless, I'm afraid. Especially as he has made threats to...to close the hospital if I don't attend to him.'

'Indeed? Why haven't you mentioned it?'

Carter shrugged, bitterly. 'To you and me, it is an explanation. To others, it would simply seem an excuse.'

Edith nodded. 'I see that. But there's no explanation or excuse for what's happening to that poor boy. And now you've dragged *me* into it. I feel sick to my stomach.'

She was right, of course, but she didn't understand; it wasn't just a case of protecting himself.

By the next day, Soulette's contusions had faded to a jaundiced yellow and by the execution date, as Edith had promised, they had all but disappeared. His face still had an odd slant to it, but the Commandant would be satisfied.

The southern beach of St Aubin's Bay had been chosen for the execution. It was overlooked by a large stone wall, which would provide ample viewing space for those islanders eager to watch the spilling of foreign blood.

Father Gillard had been called out early to perform absolution. He was an elderly fellow, arthritic and asthmatic. He was also hard of hearing. Initially, having staggered to Soulette's cell, he struggled to comprehend the situation.

'But this man is not ill,' he wheezed. 'I was instructed to perform the last rites. There must be some misunderstanding.'

Carter shook his head. 'I am afraid not.'

'But he is not dying.'

'He is set to die this morning. By firing squad.'

'To be shot? But he is only a boy. What barbarism is this?'

'I thought everyone knew: he was captured while trying to incite rebellion. The Commandant has sentenced him.'

'And you tolerate this, do you? The murder of children?'

Something in the accusatory tone forced Carter to protest, 'He is hardly a child. He is twenty-one years old.'

'Still a boy. *Look* at him, Doctor.'

Carter felt his defensive stance fade; the priest was right. For heaven's sake, how on earth could he justify this? He tried to steel himself, Father's voice in his head, mingling with the Commandant's until the two became indistinguishable: *This is war!* And yet, the truth spoken by this gentle, frail priest was so much more profound: *This is murder! He is a boy.*

Carter stared at him: mottled skin, covered in spider veins. He listened to the faint stridor on each of the priest's inhalations. He was, in all likelihood, not long for this world himself. But the conviction of his faith was like a talisman against fear.

The body carries one certainty within it, from the moment of birth: one day it will fail.

Carter managed to keep his voice calm, in spite of the accusation in Gillard's eyes.

'I will leave you with Monsieur Soulette now, Father,' he said. 'Thank you for your help. You have been most kind. I'm sure you will be of great comfort to the young man.'

Carter left the cell, walked down the corridor at a brisk pace and out into the open air. He found a secluded spot and sat down in the shade of some trees, taking out his hipflask. He drank a measure of whisky, then another. Single malt, hot and peaty, but he would have drunk rubbing alcohol with as much relish if it could have annihilated thought and care in the same way.

He closed his eyes and leant his head against a tree trunk. The bark was rough. It must have been two hundred years old, that tree. An oak. It would be standing long after he had gone. He stood, wrapped his arms around it, then struck his forehead against the trunk. Then again, a little harder. He felt the bark pierce his skin. He longed to curl his arms around himself and weep like a child.

—

EDITH hadn't gone to see the poor French boy butchered. A public execution with the crowds gawping at the blood—it was something from the Dark Ages and she'd have no part in it. She heard folk gossiping about it afterwards, of course: the young lad's bravery and Dr Carter's cowardice. But her tears and her rage couldn't revive the dead or give Carter a backbone, so she tried not to dwell on it, tried to think instead on Marthe and Claudine and her baby brother.

Francis was growing more bonny by the day. Rationing had thinned his limbs, whittled his tiny fingers to the bone, but his face was round and merry. He laughed often and was an affectionate little soul; he would often run to Edith, arms stretched high, shouting, 'Cuggwl!' until she swept him into her arms and held him close.

Children change the way you see things.

Edith had sworn to Maurice that the soldier sat at the end of the garden didn't bother her. But still, after a good few days of him watching them, Edith found herself more reluctant to go out. She'd taken to drawing the curtains at the front of the house firmly shut, and she stopped the children from going into the front garden when he was there.

Claudine was suddenly peculiar about the subject of soldiers—she shied away from them in the street, almost as though she was frightened—so Edith didn't want to put the wind up her by telling her there was one sitting out in front of the house most days.

One morning, she had to go to Hacquoil's and fetch the meat ration. There was no way around it, and she would have to use the front way because the steps at the back were too steep for her to carry Marthe down safely. But the soldier had been sat there all morning. Edith's skin was crawling with the feel of his eyes on her. Luckily, Claudine was at school.

After a morning of procrastination, Edith pulled herself together and made herself lift Marthe into the wheelbarrow. She had found an old bedsheet to carry Francis, and he sat on her hip and bounced up and down.

'Me go for ride!'

Fretful as she was, it made Edith chuckle.

She walked as fast as she could down the path, trying to keep her eyes down. Counting her steps. Just ten and she was at the gate.

She was nearly past him when he said, 'Halt!'

Her heart leapt. 'Sorry, we mustn't stop,' she managed to mumble. 'Ever so poorly, she is. *Sehr krank*. I think it's contagious. You're best to stand back, sir.'

He didn't budge. He put his hand into his jacket pocket.

Oh Lord, this is it. Maurice will never forgive me.

She was ready to claw his eyes out before she'd let him touch Marthe or the child.

But then he brought out a photograph. Himself with a woman—must have been his wife, and a baby. He indicated the woman and then pointed at Marthe.

'She is same. Also ill.'

Edith stared at him in the photograph and then looked at the man in front of her, his tentative half-smile. He had a pleasant face. Those blue eyes, so common to the Germans, but also a soft mouth without an ounce of cruelty in it. Once upon a time, when she'd cared for such things, she'd have called him handsome.

'Your wife? She's poorly too.'

He nodded.

'I'm sorry for you then.'

He sighed, sadly. 'She fall and hit on her head. After, she is not the same. Something is…gone.' He shrugged and then stroked the face in the photograph.

'Poor girl. Hard for you, is it? Being away from her. You miss her?'

'Yes. But...' He exhaled. 'I must make the Fatherland. Something good and strong. A good life for my son. Germany is a hungry place—there is much anger. My son has enough but many have nothing, and this anger is like a...sickness. I want better for him.'

He reached into his pocket again. Edith tensed, ready to clobber him if he tried anything crafty. But he drew out two apples and gave one to Marthe and one to Francis.

Then he rubbed at the tight, shiny skin on that lame arm of his—it was red where it was stretched over the bones. Close up, it didn't look so much like a withered arm. More like it had been chewed up and spat out at some point. The fingers fused together and bunched, and the whole lot of it webbed with scarring. His lips tightened in pain when he moved it.

She was about to reach out and touch it, suggest some remedy for that ruined skin, but he sat back down on the wall and waved her on.

She didn't mention to Maurice that she'd spoken to the soldier. Nor to Claudine.

In any case, Edith had other things to worry about. Much of her time was spent making remedies, now that everyone had taken against Dr Carter. She had people wanting to see her for all sorts: the usuals of cuts and scrapes and broken bones, and most of them were mended easily enough with creams and bandages and sticks to use as splints.

But then there were the other sicknesses, things that should have gone to Carter, really: the woman with the cancer growing like a child in her belly, or the man with a leg which had overnight become numb so the poor fellow couldn't walk.

Edith did what she could for them, mostly by guesswork.

She didn't charge a penny or even ask for a share in their rations, much as she would have liked some more food for Marthe and the children. But it wouldn't have felt right: taking payment for a medicine that was more hope than anything.

She said the same thing every time: 'You'd be better off seeing Dr Carter, you know that, don't you, my love? I can only do so much; he might have a cure.'

A few folk—those in so much pain that life was torture—nodded and sighed. But most people shook their heads and spat on the ground.

When she didn't have Claudine with her, Edith used the front door. The German soldier always watched her come and go and they smiled, sometimes nodded at one another, like neighbours. He reminded her of Frank: that bright humour in his eyes, though Frank had looked smarter and happier in his uniform. But perhaps the soldier fidgeted because his arm bothered him?

One morning, as Edith walked past, he winced and scratched at his left arm again, and she held up a hand.

'Wait there a moment.'

She fetched a jar with a salve in it, along with an old shirt of Frank's.

'Your arm, please,' she said.

He hesitated, then held it out.

She knelt down next to him. 'It pains you.'

'Some small pain, yes.'

'Don't give me that rubbish. I've seen your face when something touches it.'

He shrugged. 'Yes, it is hurt, but I... Sometimes I do not feel when it hurts. I do not know how you say this.'

'You're used to the pain, so you don't notice it? But that doesn't mean it's not hurting. I've something here that might help. I call it a poultice.'

He looked mistrustful for a moment. But then he said, 'You and my wife. Before she is ill... You are the same. She is also kind.'

Edith started to rub on the ointment. 'I do my best. Now, this will sting a little. Keep still—fidgeting won't make it hurt less.'

'What is this?'

'Nothing magical. Mostly onion juice and mustard seeds. The poultice keeps it compressed. It should start to break down some of this nasty scarred skin. That's what's giving you the pain. It shouldn't be hurting as much. Is it?'

'No. Some small better. And so soon!' He smiled, then he sniffed the poultice and wrinkled up his nose.

'Doesn't smell like fine French perfume, I'm afraid. And the smell seeps into your blood, so you'll be breathing out onion fumes. But it'll see your arm right, over the weeks. Less painful. I'll change it every day.'

'*Danke.*'

'No bother. A fire, was it? That did for your arm?'

'*Nein.* A big machine. On the farm. I was a foolish boy.' He shrugged and smiled again, that sweet, sad smile.

'You can't protect children from life,' Edith said. 'Things happen. One moment, and then everything is different, forever.' She patted his hand. 'I'll be back to change that tomorrow.'

———

BY the second February under German rule, every day had started to tug on Maurice, like the wrenching hand of a ticking clock. He'd nearly been caught mooring the boat a few times, though luckily he'd seen the patrol before they'd seen him. He thought about applying for a licence, but that would have meant awkward questions about why he hadn't declared the boat before.

And then there was Marthe. She'd seemed to be improving for a while, eating more and so on. Then a sickness went around, and of course she caught it.

He and Edith were up with her day and night. They took it in turns to sit with her and encourage her to take water. They had no sugar, so they gave her the brackish leftovers after boiling potatoes. She brought it straight back up, time and again, shrinking before their eyes. Watching her fading filled him with a desperate, burning rage, but there was nothing to do except sit and wait and hope.

In the end, she turned a corner, but the illness left her even weaker than before. She needed food, and plenty of it, and there just wasn't enough. Even with the black-market bits, the extra from the butcher and the fish Maurice caught, it was never enough. It struck him that he could try sneaking out at night and stealing food from the Germans' rations when they were out on patrol and never mind the risk to himself.

But that soldier made everything impossible. Sat on the wall, smoking. Watching. He was there every time Maurice set foot outside his house, and if he wasn't sitting there, he was waiting at Edith's. Wherever Marthe was, the damned soldier followed.

But he never said a word to Maurice. Just watched, as Maurice crept past him, eyes on the ground. He knew it was only a matter of time before there was a pounding at the door and they came to take Marthe away.

Edith claimed the soldier was a good sort. She'd bandaged up that bad arm of his, and it looked better afterwards. The soldier smiled his German smile at Edith, and sometimes they stopped and talked about the weather, or food. Once the soldier gave Edith a little of his bread.

But it didn't change the fact that he was the bloody Bosche and Maurice couldn't stand to look at him, sitting there as if his bloody uniform gave him the right to do whatever he bloody well wanted.

By spring, Maurice was barely going out for fear of being caught. Everyone was thinner and they were all at each other's throats. Though they had returned to their mother months before, Claudine had carried on bringing Francis over and they shared whatever food they could spare with the children.

Claudine seemed hungry and sad, but Maurice was thankful that she no longer mentioned her German friend: in fact, she seemed nervous of the soldiers and Edith took great care not to let her see the one who was sitting at the end of the garden. Nothing to be gained by making the girl fret, Edith said.

One day, Maurice discovered a different way down to the boat. It meant sneaking past one of the bunkers the Bosche had built, but there weren't any patrols behind it: they seemed to think no one would be brave or stupid enough to come that close—and at least he didn't have to walk past that damned soldier and watch the suspicion creeping over his face.

Maurice scrambled over the barbed wire and ran past the bunker, and then came to a steep hill. It was while he was trying to run down it without falling that he saw the broad, flat leaves of a potato plant.

He stopped dead and looked about. There were hundreds of the plants, sprouting in among the weeds. At first, he thought he might be mistaken: all the crops were closely guarded by the Bosche. Surely they wouldn't allow stray plants to grow without guarding them? Then he realised: he must be standing on a *côtil*, one of the steep, south-facing banks where the farmers planted their early new potatoes to give them the greatest sunlight. Somehow a farmer must have planted some potatoes and the Germans had since wired the field off without noticing the crop.

Maurice looked around. Not a soul. He didn't question his good fortune but dug down with his hands, hoping the potatoes wouldn't be rotten or blighted. He scrabbled in the soil, into the roots. Nothing. He dug a little further and his fingers closed around something hard. He dragged out a grubby little pearl.

Maurice chuckled, kissed it and put it in his pocket, then dug and uprooted seven more. All small, but they would be packed with goodness. He'd have to gather as many as he could before they were discovered by someone else or before the farmer tried to gather his crop. His guilt at stealing was momentary: starvation breeds savagery.

He hurried back home and fetched three sacks and a fork. But on his way back, the soldier stopped him, pointed at his bulging pockets.

'What is this?'

Maurice pretended not to understand. The soldier asked

again. It pained Maurice to show him but there was no refusing the Bosche. Slowly, he drew out a potato, hoping it would be unrecognisable, small and soil-covered as it was.

The soldier grinned. 'For eat, yes?'

Reluctantly, Maurice nodded.

'Where are you finding?' Bloody man was still smiling.

Maurice sighed. 'Follow me.'

He half expected the soldier to stop him from clambering over the barbed wire but he followed without question. Maurice glanced sideways: the German was just as thin as him.

When Maurice showed him the plants, he clapped him on the back.

'*Die Taschen, bitte.* Bag, yes?'

Maurice reluctantly gave him a sack and took one himself. But it was a tricky business, digging deep with the fork and sifting the soil, then picking the potatoes out and putting them into the sack—and the soldier had only his one good hand. When it was his turn with the fork, he couldn't dig deep enough to reach the potatoes. The whole business would take too long and a patrol would easily spot them, perched as they were on the face of the *côtil*. It didn't ease Maurice's mind, either, that the soldier kept looking around as if he was frightened of being spotted himself.

'Look here,' Maurice said, 'I'll take the fork. You pick out the potatoes and throw them in the sack.' He mimed the actions.

It was much easier, working together. They didn't say a word, but there was a soothing sort of rhythm in the repeated *dig-sift-throw*.

When they had filled the three sacks, the soldier said, 'This is all.' They carried one each and the third sack, the heaviest one, between them.

Maurice knew when they returned home, the damned soldier would take them all, to share out among his Kraut friends.

I'll have to creep back after curfew.

But, to his amazement, the soldier walked to Maurice's shed, stowed one of the sacks behind the door and threw an empty sack over it to hide it. He tapped Maurice's chest and smiled.

'For you.'

He pointed at the other two sacks and tapped his own chest. 'For me.'

'Thank you. That's wonderful.' Maurice forgot himself then, forgot he was a blasted soldier and shook him heartily by the hand. 'You should come in. To eat. *Essen?*' He pointed to the house and brought his fingers to his mouth in the universal signal for *eating*.

The soldier shook his head. 'Thank you. I cannot.' He pointed at one of the sacks. 'I must take this for the Commandant.'

The soldier picked up his sacks, winked at Maurice and used his foot to push the other sack into a dark corner. They smiled at each other and Maurice laid another sack over the potatoes to hide them.

'*Danke*,' he said. The unfamiliar German vowels were thick on his tongue.

Maurice took a scoop of potatoes and boiled them with a little mint from Edith's garden. They ate them with the rest of their butter ration. They were hot and rich and delicious.

Edith and Claudine stayed long after curfew and they all

gorged themselves, laughing. They even put the illegal wireless on quietly and danced around the room. It could have been years ago, when Germany was simply a place on a map.

For the first time in months, they all fell asleep quickly and hunger didn't claw at them through the night.

The next morning, Maurice thought to go fishing again. Perhaps this time, on his way back, he could give the soldier a fish, by way of thanks.

But he wasn't there.

Maurice's first thought was the potatoes.

All a trick. That Kraut bastard!

He checked the shed—the potatoes were behind the door. A clever trap, perhaps, so they could catch him red-handed? He imagined a whole troop of soldiers watching him, waiting to snatch him.

He hurried back to the house, looking over his shoulder and scanning the horizon. The long seagrass was bleached by the sun and now pressed flat against the hills by the wind. The look of the land made him think of a cold, wet dog. Flattened and miserable and ready to attack.

The soldier was nowhere to be seen.

Maurice went inside, locked the door and waited for the patrol to come and drag him away. He found his small knife, the one he used to do any quick gutting if he wanted extra bait for line-fishing—not a long knife, but sharp. It could cut through flesh and bone like soft cheese.

He crouched by the door, hunching below the glass. The rain swept on, the sun arched across the sky and fat clouds sailed high on the wind. It would have been a good day for fish.

Maurice couldn't stop brooding about yesterday and the

soldier's delight when he'd seen the potatoes. The way he'd helped Maurice sift through the soil, both of them scrabbling through the dirt together, lugging the sack back between them—as if they were on the same side.

Or, more than that, as if there was no such thing as war; as if *occupation* was a word that was simply used to describe what an honest man did to make a living.

Maurice shook his head. The soldier had smiled. Damn that man, he had *smiled* and had given the potatoes to him.

Now this. Maurice clenched his jaw. He had forgotten that they were at war. He mustn't forget that the Germans were the enemy. All of them.

He tapped the knife on the palm of his hand, tested the blade on the pad of his finger. A bright bead of blood swelled. With enough force, the knife could reach a man's heart.

Lunchtime: Marthe needed feeding. He hadn't time to mash anything, not with a patrol breathing down his neck, so he cut a scrap of ham from the bone (a few days old but it still smelt good) and they had some cooked carrot (a touch soft and sludgy) and some potatoes left over from last night's supper. He set it all in front of her. Then he fetched his knife again and sat back in front of the door.

The day was darker now. He was glad not to be out on the boat after all: rain made the deck slippery. Besides, on days like this the cold crept into his bones, so he could still feel it hours later when he was tucked up warm in bed—that lingering finger of chill that curled in his stomach all night long.

He heard rustling. A German patrol, come for him or for Marthe? Heart thudding, Maurice looked out of the window. Nothing except the broken hands of the trees, clawing at the sky. He gripped the knife more tightly. The noise again. But it was inside, behind him. How the devil had they crept into the house?

The back door. He had left it unlocked.

Maurice spun around, knife whipping the air, ready to gut the whole damn patrol. And then he saw. The noise was Marthe: she was banging on the table, looking right at him and straining towards the food in front of her.

'You want me to sit with you, my love?'

He hadn't seen it in months, but he could swear there was the trace of a smile tugging at her mouth. He put down the knife and sat next to her at the table. They ate. No plate, knives, forks or spoons, because who needed them, truly?

Marthe put her hand on top of his. It rested there for a moment and his heart jolted with sweet and painful memories. Then she twitched and the invisible tug of the disease yanked her from him again.

He clasped her hand. Cold, she was always cold. He kissed each of her fingertips.

'I love you.'

He pulled her to his chest and wrapped his arms around her. He kissed her cheeks, her nose, her mouth. He put his lips to her bony chest and kissed every thud of her heart. He closed his eyes and inhaled the smell of her: cut grass and, on her breath, the sweet-sour rot of sickness.

Before Maurice knew it, an hour or more had passed. There was still no bang at the door, but he wasn't going to risk going out. His stomach griped again. A few bits of carrot and potato wouldn't keep him going for long. He tried not to worry about dinner.

Marthe's head lolled on to her chest; she snored softly. Maurice pulled the blanket up to her chin and kissed her cheek.

He couldn't let them have her. He wondered, as he went back to the door, if he would have enough time to slit his own throat after he'd done it.

Perhaps he fell asleep because suddenly it was dark and there was a pounding at the door that set his heart hotly hammering. He couldn't find his knife in the darkness. He scrabbled around for it on the floor. The banging continued, growing louder, and Marthe woke and cried out.

Maurice found the knife when the blade stuck right into his finger. Lancing arrow of pain through his whole hand. He held it close to his face. A bad cut—a flap of skin hanging off.

He yelled, which set off Marthe's howling. He could feel the tendons tight in his neck, the blood banging in his skull.

Maurice shouted, 'Come on then! Come and take me! I'm ready for you!' And he kissed Marthe on the mouth again and again until she stopped crying. 'I'm so sorry, my love.' His voice shook. 'I'm *so* sorry.'

He pressed the knife against her throat. He could feel the hot blood throbbing under her thin skin.

'You'll have to break the door down! I'm not letting you in!'

He gave Marthe one last kiss.

Then a voice came from behind the door. 'What on *earth* are you up to, Maurice? Let me in, quickly! Before a patrol guts me like a fish.'

Edith!

He dropped the knife and opened the door.

Edith bustled in and elbowed him out the way. 'What are you playing at, sitting in the dark?'

'Nothing, I—' He went into the kitchen and took a deep breath. He wound a towel around his finger and squeezed until he was certain it had stopped bleeding.

When he moved the blackout blind aside, he gazed out of the window. The blackout made shapes sharper. The dark darker. The stars brighter, harder.

Even if the bastard Bosche have taken everything else, they've given me the stars.

Edith swept into the kitchen and tutted. 'Look, no water on to boil. *Honestly*, you men. And will you look at that finger— blood all over the place.'

He snatched his hand away.

'Hold still! You're lucky you didn't cut the tip straight off. What happened?'

'Peeling potatoes. Knife slipped.'

She raised her eyebrows. 'Oh, yes?'

'That's right.'

Edith narrowed her eyes. 'Well, at least let me bandage it for you, and salt it. You don't want an infection.'

'I need to see Marthe.'

'I laid her on the sofa. She's fast asleep.'

Maurice sat and listened. Slow and regular, her breaths. Yet another sleep when she would lose a little bit of herself, wake up a little less his. But she was alive…

Edith nodded. 'Now let's have a look at this hand.'

'Thank you.'

She talked while she worked. 'She was in a bit of a

state—Marthe, I mean. Trembling like a leaf. I had to give her a dose of valerian.'

He frowned. 'Yes. Your knocking startled her.'

'I see. My knocking was it?'

He looked away.

She patted his hand. 'There. All done. Don't be fiddling with it now. And keep it dry.'

'Expect me to go fishing with one hand in the air, do you?'

'How you catch fish is your business, Maurice, not mine.' She sat next to him. 'Now, will you tell me what on earth is the matter? Where have you been all day? I started to wonder if you'd hightailed it across the Channel.'

Her tone was teasing and Maurice could see her smiling from the corner of his eye, but he scowled.

'I—I needed to stay inside today. I had a bad feeling about things. A dread. But it's nothing you need to worry yourself over.'

'Well, I'm glad we've had that chat then. Everything is as clear as mud.'

'I'm sorry.' He clenched and unclenched his fists. 'It's simply—and I don't want you saying that I'm fussing over nothing but…it's that soldier. I *know* he's going to send a patrol for me. Perhaps for Marthe, too.'

He explained about the potatoes in the shed, how the soldier had set them as a trap and then gone to tell, Maurice was sure of it.

'So we need to move them.'

Edith cocked her head to one side, considering. 'He's always seemed quite decent to me. For a German.'

'Trust your life on that, would you? Marthe's life on a

German who *seems* decent?'

'No, you're right, absolutely right. What's to be done, then?'

'I'll wrap them in another sack and bury them in the manure pile on Vibert's field tonight. No one will go digging for them there and the Germans can't hurt us for stealing potatoes if they can't find them.'

Maurice buried them that night and then sneaked back whenever he could to grab a bagful for their supper. They ate boiled potatoes or potato bread almost every day, until just the smell of cooking potatoes turned their stomachs.

Perhaps the potatoes didn't agree with her, or maybe it was all the moving about, but at the start of May, Marthe suddenly went downhill.

Maurice didn't like to think that the seeds of it were sown on that day when they had sat indoors, waiting for that patrol. That moment with his knife against her throat… But whatever the cause, Marthe was jumpy again and spent all of her time twitching, while her groaning was higher pitched, sometimes rising to the shrieks of a flayed animal. Even Maurice couldn't block it out.

But it was the nightmares that really distressed her. They distressed the whole house. She woke up screaming and crying—clawing at her face till the blood ran. Maurice put thick woollen socks over her hands, clipped her nails as short as he could. But it didn't make a difference—every morning she had new scratches everywhere.

She wouldn't eat a bite that wasn't forced into her mouth. The skin under her eyes was the transparent blue of waterlogged petals. Her shoulderblades stood out from her back like budding wings.

And scabs everywhere from the scratches. They tried their best to keep them clean, but somehow Marthe managed to keep taking the tops from them. In less time than it took to fill a pan of water, she could open up every scab on her face.

Some started oozing yellow. It was bound to happen, even with Edith layering on poultices and creams. They washed the wounds often. Edith prepared countless ointments to rub on to them, but it made not a bit of difference. The pus seeped, and Marthe whimpered.

Then came the night she slept right through. Didn't make a sound. Bliss.

In the morning, she was like an angel lying next to him. Maurice rolled over and kissed her. Her skin was boiling to the touch. The sheets were soaked through with sweat.

He shook her shoulder. She didn't stir. He patted her cheek. He bellowed, *Marthe! Marthe! Marthe!*

Nothing.

Those scratches on her face and neck were now deep yellow. And little red lines crept out from the cuts and crawled over the rest of her skin, like a map.

The poison was in her blood. Maurice knew it, even without calling for Edith.

He ran to soak some towels with cold water from the rain bucket outside. He and Edith stripped Marthe and laid the towels on her skin. She stirred a little and groaned and her muscles started juddering. But her forehead grew hot again, as soon as they took the towels off. She didn't wake.

So he lifted her into the bath chair that Edith had somehow

found to replace the old wheelbarrow, and he ran down the garden. Marthe's body bounced; her head slumped on to her chest. She looked like one of the stuffed Guy Fawkes dolls that Maurice used to throw on to the bonfire as a boy. Spittle trickled out of her mouth and pooled on her chest.

Maurice ran faster. Then he came to the steep granite steps at the end of the garden. It was the quickest way to Dr Carter's house. He tried going forwards first, but Marthe sprawled and nearly fell. He tried to lift the chair, but it was too heavy.

Maurice would have to lift her out and carry her.

All of a sudden, the chair righted itself and it was lighter in his arms. He looked up. It was that soldier. That *bloody* German soldier had his good hand supporting Marthe's head.

Maurice felt that familiar, sickening rush of fear. *He's here to take her away.*

He put his hand to the knife in his pocket. But the soldier had a gun in his belt and Marthe needed Maurice alive.

Voice shaking, he said, 'She is ill. I'm taking her to the doctor.'

'Yes, doctor. Quick, now!' He half lifted her. 'Where must we go?'

'Don't hurt her! Please, put her down. Just leave her, will you? Please, I can manage.'

He shook his head and smiled again, '*Nein, nein*. We carry together.'

He inclined his head towards Maurice and mimed carrying her between them. Maurice wanted to scream, but he rushed to support Marthe's head before it lolled.

The soldier flashed him that smile again.

'*Gut, gut!*,' he said. 'We help together.'

'This way,' Maurice snapped. 'Hurry.'

He didn't look at the soldier, but he could hear the man breathing hard as they ran, carrying Marthe between them. He wondered what they'd say if they saw a patrol coming. But they didn't see anyone.

—

AFTER Soulette's death, the island's hostility towards Carter had festered. Apart from the odd emergency, house calls became a thing of the past. One youth in St Helier actually *spat* at his shoes as he passed.

They were his newest shoes: finest Italian leather in a chestnut tan. Painfully aware of the Jèrriais population in their thin-soled, cracked shoes and wooden clogs, Carter had tried to refuse them, despite the brutal winter and the wet spring.

The Commandant had simply smiled. 'My men must be smart, Doctor. Soldiers will not wear broken shoes. We build a better world, yes?'

Carter took care to wear the shoes only while inside the government buildings and changed into his old shoes to walk home. One day, however, when he went to undertake his routine morning examination, he found his old shoes positioned on his chair, the Commandant waiting for Carter's response.

He forced Carter to throw the old shoes into the fire and laughed as the leather began to blacken and curl.

'You must do as I tell you, Doctor,' he said, flashing his yellow teeth. 'I do not wish to look for a different doctor. And you are too thin for the work camps. You would not last long, I think. Or perhaps your friends will go with you? The old woman. She will be the camp witch. They will make her a bonfire, yes?'

He still made threats in this way. Closure of the hospital. Deportation of Carter himself or some other islander—Edith and Clement Hacquoil were always mentioned, followed by, 'Ha! *Sie haben Angst! Das ist gut!*'

When he wasn't at Royal Square, Carter spent long hours staring at the beige walls of his little sitting room, with no company but his thoughts and the mirror.

He was so lonely. *What is Will doing right now?* he'd often wonder. *Does he think of me?* His longing was like a clenched fist in his chest.

At first, he had written to Will: stilted letters crammed with the daily banalities of island life. Will's replies were effusive and unguarded: *I miss you, Tim. I think of you so often and I wonder if you will ever return to me.*

Carter flinched at the thought of someone intercepting those letters and kept his answering correspondence briskly matter-of-fact, even as he was aware that his coldness might cause Will pain.

But better, perhaps, for Will to move on, to find happiness with another, than to wait for the delivery on a promise that Carter could not make.

By the time the Germans arrived, the two men had not written in months. Carter sent Will one final note, quickly scribbled, sealed and posted before he could think better of it: *Please stay safe.* He signed it, *Ductus Arteriosis*, partly for anonymity and partly as a glimmer of the vow that he wanted so desperately to pledge.

During those lonely months, Carter read a great deal, finding comfort and not a little despair in Dante's 'Inferno'. He had read the work before, and the words had no shape or substance, but now they were branded in his mind as absolute truths:

In the middle of the journey of our days
I found that I was in a darksome wood
the right road lost and vanished in the maze.

He struggled to sleep. He found himself waking in the early hours, twisted in the sheets, soaked in sweat, mind racing. He was plagued by headaches and nausea. He took to covering the mirror in his house with a towel.

He tried to identify the exact moment when his life had peeled away in two opposing paths and he had taken the wrong one. But it seemed to him that he could not have chosen otherwise: he had wanted to stay in Jersey to help the islanders. Even now, he could not imagine himself abandoning his patients, though his act of betrayal had made them abandon him.

Then, too, there had been a certain feeling of well-deserved penance in staying. The sense of a just punishment for past sins, and perhaps his current unbearable predicament was his final atonement.

Mother, Father, Will... He had hurt and disappointed them all.

It seemed impossible to go on like this. But even when he scrambled from his bed and leant over his sink, his razor blade pressed against the frantic pulse at his throat, he lacked the impetus, the *courage* to complete the action.

Father's voice echoed in his head. *Coward.*

Carter crammed his endless waking hours with activity: reorganising his kitchen cupboards, cleaning out his chest of drawers, refolding his clothes, more reading. He was fastidious by habit and was often irked when he didn't have enough time to keep his house tidy. Again he wondered what it might be like to be married. But he had never come across a woman who moved him as he knew he should be moved—besides, it was dishonorable to marry for the sole purpose of keeping a clean house. Women should be nurtured; his mother had taught him that.

On that May morning, the pounding on his door made him jump.

Maurice Pipon stood on his step. His hair was wild, his eyes wide. His wife, Marthe, was slumped unconscious in his arms. A German soldier with a malformed arm supported her head.

'For heaven's sake, man, come in,' Carter cried. 'Lie her down, just here. How long has she been like this?'

They carried her in between them and laid her on the sofa.

The soldier stood in the doorway, waiting. Carter said, *'Danke. Sie können gehen.'* The German saluted and left.

'Found her this way when I woke,' Maurice explained. 'She's burning, Doctor. Can you help? I can't wake her. What can you do for her? You must be able to do *something!*'

Marthe Pipon was certainly pyrexic: her fever was just under 105°F. Heart rate high. Respiration shallow and rapid. One of Carter's immediate worries was long-term damage to the brain. She was unresponsive to external stimuli: she didn't react to her name or flinch when Carter pricked her finger with a pin.

His heart sank. 'You hadn't thought to take her into hospital?'

'You're closer, and I knew you'd take care of her.'

'Pass me the stethoscope, would you? You have surprising faith in me. I imagine most of the island would rather walk over hot coals to the hospital than deal with me.'

Maurice raked his hands through his hair. 'You've made some bad choices, but the war has made fools of all of us, one way or another. And if you can help her then I don't give a damn if you're Lucifer himself.'

Carter gave a grim smile but Maurice's words didn't sting as he might have expected: it was something of a relief to hear it spoken aloud. There was almost a companionship in those words—a sense of understanding, if not forgiveness.

'Well, I'm glad you trust me, devil that I am. May I?' Carter lifted the back of Marthe's vest and placed the stethoscope on her ribs.

'So?' Maurice said, white-faced. 'Will she live?'

Carter stood upright, pulled Marthe's vest back down. He spoke gently.

'I think you should take her to the hospital immediately. I'll help by telephoning ahead, if you like. They won't cure her but they may be able to make her...more comfortable, at least. I'm sorry, Mr Pipon.'

Carter felt a stinging frustration: in peacetime, Marthe's infection could have been cured and her illness managed in order to prolong her life. As it was, she was another casualty of the war.

After a moment of staring, Maurice said, 'So you can't find medicine for her yourself, then? I thought...your position with the Commandant?'

'I'm afraid not.'

'But she won't recover without the medicine? And they won't give it to her in hospital.'

'Sadly, no.'

'Damn it, what am I to do then? She can't stay like this.'

'I'm very sorry. Her coma will become deeper and her temperature higher. At some point either the temperature will... damage her frontal lobe—sorry, part of her brain. Or the bacteria itself will go to the brain stem. In either case, the...prognosis is...very poor, I'm afraid.'

'Meaning what, exactly? Plain English, Doctor.'

Carter felt the knifing pain of the words as he said them, quietly. 'She will die, Mr Pipon. I'm so very sorry. I wish I had a different answer for you.'

Maurice didn't weep, or beg, or shout at him, or thump the wall, as Carter had seen many husbands do when given such a bleak prediction.

Instead, he stared out the window at the sea, nodding slowly.

Carter went to make the necessary call to the hospital. His own car was held at Royal Square, but he might be able to persuade the hospital to send a car—he would pay for it from his own pocket.

Suddenly, Maurice said, 'Best find some of that medicine then.'

Carter felt a stirring of unease. 'As I said, I'm afraid that won't be possible.'

Maurice gave a thin, stiff smile. But his eyes were hard. 'What about *you*? You can find all sorts. You must be able to uncover medicine. Steal it, if you have to.'

Carter sat and put his head in his hands. 'I wish it were that simple.'

'It *is* simple. She will die without it. You've said so. *You're* the doctor. *You* can find her the medicine.'

Carter felt cornered. 'I can't. I'm sorry, Mr Pipon. Truly.'

Even as he said it, Carter wished there was some way he could summon the bravery to simplify matters. Some way to transform himself into a man like Maurice Pipon, who would steal the medicine without hesitation, without a single thought for his own safety. Again, Father's sneering face in his memory.

Spineless boy.

Maurice growled, 'You're a coward then.'

'Perhaps I am.' Carter flushed with the shame of the admission.

'A *damned* coward,' Maurice said. 'You should be ashamed. I hope you don't sleep at night. You're letting her die. How can you do it? You're not a bad sort. I can see that. Why are you doing this? *Why* are you putting that fat German bastard's life before hers?'

Carter drew in a breath, tried to steady himself. How could it be possible that saving a life was not the right choice? And yet what he couldn't begin to articulate to Maurice was that, in this world where other men made the rules, there were no *right choices*. At every turn, the end result was failure: it was simply a case of choosing cataclysm over apocalypse.

Carter knew his silence must appear uncaring, that his inaction would seem to be born out of selfishness. His hands were shaking; he couldn't still them.

Maurice muttered an oath and strode to the drinks cabinet in the corner. His breathing had grown ragged. He poured out two large glasses of whisky and gave one to Carter, who didn't touch it.

Maurice drained his glass, then refilled it. 'Very fine whisky.' His expression grew narrow, his voice sharp. 'I haven't seen whisky since before the war, I don't think. Gift, was it?'

Did the man have to torture him so? But, then again, perhaps Carter deserved it.

Marthe gave a moan. Maurice kissed her hot forehead and whispered, 'Stay with me, my love.'

'Here.' Carter handed Maurice a wet cloth. He fetched one himself, and began sponging Marthe's forehead, cheeks, arms. 'It won't cure the infection. But it'll bring the fever down a little. It might grant us some time.'

Maurice gave a bark of bitter laughter. 'Time for *what*? There's no medicine, remember?'

Carter shifted uncomfortably. 'The Commandant has medicine. But—'

Maurice's face brightened. 'Then surely you can fetch it—'

'I'm sorry, but the risk—'

'Come, if you went now, he'd never know. He'd never notice the medicine was gone.'

Carter turned away and stared out of the window. Dusk would soon fall and the sky was a perfect plum blue. On the horizon, the flat eye of the sea, unblinking. Strange that the sight of the endless, open water should make him feel like a caged animal.

'Oh, he would notice. He notices everything, in the end. And what if he had need of it?'

'And it means so much to you, does it? The extra food? The warm clothes? This drink? Those bloody *shoes*.'

Carter's jaw dropped. To hear that another man could believe him to be so callous.

'My God, is that what you think? That I'm looking after him for what I can gain from it?'

'Well, aren't you?'

'One of his soldiers was punished just last week—he'd disobeyed an order. He was a pianist—played beautifully. The Commandant ordered a surgeon to amputate the man's fingers. When the man woke after the operation, the Commandant made him sit in front of the piano. Made him play, with his bandaged stumps. Forced him to keep trying, until the man broke down and wept.'

'But you're hardly a soldier. Look at you.'

'It doesn't make a blind bit of difference to him. I'm his man—his *Eigentum,* his property. Everything that belongs to him obeys him—he makes sure of it. Just last month, one of his men fell asleep on duty. Before he had him put in front of the firing squad, the Commandant had the surgeon remove the man's eyelids, so he couldn't ever be off duty again. Even after he was dead.'

'He's a monster,' Maurice whispered.

Carter felt a wave of relief. Finally, someone understood his predicament.

'Yes, he is. But it's not simply a case of saving my own skin. He's threatened others too. Anyone he believes is close to me. Edith Bisson, Clement Hacquoil. And he's spoken of closing the hospital. Can you imagine it? Hundreds of sick people, dying on the streets because I've disobeyed orders.'

Carter felt stronger for saying it aloud. Every word he spoke was the truth, but somehow laying it out for someone else made it *more* true, made everything more understandable.

But then Maurice said, 'None of this makes any difference: my wife will die without your help—'

'I've explained—'

'She'll *die*. You've said so. And what about your oath, eh?'

Carter blinked. 'My oath?'

'Your doctor's promise. To heal people who are sick.'

'You're making it all sound very simple.'

'It is. *Look* at her. Will you let her die?'

Carter shook his head. Maurice sighed. Took his fishing knife from his belt, laid it on the table. Blade glinting in the dim light.

Carter felt a tingling of adrenaline. 'Is that a threat?'

Maurice gave a bark of bitter laughter. 'If only I had the stomach for it. Perhaps you'd find the medicine with a knife to your gullet.'

Carter heard a click in his throat as he swallowed. Surely the man wasn't desperate enough to kill him?

'Put it away then, would you? There's a good chap.'

Maurice's voice was steel. 'I want you to use it.'

'I don't follow.'

'If she's going to die, then it needs to be quick. Who knows what agony she's in right now? I won't have her dying in pain. Like some sickly animal.'

Carter gasped. 'Are you mad? I can't do that! Think what you're asking of me, man.'

Maurice spoke calmly. 'Not only that. Me too. After you've— after she's gone. I can't live without her, so you'll have to...to do me, too. You'll know how to make it quick for both of us. Where to cut.'

Carter's mouth was dry. 'Good God, you're serious.' But along with his disbelief, Carter felt a tiny glow of understanding: better to choose one's own death than suffer at the whim of a disease or the caprice of a tyrant.

Maurice pushed the knife towards him. 'Go on. Do it now.'

'Christ!' Carter picked up the knife, calculating the location of the incisions, the volume of blood that would be lost, the time it would take. He thought he might vomit.

Maurice lifted Marthe out of her bath chair and on to his lap. Her head lolled back and her neck was exposed: the blood, battering away under that pale skin. Maurice kissed her again and again: eyelids, lips, hair, cheeks, mouth, nose, throat, mouth.

Maurice rasped, 'Make it quick.'

Carter drew back the knife, then dropped it. It clattered to the floor. 'I'll do it.'

'Come on, then,' Maurice hissed. '*Now!* Before I change my mind.' He kissed Marthe's mouth again.

'No, not that!' Carter snapped. 'For God's sake, man. The medicine. I'll take the medicine. From the Commandant.'

Because there was no way he could do it: murder another human. He couldn't bring himself to kill the Commandant, so there was nothing under heaven that could make him harm Maurice or Marthe. He would rather die himself. Embrace the inevitable.

Maurice stared and smiled and Carter could sense the tiny hope forming within him, brittle and brimming as an egg.

'I may not be successful,' Carter said, 'so you must temper your expectations. I'll go now. If I'm stopped then I'll say I'm going to attend the Commandant. They won't dare to question me.' He put on his coat and hat. 'They should have you negotiating with Hitler. We'd have the whole lot of them back in Germany by the end of the month.'

It was easier than Carter expected. He wasn't stopped or questioned. He took the tablets from the cabinet in his office, stuffed them deep into his pocket, and returned within the hour.

But even in that time, he could see that Marthe had worsened: her skin was hot but her nose and the tips of her fingers were laced with blue. Maurice was squeezing her hand and talking to her as though she could hear him. But she was barely breathing.

Carter frowned and listened with his stethoscope. 'Has she stirred at all?'

'No. How does she sound?'

'Not promising.'

'You have the medicine?'

Carter held up a small bottle, feeling a tiny surge of victory. 'Sulfa tablets.'

'They'll do the trick?'

'We can hope.' He opened the bottle. 'You will need to grind two tablets up and dissolve them in water. Then we must revive her enough that she can swallow—otherwise the fluid will go to her lungs. You'll find a pestle and mortar in the kitchen.'

Maurice did as he asked and brought Carter the solution, retching at the stench of rotting eggs.

'Unpleasant, I know.' Carter pulled a little syringe out of his pocket and filled it with the mixture. 'Right, then. We must rouse her and then give it to her slowly, one drop at a time. Any more and we will effectively drown her.'

Maurice's eyes were wide with panic. 'How am I to wake her? She's out cold.'

Carter, on familiar territory, kept his voice calm. 'Pain, I'm afraid. Intense pain. Strike her, shout at her, anything to revive her, just momentarily. Pinching the earlobe is effective.'

Maurice blinked. He put the syringe to the corner of her mouth and depressed the plunger.

Carter said, 'That's good, now *very* gently...yes, perfect! Right, now you must wake her. Go on, man! Be quick about it or she'll choke.'

Maurice struck her face. 'God forgive me,' he muttered.

Marthe groaned, stirred.

'A little more,' Carter said. 'Quick, while she's able to swallow.'

But her head had drooped back on to her pillows and she was unconscious, a red handprint across her cheek. Carter nearly said, *Strike harder,* but he could see that Maurice was only just holding himself together.

But somehow he kept repeating the actions. Twice Marthe choked and Maurice, grim-faced, muttered, *Oh dear God. Breathe! Breathe!* But Marthe always swallowed and then started breathing again, as if the force of her husband's will, his sheer desperation, was the only thing keeping her alive.

Carter watched with a sense of awe and loss: the action was futile and Marthe was doomed, but Maurice was willing to risk everything for the sake of a few more weeks or months. It was baffling and wonderful. No other species forms such irrational, selfless attachments.

The depth of Maurice's love for Marthe was such that hurting her wounded him—Carter could see that quite clearly.

But Maurice didn't question Carter, simply followed his orders, doing what he must to keep her alive: bending her fingers back until it seemed they must snap, wrenching her arm up behind the back and pushing until her shoulder joint groaned, twisting the skin on her wrists and chest and the backs of her arms.

Bruises blossomed deep under Marthe's skin and Carter saw her for a moment through Maurice's eyes: beautiful, even when she was broken.

When the syringe was empty, Maurice stood and waited for the next instruction, chest heaving.

'You can stop now,' Carter said. 'Well done.'

Maurice threw the syringe across the room and it rattled against the wall. He collapsed on to the floor and wept in rhythmic, shuddering gasps.

'I'm sorry, Maurice,' Carter murmured.

Maurice wiped his eyes, cleared his throat. 'It had better bloody work.'

Carter sat on the floor next to him. 'She may not recover, you must understand that,' he said, gently. 'She needs the sulfa every four hours. Day and night. And ask Edith for any concoction she can cook up too.'

Maurice put his head in his hands. Behind him, the orange glow of the fire died.

Carter leant forward and put his hand on Maurice's shoulder. The other man was tense, his muscles hard.

'*If* she recovers, you need to think on this: she needs help. Expert help from specialists who have studied and researched her condition and know how to treat it. There is no cure. You must understand that. But there is a chance, a small chance, that they may be able to delay this rapid deterioration she has been experiencing. There was ongoing research in London prior to the war…'

Maurice looked up. 'But *London*?' He had the wide, baffled eyes of a boy.

Aware of the risk he was taking, Carter said, 'Yes. I am saying you should leave. Escape. Go, when you next have the chance.'

Carter didn't think Maurice would betray him but he *had* to give the advice, whatever the outcome for himself: it was his duty, as a doctor. As a man.

'She will die, Maurice. I need you to know that. Eventually, the disease will kill her. But this rapid degeneration, these secondary infections—I can't help feeling that they must be preventable, with the right treatment.' He took Maurice's hand between his own, felt the strength there. 'You've been admirably heroic. You can't let it beat you.'

'Her illness, or the occupation?'

'Both.'

Part 4

CLAUDINE'S mother had stayed in hospital for weeks. But even after she returned home, she kept coughing, a noise like the stuttering rattle of a far-off car engine. Sometimes it startled Claudine awake, and she clenched her fists, willing Maman to draw her next breath.

Spring was wet and cold. In April, Dr Carter came to see them again, and when he listened to Maman's chest he frowned.

'You need decent food and you need some warmth in this house,' he said. 'It's not good for your lungs, the damp and cold.'

Maman's smile was all teeth. 'And where, pray, am I to find wood?'

His face was grave. 'Have you any trees on your land that might do?'

She shook her head and tried to talk but the coughing stole all her breath.

Claudine said, 'We saved some trees through the winter to use in spring, but the soldiers came and chopped them down while Maman was poorly in hospital.'

Dr Carter nodded. 'I happen to have some extra wood I'd be very happy to give you.'

'From the Commandant?'

Maman slapped her hand on the quilt and hissed, 'Claudine, don't be rude!' She directed a tight smile at Dr Carter. 'My apologies. And thank you, but we really can't—' She started coughing again.

Claudine looked at her feet. She hadn't *meant* to be rude.

Dr Carter looked tired. 'It's a perfectly reasonable question. Yes, it is from the Commandant, and it is more than I can use, really. I would be glad to give it to you.'

'Truly?' Claudine smiled.

Maman glared. '*Clau*dine!' Her face was hard. 'Thank you, Doctor, but that won't be necessary—'

'Maman! We need more wood, you know we do—'

'That's *enough*, Claudine!'

Claudine bit her lip and risked a glance up at Dr Carter. His face was white, apart from two bright spots of colour burning in his cheeks. His eyes met hers and she experienced a momentary flicker of recognition that she had never felt towards an adult before. She suddenly saw his sadness and how hard he worked to hide it. Then he blinked and it was if the shutters had dropped back down and he was the doctor once more.

'I understand entirely,' he said. 'Please let me know if you change your mind. I'll be back tomorrow.'

After he had gone, Maman's voice was sharp. 'We'll not be taking wood from that man, do you hear?'

Throughout the slow, wet spring, Maman kept on coughing and growing thinner and thinner. The shape of her skull crept out from beneath her yellowing skin. Claudine tried to go cockling on the way home from school, but the seabed was empty. Sometimes she found one or two, but she always gave those to Francis.

Then, one afternoon in May, there was more light and warmth in the air and Claudine felt the chill fade from inside her bones. She stretched in the sudden sunlight on the way home from school, but when she saw the house she could tell that something had changed. There was smoke coming from the chimney and a smell like Sunday roast dinners from a long time ago. Before Papa left.

The kitchen was steamy, and Maman was humming when Claudine walked in.

Maman whooped, a sound she hadn't made in years.

'Darling!' she cried. 'We've been waiting for you! Where have you *been*? I thought the chicken was going to burn!' She hugged Claudine so hard it took her breath.

'Chicken?'

'*Real* chicken! A *whole* one! Fresh. With potatoes and carrots, parsnips and gravy. And bread and jam for pudding. *Pudding!* With butter—*real* butter! I hope you're hungry, my love.'

'I am! But how…? Where did you find a chicken?'

'I didn't *find* it, my love. I—well… Hans is going to…*share* it with us. Hans, this is Claudine. Say hello, sweetheart.'

That was when Claudine saw the soldier standing over in the corner by the sink.

'*Hallo*, Claudine,' he said, smiling.

She froze. It was the soldier with the pig-snout nose who had eaten all of the sand eels and pulled her on to his lap and put his hands all over her and inside her knickers with his hard fingers.

Claudine backed away.

Maman dragged her forward by the wrist. 'Stop being shy, you silly goose! She's having you on. Come *on!* Here, you can drain the potatoes for me. We've even *butter,* Claudine! Did I say? *Real* butter—four ounces—can you *imagine?*' Her voice was falsely bright, like a stone made shiny with spit.

Claudine took the potatoes and drained the pan. The steam billowed around her face so she could see her breath going in and out and in and out. She put the potatoes in a dish next to Hans.

'*Danke, Liebling,*' he said.

When Claudine said nothing, Maman snapped, 'Manners, Claudine!' and she finally muttered, '*Bitte.*'

But you wouldn't take the firewood from Dr Carter, she thought.

It didn't make any sense, this world of loyalties that shifted like steam.

Maman smiled and laughed and wolfed down the chicken, while, sickened, Claudine stared at the food on her plate. All she could see was Hans's face, his white teeth, and his long, hard fingers.

The beach was a fine place to be wretched. The sea sometimes blue or green or purple or grey. Never the same but always there. Everything smelt bitter and fresh and clean. Time slipped away and thought disappeared.

Claudine could breathe easily there. She dug holes until they filled with water and she watched the sandhoppers drown. Then she rescued them one by one and they leapt away to safety.

Suddenly she felt a hand on her shoulder. It was Gregor.

Something inside her broke and she started to shake and she couldn't stop sobbing, wave upon wave of grief and fear. At first she put her arms around him. He felt safe and warm, like home or Papa. But then she remembered how ashamed she was and she thought of everything he had done and she pulled away.

'I'm going home.'

'What have I done that you are so sad, Claudine?' he asked. 'I have not seen you. You are running from me, I think.'

He went to put his arm around her again, but she flinched and moved away.

'Why were you mean?' she said, suddenly, as she stared at the bruise-black sea.

He sat next to her. 'Mean? What is this?'

'I saw you. You were so mean to those poor prisoners, just before the execution of the Frenchman. Why?'

'You saw this Frenchman killed?'

'No. But I saw you shouting at the prisoners. And you watched while the other soldier...' Her voice cracked. 'It's rotten, you're all *rotten*!'

Gregor was quiet for a long time. Then he took an apple out of his pocket and offered it to her. She shook her head.

His face was thinner and his skin was like old paper. She remembered that night on the beach, when the other soldiers dragged him away. She felt a surge of pity for him, swiftly followed by shame at what had happened to her, at what he had *allowed* to happen to her, and anger at how he had treated the prisoners.

'The men,' he said. 'The *Häftlinge*. I think this for a long time. It is *mean*—this is your word, yes? *Rotten*. Yes? So I try not to hurt them. I am good man to them.' He crunched on his apple.

Claudine frowned. 'But you *shouted*. And then you let a man get beaten and then...' She spread her hands, unable to speak.

'It is a hard thing,' Gregor said, at last. 'Before, for a long time, I am good to these men. And the men do not work hard for me. They are lazy for me. The soldiers, my comrades, they laugh at me. I am soft, like a woman, they say. They hit me. They tell me to hurt the *Häftlinge*. This will make them work better. I am not hitting. I never do this. But now I see other men hitting and I am not stopping them...'

'But hurting people is wrong.'

'But these are not men, *Liebling*. I know this now. They are like animals. A cow works and she pulls for us, yes? And if she is too slow, we teach her to be fast.'

'But...that's different.'

'No, not different. The cow works, yes? We strike her and she works harder. She makes something for us. She is then more than a cow—she is a...how do you say it?...*Bildner*.'

'Builder?'

'Yes. So she is now more, better. You understand?'

'*Ja*. I think so.'

But she didn't—not really. How could good, kind Gregor believe such terrible things? It was so confusing, the twisted line between right and wrong, good and evil. Gregor was good, she knew, and yet he could behave like a monster. Was everyone such a confusing mixture? In Hitler's black heart, was there a tiny glow-worm of tenderness that made him kind to children? She thought of Dr Carter, who was so good, so kind, and yet he helped the Commandant, which was wrong, surely?

Gregor held out the other half of his apple, with a smile. Hunger scrabbled in Claudine's guts.

As she ate, she spoke haltingly about Maman and how she had been miserable and poorly all through the winter and into spring. She told him about Hans being at home. She wondered how much he knew of what had happened on the beach that night.

'He scares me, Gregor,' she said quietly.

Gregor's mouth was set in a thin line. 'This is not a good thing. We must help you. We must think of...something for help you.'

Claudine said, 'I don't understand about you.'

'Warum?'

'You are so kind and yet—' She nearly said it: he was kind to her but so awful to those poor men. Instead, she said, 'You are good to me, even though you are a soldier.'

'How can I be rotten for you?'

He grinned, pleased with himself for using the unfamiliar word. Then his face grew serious.

'I have a boy, a son. In Germany. I think that I want him happy. You are a child. War is cruel.'

He shrugged, an open-handed gesture that contained the difficulty of all the ideas he couldn't say in English, or perhaps couldn't say at all. 'It is good for being kind to children. This is what I hope for my boy.'

After a long time, the air became ragged: biting gusts

scraped their cheeks. The sea turned slate-grey and Claudine could feel rain waiting in the cold wind.

She didn't talk about the night on the beach. The sand eels. Hans.

Claudine knew she had to go home.

As she stood up, Gregor reached out to her. 'This Hans,' he said. 'I will not let him hurt you. Don't be frightened.'

But Hans came to their house every day, all through May. He brought bags of food and he brought medicine for Maman, too. She stopped coughing and started singing while she cooked. Her piano-ribs faded and filled with plump flesh. By the summer, her face was round and happy.

Francis started to sleep instead of crying. Claudine's stomach didn't gripe all the time. It was easier to run without feeling dizzy.

Hans brought her a wooden hoop and a stick to play with outside so that he and Maman could go and lie down together. A toy for a child, but she played with it anyway. She tried not to listen to the grunts and groans from Maman's room.

She wondered where Papa was fighting. They had received one tattered letter, via the Red Cross nearly ten months ago (and it had been dated from two months before that, June 1941), which had been very bright and talked about the heat, as if Papa were enjoying a holiday. Some sentences were black blocks of the censor's pen. Papa had written, *I like to think of you, safe in Jersey.*

Maman had scowled when she read that and thrown the letter to the floor. Claudine had picked it up and tucked it into her pocket. She had read it again and again, trying to understand what had made Maman so angry.

Hans was kind to Claudine. Called her *Liebling*. Sometimes, he patted her on the head or stroked her hair. Sometimes, he stood behind her and squeezed her shoulders. Or he put his hands on the back of her neck and rubbed it, very gently, so that it almost tickled. His touch sent spiders skittering into her stomach.

Maman watched. Once, after he had gone, she said, 'Hans is very kind to you, my love.'

'Yes, Maman.'

'He's never hurt you, has he?'

Claudine imagined the shock and disgust on Maman's face if she told her. Perhaps she would make Hans go away. But perhaps—and this thought was more terrible—perhaps she wouldn't. Might she *blame* Claudine somehow, for making Hans do those terrible things to her?

'No, Maman,' she replied.

'Do you like him?'

Claudine looked at her face. Maman was smiling, truly smiling. Her cheeks were pink, her eyes were bright, like they used to be before Francis was born. No trace of her black mood. If Claudine told Maman what had happened, she knew that Maman's darkness would return, along with the squeezing hunger.

'Of course I do.'

'You'd never know he was a soldier, really, would you? Not a German soldier? To look at him, he could be English or French. Or even from Jersey, except that his hair is a little light.'

'Shall I peel the potatoes?' Claudine said.

One day, Hans brought another chicken then took Maman to the bedroom.

Claudine knew how to cook vegetables and fish, but she had never cooked a chicken before. She didn't know where to start with it: what to do with the feathers and feet and head. So she took it to Edith's house.

'Goodness, child, I must be dreaming. A chicken? A *real* chicken. Come, let me hold it.'

Edith was showing Claudine how to pluck the chicken when she suddenly stopped.

'What's this then?'

She was pointing at the chicken's foot: the skin was green.

Claudine grimaced. 'Is it bad?'

Edith's voice was hard. 'Where did you find this bird? Or *who* did you steal it from, I should be saying.'

'No one. I *didn't* steal it.'

'Well, what's this?' She beckoned Claudine closer so she could inspect the foot. It wasn't mould but green paint.

'There's only one man I know who paints his chicken's feet green so they don't go missing. This is Oliver Le Marchand's bird, stolen from his coop just yesterday morning. Making a right old song and dance about it, he was.'

Her cheeks burning, Claudine told Edith how a soldier had become friends with Maman. How he had been giving them lots of food. How Maman was happy.

'She *sings*, Edith. And she hums and laughs for no reason.'

Edith stood and looked out of the window. The wind was flattening the grass and shaking the gorse bushes.

'Are you angry?' Claudine asked.

Edith shook her head.

'Do you think Maman is a bad person?'

Edith shook her head again and gave a sad smile. 'Those that live on hope die of hunger, my love.'

'Should I take the chicken back to Mr Le Marchand?'

'Take it back,' Edith laughed. 'Are you mad, child? First thing he'd do would be skin you alive. Second would be to eat that chicken. Which I must say, I quite fancy a bit of. It would also do Marthe the world of good.'

After that, whenever Hans brought a chicken, Claudine took it to Edith and helped her to strip and gut it. Edith kept the innards for paté and stews. Maman never asked where the giblets had gone, but she must have known that Claudine was taking the birds to Edith's house. Perhaps it was because Maman knew Edith had cared for the children when she had been in hospital, or perhaps it was because Hans and the food had turned her into a different person, but she didn't seem to mind.

When Claudine watched Edith and Marthe and Maurice eating the paté, it made Hans's eyes on her body and his hands on her skin seem to matter less.

———

EDITH had thought Maurice a fool for fretting when the soldier disappeared for those days. What was the worry? But then, after she'd seen him help Maurice take Marthe over to Dr Carter's, she started to bother over it. It kept her up all that night and worried her over the weeks that came after: was he a spy, reporting back to the Commandant? The darkness makes monsters out of thin air. Still, what with fretting over Marthe too, Edith didn't catch a wink of sleep.

Three weeks later, at 5am and with the air still freezing, Edith stamped outside to fetch some wood. The shed was thick with the darkness—her little candle blinded her to anything past the reach of her arm. But she could see the pile of oddments that she'd heaped in the corner to hide the wood.

She took one of Frank's old rakes and prodded off the old newspaper and the sacks (they could use them for fuel once the wood ran out). She was just poking the last piece of newspaper when it moved and gave a moan.

Edith screeched and ran from the shed back into the house. Was it an ambush? Or an escaped prisoner of war? They could be violent, half starved and desperate as they were.

She leant against the door, trying to think where she could find her sharpest kitchen knife, her heart still going ten to the dozen when there was a *rat-a-tat-tat* at the door.

'Leave me alone. I've nothing for you.'

'Helfen Sie mir!'

She opened the door a crack. There he was, the soldier: crouched on her doorstep, that ruined arm held up like an offering.

She gasped. 'You frightened the life out of me.'

'Sorry.'

'I suppose you want to come in?'

'Thank you.' He rushed past her into the house and then cowered in her kitchen, looking all about as if he was the one with an army after him.

'You look dreadful. Whatever's the matter?'

'I must…hide.'

'Hide? From whom?'

266

He laughed but there was no joy in it. 'My countrymen. They take me, I think.'

Edith frowned. 'But why?'

He held out that arm again. 'This. I take the potatoes for the Commandant. He is happy. Then he see my arm. Before, he has forgot it.'

'How?' Edith grinned. 'It's not the easiest thing to miss, that arm.'

The soldier's face was serious. 'Not *forgot*. But my father is a big man with much power in Lübeck. Before, I am safe because of him. But now Lübeck has bombs, many deaths. My father...'

The soldier's eyes filled with tears and Edith took his poor, broken hand and held it. But he pushed her away.

'The Commandant say I am only in Jersey because my father was big man. Now this is all change. He tell me to stay in my house, not move. He will send men. I ask why. He say I am better for going to Germany. But...I know what this means, so I must hide.'

'He wants to deport you? But then you would be going home.'

'No! Not home. To...I do not know how you say... *Konzentrationslager.*'

'Not to the work camps?'

'Perhaps. The Führer does not like men who are...broken. Since long before war, *bihindert* people are killed. They pretend secret, but many people know this.'

His eyes were bright with tears.

'Come, come.' Edith put her arms around him. No other way to give true comfort. His shoulders shook like a child's. 'There, now. So you were hiding here? Stealing food where you could find it?'

He nodded. 'But I do not take food from you. From other field or garden, yes, but not from you.'

'Well, I suppose that's a compliment of sorts.'

She sighed, was about to tell him to go and find some other house to bother, but the hunted look in his eyes stopped her. How many people had war devoured over the years? There were those it had killed outright, like Frank and that poor French boy. It had disfigured Clement's body, distorted Dr Carter's mind beyond all recognition. Then there were those who were fading fast because war stopped them getting the help they needed: poor Marthe and little Francis, who, sweet as he was, would always be scrawny and seemed backward.

Edith made up her mind: her own private protest against the evil beast that was war.

'Now listen,' she said. 'If you're going to be hiding then there are better places than my wood shed. You'll stay in my larder.'

He shook his head. 'This I cannot. If they find—'

'They *will* find you in my wood shed and then we'll both be for it.'

'I can find other place. In woods or cave. You are good woman. I can't—'

'You *can't* keep disagreeing with me or I shall give you a clip around the ear. You will sleep in the larder and that is that.'

It felt good to be saying it. Two fingers up to Hitler and all his ilk. Violence and hatred and suspicion had tilted the world off its axis, but she had to believe that, somehow, all the little acts of kindness would serve to right it. The alternative was chaos.

Edith smiled at the glimmer of hope in the soldier's eyes.

'But first I'll have your name. I'm not having a strange man bedding down under my roof.'

'Gregor.' He held out his good hand. She clasped it. Warm, like the body of any other human.

She settled him in her larder with some blankets. He was thin and pasty and looked as if he hadn't slept in a week. She made him eat some bread and butter.

'I shall go to the butcher tomorrow for more meat. In the meantime, this will have to do.'

He ripped into it like a dog, wincing as he swallowed—the hunger in his guts must have been like fire for him to gobble so. Between mouthfuls he said, 'You ask for meat. The butcher, he will know something is strange?'

'Ha! Even if he does suspect, he's in my debt for life. And he's a decent chap really, though his wife is straight out of the River Styx. A bad woman.'

Gregor nodded. He'd finished his bread and Edith could see his eyelids beginning to droop so she settled him down with a cushion under his head. When she tried to give him a blanket, he pushed it away, saying, 'I will make dirty.'

She stayed nearby until he began to snore, then she tucked the blanket in around him. Thin as a rail, he was. He looked like not much more than a boy, limbs uncurled in sleep, face smooth with not a trace of cunning written upon it.

Frank had looked similar when he was asleep. Strange how such big, rough men, with their guns and their uniforms, turned back into guileless children the instant they closed their eyes, as though it was all a pretence they could shrug off in sleep—boys caught up in war games.

The next day, two soldiers came marching up Edith's path and hammered on her door. She opened it and they barged in, stamping their muddy boots all over her floor. Then they sat her down and pulled out a piece of paper, waving it at her and bawling in German.

'You're wasting your breath,' Edith said, calmly. 'I could sooner understand a barking dog.' But she felt the beginnings of fear and prayed that Gregor wouldn't sneeze.

Eventually, she called for Claudine, who had been hiding in the kitchen. The girl crept out and stood in the corner, shoulders hunched, eyes wide—terrified of any soldier, she was.

Edith said, 'Tell me what they're so hot and bothered about, would you, Claudine, my love?' Praying they didn't suspect that Gregor was crouching in her larder.

The girl nodded and, startled rabbit that she was, came out with a mouthful of gibberish, which might as well have been her own creation for all the sense it made to Edith. But the soldiers nodded along and spoke back to her.

Edith thanked the skies above that she hadn't mentioned Gregor to Claudine. The girl looked the picture of innocence. But after they'd finished talking, Claudine's eyes shone with tears and Edith felt her stomach thud into her boots.

'Someone has reported you for having a crystal wireless,' Claudine whispered. 'They want to search the house.'

A chill prickled over Edith's skin, but she made her voice light and fixed her mouth into a smile.

'Oh, is that all? Well, nothing to fuss about. You tell them I'll fetch the wireless out and no bother at all.'

The girl stared, aghast. 'But Edith, I can't tell them that. They'll put you in prison.'

'Well, then, tell them they're mistaken but I'll give them something for their troubles, for coming all this way.'

'I don't think they'll believe me.'

'You're giving them too much credit: tell them anything you like, they'll not ponder or question. Great oafs, look at them. If they fell into a barrel of nipples, they'd come out sucking their own thumbs.'

Claudine gave a tiny snort of laughter. '*Edith!*'

'That's better. You keep on smiling. Now, be a good girl and fetch some dandelion tea and one of the jarred chickens that I have in brine on the shelf in the larder.'

She looked again at the soldiers. They were gaunt, skin stretched tight across their hands. The shape of their skulls was sharp under their skin.

'Best fetch *both* chickens.'

'But you're saving those chickens for Christmas.'

'The soldiers are hungry now, Claudine, my love.'

Claudine set her mouth in a thin line. 'I *shan't* do it. We'll eat those chickens at Christmas, as you said we would. All of us together.'

Edith pulled her into a tight embrace and whispered in her ear, 'There's a soldier in the larder. He has a bad arm, try not to stare. But we can't have the Germans searching the house. Don't tell Maurice, either!'

Claudine's mouth hung open, but there wasn't time for Edith to explain any more so she gave the girl a quick kiss.

'Fetch those chickens out then and give them to the good soldiers. Chop chop.'

They took the chickens, of course, promising to return soon. Edith knew she would have to find a better place to hide Gregor.

~

AFTER the soldiers left, Claudine and Gregor sat in Edith's kitchen and talked. She could barely believe it when he said he had been sitting outside Edith's house for much of the time, watching over her and Marthe. 'You did not see me?' he asked.

Now that she thought about it, perhaps she had seen a flash of green uniform at times, or a face that looked like Gregor's. But after that night on the beach with Hans, and then seeing Gregor with the prisoners of war, she had closed her mind off to the sight of any German soldier at all.

But looking at Gregor now—thin, vulnerable, shaking with fear—made her think again. He explained how the other soldiers had always used his arm as an excuse to shout at him or beat him and the beatings had got much worse since the news of his father's death.

'You are kind child,' Gregor said. 'You do not look at me as monster because of this.' He gestured at his arm.

'I haven't noticed it very much,' Claudine said. And she hadn't. It was simply part of him, like the colour of his hair or the shape of his nose. It didn't change who he was, she thought. He had done that himself, when he had started behaving like all the stories of heartless German soldiers.

'Why did you stay outside Edith's house?' she asked.

Gregor shrugged. 'After time, I do not like to be with the soldiers. I like to watch the woman, Marthe. My heart hurts for her. She is ill, like my wife.' His face darkened. 'I fear for my wife. I fear for Marthe, and for you. You are sweet child. I do not want bad things for you. And then I see Edith is good woman. So I watch and keep other patrols away—they avoid because of my arm and...my father.' He sighed. 'And now my father is dead and the Commandant has remember me and I hide.'

Claudine tried to untangle her anger at Gregor from her concern for him. It seemed that he was a different person from the man who had played with her in the bomb shelter. She had been different then, too. A child who would believe anything.

'I am glad you are here,' she said, realising that she meant it. 'I am glad you are safe.'

Edith made Claudine promise again and again not to breathe a word to Maurice about Gregor.

'He won't understand. You know how he is about the Germans. He'll have a blue fit if he knows I'm sheltering one.'

When she discovered that Gregor was the soldier Claudine had spoken of before, Edith was delighted and kept shaking her head, saying, 'Just imagine it.'

Then she gave a puzzled frown. 'Why have you been so skittish about the soldiers all this while, then? You can't have fallen out with Gregor—he wouldn't hurt a fly.'

Neither Gregor nor Claudine could answer this, so they sat in silent shards of time, unspoken words tattooing around them like trapped moths.

But sitting with Gregor in the quivering silence was still better than the slow poison of watching Hans and Maman. Claudine lingered at Edith's house, though she always went home before curfew.

At first, Hans brought home lots of meat and butter and even sugar. In June, for the first time since the bombing on the beach, Claudine and Maman made biscuits while Francis ran around, waving his skinny arms and shouting, 'My tummy burst! *More!*'

They all laughed and feasted until they felt sick—Maman

and Hans too. Claudine tried to close her eyes and pretend that Hans was Papa.

But he sounded different. He smelt different. Like old rust and the cloying, mushroomy stink that seeped up from the roots of fungus-covered tree stumps. Claudine imagined spores, wheeling through the air, filling her lungs.

Some weeks later, Hans came to the house without any food. Maman frowned.

'I thought you might bring a chicken?'

Hans turned and walked out. They didn't see him for a week. They had to go back to living off their rations, but their flour was full of weevils, their potatoes were mouldy and their meat was greenish, even when they had boiled it for hours. They forced it down.

'Hold your nose,' Maman said, 'you'll barely taste it.'

After the meal, she scrubbed the sticky grey meat residue from the pan, her face hard with unshed tears.

'Don't you see, they've done it on purpose?'

'I don't understand,' Claudine said.

'Our food being like this. They're punishing us.'

Claudine couldn't comprehend how such malevolence was possible, and yet she knew it was true: war made people ugly.

They were awake all night, vomiting.

The next time Hans arrived, Maman made a fuss of him: cooked the last scraps of their food into a potato peel pie and gave him all of the wine ration she had saved. They spent the night in her bedroom, laughing and gasping and making those animal groans. Claudine sang Francis to sleep so they wouldn't have to hear.

Hans started coming every day again. Most days he brought

food. Maman always smiled at him; if he came empty-handed then she beamed wide enough to crack her face in two and nudged Claudine to do the same.

One day, he brought something that he had already skinned. When Claudine asked him what it was, he gave a sly smile and said, 'A rabbit I have this morning catched.' But later she heard him tell Maman that it was a squirrel. It didn't taste like squirrel or rabbit.

After they had eaten it, there was a banging at the door. It was Madame Du Feu with her little boy Mark, who was hiding his face in her skirts. His shoulders were shuddering. She was crying too.

Claudine heard shouting and when she went to look, Maman was saying to Madame Du Feu, 'You must have misunderstood.'

'Don't you give me any of that,' Madame Du Feu snapped. 'I'm no fool.'

Maman pressed her hands together, her eyes pleading. 'I'm sorry, but we can't help you.'

'Of course you can't! We all know you for what you are. Cosy, is it? Nights must be warm with a full stomach and a soldier in your bed. Filthy Jerry-Bag! Whore!'

'Get off my doorstep.' Maman's voice shook.

Madame Du Feu started sobbing again, and her voice was high and quaking.

'Please, we only want Tom back. *Please*, give him back.'

After they had gone, waves of nausea washed over Claudine. Tom was their cat's name. He was black and white with green eyes. He always used to run to Claudine and rub his head against her legs and purr.

She went outside. It was cold and windy, no glimmer of the

July sun, just a smoky, barbed light and the shadowy trees like twisted limbs. She bent over behind the shed, convulsing. Her stomach clenched and flipped. The vomit burned her throat.

When her stomach was empty, Claudine scrubbed her mouth with a dock leaf and dried her eyes. Then she went back into the house, because Maman and Hans would need her to look after Francis while they lay down.

Claudine tried to find as much extra food as she could for the days when Hans didn't come to see them, or didn't bring food. They ate winkles, which tasted salty and sour. She went to the rock pools and caught bitter-tasting fish and shrimp so small they had to be eaten with their heads and legs on. Trying to chew them was like grinding your teeth on straw. Francis coughed and gagged and was sick, bringing up six whole shrimp, still with their prickly legs outstretched.

Claudine caught shore crabs, too. They ate them with seaweed, which was like chewing on car tyres, even after Claudine had boiled it for hours.

She watched Francis shrink again. His eyes were dark tunnels, full of tearful confusion. He had a high-pitched wail: 'My tummy hurt!'

'Child should be with mother,' Hans said, one day. 'He will not cry, I think, in your bed, Sarah.'

So Francis began to sleep in Maman's bed.

When the creaking floorboards woke Claudine in the middle of the night, she knew. He stood in her doorway, a blacker shadow in the muffling darkness. She could hear the rasp of his breath, feel the heat in it. A tiny glint of light as he smiled.

What big teeth you have.

Her heart scrabbled in her chest. He leant forward and wrapped his hand around the back of her neck.

'*Ist dir kalt, Liebling?*'

'*Nein.*'

He lay down on the bed and coiled his arms around her. They were big and hard and covered in hair. His body was hot as he pressed against her. She closed her eyes and tried to breathe quietly. Perhaps he would think she had fallen asleep. Perhaps he would leave her alone.

He kissed her cheek. His face was spiky. She stayed very still. He kissed her lips. She squeezed her eyes shut. She imagined that she was like a cockle, shut up tight and buried in the mudflats.

He moved his hands down over her stomach. Up under her nightdress. He pressed himself against her and held her tight, all the while his fingers moving. Hard. Something deep inside her tummy punctured. She screamed into his mouth.

'*Still sein,*' he whispered. '*Du bist so schön, Liebling.*'

He slept all night with his hairy hand on her chest. She counted her breaths and watched the shadows creeping over the walls. In the morning light, he woke, stood up and crept back into Maman's room.

He came to her bed most nights. In the day, he rarely looked at her. But when he did, he smiled or winked. It was like someone tipping iced water into her lungs. And it ached inside when she moved.

One day she said to Maman, 'I don't like Hans.'

Maman's hands froze over the sock she was darning. Her mouth twisted downwards, as if she was chewing on a sour winkle.

'I know you don't, my love.'

'He isn't very…kind.'

Maman sat down next to Claudine and held her hand. 'Sometimes you will meet people you don't like. And that's perfectly normal. You don't have to like everybody. But some people…some people you might *need*. So you have to grit your teeth and put up with them. It's part of growing up. You don't want Francis to starve, do you?'

Claudine shook her head.

'Hans doesn't hurt you?'

She made herself shake her head again.

'And he *is* kind to you, isn't he? Even though you don't like him?'

Maman's eyes were wide with wanting her to say yes.

Claudine nodded.

'Good girl.'

All through the summer and the early autumn, Hans came into her bed. Sometimes he didn't hurt her, but he started to put her hands on his hot, hairy body instead. He groaned when she touched him.

It was in September when she first bled. Edith gave her some cloth to put in her flannel drawers; she scrubbed them clean in the tub in the garden when no one was looking. But she had read books about it: the way the man's seed swims into the woman's body and makes a baby. Her body could do that now.

When Hans found that she was bleeding, he didn't touch her. But, lying next to her in the darkness, he said, 'You are a woman now.' And there was something new in the way his hands rested on her, possessive and full of promise.

That was when she decided to run away. She had seen the cows and what the bullocks did to them. She understood the harsh animal cries from Maman's room when she and Hans lay down in the afternoons. Grunting. Claudine knew what men expected women to do.

At first she thought she could hide with Edith. But they would find her there. Then she imagined hiding in the sand dunes, or in the caves at Devil's Hole: nobody ever went there, because the spirits of dead fishermen haunted them. But she wanted to take Francis with her so that Hans couldn't hurt him in her place.

In the end, Claudine decided she would find a boat and row to England, just her and Francis. With Gregor to look after them—and Edith too, if she wanted to come.

That was when she thought of Maurice.

Early next morning, when everybody was still asleep, Claudine lifted Hans's heavy hand from her chest and tiptoed from the bedroom. When she walked past Maman's room, the floorboards creaked and Maman opened one eye. She smiled at Claudine, made her lips into the shape of a kiss and then closed her eye again.

Claudine ran all the way, muscles burning, and tapped on Edith's door. Claudine thought she might be asleep, but Edith opened the door straight away, almost as if she had been waiting. Her face was puffy but she was wearing her housedress and her eyes were bright and sharp. She looked relieved when she saw Claudine.

'Is Maurice here?' Claudine whispered.

'Out on the boat, my love, but he's due back shortly. You look pale. Whatever's the matter?'

'Where is Gregor?'

'See for yourself. Gregor! You can come out, dear.'

The larder door swung open. 'Hello, Claudine.'

He was smiling; his face was a little fatter, more like the old Gregor. He looked handsome, with his dark hair and his blue eyes. Somehow, Edith had managed to hide him from the patrols, or throw them off the scent or bribe them into looking the other way.

His smile faded when he saw her face. *'Was ist los?'*

'Nothing, I...' Claudine shook her head, fought back tears. She didn't want to say anything before Maurice arrived. They might think her a fool or try to stop her from asking for his boat. She didn't want to have to explain everything. She didn't know how to form the words for the leaden ache in her stomach.

'I don't want to say,' she finally whispered.

Edith and Gregor nodded. Claudine saw them exchange a look, but neither of them pressed her. They all sat for a long time without saying anything. The skeleton clock on the mantelpiece ticked.

When there was a knock at the door, they all jumped. Gregor and Claudine both dashed to hide in the back of the larder.

'Calm yourselves!' Edith hissed. 'Not loud enough for a patrol. But Gregor, my love, you'd best hide.'

Edith let Maurice in and cut him a slice of bread too. She didn't eat any herself. Claudine could almost count the bones under the thin, yellowing skin of her hands, but Edith always said she wasn't hungry.

Maurice ate his bread in three big mouthfuls, without saying anything. His hair stuck out in all directions; his face was pouchy with exhaustion.

Everything was quiet except for the sound of hungry chewing.

Claudine felt the need to fill the silence. 'Do you truly believe Marthe will die, Maurice?'

'Goodness me, child,' Edith cried. 'Say what you mean, don't hold back.'

But Maurice gave a sad smile. 'The medicine's done her the world of good,' he murmured. 'Thank you for asking.'

It was quiet again until Claudine clenched her fists to give herself courage before saying, 'I want to borrow your boat. Please.'

Maurice and Edith stared at Claudine and then looked at each other and laughed. A loud, grown-up laugh, from before the war.

Then Edith said, 'Well, then, Maurice, I can offer you a little acorn coffee, if you've time to stop?'

'Thank you, I think I will today.'

As Edith went to fill the pan, Maurice sat down at the table and gazed out at the sea. Claudine could see the reflection of the clouds in his troubled eyes.

'Maurice, please can I borrow your boat?'

He frowned and scrubbed at his eyes. 'I'd laugh, Claudine, love, honestly I would. But I've spent these last few months nursing Marthe and I'm tired to my very bones.'

'But I mean it! Why won't he listen, Edith? I *need* to borrow his boat.'

Edith gave her a blank look: the same one Maurice had given her.

'Now, child, you're not normally one to be an irritation. I

know you mean well. But we're not laughing now, are we? So stop jesting and sit quietly. I'll even give you a drop of acorn coffee if you won't say a word to your maman.'

'But I'm *not* jesting and I don't *want* to sit down and I don't *want* any acorn coffee! I want Maurice's boat!'

She started to cry. She couldn't make herself stop, not even when she dug her nails into the palms of her hands and chewed on the inside of her cheek and counted her teeth with her tongue.

Edith took Claudine on to her lap and held her and stroked her hair. 'Shhhh, shhhhh, there now,' she said, until Claudine's breath had stopped shattering out of her chest in gasps. Edith kissed her cheeks. 'Come then, what's this?'

'I have to leave because I don't like Hans. And I need the boat because England is too far for me to swim.'

She could see Maurice's mouth curling into a smile. Edith frowned at him.

'Slow down, my love,' she said. 'Why this sudden worry over Hans? I know he's a soldier, but they're not *all* bad. And the food he brings. Why, you'd have starved if your mother hadn't—'

'I just don't like him. He's not very…kind to me.'

It grew quiet once more. No sound but the ticking clock and everyone breathing and thinking. Claudine stared at her fingers in her lap, which had crescents of dirt under the nails where she had scrabbled at the rocks, trying to lever limpets free. She knew that Maurice and Edith were looking at each other and saying things with their eyes, so she waited for them to finish.

Maurice eventually sighed. 'Claudine, all of us have to be around people we don't like sometimes. You can't simply row off in a boat and leave folk behind. You'll spend half your life rowing; you'll end up with arms like a sailor. And who will want to marry you then, eh?'

Edith chuckled.

'I don't *want* to row away from everyone,' Claudine hissed. 'Just Hans. And I want to go to England because they haven't been invaded and they have more food. Here I have to find cockles for our dinner. But there aren't any cockles left. So we have to eat the food Hans gives us. And I don't *like* eating his food.'

Edith stroked Claudine's hair. 'It shouldn't be up to you to find food, my love.'

Claudine nodded because her throat was aching.

'The war means that lots of us do things we'd rather not,' Edith said. 'And I suppose you worry about people calling your maman a Jerry-Bag?'

Claudine stared at the cracks in her shoes.

'I think, Claudine, if we're candid…I think we're all simply doing what we must. To stay alive. Your maman has herself and two children to think about. And there's none of us that haven't helped the Germans out one way or another. Or taken something from one of them. Isn't that right, Maurice?'

He snorted.

Edith continued. 'So you mustn't be too upset about all the rubbish about traitors and Jerry-Bags. Do you hear me?'

'Yes,' Claudine muttered.

'No more talk of running away, do you hear me?'

'But I *still* want to go to England. I *hate* being in Jersey.' There was a quivering, childish fury in her voice once more.

Edith and Maurice looked at each other again and said more things with their eyes. Claudine dug the dirt out from under her fingernails and waited.

Edith took Claudine's hand in hers. Her skin was leathery and sun-spotted, but her grip was strong.

'We can't take you from your mother, my love. I'm sorry. She'd never forgive us for putting you in danger. And you'd miss her, wouldn't you?'

'I would. But I wouldn't miss Hans.'

Claudine started to cry again. Even though tears didn't help anyone or change a thing. Even though she was nearly a woman and tears were for babies.

Maurice sat straighter in his chair. 'Come now, Hans can't be so bad, even if he is a Kraut.'

He put his hand on Claudine's shoulder and squeezed. Memory of Hans, his hard hands, his moving fingers that were all over her and inside her, sent spiders skittering into her stomach. Claudine stopped crying and froze, squeezing her eyes shut.

Edith took a sharp breath. 'Claudine, my love,' she asked, 'has Hans ever hurt you?'

Through the roaring in her ears, Claudine heard herself reply, 'Every night. Even though I never talk to him or look at him. I *try* to be good… But I must have done something *terr*ible to make him do that. Why does he want to do those horrible things to me? What have I done to—'

Edith pulled Claudine into her lap again and held her tight. She smelt of the sea and clean air and fresh new plants. Claudine sobbed.

Edith's voice was fierce. '*Never* think that! *Never*! You're a wonderful girl, there now, no need to cry, hush. Go on through to the sitting room and let me have a little chat with Maurice. Take Marthe with you, there's a good girl.'

So Claudine wiped her eyes and wheeled Marthe through and started reading a book about plants, which had lots of long names in it. But all the time her ears were straining for Maurice's and Edith's words.

As if from very far away she heard Edith say, 'Evil bastard, I'll *kill* him. I'll—'

'Not if I do it first,' Maurice spat.

'We'll do it together. I'll make him a nightshade tea and you can cut his throat. We can fight over which of us is allowed to gut him.'

'This isn't a time for jesting, Edith.'

'I'm not.' Her voice was savage.

Eventually Edith said, 'Her *face*, poor love. Did you see her face? She can't stay there. I won't have it.'

'No.'

Edith's voice was firm. 'I'll go to Sarah today. Tell her Claudine is staying with me. Helping me with Marthe. And Francis is here to keep her company.'

'You think she'll agree to it?'

'Who knows? She's all muddled, that one. Never the same since the boy.'

Maurice grunted. 'Doesn't excuse her letting that sort of thing go on. If she knows, that is.'

'Most folks know more than they'll admit, even to themselves—whether she knows or not is beside the point. It's happening and we must get the child away.'

'Perhaps taking her from the house might be enough?'

'What if Hans sees her on the way to school? Or we come a cropper because he knows that we're on to him? A soldier can do anything he likes, and there's nothing we can do to help her as long as she's near him. I think England might be the best place for her.'

'But how could I take her?' Maurice said. 'I've enough to worry about with where to go and what to do with Marthe, let alone two children. The news on the wireless doesn't make me jump for joy, you know. England's no better than here for a child. Bombs and the like. Then there's food and water for the journey. Finding and storing enough to last all of us. That's if we don't find ourselves captured and shot on the way over. And the children, imagine the noise! We'd be arrested before we ever reached the boat.'

Another stretch of silence and then a chair creaked.

'Well,' Edith said. 'What if I was there to help?'

'What if you were where?'

'On the boat, you great oaf. What if I came with you?'

—

CARTER had always been a fitful sleeper. As a boy, his mother blamed his chronic insomnia on his overactive brain. He could still remember curling up with his head on her lap, whiling away the shadowed hours between night and morning by reciting all the battles of the Wars of the Roses or all the capital cities in Europe.

She had been a good woman: a gentle mother and a devoted wife. She coddled both of them terribly, husband and son alike, and Carter's father had never recovered from losing her. She'd died of a heart attack after a particularly nasty episode of pneumonia.

286

Father had glowered at him after the funeral. 'Disappointment took her,' he said. 'All she wanted was the hope of grandchildren.'

Exhausted and grief-stricken, Carter had snapped, 'People do not *die* from disappointment.'

'Still, if you'd shown but the slightest interest in *any* girl, it might have given her something to live for.'

Carter hadn't been able to meet his baleful glare, had tried to ignore the mounting guilt and shame he felt, and the suspicion, ridiculous as it was, that Father might be right.

Carter was unsurprised that his sleep was disturbed in the weeks that followed the incident involving Maurice and the medication he had procured for Marthe. She recovered from the infection, so it had been worth the risk, in that sense.

Nonetheless, it terrified him that he had taken the sulfa tablets that were intended to treat the Commandant. Every single one of them—four or five months' supply. At some point, the Commandant would discover they were missing and would know he was responsible.

But the summer blew past in a daze of sunlit days and very little of note occurred. Carter began to feel like he could afford to breathe again. Perhaps the Commandant would have no need of the medication, after all?

Then, one morning in September, Carter arrived at Royal Square later than usual, having overslept for once. He walked briskly to his office, expecting the Commandant or one of his cronies to be there waiting, ready to reprimand him for his tardiness.

But his office was empty. He set down his bag and prepared to sort through some prescriptions and old patient cases. It was then that he noticed that all his paperwork had been moved. Only marginally. As though someone had rifled through the papers and then attempted to return them to their original position. Some of his books had been moved too.

He opened his drawers. The same.

He knew, of course, that the Commandant occasionally asked one of his soldiers to examine the office and report back to him; the German had the paranoid nature common to most egomaniacs and demanded regular reports on all the men under his command.

But this was different: the furtive way in which every area of the office had clearly been closely examined and then objects returned to their—almost, but not quite—original position. *Some*one had been searching for *some*thing specific.

Carter checked the whole office again. Nothing had been taken. Even his wastepaper basket contained the same collection of aborted correspondence, old receipts and prescriptions, though all had been removed, smoothed out, read and then replaced. He couldn't, for the life of him, fathom what the Commandant would have wanted.

Then came the dull thud of realisation: what if the Commandant wasn't having his soldiers search for something that *was* there but confirming that something *wasn't* there?

Of course: the sulfa tablets.

Carter's mouth was dry, heart pulsing hotly in his throat, his fingertips. He took a steadying sip of water, tapped his pen on his desk. He resisted the urge to take a gulp of single malt, to drain a bottle dry, and instead sat, waiting.

Within ten minutes, a tall and well-muscled soldier appeared in the doorway and indicated that Carter should follow him.

'Never a moment's peace, eh?' He forced himself to laugh, but the soldier simply scowled.

Carter walked down the dark corridor with the sinking feeling of a man edging towards the precipice of a cliff. But when he entered the office, the Commandant was doubled over, clutching his stomach and moaning: clearly an attack of diverticulitis—his gluttony had precipitated the condition some months earlier. Abandoning all concerns about his own predicament, Carter rushed to his side and encouraged him to lie supine on the chaise longue.

'Don't talk for the moment. I will find you some morphine and water and then examine you.'

The soldier who had escorted him was still standing to attention.

'For God's sake, man,' Carter snapped. 'Don't just stand there. Fetch my medical bag! *Meine Tasche!* Run!'

The lout lumbered from the room, leaving Carter alone with the Commandant, who was still breathing heavily and clasping his abdomen. In spite of everything, Carter found himself pitying him—diverticular pain was absolutely agonising. Then, too, there was the possibility of a ruptured diverticula, an abscess or even a fistula forming, all of which would increase the man's pain and might even threaten his life.

Watching the German's pinched face, Carter couldn't help imagining this outcome: the wall of the intestine swelling, bulging, bursting. The poison spreading through that huge body. He visualised the Commandant's face, slack and innocuous in death…

But Carter felt nothing approaching the excitement and eagerness he would have anticipated in such a scenario. In fact, he felt the usual pulsing urgency that came with knowing that a patient's life was in danger; he felt, as he would have felt for any man, a desire to save his life. It was not simply a case of the Hippocratic Oath and his vow to *take care that patients suffer no hurt or damage.* It was the years he had spent battling that other enemy, Death, who was far more merciless than any man could hope to be.

Thoughts whirring, Carter started to examine the German, palpating his abdomen to find the area where the bowel lining had pushed through the muscle wall. The first thing he noticed was that the abdomen was softer than he might anticipate for someone with an inflamed or infected diverticula.

He asked a series of questions. Have you vomited? Have you experienced diarrhoea or constipation? When did the pain start? Indicate the level of pain you are currently experiencing, if ten is unbearable and zero is no pain at all.

The Commandant's answers were puzzling: yes, he had vomited, had been constipated for some days now; the pain had started just that morning and he would currently class it as nine on the pain scale—a point at which, Carter knew, patients were usually incapable of speech or coherent thought.

Then there was his temperature: normal, when everything suggested that he should be pyrexic. The German was not sweating excessively, and he did not have that fixed and staring look which patients often exhibit when their pain is so extreme that they can't function.

Carter busied himself looking into the mouth, ears and eyes, allowing himself time for thought. The Commandant's blue eyes were watchful, lucid. In spite of the occasional groans of pain that he gave, Carter noted that he continued to observe his every move. Sometimes, he even looked vaguely smug. Or amused? The slight shadow of a smile on his lips, when his mouth should have been a rictus of pain.

Carter felt a prickling fear across his scalp. *This is a performance*, he thought.

Just then the soldier returned with his medical bag. The Commandant sat up a little straighter.

'So, Doctor? What medicine will heal me?'

Carter blinked. The Commandant expected the sulfa tablets, but quite apart from the fact that Carter no longer *had* the tablets, the man's condition did not demand them. Yet, if he was challenged, the Commandant was liable to fly into a rage and have Carter punished for insubordination.

The image of a dark, damp train carriage flickered across Carter's mind—the crush of bodies swaying with the forward momentum of the train, passively waiting and absorbing every movement as they clattered towards Ravensbrük.

So he decided on a compromise. 'I will give you a painkiller, Commandant, to provide relief while your body battles the infection.'

'Painkillers, these will cure me? Make better my stomach, yes?'

'No. But you will be more comfortable. I believe you will recover in any case, without the need of further medication.'

Eyes bright, the Commandant chuckled. He seemed to have forgotten about feigning pain. His hands dropped back to his sides, and his breathing became regular, his expression triumphant.

'So I do not need medicines?'

'Goodness, no! It would be a waste—I would like to ensure that the sulfa tablets are reserved for...*emergencies*.'

The Commandant straightened up and clapped his hand on Carter's shoulder. 'I think I am feel better already.' He turned to the soldier and said, 'Is he not a wonderful doctor?'

Carter had a queasy moment of comprehension: in playing along with his pretence but refusing to give the Commandant his sulfa tablets, he had confirmed his responsibility for their disappearance. He should have either challenged the man outright when he found no evidence of illness, or he should have made a pretence of wanting to give him the tablets but finding them gone. By doing neither, he had revealed himself as guilty.

'If you need me,' he finally muttered, 'I'll be in my office.'

Usually, Carter would have been prevented from leaving until he was dismissed, but the Commandant simply watched him leave. As Carter was going out the door, the German called, 'You must go to your house and wait there, yes. I have no need of you, Doctor.'

'Of course. As you wish.'

Carter tried to press his trembling mouth into a smile, wondering how on earth he was going to escape the island.

—

SHE knew Gregor would have heard every word of their plans to escape, so after Maurice and the girl had gone, Edith opened the larder door and said, 'Go on then, arrest me!'

His expression was so aghast, and the idea was so ridiculous that they both giggled. Then his smile faded.

He sat at the table. 'I hurt for Claudine,' he said. 'This Hans, he is a bad man and my heart pains for her but…this is a dangerous thing. Escape. Many people try. For some, it is easy. But so many people? And children?' His eyes were wide, beseeching. 'I do not want them to catch you, Edith. They will not harm children if they catch, but they will kill you—' His voice cracked.

She smacked her hand on the table. 'No more talk of killing. Or catching, for that matter. If you're going to tell me anything, then talk to me about how to escape.'

He took her hand in his. 'I can help. I try. But if you go…'

She pulled her hands away. 'You mercenary bastard! You're fretting about how to save your own skin, not mine! Worried about where you'll hide? Where you'll get your food.'

'No! It is not this. I worry little for me, yes. But I think more for you—'

'You lying sod!' She was not usually one for huffing, but she stood up to go, ready to stamp out and slam the door.

He seized her hand again, pulled her back to the table. His skin was rough, his grip strong. 'You must not go!'

Before she could move away, he wrapped his arms around her waist and held her.

'You stay.'

She went to slap him off, but then she brought her hands to rest, first in his hair, then on the back of his neck. His skin was smooth. She ran her fingers over the fine shadow of light fuzz that ran down his neck and disappeared into his shirt. She had imagined that holding him would be like embracing a sack of bones. But she could feel the corded muscles under his skin and, as she closed her eyes, she could sense the thrumming of his heart. Or was it her own?

They stayed like that, for a long time. He was very warm. Then she leant down and pressed her lips against his rough cheek and untangled his arms from around her waist. She felt the sudden rush of cold. A tug of longing as she pulled her hand from his, but she paid it no mind; instead she went to gather some bladderwrack from the shoreline. Wonderful for arthritis.

His face, from behind the window, was small and white and sad. But she couldn't think on that now. She had to see Sarah.

They'd not spoken in so long—Edith felt a clutching of nerves as she tapped on the door. Claudine's maman opened it warily. She was plumper than Edith expected, but her eyes were lifeless. No more the young girl she'd once known. Time rises up to meet everyone.

Sarah raised her chin and narrowed her eyes. Edith smiled, though she half expected the woman to screech her off the step and slam the door.

But she simply folded her arms across her chest and said, 'What are *you* after, then?' She didn't ask Edith in, which was just as well, because Edith didn't know if she could trust herself not to claw Hans's eyes out.

Edith had a little speech prepared. She explained how she needed Claudine's help. She was ready to argue until she was blue in the face, but Sarah was nodding before she'd finished speaking and there was a glint of life in those eyes. She even smiled and said, 'Thank you,' and promised to send the children's rations over, along with any extras—meaning what Hans gave her.

Then Hans appeared. Pig-faced, just as Claudine had said.

'Where is Claudine?' His voice was cold.

Sarah flinched at his tone, but she said, 'Claudine and Francis are staying with Edith. She looked after them when they were young and she misses them. They're having a...holiday with her. Isn't that so?'

Edith looked Hans right in the eye. 'That's the way of it. Good to have children about. And she's lovely, Claudine. Such a good girl.'

'Yes, she is,' Hans said, and turned away.

But not before Edith had seen a flicker of *something*. A bleak rage, a craving. It was enough. She couldn't let the girl come back to the house—her mother couldn't protect her. And she mustn't stay on the island. She would be better off in England, where Edith could care for her. A place where the Germans had no sway.

As Edith turned to go, Sarah clasped her in a quick embrace. She whispered, 'Thank you,' again. It chilled Edith, that hasty clutch of her arms, that searing fear in her voice.

How much does she know? But some things are too terrible to dwell upon, so Edith didn't let herself ponder it for long. The knowledge of something doesn't change the fact of it.

She walked back along the shoreline, gathering bladder-wrack and counting the new buildings the Germans had slapped on to the seafront, blocks of grey amid the greenery. As if patches of the landscape had given up and turned into tombstones.

When she returned to the house with a sackful of seaweed, she couldn't find Gregor anywhere. Not in the larder, the garden, the shed. Remembering how she'd left him, full of sudden fear that he'd run away, she raced through the house, calling his name. She finally found him, curled up on her own bed, facing the wall.

He didn't move when she came in. She sat on the edge of the bed. She could feel the heat from his body.

'Please do not leave me,' he said.

She lay down behind him and put her hand upon his back. The warmth rested between them, something newly born and barely breathing.

Neither of them dared move for fear of smothering something so fragile and precious. Light seeped from the room. They slept, the burning space of a finger width between their bodies.

When Edith woke, it was dark and he was shouting, voice taut with fear. She flung her arms around him.

'Hush now.'

He turned to her. She kissed his cheeks. They were rough and wet and tasted of salt.

With Frank, it had always been eyes shut and count to twenty and roll over and go to sleep. This was different. The unpeeling of clothes. The unspooling of thought. Kisses tugged from the roots. Eyes open. Breath hot and gasping. The weight of him. The way she stretched herself to meet him. The way she pulled him closer, closer and then, even when closer wasn't possible, she wrapped herself around him, pulling him closer still, until she didn't know where her body ended and his began.

There were no lines in the darkness. No words or thoughts of young or old or Jèrriais or German.

In the grey light of the morning, Edith felt a panic where she thought there might be shame. Or worse, disgust. He smiled and stretched out his arm and pulled her towards him.

But by the time the sun was fully up in the sky, Edith knew she had to be out collecting more herbs and bartering for meat because they were still leaving.

It was a wrench even to be thinking of abandoning it all. Her little house. The sea. The size of the sky. That salt smell that bled into her very skin and was as familiar as the breath in her lungs.

Gregor.

But it was a different place, Jersey, since they had taken over. They had built grey walls and shelters. They had slapped concrete on to the beautiful old castles. They had chopped down whole areas of woodland. The land was butchered. Scarred.

They had changed the people, too.

Of course, Edith had noted the difference as soon as they started evacuating, even before the Germans arrived. Folk raiding their friends' houses the moment they'd left: making off with their good china, their kitchen table, even the pictures off the walls. The rugs that had been there for three generations of babes to lie on—all of it gone in an afternoon.

The Gallichans weren't even evacuating, just went to the harbour to watch. They came back within the hour to find their neighbours 'borrowing' their rugs and saucepans—the sheets from their beds, for heaven's sake. No room for sentimentality when the sky is on fire.

After the empty houses had all been stripped bare and folks had taken whatever they could carry, the rooms didn't stay unfilled for long. They were overrun by the soldiers as soon as they arrived. Four or five of the Germans, crammed in together in the tiniest of houses, living like animals in muck.

Suddenly, Edith couldn't think of leaving her little house.

Couldn't imagine letting soldiers come to squat in it and inviting the vermin in, and pissing in her good kitchen sink. The very thought of it made her shudder.

She tried to explain that to Maurice, but he said, 'What will it matter? You won't be living here to see it.'

'But where would we go in England?' Edith asked. 'Who would know me?'

'Why the worry? You're useful and you've a friendly sort of face.'

She snorted. 'Good of you to say so.'

'Now, don't be like that. I simply meant that you'll have no trouble talking to people.'

'At my age, though. I've birthed two generations of some families here.'

'You should have time for at least one more batch of babes then,' Maurice grinned—there was wickedness in his eyes since he'd seen a chance of escaping. A humour fashioned from hope. 'Somewhere new, before you're gone.'

'Charmed, Maurice, I'm sure. *You* can jest. You're still young.'

'Ah, come now, Edith. I mean no harm. It's only...I *have* to go. I knew it all along, but I didn't think I could put Marthe through it, knowing she might not survive the journey. But the girl made me think on how it is here for all of us—the pain of it. Like living in a furnace. It's changed everybody. War's blackened our hearts. And if Marthe is set to...to die...then I won't have it happen here, under this. I'm not saying you must come along for me, or for Marthe, but leaving you—well, it would be like leaving family.'

She waved a hand at him, wiping away the prickling sensation in her eyes.

'Stop it now. What do you think you're doing to me? You're a cunning one, Maurice Pipon.'

'I mean every word. You're the closest to family we have. It would break my heart to leave you here, Edith.'

There was a wrenching in her chest, a burning ache in her throat. She scowled at her knitting until she could talk again.

Then she said, 'I haven't made my mind up between staying and leaving yet. But what about the land? Won't it hurt you? Leaving the place that birthed you?'

Maurice shrugged. 'No beating heart in sand and soil, is there, Edith?'

Those words drove her to thinking. She took to walking out, in all weathers and times of day. Rambling over the beaches and along the cliff paths and across the fields. Anywhere they wouldn't have laid bombs in the soil.

Sometimes she carried Francis with her, if he was sleepy. He pointed at the sea, the trees. They watched seagulls together, screeing across the free and open sky. And, in the end, if she walked next to the sea for long enough, the wombing of the waves lulled him, and he nodded off.

She trudged for miles: only her thoughts and that little child's heavy body in her arms. Then came the sudden realisation like a detonation in her head. She never expected the remembering to steal up on her like that and snatch the breath from her mouth.

That babe of hers. Born warm, but quickly cooling and cold. Close-eyed and screwed-up bud picked too soon.

Edith had stowed that scrap of her flesh in the ground without a name or a stone to mark the place, but she knew it as well as she knew where her own eye was, her mouth, her heart.

But for all the times she'd thought of it—that cold little body, with the tiny hands and feet and the lips quite blue—she hadn't thought what it would be to abandon it. To travel across the water to another country, perhaps never come back. Who would be there to lay flowers in the spring? Who would know to put a holly wreath down, come Christmas? That piece of her body would lie in the ground. Frozen, forgotten. Once she was dead, there would be no one to know it had ever been at all.

So she poured herself into the thought of staying. When Gregor saw her unpacking her suitcase, he seized her and kissed her from top to toe.

Laughing, they were always laughing. The sound gusted out of her mouth and into his and then back again. The warmth of sharing that laughter. The warmth of being known, being understood. It was strange to find home in another body from another country.

Strange, too, how life could change through a few moments. Weeks ago, she barely knew who he was. Now she couldn't imagine taking a breath without him.

It was bad timing; that was all. Claudine came running to find her on the beach when it happened. Edith had been picking through one of the deeper rock pools, looking for anemones and dead men's fingers when she heard the girl shrieking from the beach. Something in her voice made Edith drop her net and run.

Claudine kept up her screaming. When Edith was close enough, she could hear her shouting, 'He's found him! Maurice! He's found him.' And Edith knew, from the dread in Claudine's eyes, what she meant.

They raced up the beach while the girl puffed out what had happened: Maurice had brought Marthe around. She was sleepy, so he'd taken her to Edith's room—and found Gregor crouched in the corner, gun in his hand.

'Bloody foolish men. What was Gregor doing with his gun?'

'I think he thought it was a patrol. Now they're both shouting. Maurice said he'd kill him.'

When Edith ran into the room, she half expected to find both of them bleeding or one of them with a bullet in him. But they were facing each other, gun and knife in hand.

Edith said to Claudine. 'Go and fetch some wood from the shed, will you, my love?' When the girl didn't move, Edith snapped, 'Go now. No need for you to see this.'

Claudine scampered from the room but Edith saw her crouch behind the door to listen.

'Don't come any closer, Edith,' Maurice growled. 'I found him here. Waiting for you with a gun, he was.'

'Put the knife down, Maurice.' She stepped between them, trembling hands raised.

'Don't be a fool, Edith. Move over. Now.'

'Gregor, put the gun down. Drop it.'

Gregor grunted, let his hand fall to his side. He didn't drop the gun, of course—but then Maurice was still pointing that knife at him.

Edith reached out and took Maurice's arm, pushed it down. He glared, but he too let his hand drop.

Edith took a breath. 'Now, that nonsense is done with. I'll not have guns or knives in my house, do you hear?'

Maurice said, 'You called him Gregor.'

'Well, his name isn't Albert.'

'You know him by name?'

'He came to me for help. What was I to do? They'll ship him off to Germany. The Commandant's got it in for him. That arm of his.'

Maurice narrowed his eyes. 'You've been *sheltering* him. A German soldier? *Helping* him?'

Edith kept her gaze steady. 'As you see.'

Maurice threw his knife to the floor, turned and stamped out of the room and into the garden.

Edith turned to Gregor, pressed a quick kiss on to his lips. 'You fool. A gun?'

He shook his head. 'I am sorry—'

'No time for that now. There's a half bottle of whisky on the top shelf in the larder. Three glasses. Wait in the kitchen.'

She clasped his poor arm as he walked past her, crammed all her feeling into that quick compression of her hand. But there's no way to convey the fierce burn of love through a momentary touch.

Maurice was sitting at the end of the garden, in Gregor's old spot. She'd thought she'd find him furious, but instead he patted the stone next to him. She sat.

'You're staying?' he said.

Edith hesitated. 'Perhaps. As I said, I'm torn on it.'

'The reason you're torn—it's *him*, isn't it?'

'Among other things. You're angry.'

'A little. For the most part I'm thrown. You're the last person I'd have suspected of bedding down with the enemy.'

Her stomach jolted. 'I'm *not*—'

'Ha! I didn't mean it like that. I'm not accusing you of being a Jerry-Bag. Not at *your* age.'

He laughed, but there was something in the way he looked at her: a watchful, attentive sort of scrutiny.

She couldn't remember the last time she'd felt a heat in her cheeks like it. There was a flash of recognition in his eyes; he gave a sharp intake of breath and then coloured himself, and looked away.

Edith fixed her eyes on the shrieking gulls, sailing the wash of the wind across the sea. She made her voice brisk.

'Well, enough fussing. It is what it is; I'll not have the Germans doing harm to anyone, if I can help it. Even one of their own. Now will you come and talk with him? He's a good man. But you know that already.'

She marched back inside, cheeks still blazing. Maurice followed, slowly. When she risked glancing at him, his eyes were wide with incredulity.

'Come on out from behind that door, Claudine,' she called. 'No danger now, and you're old enough to hear this.'

Claudine fell in next to her and held her hand. Edith felt a glow. What it would have been, she thought, to have a child of my own.

Gregor was standing in the kitchen, scowling. Maurice stood across the table from him, glaring back. Eyeing each other like wary dogs.

'For goodness sake, sit!' Edith cried. 'Both of you. Here. Drink.'

They didn't take their eyes off each other as they sat down.

Edith sighed. 'I'll start, then. Maurice, this is Gregor. He's hiding here so that he's not dragged back to Germany and shot for the sake of some scars.'

They all stared at his arm.

'Claudine's soldier friend was named Gregor,' said Maurice.

'The same,' Edith said. 'He's been good to both of us. And to you too, if you recall.'

Maurice snorted. 'Why didn't you tell me he was here?'

'I knew you'd not like it. In your mind, every soldier is a villain. Even one who has helped you gather food enough for months and carried your wife to Dr Carter's. You think every soldier on the island is Hitler's own disciple. But they're boys caught up in it, most of them. Just doing what they must to save their skins. Same as us.'

Maurice glared, but he didn't contradict her. 'And you're staying here for *him?* This soldier? His life means that much to you?'

'It isn't *only* him. But if I leave, he dies.' She didn't mention that little body in the ground, or the way the land tugged at her. It never paid to sound like a foolish old woman.

'And without you to help us,' Maurice rejoined, '*we* will die. Rowing across the channel with Marthe and the two children? It's laughable. Even if I reach the boat, I'll be shot before I've rowed three strokes.'

'And what will you do if…when you are in England?'

'I'll fish. Find myself somewhere to live on the coast. Where Marthe can sit out on the beach without me fearing for her. She used to love dabbling her toes in the sand—'

'And what if they sign you up to fight? Had you thought of that?'

His face was grim, his lips pulled back into a snarl. 'I won't leave Marthe. They can't make me. But once she is gone, I'll do whatever they tell me. It won't matter anymore. Nothing will.'

Edith nodded. She could understand that sensation: life like sudden gold between the fingers because of the beating heart in another body.

'But at least we're not being bombed,' she said. 'Surely it's safer here, if you know what you're about, which you do—'

'*Safer?* Nothing is safe here. Not for any of us, but especially not for the women. We've seen what the Germans have done to—' He looked at Claudine and said, 'Sorry, my love, I didn't mean—'

Claudine said, softly, 'It doesn't matter. You're right. We can't stay. I shan't stay.'

Sometimes, when someone is right, there's nothing more to say. They sat and they drank, refilled their glasses, drank again.

Edith didn't look at Gregor, couldn't meet his eye in case he saw her weighing his life against the child's.

There's a reason the hangman wears a mask.

She closed her eyes, balanced the scales in her mind. I could always come back, she thought. Maurice had said it— no beating heart in sand and soil. He and the children needed her more than she needed the island. Jersey had been around for thousands of years; it would be there to return to, after the war was over and Hans and his ilk were gone. She tried not to imagine a future when all the world might be German.

She tried to imagine a life without Gregor's smile, his warmth, his arms around her in the darkness.

But it would happen, one way or another, the separation. His sickly wife back in Germany needed him more than Edith did. It's a peculiar feeling, measuring out *need* and *hope* and *love*, as though they are liquids that can be crammed into cups.

Edith knew that life without Gregor would be hard to bear. After he returned to his wife, she would feel his absence like the exposed skin of a raw wound. The thought of that pain was enough to make her want to hold him here on the island as her own hostage, her moment of stolen peace.

But it is wrong to seize ownership of something simply to fulfil a yearning. Doing that would make her no better than the Germans themselves.

After countless ticking minutes, Gregor put his good hand on hers. 'You will do best thing,' he said. 'I cannot think bad of you for this.'

Edith clasped his hand, stroked his fingers. A thought sprouted, blossomed.

'Maurice,' Edith said. 'Your boat, it's big?'

He held up his hands and shook his head. 'Oh no. Don't think of it. The last thing I'm having is a bloody soldier in on it.'

'Why ever not? Another pair of hands at the oars.'

There was a short silence, then Gregor said, 'I have actually only one hand.' He grinned.

The air whooshed out of Edith's lungs. Before she knew it, they were all laughing, bent double, tears streaming.

They talked long into the evening. Gregor had some paperwork he could give Maurice: a fishing licence and a late-curfew pass he had stolen.

'I take for bribe people,' he admitted. 'And I know where we can find a motor for your boat.'

Maurice jumped to his feet, almost knocking over the chair. 'I don't know what to say. Edith, are you hearing this? We might actually make it across! Alive!'

'Marvelous, isn't it?'

But after Maurice had gone and she was lying with her head on Gregor's chest, running her fingers over his hard muscles and harder bones, listening to the insistent thump of his heart, she said, 'What will you do, eh? A German soldier in England?'

'They will hurt me?'

'Hurt you? I hope not. You'll be a prisoner of war. But the English aren't brutal like—'

'Like Germans?'

'Sorry, I didn't mean—'

'It is not bad for you saying. I know this.'

He kissed her cheek, then her lips, pressing her against him. She could feel his need, his desperation, his simmering fear.

—

TURNED out Gregor wasn't a bad sort—for a German, anyway.

The night after they decided he would help them to escape, Maurice found himself creeping out at midnight with Gregor to steal the boat engine from one of the guard outposts while the soldiers were out patrolling.

Gregor kept watch, while Maurice ran and snatched the engine. They hid it in Maurice's boat, in the caves at Devil's Hole.

Scrambling down to the caves was difficult, even for Maurice: it was a sharp drop and the sound of skittering stones shattered the silent, yawning darkness below; he gripped Gregor's hand when he thought he might fall.

Time was past when he would have pushed the soldier and been glad to watch him smash on to the jaws of those rocks, broken body wrenched away by the sea, blood pluming out into the brackish water. But no more—Maurice was done with that corrosive hatred.

They sat and shared a cigarette and the last of the whisky from Edith's larder. The darkness hid his face and his arm. He could have been Maurice's friend of many years, out to help him poach oysters from the French.

The next thing Maurice had to do was meet with the French fishermen and ask them about the German boats. They agreed to keep an eye out and to draw the patrols away if the group were sighted escaping. They had their fee; Maurice expected that.

They asked for payment in medicine. Their children were catching sicknesses in their blood from a scratch on their leg because French doctors had nothing to give them.

The guilt kept Maurice awake some nights: the thought that, after they'd gone, the Jèrriais would have less medicine because they'd traded it to the French in return for safe passage. But everyone did what they must to survive.

Maurice planned to ask Carter for the medicine. He pounded on Carter's door early the next morning. He gave it a minute or so and then he hammered again. Maurice knew he was there because his fancy shoes were sat outside the door, almost as if he *wanted* someone to run off with them.

Strange.

Another minute and he knocked again. He kept banging on

and on, until he heard the scratch of the key.

The door opened a crack. Carter peered out, watchful eyes of a cornered animal, hair standing in all directions.

'Oh, Maurice,' he said. 'Come in, won't you. My apologies for all this.' He gestured at his chaotic living room: clothes and papers everywhere and the sort of damp and fusty smell Maurice associated with stables.

Carter looked like he'd hardly slept in the months since he had seen him last. His face was rough with a straggly beard and his clothes had that sour animal stench of being worn day-in, day-out without washing.

Carter rubbed his eyes. 'How is Marthe? Recovering well, I hope?'

'Yes, she is much better, thank you. Though we're down to the last tablets. I don't know what we'll do if she becomes ill again...'

'I'm sorry.'

Nothing for it but the truth. Maurice took a breath and let it all out in a rush.

'We're...off. Escaping. I've taken your advice. And I came to ask...if you'd help?'

'Tea!' Carter jumped up. 'My dear fellow, please do forgive my rudeness. Would you like a cup of tea? Only rosehip, of course—haven't had the real stuff in an age. I'll put a pan on right away. I don't have any sugar, I'm afraid. But who expects sugar these days?'

And he rushed off to the kitchen before Maurice could say anything more.

Very strange. Maurice sat, frowning, a little dazed. From the kitchen he heard pans banging and some muttering.

'Is everything all right in there?' he called.

'Yes, I'm just—no bother. I'm...'

Maurice shook his head and went into the kitchen. Carter hadn't even put water in the pan. He was leaning over the hot stovetop, dry pan scorching. Eyes streaming from the smoke and he was coughing.

'For God's sake! You'll burn the place down!'

Maurice pushed him aside, took the pan off the heat, shut the stove and sat him down at the table. As he opened the door and waved the smoke out, he felt the beginnings of fear. What on earth was the matter with him? Was he ill? Drunk? Maurice couldn't smell alcohol. The doctor was behaving as though he wasn't all there.

Carter blinked, stared at Maurice like he'd just this minute noticed him.

'Forgive me, how rude of me not to offer you a cup of tea. It's a devil to acquire these days but I have some rosehip in. No sugar. Rationing, I'm afraid.' He shambled across to pick up the red-hot pan and replace it on the stove.

Maurice caught hold of his arm just in time and wrenched it away. 'What the *devil* has taken over you?'

But Carter didn't say a word. He just stared at Maurice's hand clutching his arm, as if it was nothing to do with him. It must have hurt, Maurice's grip, but he kept on smiling in that same vacant way. It made Maurice think of the fixed grin he'd once seen on the corpse of a fisherman. The man had become tangled in his nets and been dragged from his boat and under the water. When they'd pulled him out, he'd been quite dead, but the pain and fear of drowning had set his face into a ghastly smile.

So Maurice treated Carter as he did Marthe, when she was having one of her bad spells: he sat him down in a chair, gave him a blanket and tucked it right up to his chin. He boiled the rosehips, though he could have done with something stronger himself. He made Carter sip the tea, and sat and waited for the man to come back to himself.

After a while, Carter lost that blank, empty look. Stretched and yawned as if he'd been asleep. When he shivered, Maurice fetched another blanket, tucked it around him. He was thin— thinner than he should have been, in the pay of the Germans.

'Thank you so much,' he finally said and gave an unsteady smile.

Maurice nodded. 'What's troubling you then, Doctor?'

'I've taken the Commandant's personal store of sulfa tablets.' Carter's voice was barely a whisper, his eyes empty. 'I'm a dead man.'

'But there's no reason the Commandant should find you out, is there?' Maurice said. 'It's been months and nothing has happened.'

'He *knows*. He's dismissed me.'

'How could he know *you* took them?' Maurice's throat tightened with fear. 'You're sure?'

'Quite sure.'

'Well, then—and I don't mean to give you more of a scare, Doctor—but why are you still alive? You must be mistaken. It's easy to grow jumpy when you're hiding something.'

Carter ran his bony hands through his hair and made a noise somewhere between a sob and a howl.

'That's the worst of it! I don't know *why* I'm still alive. I suspect he is delaying the inevitable to torture me. He will enjoy the thought of me suffering. It's the worst part, isn't it? The waiting? And he'll be laughing about that. But it will happen at some point. The firing squad, I expect. Ravensbrük, if I'm lucky.'

He laughed—a savage shredding sound. There were tears in his eyes.

Maurice felt a chill in his gut. 'Don't talk like that.' But guilt had made him breathless; if Carter was right then the other man might die because of the medicine he'd forced him to steal.

'It's the truth. He *can't* let me live.'

Carter looked up at his window as if expecting to see a patrol there, waiting, guns poised.

Maurice found himself saying, 'Come with us then. To England. I'm taking Marthe and Edith and the two Duret children. And…a soldier.'

'A *German* soldier? Escaping with you?' Carter's eyes were round. 'But that is lunacy. Can you trust him?'

'I don't know if I can trust anyone, German or Jèrriais. But he's better off with us than with his own lot, and that's surety enough for me.'

'And am I to translate?'

'No, he speaks English. You can care for Marthe on the journey and I could use another pair of rowing arms—'

Maurice wavered then. Carter didn't look like much of a rower—he was gaunt and slump-shouldered with despair. The last thing we need is more weight in the boat, he thought.

But it was too late to take it back. Carter's eyes had brightened, his back straightened.

With some of the strength of his old voice, he said, 'But how the devil will you manage it? With a soldier and children? And

Marthe? I don't mean to be cruel, but…it's absurd. You'll be shot, the lot of you.'

'And you'll be shot if you stay.'

Carter put his head in his hands. 'How do you propose to evade the patrols?'

'I know most of the patrol times—from the fishing, you see. The problem will be keeping the children quiet.'

Carter gave a feeble smile. 'So I'm to play nursemaid, am I?'

Maurice sighed. No point in lying. 'In a way. And you can help Marthe, once we reach the mainland. But we need supplies. I've persuaded some of the French fishermen to distract any patrols and to help us navigate through some of the reefs out past Guernsey so I don't take the bottom out of the boat. But they want medicine.'

'And you want me to obtain it for you?' Carter's eyes were hard.

Maurice met his stare. 'Yes.'

To his surprise, Carter gave a strangled laugh and stood up.

'As if obtaining medicine for you hadn't landed me in this mess in the first place. What do you need?'

—

THEY waited for two days for Dr Carter to bring the medicine. At the end of the second day, he knocked on Edith's door. But, Claudine saw, he was empty-handed.

'I'm sorry,' he said. 'Truly I am. The hospital won't allow me anything. And taking medicine from the Commandant's personal supply is too great a risk.'

'You must have contacts in there?' Maurice said. 'A man like you makes friends.'

'*Friends?* You're talking about German soldiers.'

'Yes. And *you've* spent the war cosying up to them. So there must be one of them you can trust?'

Dr Carter looked at the floor. 'I'm sorry. It wasn't worth the risk. It might have given everything away.'

'Don't give me that. It wasn't about the risk to *us*. You're always about saving your own skin, aren't you?'

'Leave him be, Maurice, can't you see he's in pieces?' Edith muttered. She addressed Carter brightly. 'Come, sit, Doctor. I've just boiled up some nettle leaves for tea.'

Carter sat down. He looked shaky and smaller than Claudine remembered him.

'I'm not sure I would hold up under interrogation,' he said. 'I feel I can't trust myself... You must think me a coward.'

Maurice snorted and went back to mending some rope.

Edith's voice was kind. 'Of *course* not. You're right to worry about keeping your mouth shut—I've heard they don't hold back during questioning, and pain is enough to start anyone's tongue wagging. And we're none of us keen to be put in front of a firing squad. Isn't that right, Maurice?'

Maurice scowled and didn't look up from his rope.

Then Claudine had a thought. A silly idea, probably, but still...

'Why doesn't Edith simply make up some of her plant medicines for the fishermen?'

'Don't be foolish, Claudine,' Maurice said. 'I know you're trying to help, but you're best to hold your peace until we have things clear. There's a good girl.'

314

'Well…but wait,' said Edith. 'Why didn't we think of that? She's on to something there, Maurice. I've plenty of remedies. We're running out of other ideas. It can't hurt.'

Maurice's voice was loud and sharp. 'Well, of *course*! Why didn't I think of that before? I'm *sure* the French will risk their necks for a few ground-up leaves and sticks. I know *I* would.'

'Mocking doesn't suit you, Maurice. And we have precious little choice. So you're best to hold your peace, just until we have things clear. There's a good man.' Edith gave Claudine a wink and Maurice let out another exasperated sigh.

Edith filled a sack with all her different powders and teas and poultices and gave it to Maurice.

'We'd best hope none of us are ill,' she murmured.

Maurice and Edith had made Claudine promise not to tell anyone about escaping. She knew that Maman might try to stop her going, and then she would have to stay at home forever, with Hans wanting her to be a woman.

When she knew Hans would be out on patrol, Claudine went home to visit Maman. Inside, in the kitchen, she held Claudine's face between her hands and squeezed her cheeks.

'Are you eating? The extra meat I've sent?'

'Yes, Maman.'

'I can't stand to see you thin—you know that.'

'I'm eating, Maman. The meat. The butter too.'

The tightness in her face softened. 'You're happy with Edith? You look happy.'

When Claudine thought of leaving Maman forever, everything grew dark. She walked down to the beach and looked out across the sea. It shimmered and glittered with sunlight and shadows. She imagined the yawning miles of black water breathing beneath the surface. If she looked towards England, she could only see the sky and then the stark, flat line of darkness where the horizon disappeared. It was where the wind and storms came from. Fear and anticipation made her quiver.

She wondered where they would go in England, what they would do. Would there be bombs? At the start of the war, when the Germans first arrived, Claudine had wanted to go to England, to see Papa. But now, time and pain had taught her better: she knew he probably wasn't there anymore. Perhaps he wasn't anywhere, and even if he was he would be a different person now. Like Dr Carter, like Maurice. Like Maman.

Claudine watched the waves beating against the rocks again and again. They had taught her, at school, that over millions of years, water could wear a cliff face away until it was nothing more than specks of sand to be blown about by the wind. Anything could change, they said: it was all a matter of time and pressure.

—

UNDER the circumstances, Carter had thought it best to maintain a low profile. So he had stayed at home, even when he felt the walls were closing in on him.

Whenever he thought about returning to England, he tried to picture Father's face. But he could see only his back: the hard lines of his head and shoulders, like the crenellated walls of a fortress, dressed in his Warwickshire regiment uniform. Ypres.

Amiens. The Somme. He had survived them all and returned home to the disappointment of a son who cried over a scraped knee and never took his nose out of a blasted book.

Carter could recall the exact timbre of Father's voice when he'd told him to get out of his sight.

He would have to stretch the truth, he knew, when accounting his experience of the war. Any details of his care for the Commandant would be best left unmentioned. None of the English doctors, who would no doubt judge him *a traitor* for his actions, *none* of them had been on the island, under the suffocating weight of occupation, had been trapped and bullied until they no longer recognised themselves or their actions.

Father would judge him, too, if he knew the truth.

Sometimes, in the dark belly of the night, Carter was convinced they would all be captured. He found himself pacing the length of his hallway, as if he was already imprisoned and awaiting the German guns. At other moments, he daydreamed about what he might do if they arrived safely on the mainland.

Will.

Would he have forgiven Carter for the years of abandonment and silence? Perhaps he would have made a life with someone else? The thought was agonising. Still, Carter couldn't help wishing for Will to be there, waiting for him. He couldn't help fanning that small spark of hope, that somehow, this time, he would return to England and find himself braver.

While Carter was in search of some sort of distraction from these thoughts, an idea evolved. It came to him in the dead of night, when his ravenous guts kept him awake. He had failed to procure medication for the French fisherman and he wanted to make a contribution to the escape—and now it occurred to him that he could barter his newest shoes for food.

The offending footwear had remained on his doorstep for over a week. He had hoped that, by leaving the shoes in plain sight, he might have encouraged some opportunist to steal them. At least then somebody would benefit from the 'reward' the Commandant had pressed upon Carter.

The shoes—glowing, mahogany leather—would have cost a fortune even before the war. In a situation where most men had been forced to wear wooden clogs or shoes that had been resoled with old bicycle tyres, Carter's were invaluable.

Clement Hacquoil was the man to go to, Carter was sure of it. Not just because of their shared past, but because he was one of the few men on the island who didn't condemn Carter as a traitor. The butcher himself had been the subject of no small amount of haranguing from the islanders after openly supplying meat to the Commandant.

Hacquoil had never intimated to Carter that he condoned his position with the Germans, and Carter had never demonstrated any approval of Hacquoil's actions.

But at some moments when they exchanged meat for money, with a queue of bone-thin faces clamouring outside the shop, something had passed between them. A look of perhaps not camaraderie but *comprehension*.

Carter went to Hacquoil's early in the morning, once the usual post-curfew rush had died down.

Clement didn't look up from sharpening his knives when Carter entered the shop.

'Bouônjour.' The butcher's water-logged voice crackled but

Carter had become accustomed to ignoring these sounds that punctuated his speech.

'Good day, to you, Clement. How are you this morning?'

'Weary, Doctor. It's this arm, keeping me awake. I thought scars had no feeling in them, but these itch in the night. I have to wear mittens to keep from scratching myself raw.'

'I'll see what I can do. It may be that Edith Bisson has something to help you.'

'I appreciate that, Doctor. Thank you. I'll have a half a chicken sent over to Royal Square later. Can't spare a whole one, but the Commandant will be happy with half. And I'll let him know it's on account of you. Your help.'

'Many thanks, but that won't be necessary. I don't find myself at Royal Square much these days.'

Clement stopped sharpening the knives for a moment. 'Oh?'

Carter affected a light-hearted tone. 'Yes, he has no...need of me at present.'

'No *need* of you?' Clement leant across the counter. His fixed grin gave the impression that he found everything amusing, but his eyes were dark. 'That's not a position you want to find yourself in, is it?'

Carter managed to squeeze a chuckle through gritted teeth. 'Oh, I'm not concerned.'

Perhaps it was just the slant the scars lent his face, but Clement suddenly seemed to be assessing Carter, weighing him as one might judge a lamb shank. Then his lips stretched as wide as his tight, shiny skin would allow.

'Good man. Can't change a thing by worrying, can you? So, what can I do for you then, Doctor?'

Carter drew the shoes from his medical bag, placed them on the counter, between the chicken necks and the pigs' trotters.

'I wish to exchange these for as much meat as you can give me. Preferably dried stuff.'

Clement laid down his knives and looked at Carter as if he had never seen him before.

'And what would I be doing with those fancy shoes then? Up to my ankles in sheep guts in finest leather? A right picture I'd make.'

Carter flushed. Why was the man being so obtuse? Perhaps this was some sort of test?

'Well, of course I did not...intend them for *you*. I merely hoped you might be able to...*trade* them. On the black market. For some decent meat.'

Clement glared. 'I don't know what you're on about, Doctor. Now, I'm busy, if you don't mind? *À bétôt.*'

And damn the man if he didn't turn and walk back behind the curtain and into his own house. Left Carter standing there, staring at those bloody shoes. It was as if Carter had proffered the decomposing carcass of a rat, squashed by a bicycle.

Briefly, he considered shouting after Clement, but instead he made an obscene gesture at the curtain and felt immediately foolish, even though the shop was empty. He stuffed the shoes back into his medical bag and left.

Once outside, a sudden chill twisted his guts. He leant against the wall and wondered how he could have committed such a grave error. If Clement was not involved in the black market then he'd essentially just incriminated himself.

You damned fool.

He was under enough suspicion because of the sulfa tablets.

Once news of this event reached the Commandant's ears, Carter's death sentence would be expedited; he was quite sure of it.

But *how* could he have been so misinformed? Before the islanders had stopped coming to him altogether for medical care, numerous patients had mentioned Clement's involvement with the black market. And Carter himself, while he was collecting meat for the Commandant, had seen Clement whispering to islanders: the sort of back-alley mutterings that had left him in no doubt that an illicit bargain was being made.

He began perspiring most unpleasantly, a trickle of sweat creeping down his spine. He removed his coat. However, the sun wasn't yet up and the sea seemed to radiate cold. He quickly grew chilled and began to shiver as he walked home.

Along the seafront, the sky was a tarnished, metallic grey, and the land, too, seemed to be shaded a dull monochrome: loops of barbed wire marked the *verboten* areas, overgrown by sprawling weeds; nature cared nothing for man's edicts. The wire was coiled in neat spirals: a jagged reminder of the unspooled viscera of Hitler's dream.

Suddenly, Carter felt a hand tap on his shoulder. It was Hacquoil's young daughter, a small, sickly looking child, who had run barefoot after him and now stood, shivering.

Her voice was barely more than a whisper. Carter strained to hear her above the wind.

'Does your mother or father need me?'

He pointed at his medical bag and mimed putting on a stethoscope, as though he was talking to a deaf-mute.

She shook her head. Carter leant in closer and caught her words: 'Papa says to come now. But through the back door, sir. Into our house, not the shop. Don't be seen, he says.' And then she ran back, her feet slapping on the cobbles.

Carter stared after her, then glanced about. The street was quite deserted.

After a jittery minute of hesitation, he walked around to the back door of the butcher's house. It was bordered by a small garden, immaculately kept rows of vegetables, untouched by the soldiers. He knocked lightly on the door, which was opened immediately by the same girl.

Hacquoil was seated at the table in the cramped kitchen, staring off into the distance. He rubbed at his hands repeatedly, at that skin that had melted and fused together.

'Doctor,' he said, standing up. 'You're a bright man and I owe you my life…but what on *earth* were you thinking?'

'I don't follow.'

'Coming in like that. Setting your shoes—*those shoes*, which the Commandant gave you—on my counter, bold as brass, and then shouting about the black market for all to hear.'

Carter's stomach dropped. 'Forgive me. I've clearly misunderstood. I believed you had dealings with the…black market. I apologise if…'

'For Christ's sake man, stop quibbling. Sit down.'

Hacquoil wiped his chin and gestured at the chair opposite him.

'You've not caught the wrong end of the stick. I buy and sell and trade without the Germans knowing—or sometimes with the soldiers themselves. It takes all sorts.'

'I see.'

'But there's a *way* of going about it. What if some fellow had seen those shoes—'

This was too much; the butcher was treating him like a

bloody idiot. 'But there wasn't a soul there, Hacquoil. I made sure of that. What sort of clown do you take me—'

'And what if someone had walked in at that moment, eh, with us having a cosy chat about the black market, and *those* shoes, those *bloody* shoes, sitting on the counter?'

A vein pulsed at Hacquoil's temple. On his disfigured face, it gave the impression that the thickened skin itself was shifting.

'So,' he said, finally. 'It's meat you're after then? Dried stuff, you say?'

Carter felt a hot surge of relief. 'Oh, so you *will* trade then? Thank you.'

'I'll do what I can. No promises. It's short notice.'

Carter nodded vigorously. 'Of course.'

'It's risky. Putting a rush on things. But as it's you and…' He held his hands out again, gestured at his distorted face.

'Thank you. I'm most grateful.'

'You haven't seen what I can find you yet. But it's meat you're wanting?'

'Yes, yes…ah, mostly. Dried—cured where possible. In any case, meat which won't spoil easily.'

Silence for a beat or two, Hacquoil's eyes suddenly watchful. 'Need it to last a while, do you?'

Carter leant back in his chair, tried to look nonchalant. 'Putting a bit by, you see, for winter. But I'd like a decent amount. Enough to give out to patients, if they need it.'

Hacquoil blinked.

'Or anything you can find,' Carter said, hurriedly. 'I know times are hard.'

The butcher drew out a pencil and notepad from a drawer and, after wedging the pencil into his shiny claw, scribbled a few notes in what looked to be some sort of shorthand.

'Tomorrow morning,' he said, 'before curfew—so you'll need to tread quietly, keep a lookout.'

Carter nodded, mouth too dry to speak.

Hacquoil narrowed his eyes and gave him that measuring look again. 'You could have it over a few weeks, you see, the meat? You'll get a good amount for shoes like those. The parcel will be heavy.'

Carter squared his shoulders. 'I would like it all together, please. I will manage.'

Hacquoil nodded, scribbled something else illegible. 'Off on your travels somewhere then, are you?'

Carter went cold. Then he saw Hacquoil had shaped his face into the grimace that now passed for a smile. Carter forced himself to chuckle.

'Haha! Ah, yes. Fancied a short holiday—while the weather holds.'

They laughed together at that, though Carter felt queasy.

Despite his trepidation, the next morning went smoothly as Carter collected the large, heavy parcel and returned home. He walked briskly and managed to avoid the patrols.

Once home, he drained the dregs of his last bottle of whisky. High tide was two days away.

—

THE day before they were set to leave, Edith walked halfway

around the island, seeing as many folk as she could. She gave Mrs Fauvel some bladderwrack for her arthritis. The old woman wheezed and scowled as she told Edith that Lucy Tadier had been caught sheltering a Russian prisoner of war.

Mrs Fauvel's hands were like claws. They quivered as she spoke and her eyes were bright with horrified excitement.

'Battered her door down in the middle of the night, if you'd believe it? Hundreds of soldiers, so they say. Dragged them out into the street—her kicking and screaming; him yelling fit to raise the dead. They'll shoot him and it'll be a boat to Lord knows where for her, poor love. Bailiff Coutanche tried to persuade the Commandant to send her to Gloucester Street Prison instead, but he was having none of it.'

Edith tried to keep her face smooth, but the tale cut close to the bone, and her voice sounded too high-pitched—she knew it.

'How did they find out? The soldiers?'

'Ha! Well, how does anyone find anything out these days, my love? There's those with poison pens that spend their days writing letters to the Commandant.'

Edith hurried home to make sure a hundred soldiers hadn't battered down her door in search of Gregor. But all was quiet, apart from Maurice fretting, packing and repacking.

The darkness plummeted from the sky, same as ever. Edith wondered if it would do the same in England, or if she might have to live the coming months and years without watching the sun sinking into the sea every evening, as if the ocean were extinguishing it. Long ago, people on the island used to believe that the sun drowned itself daily and was born afresh each morning. Did English folk have such beliefs thrumming in their blood? She'd never asked any of the sunbathing tourists, before the war.

When Edith tried to talk to Maurice about how things might be in England, he grunted and kept on with his fussing. About the children giving everything away with noise and chatter, and how they were going to gather enough food to last the journey and so forth.

In the end, Edith said, 'The children will hold their peace and we've plenty of food. Stop faffing.'

But when she thought on it, taking Francis with them was foolishness. Besides, they'd be stealing him from his mother and the idea didn't sit well with her.

She found Claudine out in the living room: the girl was using scraps of fabric to teach Francis his colours but he shouted 'Bloo!' for every colour and then Claudine tickled him under the chin.

Edith took Claudine's hand and told her, without mincing her words, that Francis would stay. Edith had expected hysterics and protestations and bargaining, but she'd forgotten how quickly the war had forced Claudine to grow up.

The girl nodded. 'I knew we couldn't take him.' She used her grubby sleeve to scrub the tears from her cheeks. 'I *knew*... I just wanted to make believe for a while.'

Edith leant in and kissed her wet cheek. Her heart could have cracked in two at the girl's bravery. 'He will be safe here. Hans won't hurt him. And we'll come back one day, you'll see.'

The darkness in Claudine's eyes struck Edith to the quick. 'Make-believe is for children.' She wiped her eyes again and gave a shaky sigh. 'I'm not a child anymore.'

When Edith returned to the kitchen to tell Maurice that Francis would stay, that they would return him to his mother in the morning, he nodded and went back to counting the loaves of bread for the hundredth time.

'For heaven's sake,' Edith snapped. 'We've enough to last us.'

'Have we?' He stopped counting. 'What about when we arrive in England? Do you imagine they'll just hand out a ration to each of us?'

'Well, why not? We need their help and that's the end of it. Can't see them turning us away.'

Maurice chuckled quietly to himself.

'What's tickled you then?'

'I couldn't see the English abandoning us—letting the Germans drop bombs, waltz on to the island like they owned it. But there you go. People always surprise you.'

'Well, now you're being ridiculous,' Edith huffed. 'It's hardly the same thing.'

'It's *exactly* the same thing. The English would leave us to rot if it wasn't for the smell we'd make when the wind blows their way.'

'You're winding yourself up over nothing, Maurice. Honestly, you have to trust that they'll look after us once we're there. Or why go? Might as well sail across to France. Or Germany. Trust that things will work out right, can't you?'

'I'm sorry, Edith. I can't. We look after ourselves—no one is going to play nursemaid to us. Now, I'm off to try to find some more loaves and some cheese.'

Sometimes Edith caught herself thinking that the Germans weren't such a bad bunch after all. Those like Hans were monsters, with darkness in their hearts that most people couldn't dream of. But many of them struck Edith as just boys with guns, simply doing as they were told. Of course, there was the odd one with a nasty streak, but in the main they were following orders, and who could blame them?

And at night, Edith massaged ointment into Gregor's arm and pressed her lips along his chest, on to his stomach and then all the way back up to the heat and the breathlessness of his open mouth.

—

THEY were set to leave at ten on Friday night. The clock reached half past nine and they were all of them jumping out of their skins at every whisper of the wind.

Maurice felt sick. Even Gregor, he observed, who never batted an eyelid, looked queasy.

Claudine was weeping over leaving Francis, even as she said, time and again, 'I know it's for the best.' She and Edith had taken him back to Sarah that morning, under the pretence of some chest cold Marthe had: *'We don't want him catching it.'*

The fib hadn't worried Maurice at the time, but now that Marthe was fast asleep and he couldn't rouse her, he started fretting that their words had tempted Fate to strike Marthe down with another illness.

Edith seemed not at all troubled. 'Hush, Maurice, it's easier this way. At least she'll be quiet.'

Then Maurice understood. 'You've *dosed* her!' he snapped. 'What the *devil* were you thinking?'

Edith leant forward and patted his head. 'It'll make every-thing easier, Maurice. You know it.'

'Why didn't you *ask* me?'

She gave a laugh that made him want to punch his fist into the wall. 'Well, yes, Maurice, my love, but what would you have said?'

It was lucky that at that moment Carter arrived, looking like some bearded vagrant from the hills. His eyes were wild and he was sweating. But he grinned and looked instantly youthful.

'I thought I had better contribute *something* to this expedi-tion.'

He heaved a huge sack on to the table and they all crowded around. Maurice dug his hand in and started to draw things out, one after another, and for a moment they all forgot themselves. There were things in there that none of them had seen in years: a whole bag of sugar, a small bar of chocolate, powder for clean-ing teeth. And a good two pounds of dried meat.

Maurice laughed as he had not laughed in months: an unfet-tered sound, like bursting bubbles from his chest, and he shook Carter by the hand.

Once everyone had quieted and the nerves had slunk back into the room, Maurice said, 'So I don't need to warn you to keep quiet as we go. Patrols will be out tonight like any other. We don't want to bring them down on our heads because we've forgotten how to whisper. And remember: if anyone is taken, you don't know anything about any escape. You were out for a walk, scavenging for extra food.'

They all nodded again.

'There's a big field on the way to the beach,' Claudine said. 'It used to have all sorts in it but now it's potatoes for the soldiers.

Perhaps we could say we were going to steal potatoes?'

'Clever girl, Claudine.'

Her face was still blotchy from her crying about leaving her maman and Francis. Maurice felt a tug of guilt: while she was sobbing, he had muttered, 'For goodness *sake.*'

He gave her an extra smile now. 'So we'll be going quietly and not all at once,' he continued. 'Less chance of being spotted than if we're together. I've been hiding a few bits and pieces down in the caves for a while now—blankets and so on. It'll be bitter out at sea.'

'Just a moment,' Edith said, rummaging in one of her cupboards. 'Here we are.' She pulled out a bottle of wine. 'I've been saving this for years. And I'd rather not leave it for the Germans.'

She opened the bottle and poured a glass out for everyone, even Claudine. Glug of red liquid pooling in the glasses; for a moment it gave Maurice a chill and then he shook his head to rid it of foolishness; it was the nerves making him whimsical.

Edith held up her glass. 'To escape.'

Maurice clinked his glass against hers. 'And freedom.'

Gregor said, *'Prost!'*

The wine was dreadful—cheap, acidic stuff—but it was years since Maurice had tasted wine, and the sudden vagueness in his head was exhilarating. He could have gulped the whole bottle. But he needed his mind clear so he stopped after two small glasses, drunk in such quick succession his gullet burned.

Then it was time to leave.

That was when Edith wouldn't budge. 'I've a bad feeling

about the whole business,' she said from the armchair.

Maurice felt a seething impatience. 'Fine time to choose to tell us that.'

'It's only hit me now. It's all been too hurried. We oughtn't to go.'

'For Christ's sake! Are you mad, woman?'

'Save it for another night. Not as though the Germans are going anywhere. There will be other chances for escape. When we've had more time to prepare.'

Maurice threw his hands in the air, then balled them into fists and made himself turn from Edith.

'She's hysterical!' he snapped, to the room in general. He raked his hands through his hair and fought the urge to scream. 'Someone else talk to her; I'm tempted to drag her to the sea and drown her.'

He forced himself to go outside for a lungful of the fresh, dark air. No moon in the sky, just the watchful eyes of a billion stars.

When he went back inside, Gregor was sitting on one side of Edith, Claudine on the other.

Maurice shook his head. 'Don't tell me: you're not going either?'

Claudine's eyes were wide. 'It isn't that. Edith thinks we haven't enough protection to leave tonight. If they catch us—'

'I'll tell you something, we *must* leave *now*. Imagine if a patrol marches up and finds us sitting here with a runaway soldier and enough food for a week, not to mention the traitor doctor...'

Carter shifted uncomfortably.

Edith knitted her fingers together, her knuckles whitening under the pressure.

'Maurice, I'm not trying to be a difficult old woman,' she said. 'But this doesn't feel right. If we're caught—the *risk*, Maurice. With Claudine involved. And Gregor. We've no defence, none at all. We'll have to simply put our hands up and let ourselves be taken. It's *lunacy*, the whole thought of escape like this, no protection…'

Gregor said, very gently. 'You worry about hurt, yes? And catching? I have my gun.' He took it from his holster.

Edith's eyes slid from his. 'Much good that will do us when we've no bullets for the thing.'

Gregor blinked. 'No bullets? Where——?'

'I threw them into the sea. After you waved that thing at Maurice.' She blushed. 'Good riddance, I thought at the time, and all for the best. But now we've a gun that's as much use as a croissant.'

Edith dug into her pocket and fetched out something white and pressed it into Claudine's hand—looked like knitted baby shoes but perhaps Maurice was imagining it, for why would she have such a thing? Then she fiddled with the gold band on her finger, worked it over her knuckle until it came loose.

'Go on and run to Clement Hacquoil, will you, child?' she said. 'You're to take this gun. We need bullets for it. As many as he has.'

Maurice held up a hand. 'But Edith, we've no time.'

Her voice was brisk. 'We've plenty of time if Claudine runs. And you're quick on your feet, aren't you, child?'

The girl nodded, but her mouth had crumpled with fear.

'What if a patrol catches me? And what if Monsieur Hacquoil doesn't have the bullets?'

Edith gave a humourless laugh. 'Oh, he'll have them—that man has fingers in every pie in the island. If you hear a patrol then you throw the gun away and you run, fast as you can. We're depending on you, my love. Remember, it's safety and freedom for all of us if we can get away. But we need these bullets. So off you go.'

Claudine was gone before Maurice could stop her.

The minutes ticked by. Maurice sighed. Paced. Glared at Edith. Packed and repacked the bags. Divided the meat so everybody had a little each. Glared again and refilled the canteens of water.

Claudine didn't return.

Maurice boiled a pan of water, shared around the last of the acorn coffee. He counted the slow *tick tock* of the grandfather clock—unravelling of time, which couldn't be recalled—and then checked again that there were enough warm clothes for Marthe.

'There's plenty of time,' Edith said.

'What if she's been caught out with a soldier's gun? What will the Hacquoils say?'

'Just sit tight. She's too fast for soldiers to catch her. And they'll not talk—Clement owes me his life.'

In the end, nearly an hour had passed before Claudine crept back in, clutching a rattling sack. Maurice was shaking, barely able to gather the breath to speak, but he could have danced a jig and kissed the girl, honest to God.

'We thought you'd gone to make those bullets yourself, Claudine.'

She didn't smile at him, and her face was pale, even though she was panting from running.

Something is wrong.

Edith must have felt it too: she stood up and clasped Claudine's arms.

'What took so long? We were worried sick, imagining all sorts.'

Claudine whispered, 'Sorry. I...' She shook her head.

Edith's voice was bright. 'Well, no matter now. You're here and we've no time for chattering. Go to see your maman and Francis, did you? They didn't suspect anything?'

Claudine shook her head again; she looked close to tears.

Edith pulled Claudine into a quick embrace. 'Let's have them, then. We don't want them going off in your hand.'

The girl opened the sack: five bullets in a tin, hard and bright and shiny as jewels. And there was more: two eggs, bread, a little sugar. Even some real tea leaves.

Edith gasped. 'Claudine, you marvel! How on *earth* did you come by this lot?'

'Madame Hacquoil. I—I don't know why.'

'Gracious. Well, don't look a gift horse in the mouth. Wonderful, Claudine, well done.'

'Perhaps Joan finally grew a heart,' Maurice said.

'Either that or Claudine sold her something.' Edith smiled. 'You didn't promise her Francis, did you, love?'

Everybody laughed.

Maurice drew a deep breath. 'Time to go.'

—

THEY had planned for Maurice to leave first, to make sure that the way was clear of patrols. Claudine was to follow with Edith, Dr Carter and Gregor.

Claudine wished, once again, that she had Francis's warm hand in hers. But it would have been too dangerous. She wondered if he would remember her if they met again, if the war was ever over. She wondered if Maman would forgive her for leaving.

Maurice set off. The rest of them waited, watching the flickering flame of Edith's oil lamp. No sound except the creak of the house as the wind from the sea rubbed against it.

In the quiet, Claudine couldn't help thinking of Maman and what she might believe tomorrow when Claudine didn't visit her.

Will she cry? How long will she search for me? I should have written a letter, telling her not to worry.

Claudine tried not to think of Hans's red-faced rage: when he was angry, his hands seemed larger, his fingers harder, his mouth bigger and wetter, his breath hotter.

Poor Maman. Claudine stifled a sob.

Her throat was still raw from running, her mouth acrid with the tang of blood. The gun had banged against her hip with every step to Monsieur Hacquoil's. The pain had made her run faster, like a flogged horse.

She had knocked quietly because of the curfew. When there was no answer, she had tapped on the window with a pebble. At last, Monsieur Hacquoil had opened the door. He scowled.

Breathless, Claudine gabbled, 'Edith needs bullets. For this gun.'

She put the gun on the doorstep and pressed the ring and woollen booties into his hand. She tried not to touch the skin where the fire had melted it and made it pink and shiny. The ring and the booties looked tiny in his crab-claw hand.

When Clement frowned, Claudine's stomach somersaulted: perhaps he meant to give them back?

But his mouth stretched wider; she supposed he was trying to smile.

'Come out of the cold, will you, child? Sit down.'

Her insides were vibrating with the need to leave, but she did as she was told. She tried to sit still. Tried not to think of everybody waiting for her.

'It is after curfew. I must—'

'Yes. You shouldn't be out and about. What if they catch you, eh? And looking for bullets. For a German gun? I've seen all sorts, but a *child* asking me for bullets for a soldier's gun? Now that's a first.'

There was something light in his voice, almost like laughter, but it was difficult to tell. He gave Claudine a glass of water and then he sat down opposite her and rubbed his melted face with his hands.

'So, little Claudine, what exactly are you lot up to then?'

It had become hard to breathe.

'Can I have…what I came for, please?'

'But *bullets*? Why does Edith need bullets? And why is she sending you out after curfew to fetch them? Hoping for a night in prison, are you? Or worse?'

She traced the whorls of the wood on the table. 'I don't know.'

Clement leant forward and put his pink, shiny hand on top of hers. She tried to pull away, but he kept hold. His skin felt smooth and hot and hard, reminding her of Hans.

She said, fast and low, '*Please* let me go.'

He shouted, 'Joan!' and Claudine jumped. She pulled her hand free and rubbed away the sensation of his fingers from around her wrists.

Madame Hacquoil came into the kitchen. Her face was puckered, as if she was chewing on a mouthful of sand.

'Joan, you know Claudine. The Duret girl?'

'Of course.' Her smile was all teeth; it didn't touch her eyes.

'Claudine has come for *bullets*. For this gun. For Edith. And I thought you might like a word or two?'

They stared at each other for a moment, time stretching like elastic—the promise of stinging pain when it snapped back together.

Finally Joan nodded, her smile stretching wider. 'Of *course*.'

Clement patted her on the shoulder and went through to the shop.

'A cup of tea for you, dear?' asked Joan.

Claudine shook her head.

'Come now, don't be like that. Hasn't your maman taught you your manners?'

Claudine's voice was faint, barely more than a breath. 'All right. Yes, please.'

'That's better.' Joan boiled the pan of water. Then she found the heel of cabbage loaf and a little pat of butter and set them down in front of Claudine.

Hunger unfroze Claudine's limbs and she grasped the piece of bread. She didn't want to gobble her food because that was rude, but she couldn't stop. She tore at it with her teeth. The bread felt warm in her stomach, even though it was days old and hard as a stone.

Joan sat down next to Claudine. 'Do you know,' she said, 'I remember when you were nothing but a babe in arms, such a good child. The sweetest, quietest baby a mother could wish for. I used to see your maman often.'

Mouth crammed with bread, Claudine nodded again to show that she was listening.

'We laughed a lot—we were great friends.'

Claudine swallowed. 'Did Maman laugh?'

'Yes, your maman was quite the entertainer, back then. Quite the life and soul, she was. But children are hard work—don't let anyone tell you different. Then, of course, there is rationing. It's difficult to feed a hungry family, let me tell you that.'

'Oh.'

Claudine realised it must be true. Maman used to be happy, but the war and looking after children had stolen that. She laughed with Hans, but it was a tight laugh, like Madame Hacquoil's smile.

Claudine stopped chewing the bread, her vision suddenly blurred. She blinked.

Joan put her hand on Claudine's shoulder. 'You mustn't blame yourself: children can't help but be burdensome. Come, wipe those eyes. But she's taken up with that soldier now, your maman?'

Claudine nodded. 'Hans. I *hate* him.'

'Of course you do. But you've heard what people say, haven't you? About women who take up with soldiers?'

Claudine wiped her eyes. More tears kept on coming, even when she dug her nails into her hands so hard that she broke the skin.

'People talk, Claudine, I'm afraid. An important thing,

your reputation. And once it's ruined… Well, it's like throwing blood over white sheets. You can scrub them as much as you like, but that stain won't budge.'

Claudine gulped. 'So will people always think badly of Maman?'

'I'm afraid they just might. Now, *we* know the truth, don't we? We both know that your maman is keeping you and your brother safe and warm. Keeping your bellies full. But people can be cruel, and memories are long.'

Claudine sobbed. 'I don't *want* them talking about her forever simply because…' And then she realised it was all her fault that Maman had brought Hans into the house. If Claudine hadn't been so *hungry* all the time. She ate far more than Francis. 'I've tried…'

'You're a good girl, *I* know that. And you couldn't help it; children never *mean* to be selfish. But you can make things better now. Do you think you might like to help your maman?'

Claudine nodded.

'*I* don't think she's bad,' Joan said, with a sideways glance at Claudine. She placed her hand over her heart, as if the words she was speaking pained her. 'I'm simply saying what others will think. But do you know, *you* can stop them? *You* can change what they're saying.'

Claudine sniffed. The handkerchief was sodden; she wiped her nose on the back of her hand.

'How?'

'Well, you must remember that I'm only trying to *help* people. You know that now, don't you?' She pressed her hand against her chest again. 'Good. I want people to stop getting themselves in trouble, and I've a feeling you might know some more people who could be doing something silly. Something that could cause trouble. Yes?'

Claudine sat with her hands in her lap, twisting the handkerchief around her fingers. There were four little bloody half-moons on her skin.

'I thought we were talking about Maman.'

'We *are*.' Joan's eyes were wide and sincere. 'We're talking about how you can help her, and also how you can help your friends. You don't want your friends to be in danger, do you?'

Claudine shook her head.

'And we can help. Clement and I. We like to help people to stay safe. Your maman—we can look after her. We can look after your friends too. Anything they need.'

Claudine kept staring at her hands. The wounds looked like broken little mouths now, dribbling blood. Right and wrong were like that: one minute the truth was one thing, the next minute it was something else. The Germans had done that when they arrived, turning everything upside down.

Joan's voice was soft, crooning. 'Imagine it: bread and butter for your maman and your little brother. And your friends. But you must tell us *every*thing.'

'That's all you want?' Claudine asked, quietly. 'So you can help? You won't tell the Germans anything?'

'Goodness, *no*, the very idea!'

Claudine remembered how she had trusted Gregor. He had been good and honest, even though he was a German soldier. And they really *needed* the bullets. Claudine also needed to know Maman would be safe and her reputation wouldn't be ruined. Madame Hacquoil was in charge of people's reputations: Claudine knew that.

So she told her everything.

About Maurice's boat and how Gregor was helping them to escape. How they were all going to escape to England and be happy. How she was scared to leave Maman with Hans and how she wanted her to have extra help because Claudine would miss her and Francis so.

Joan listened. Sometimes she nodded. When Claudine had finished, Joan smiled her smile full of teeth and embraced Claudine, gripping her hard.

'Thank you for telling me, Claudine. That's very brave of you. You're a very good girl, you really are.'

'You won't tell, will you?'

'No! Of course not.'

'You'll look after Maman for me? So that she doesn't have to do…bad things?'

'Yes.' Joan squeezed her arm. Her fingers were cold and bony. 'You've done the right thing.' Then she stood and clapped her hands. 'Now, you must be off, sharpish, young lady, or you'll miss the tide.'

As Claudine stood, she pressed a small sack into her hands. But before the butcher's wife could move away, Claudine gave her a quick kiss on her cheek, which held the bitter smell of blood.

'Thank you. For looking after Maman. And for not telling.'

Claudine ran all the way home, her heart rattling to the staccato clatter of five bullets in a tin.

—

CLAUDINE was safe and they had bullets for the gun.

Edith tried to keep her thoughts on that and pay no mind to the fist of fear compressing her chest. She fixed her eyes on the blue-black sky and its uncountable stars. Maurice had chosen a night when the moon was but a thin paring of silver, so they had to pick out their path from memory. But Edith could have walked the whole route blindfolded: she knew the shape of the land as she would have known her own child's skin.

Maurice had gone ahead, carrying Marthe. He would be the slowest, he'd said, and he didn't want the others captured because of his noise.

He'd taken a route that had only one patrol near it. At the tramp of German boots, they all crouched behind a bush. Edith glared for quiet. The patrol was too noisy to hear anything but their own voices anyway: great lumbering louts, chattering and laughing. They trampled by without stopping and the group stood up again.

Edith had only taken two steps when she heard Claudine's voice, shrill with panic.

'Edith! Something is wrong with Dr Carter!'

And, impossible to credit as it was, the man was lying down, pressing his face into the soil, as though he'd been shot.

What on earth is he doing, risking everything like this, and with the patrol still so near?

'Come on now,' she snapped. 'Up you get.'

'Oh Christ, I can't do this,' he groaned.

Edith felt a stab of fury. 'Oh for goodness sake, *up*! Of course you can do it, pull yourself together.'

He didn't shift a muscle. 'I'm not moving, I tell you. It's madness. They'll catch us, and that'll be it.'

'Well, they will if you stay sat here.'

'You don't understand. The Commandant has informants everywhere. And it's not only me he'll punish. Good God, the hospital. He'll incinerate the place. Or he'll have Hacquoil shot. What was I thinking? Trying to save my own skin and putting everybody else in danger. It'll be disaster for all of you too, if you're caught with me. He'll show no mercy. I *must* go back and turn myself in.'

Edith crouched next to him and dug her fingers into his arm. Her voice was a rattle of rage.

'You'll do no such thing. Now, up!'

'You don't know what he's capable of. He could torch the whole island and everyone on it and he'd think it a fine joke.'

She stared at the others. Claudine's face was pale; she looked set to cry, and Edith was about to tell her not to worry, they'd think of something, they'd move him somehow, even if they had to carry him down to the sea, when Gregor pushed past and pressed his gun against Carter's skull.

'You move. Now.'

Edith gasped and tried to wrench his hand away. 'Gregor! Stop!'

'Gregor, no!' Claudine said.

Gregor didn't shift his eyes from the point where the gleaming metal of the gun rested against Carter's head. His hand didn't tremble; his voice was cold, clear.

'He must move or he will kill us.'

Edith's hands fluttered to pull Gregor's arm away, but she knew he was right: Carter had to move or they would all die. And yet the poor man looked broken, his face twisted in pain and fear.

343

The gun clicked as Gregor pulled back the hammer. His next movement would kill Carter.

Carter groaned, heaved himself upright and stumbled onwards. The rest of them followed, shakily. Strange, the sensation of your heart hammering inside the roof of your mouth, Edith thought as she swallowed. A chill hush over everything, apart from their footsteps and Carter's sobs.

The sea was still. A thousand memories of the sand beneath her feet at night. The beach had swallowed the gnawing cold from the air and the sea. It took Edith's breath away every time, the bite of it.

She closed her eyes for a moment: every step was like trawling through mud, as though the land had tangled the fine thread of a fishing twine around her soul and was tugging her back. It set an ache in her insides, but she pushed on.

The others crunched behind her. She held up a hand. The faint sound of something scraping over the sand over by the rocks.

They followed the noise, tripping over sand and stones and stinking *vraic* until they found the cave where Maurice's boat was hidden.

Maurice had settled Marthe in the bottom of the boat. She was sleeping; her hair was frowzy and the poor love had sand on her cheek.

Edith whispered, 'Well, no sense in hanging about.'

Maurice and Gregor pushed and heaved, but they couldn't shift the boat over the hillock of sand made by the tide. They kept on shoving until Maurice fell, and before Edith could hush them, both men were sniggering like schoolboys.

'Shhhhhh!' she hissed. 'Buffoons, the lot of you. Go on,

Doctor, don't just stand there! Help them, or we'll be here until the morning patrols come.'

Carter pushed, but he was as weak as a kitten and he tumbled over too. Giggled right along with them.

'Oh, for heaven's sake!' Edith started pushing on the boat. 'Lend a hand, Claudine, love.'

The three men were holding on to each other, laughing: that silent laughter that makes no noise except the sucking of more air into the lungs. Edith couldn't help smiling.

But this wasn't getting them anywhere. So she hurried them along to unload the boat and lay everything on the sand: Marthe, the engine, the petrol, the food and drink. They all pushed as hard as they could and then, like a cork from a bottle, the boat shot forwards and up over the little sand-hummock and splashed down into the sea, leaving Edith flat on her face with a mouthful of sand.

The men lifted her to her feet, apologising, but now Edith couldn't help it—the laughter pealed out of her in waves and the sound bounced out across the water. For a moment, the days and years stretched out ahead of her and she could see all of them in England, happy and safe and together. No hunger. No bloody soldiers. Except Gregor.

Edith clutched his hand. He kissed her palm, her fingers, one by one, his mouth warm and alive.

They waded out into the sea. The icy undertow tugged at their clothes like a greedy mouth. Edith clasped Claudine's arm tight. There was no going back now and, for a moment, Edith feared that Claudine might try to stay, might sit on the sand, bawling for her maman and Francis.

But the girl fairly flew into the boat. The glimmer of water on her back in the near dark; she put Edith in mind of a dolphin, leaping free for the joy of it. Then Gregor lifted the bags of food and water in.

Maurice said, '*Danke schön.*'

'You're welcome,' Gregor replied.

Maurice lifted Marthe, ever so gently, from Gregor's arms and Claudine laid one of the bags beneath her head. A kind child. She would survive; she would flourish, Edith was sure of it.

Edith turned to Carter. 'Well, what are you waiting for? A marching band?'

'Well, I was rather hoping...'

They shared a grin. Then Carter waded out and tried to pull himself up into the boat, but he kept slipping back into the water. It was too loud, the constant splashing and grunting, and Edith felt that cold, clutching dread from earlier. How long before a patrol heard them? She cringed at the memory of her loud laugh.

'Hurry!' she hissed.

All around Edith, the land was inky black. The sea was black too, and breathless. No light, except for the pitiless, unblinking stars, but that didn't mean there weren't eyes out there, watching.

'I find kicking helps,' Maurice offered.

Carter jumped and kicked. He almost managed it, but then he slipped and splashed back into the water. His head went under and he came up spluttering.

Maurice and Edith hissed, 'Shhhhh!' at the same time.

'Well, would you rather I choked to death?' Carter's voice was squeaky with trying not to cough. He flailed his legs and jumped, then Gregor gave him a good shove on his backside and he tumbled into the boat.

Edith waded out and readied herself to leave.

~

MAURICE rowed steadily. Claudine searched the blank face of the land and tried to imagine where Francis would be. Asleep in bed, she hoped. Was he crying for her? Edith had told her earlier that small children were *tough little things. He won't fret for long*, she'd said. Claudine wanted to be reassured by that, but her own aching grief swelled like a sickness with every pull on the oars.

She wished Maman was with her. The old Maman, before Hans. Before she started trying to make everything better by doing the wrong things. Then, perhaps Claudine could sleep, curled in her lap, and when she woke up time would have changed and healed everything.

But Maman could never have come with them because Hans might have found out—and, of course, it would have been too dangerous to take Francis.

Dr Carter's voice cut across her reverie: 'Do you need a hand with those oars then, Maurice? Must be hard work, rowing all of us. I'm happy to help—did a fair bit of rowing, you see, back in the day. London rowing club and all.'

'No, thank you, Doctor. I'll row until we're out of earshot of the bay. Then I can set the motor up.'

'Righty-oh. I'll dig out the petrol canister for you.'

'Under those blankets.'

But Carter couldn't find the canister. He looked everywhere. They all searched around their feet and under the rest of the bags. No petrol anywhere. Claudine could see the same terror and disbelief on all of their faces. She felt it too: a sinking sensation, like cold water draining out of a bottle.

'I don't believe it,' Maurice said. 'It was *there*, I put it in the boat yesterday—'

'I don't remember seeing it,' Edith said. 'We took everything out when we pushed the boat down to the sea and I didn't see a canister.'

'Someone must've taken it,' Maurice said, savagely. 'Some bastard wants to see us shot—'

'That can't be right.' Edith laid a hand on Maurice's arm. 'No one knows we're leaving.'

'Someone has found out somehow and they're setting us up, I tell you.'

Claudine's stomach jolted. Surely the Hacquoils wouldn't have done this? They wouldn't have had time, would they? Unless… She imagined a small, dark shape. A girl, only a little younger than Claudine, running barefoot through the night, heaving a petrol canister home to her waiting parents.

Mary Hacquoil.

Claudine closed her eyes and shook her head to dispel the image. The Hacquoils wouldn't do such a thing. Maurice must have forgotten the petrol, somehow.

'Can you row all the way?' she whispered.

Maurice laughed. Fierce and raw. 'No.'

The waves slapped against the boat, as if the sea itself were telling them *hurry hurry hurry.*

'We'll take turns to row,' Edith said. 'Give you a rest. We can do shifts. We're in this together. Even Claudine can do a spot of rowing, can't you, love?'

348

Maurice shook his head. His mouth wobbled, as though he might cry, even though Claudine knew grown men didn't cry.

'Think about when the sun comes up.'

There was a silent moment as they all pictured it: the little boat, bobbing on the vast sea. Claudine wondered how many German planes and warships travelled across the channel every day.

'Perhaps we could go back,' Edith said. 'Try again another night?'

'We were lucky enough not to be caught on the way down to the boat,' Maurice said. 'It would be a miracle if we made it back unseen.'

'Let us hope for some crisis on the island that keeps the patrols off the water,' said Carter.

Maurice started pulling on the oars again.

When Claudine looked back, Jersey was like a shadow in a dream or a bank of storm clouds, where thunder was brewing.

A cold wind picked up. She wrapped her arms around herself. She knew they were all imagining the alternatives, as she was: captured by a German patrol or rescued by the British. Or somehow, evading all the patrols and landing safely on allied shores. The very idea was make believe; she knew it.

—

SUDDENLY Maurice's stomach alarmed to a far-off sound. He stopped rowing and put his finger against his lips.

They were all silent—the only noise was the splashing of the water as the sea gulped around the boat.

He watched their faces in the darkness, and he could see each of them registering the sound, the horror creeping into their eyes. Quite distinct now, the hum of a boat's motor, far away, like bees swarming in the distance, but growing louder.

Maurice hissed at Gregor, 'You said there would be no patrols on the sea tonight.'

Gregor's face was pale, panicked. 'I do not know—'

'And where are the bloody French?' Maurice growled. 'They're supposed to be keeping an eye out, drawing any German boats away.'

Christ!

Maurice started pulling on the oars as hard as he could. He could hear his own breath, coming out like a whistle, but the sensation he had was of remaining still in the water, or of going backwards even. Yet the harder he rowed, the louder the roar of the engines grew, until it pulsed alongside his blood.

'Perhaps it's someone fishing?' Claudine said. 'From Jersey? Or one of the French fishermen? Someone who will help us. Perhaps they will give us a motor?'

Maurice gasped, 'The French don't…use motors. Too… noisy.'

Maurice rowed harder, his breath escaping in sobbing gasps. A darkness had started to creep in at the edges of his vision.

Where was Marthe? Perhaps he could cover her in a blanket? He could hide with her? The Germans might not see them. Even as the thought flickered through his mind, he was aware of how ridiculous it was, how desperate. Yet he couldn't let them take her. He'd given up everything to keep her safe. The wretchedness of being captured now, of watching them take her away, it was unbearable.

He pulled harder on the oars. His back was aflame but it wasn't enough; it could never be enough.

'Maurice, dear.' Edith's voice was quiet but firm. 'Stop.' She put her hand on his back.

He shook her off and shouted, 'No! No! *Fuck!*' The wind whipped his words away and they mingled with the growing growl of the engines.

'Maurice, love, it's the finish for all of us, I'm afraid.' Her voice was level, as if she was telling him there was fish for supper. 'You've done your best.'

He stopped rowing, bent double, gasping. His cheeks were wet with salt spray and tears. He reached out to stroke Marthe's hair.

The boat engines fell silent and, in the new soundless darkness, he listened. Without the engines, he could hear the blur of voices all around. Too far away to catch the words, but certainly German spiking through the gloom. Then glaring lights on the figures in the boat so they threw up their hands and turned their heads away.

Maurice shut his eyes. 'I'm so sorry, my love,' he whispered. But even if Marthe had been awake, she wouldn't have heard him.

He had been saying goodbye to her, an inch at a time, for years. Now they were both gone.

He opened his eyes only to be blinded by the lights.

'No!' he cried. He felt the rage like fire in his bones. 'I won't have it. I *shan't* let them take her. They won't lay a finger on her. *Damn* that double-dealing Kraut!'

'You can't blame Gregor!' Edith cried.

'Gregor wouldn't tell!' exclaimed Claudine.

'Who else would have given us away?' Maurice snarled.

Suddenly there was a loud German voice bellowing, 'Halt!' and then something indecipherable, jagged words rebounding off the water.

'What's he saying?'

Gregor's face was grim. 'We are to put hands on heads. Like so. Or he will shoot.' He dropped his own gun and laid his hands on his head.

Maurice felt a wave of disbelief. It wasn't real; they couldn't possibly be surrendering, after all they had been through. Putting his hands up would mean the end for all of them. God knows what it would mean for Marthe, where they would send her.

He stood and shouted, 'Stay back! Stay back or I'll have the lot of you, I swear I will. You'll not lay a finger on her! I won't let you.'

'Maurice!' Edith hissed. 'Sit down, for God's sake. Please *sit down!*'

'They're not having her!' he roared. He heard his own voice as a raw, animal growl. Then he drew out his fishing knife and pointed it at the German boat. The blade was only as long as his little finger but any knife will reach a man's heart with enough force behind it.

'You'll have to go through me first! I'm not afraid to use it, this knife. I'll gut you all before you touch a hair on her! I swear it!'

The German voice from the boat barked, '*Sit!*'

Maurice felt a ferocious surge of fearlessness; he almost laughed. He was doomed, whatever he did. Whether he sat or stood or shouted or was silent, the Germans would kill him one way or another.

'I'll stab you through your Kraut hearts,' he bellowed. 'Every last one of you, before I'll let you take my Marthe! I swear to God, I'll—'

There was an explosion and a *crack* like thunder. Something punched Maurice backwards and he sprawled in the boat, half across Claudine's lap. He tried to sit up but his body was too heavy, and a sound like an alarm bell tolled in his ears. Over the ringing, he heard Claudine's cry: 'Edith!'

'Maurice!' It was Carter. 'Maurice, get up.'

Maurice tried to protest that there was nothing wrong, he was just a little winded, but before he could find the words, Carter said, 'Christ! It's in his chest.'

'Prop him up.' It was Edith, her hands strong around him.

'What's wrong with him?' Claudine's face was like a pale coin above him.

'On the count of three, lift him. One, two, *three*.'

Maurice felt a gust of air and then, for the first time, pain. Searing agony in his chest. He cried out and looked to find the pain, but he could only see a blackness seeping from a gaping mouth in his chest.

'Maurice! *Maurice*, say something!'

He moved his lips and a whisper gurgled out: 'Marthe?' His mouth was full of a warm, thick liquid and the sour taste of rust.

'She's here, Maurice, right here. Look, I'll lie you next to her.'

He felt the warmth of Marthe's body next to his. He closed his eyes for a moment, wished himself closer, wished himself inside her skin. How could she ever understand how much he loved her? Some feelings go beyond language.

Edith took Maurice's hand and put it on Marthe's. 'There. Feel that. She's there. She's safe.'

He clung on to the sound of Edith's voice, although it was harder and harder to hear her: like searching for smoke from a fading fire. He felt Marthe's hand in his own—her skin was hot and vital and teeming with life, and he squeezed her fingers; he thought he did… Or perhaps he wanted to but couldn't quite manage it.

Part of him wanted to shout and rail against the way that everything was slipping away, like a rug being tugged from under him, no matter how he tried to grasp at it. There was a tingling over his hands and feet, a sensation that crept up his arms and legs, as though he were sinking into icy, black water.

Slowly, the need to shout and rail faded too, and with the chill that crept through his body came a kind of stillness from yearning. Like a raging thirst, gently quenched.

It reminded him of those mornings when they were first married: he would wake up with Marthe's body warm next to his, his arm always numb and useless where she had lain on it all night. But like those times, there was no need to shift away. He had no desire to move.

—

THERE was a gurgle in Maurice's throat, then he slumped back and was still.

'Oh Lord,' Edith murmured.

Claudine doubled over; dimly she was aware of a voice crying, 'No! No!' over and over again, and it was only when she felt Edith's hand over her mouth that she realised the voice was her own. How was it possible for a person to be alive one moment and then gone the next?

More echoing cries came from the German boats.

'We must stand,' Gregor said. 'Hands on head.' He stood, slowly. The boat wobbled. Shaking, they all did the same. More shouting, a shock of senseless percussive rumbles.

Gregor said to Claudine, '*Liebling,* you must stand now. I will help you. Come, Claudine. Hands on head. Like so.'

She shook her head. 'I shan't.'

Edith said, 'Come on, my love. Stand up.'

'Please!' Gregor's voice was sharp with fear. 'They will shoot, they say. You stand. Now!'

Carter knelt next to her and put his hand on hers. 'There now.' His voice was calm and soothing. It made her remember the beach and Monsieur Hacquoil and the sour-sweet smell of burning—and how Dr Carter had made everything better.

'Claudine, I need you to stand. I shan't let them hurt you, I promise. You must trust me now.'

She took Dr Carter's hand and eased upright. The boat wobbled. She cried out, flailed, nearly fell. More growls. Metal clicks of guns all around. Every one aimed at her heart or her head. Her whole body tingled.

Dr Carter squeezed her hand. He looked into her eyes and she saw something gentle there.

'You have my word. I won't let them hurt you.'

She nodded, put her hands on her head.

Then everything sped up. The Germans began shouting again and Dr Carter cried out, 'Lean right and jump clear!'

He threw all his weight to the right of the boat. Claudine hadn't time to do anything more than take a gulp of air before the boat flipped over and the freezing water stamped the breath from her lungs.

She broke the surface, gasping. There was solid darkness all around and everything was muffled. She reached out and touched hard wood in every direction.

She had come up *under* the boat.

Edith? Gregor? Breath ragged, she trod water and listened.

She could hear the German voices shouting and then Dr Carter calling, 'Here! Take me, I'm here.'

Then, the thud of fists landing on flesh and Carter's grunts and cries and moans. Claudine felt sick.

He'd saved her. He must have known what the consequences would be and yet he'd chosen to give himself up.

Then came a German voice she knew, raised in pain.

They have Gregor too. No!

Noises like the slapping of bread dough. A sound like the drumstick being ripped from a well-cooked chicken, followed by a shriek, cut short. Not a noise a man could make, surely?

Claudine heard herself sob. She tried to make her mind blank because crying wasn't going to change anything.

Then there was someone in the water next to her; hands gripping her arms. Claudine gasped and thrashed out.

'Hush now or they'll hear us.'

Edith.

Her hands were strong; she wrapped her arm around Claudine's chest and held her.

Claudine struggled but she couldn't break free. 'We must help Gregor! And Dr Carter. The soldiers have them.'

'Quiet now!' Edith's arm was iron around Claudine's chest.

Her insides jumped with a sick terror. '*Edith!*' she hissed, 'Edith, they have Dr Carter. And Gregor. They're hurting Gregor!'

'I know, love...' Edith's voice fractured. 'But you must hush.'

How could she, when she could hear two men being broken? When their screams and the cracks and groans of their splintering bones echoed over the water.

'We *must* help them,' she wept.

The German voices sounded triumphant, and somehow closer. They had heard her.

'Take a big breath' Edith said. 'Now!'

She gripped Claudine's shoulders and suddenly they were underwater, Edith's hand tugging on hers. Claudine followed— what else could she do?

They swam until her chest was all tearing claws. Claudine saw the blink of the searchlight above them, the shadow of the German boat as they swam beneath it. She could still hear the shouting, but it was dull, like the leaden grumble of far-off thunder.

The burning crawled from her lungs into her arms and legs, then heaviness, until she felt she could no more move her body than heave one of the rocks from the sea bed.

Just as she was about to wrench her hand free and open her mouth, they broke through to the surface, next to an outcrop of rocks. Claudine wheezed.

'Hush now,' Edith said as she propped her on the rock. 'Here. Some *vraic*. On your head. Like this, see? Lean into the rock—but silence. Or it'll be a bullet for both of us.'

'Marthe—?'

'The Germans must have pulled her from the water too,' Edith hissed. 'They'll not hurt her. Now quiet.'

'But Gregor—'

Edith's voice was hard. 'You can't help Gregor by getting

both of us killed. Not another word!'

There was no space for thought, only Edith's voice. The searchlights and the boats and the German voices shouting were all around but at the same time, they were years and lifetimes away. Claudine slumped against the jagged rock and closed her eyes.

Perhaps she slept. Her head was full of screaming. Maurice and his chest like a shouting mouth, hungry and belching blood. The tattoo of fists on flesh, the sharp clap of shattering bones. Cries of pain like the desolate shrieking of gulls in the sky.

But when she opened her eyes, everything was silent.

'Edith?' Claudine whispered, to see if they were still alive.

'Here.'

'Where are the boats?'

'Gone.' Her voice was flat.

Dr Carter, Gregor and poor Marthe—gone? It was impossible to imagine.

'Will they…kill them?'

Edith sighed. 'I don't know. I pray… I pray not.' Her voice faded to a whisper and Claudine realised Edith was choking back tears herself.

'They'll hurt Marthe, they'll—' Claudine began.

'Marthe was fast asleep with what I'd given her.' Edith's voice shook.

'But you said they would have pulled her out…'

'I didn't see. Perhaps they did.'

'You think she drowned?'

'I'm sorry, my love. She was asleep. She wouldn't have known a thing—' Edith gave a strangled cry. When her breathing had steadied again, she said, 'I don't think they'll be back for us. They didn't search for long. Suppose they thought we'd drowned. We were well hidden. They've trophies to take back to the Commandant anyway.' Her voice was bitter.

Claudine closed her eyes again. Everything seemed far away, as if it had happened a long time ago to somebody else. The past, viewed through ten different telescopes, each one telling a different story. She listened to the placid splashing of the sea against the rocks.

'Will we die, do you think?'

'I've not planned for it, no.'

She could hear the smile unfolding the edges of Edith's voice. Claudine stretched out in the dark and found Edith's hand; she was already reaching for her. They held fast for a long time. Time measured in slow, shuddering breaths.

Finally, Claudine said, 'What will we do?'

Edith sighed. 'Swim back to Jersey, I suppose. Then try to hide. We're half a mile out, I think. We'll swim until the current catches hold of us and pulls us back.'

'But they'll find us. And they'll kill us. Like Maurice. And Gregor.' Claudine couldn't quell her frantic panic: there was no escape.

'There now. No noise, do you hear? Crying won't help us— plenty of time for tears later.'

Claudine tugged on her hair and counted her teeth with her tongue until the roiling spinning terror in her head stilled. Then she said, quietly, 'Could we swim to England? People do.'

'How far would we get, do you think, before we drowned?' Edith laughed. It was a raw, desperate, savage sound that Claudine had never heard from her before. More like Maman's laugh. Then Claudine heard something else.

'Hush, Edith!'

And there it was: a musical *splash, splash, splash*. The watery march of approaching capture and death.

Edith and Claudine both breathed the word 'Oars' and Claudine gave a desperate cry because she knew it was the Germans, come back to take them away, to send them to a prison or to shoot them. Their blood would ooze into the black mirror of the sea.

She hid under the *vraic* again, because she suddenly felt a fierce, hopeless longing to lie down next to Maurice and Marthe, deep under the weight of the sea, eyes closed, head calm and quiet. She didn't want this terror squirming inside her, she didn't want to be dragged into a boat or shot in the sea or to starve to death in Germany or go back to Hans.

But then Edith called, 'Hi there! Over here!'

The splashing stopped and a voice called, *'Où êtes-vous?'*

—

THE fishermen gave them blankets. Edith cocooned Claudine in the soft wool and pulled the girl into her lap—she was shaking so hard Edith could hear her teeth rattling. She stroked her hair and pulled her in close and kissed her forehead.

There, there, my love. We're safe now.

She watched the rhythm of the girl's heartbeat under the skin at her throat: pounding like a desperate drum, but gradually it slowed.

Edith told the Frenchmen what had happened. No purpose in mincing words. When she told them Maurice had been killed,

360

their faces fell and, gravely, they pulled out a bottle of brandy and took a swig each, before pouring a measure into the sea and muttering a blessing. Edith took a gulp and gave Claudine some too; she coughed a little, but the last of her shaking passed.

As the warmth of the drink sank into Edith's belly, she gave up a thought for Maurice and Marthe, lying somewhere beneath them. She felt a pressing on her chest, but she breathed until it drifted off; it wouldn't help Claudine if she fell apart now.

Her thoughts snagged on Gregor. His face, his slow smile, his kind eyes. The warmth of his breath against her ear in the dark as he held her body to his, sweating, smiling, pressing kiss after hot kiss against her flesh.

Death lasts as long as life. She would forever be left gasping by the familiar angle of a stranger's jaw in the street, or by eyes a certain shade of blue in the face of someone she had never met. She would always clutch at a ghost in the dark, wishing she could call him into being with the heat of her longing.

Sitting on the boat, Edith clasped the grief to her heart for a moment, then forced herself to straighten, to breathe, to turn her mind to the clunk of the oars and the creak of wood beneath her. *Safety*.

The fishermen said they had been late setting off: a patrol on the French coast had delayed them. *If only we had been delayed an hour longer ourselves*. Pointless to say *if only*. If only the Germans had never bombed them; if only they had never invaded. If only people's hearts weren't so crammed full of darkness that they'd trade with the enemy for a pound of extra flesh.

'The Germans must have had a tip-off,' Edith said. 'Heaven knows who talked to them.'

'Joan Hacquoil,' Claudine whispered. 'I...told her everything.

For the bullets. She *promised* she wouldn't tell. And she said she wanted to help Maman. But her smile... I *knew* she... I'm so sorry, Edith. I'm so, *so* sorry—'

Her voice splintered and she wept. Poor child. Edith held her fast to her chest, as the girl's maman would have done, once upon a time.

'There, now, you're not to blame. I should never have asked you to go. You're but a child. A child. There, my love, there.'

Edith kissed the top of her head again and again. The girl's hair was wet and smelt of salt and blood—scents of a baby, freshly born. Edith laid her down, Claudine's head upon her lap.

'You're safe, my love. Just try to rest.' She stroked her cheek and sang:

> *Lavender's green, dilly, dilly, Lavender's blue,*
> *If you love me, dilly, dilly, I will love you.*
> *Let the birds sing, dilly, dilly, And the lambs play;*
> *We shall be safe, dilly, dilly, out of harm's way.*

After Claudine had fallen asleep, Edith said to the Frenchmen, 'Is there somewhere we can lie low in France? I know you're as riddled with Germans as we are, but I hoped...I can't let her go back, you see, to Jersey.'

They looked at each other. Some current of understanding passed between them and they dipped their heads. The younger of the two said, 'We take you *en Angleterre*. We must. For Maurice. He want this for you, I think.'

'But what about the risk to you? Patrols and the like?'

'They catch your friends. They kill Maurice. This is enough work for them this night. I think no more patrols.'

Edith thanked them, and then fixed her eyes upon the horizon. She liked Maurice's thought of staying on the coast. They must have some of the same plants in England, surely? She would be able to sit on the beach and gaze out at the endless blue of the sea and listen to the promise it made daily: *things could change.*

Then too, she would know that, even though she couldn't see it, she was staring towards Jersey, just out of sight, over the horizon. And she would give her own promise back to the whispering sea: one day, she would take Claudine home.

The Frenchmen started rowing again.

CLAUDINE dozed while they took it in turns to row. Sometimes her head was filled with the noises of flesh slapping flesh, or of black blood glugging from a wound, and she cried out: an infant howl, arms beating the air in panic.

Edith held her hand and told her stories until she drifted back into a fitful, tortured sleep. Day and night bled into one another.

Edith told her that while Dr Carter might be sent to Germany, he would care for the people in the camps. Her voice trembled as she told her about Gregor, and how the Germans wouldn't have hurt him badly after all, because he was one of their own. They would let him go back home to care for his sickly wife, poor love. Perhaps he would meet Dr Carter in Germany and they would find medicine for Gregor's arm and for his wife's head.

'There's a remedy for everything, you see. You only have to know where to look.'

Claudine slept. She dreamed of Francis. She called his name; he turned but he didn't recognise her and he hid in Maman's skirts. *Maman.* Her eyes were empty when Claudine tried to explain why she had left.

Claudine woke shuddering, grief-struck, but Edith told her that Maman would understand. It hadn't been Claudine's fault, none of it. Some folks had evil in their hearts that couldn't be fought. The only thing left to do was to flee from it. One day, not so far away, they would come back to Jersey: the soldiers would be gone and Maman would take Claudine into her arms and Francis would clap his hands at seeing his sister and kiss her and Claudine would hold him close and tell him how leaving him had been like severing a limb. How she had only done what she thought best. Claudine would be home again. Edith would live in her little house and Claudine would visit her every day and everything would be as it had been before the war.

Edith stroked Claudine's hair while they looked up at the stars. She told Claudine to imagine that they were all part of the stars now, all those who had died. They were part of the sky, part of the sea. Part of the land. She made Claudine draw a breath deep into her chest and close her eyes and picture their faces.

'See now. They are there. You see them. In here. And *here.*' She tapped Claudine's head, her chest. 'It's no different to if they were in another room. Or another country. You simply close your eyes and think on them, and there they will be.'

The sky paled and brightened and was whole again. The stars dissolved. When Claudine felt a warmth seep into her, she felt strong enough to sit up. A black shadow stretched along the horizon in both directions, as far as she could see. Behind it was an orange glow, almost as though the sun might rise after all. She closed her eyes and imagined the rich burst of sunlight, like the yolk of a cracked egg.

When she opened her eyes again, the sky was lighter, the shadow more solid, as though it was more than clouds banked on the horizon. It was something real and rooted and touchable.

She whispered, 'What's that?'

'England,' said one of the Frenchmen.

'That, my love,' Edith said, 'is freedom.'

She kissed Claudine's cheek and they clasped hands and gazed at one another. Claudine could see the hope and the terror in Edith's eyes and she tried to smile.

AUTHOR'S NOTE

While some of the characters that appear in this book are based on historical figures, and while many of the events described bear similarities to actual occurrences, this is a work of fiction and these characters and the related action are very much fictional creations.

Between the years of 1940 and 1945, the people of Jersey and the other Channel Islands endured unspeakable hardships and horrors under the German Occupation, and some of those (rationing, deportations, failed escape attempts) have served as inspiration for this novel. But I have also taken liberties with the history and geography of Jersey for the sake of storytelling. Neither of the Commandants who ruled over Jersey were as brutal as the man I have depicted here. There was no last-minute evacuation from La Rocque pier, and it is unlikely that Maurice would have moored his boat at Devil's Hole, especially as I've placed his home on the opposite side of the island. Edith would not have been able to walk from St Clement to the sand dunes, or, if she had, it would have taken her all day.

All other errors are my own.

There are, however, many excellent resources that were invaluable in making this novel what it is.

The Jersey War Tunnels, the Jersey Museum and the Maritime Museum (which houses the wonderful Occupation Tapestry) provided both inspiration and invaluable sources when I was first researching the novel.

A number of books also proved helpful: Charles Cruikshank's *The German Occupation of the Channel Islands*; Roy McLoughlin's *Living with the Enemy*; Dr John Lewis's *A Doctor's Occupation*; L.P. Sinel's *The German Occupation of Jersey* and literature from the Jersey War Tunnels were all brilliant and harrowing, in equal measure. I also drew inspiration from some of the anecdotes on BBC Radio 4's *The Reunion*, which ran an episode on the Jersey Occupation in September 2013.

My gratitude goes to the people of Jersey—and especially to those who suffered and died, or somehow survived the Occupation years.

Caroline Lea
FEBRUARY 2016

ACKNOWLEDGMENTS

First thanks and a debt of gratitude and love must go to my much-missed dad, Peter Lea, who wanted a peaceful life and to 'shut those bloody kids up!' The quietest occupation I could find was reading, and an obsession with books was born. Thanks must also go to my wonderful mum, Sue Lea, who spent hours trawling bookshops for the fattest books she could find and has also always offered so much support and enthusiasm for my writing. Love and thanks to my big sisters, Sophie and Annabelle, for making me so fiercely competitive and determined (and especially to Annabelle for being such an enthusiastic reader of my work and for the editing of Carter's *ummmms* as well as the brilliant suggestion of potatoes).

To my most critical (and therefore most wonderful) readers and friends, Bill and Nettie Gurney: endless thanks for your unceasing enthusiasm and continued support of my writing. Thank you also for the detailed critiques, notes and ideas. A special thanks for the four A4 pages of blasting criticism on the first draft, Bill—you were absolutely correct on every point!

To the other friends who have been kind enough to read my work and offer suggestions: Emma Searles for your encouragement and support on that messy first draft, Cathy Thompson-Jones for your endless patience and detailed notes on my short stories, Penny Clarke and Sachin Choithramani for your words of encouragement. Thanks also go to other friends who read the first section, or first drafts, and gave advice: Katie Purser, Robert Ward-Penny, Roger McBrien, Jonathan Pettifer, Stephen Richards, Holly Alexander, Becky Kemp, Christina Athens-Davies, Pav Dhande, Michael Swann and my sister Penny Mourant. Thanks also to Jean McGrane and all the Bédar Writers for your kind words of encouragement. Apologies to anyone who I have forgotten to include here.

To my lovely brother-in-law Charlie Mourant: thanks for your wonderful enthusiasm about the novel and for the anecdote of the Christmas turkey under the duvet.

To Monty Tadier, thanks for the correct spelling of *Jèrriais*, for the suggested reading material, and for everything fifteen years ago.

Huge thanks to my wonderful school English teacher, Graham Crosby, who first believed I could write and was both encouraging and inspirational. I haven't met an English teacher to equal him yet.

Much love and gratitude to Doug and Liz Day, who have both encouraged me and been so generous with their time and care of my two small boys.

At Peters Fraser and Dunlop, I am eternally indebted to my agent, the wonderful and brilliant Nelle Andrew, who worked until midnight and beyond for me, tirelessly championed my novel across the seas and then told me, quite rightly, to 'stop being such a mare'. You are a force of nature and I so appreciate everything you continue do for me. I also owe a debt of thanks to Rachel Mills and Silvia Molteni.

An enormous thank you to my fantastic editor at Text, Rebecca Starford, who was utterly brilliant to work with and made the potentially laborious process of editing so enjoyable. Her sharp eye, wonderful suggestions (always phrased as thought-provoking questions) and delicate touch have helped me to shape the novel into something far beyond my expectations.

Finally, a giant thank you to my long-suffering husband, John Wood, who reads my work (and feigns interest most convincingly), endures the roller-coaster of my various writing-related mood-swings and ungrudgingly provides support and encouragement...as well as practical help and easily forgotten inconsequentials like food and cups of tea. Sometimes I wonder why you put up with me. And then I remember that I put up with you. x